D1257595

MOULDED IN EARTH

MOULDED IN EARTH

By

Richard Vaughan

NEW YORK

E. P. Dutton & Co., Inc.

1951

TO MY MOTHER

BOOK ONE

Chapter 1

WHEN I got to Graig Ddu it was so dark that the outlines of the firs were lost against the blackness of the sky. Walking along the dark road you could hear nothing but the sound of the river. And there's terrible at night is the sound of black rushing water in a gorge that is only a few yards away from the road. I suppose I must have been fascinated somehow by the wild terror of the place, for I stood there for a minute or so holding the horses and listening to the roar of the river and the sounds of the night. Down there, below the blur of the thorn hedge, was the black, whirling flood. I could not see it, but I could hear its churned anger, and I imagined the white foam-cakes circling round and round the edge of the whirlpool under the bend of the road. Overhead, a star or two raced across a rent in the clouds, and all around me the air was sharp and sweet with the smell of the fir trees. From time to time a little push of wind would make a dry, rasping noise in the trees.

Presently, I moved on and led the horses to the gate at the bend of the road. It was here I had promised to meet Justin. He had left home at daybreak with the cart to fetch the winter coal from Brynamman. Ever since I could remember, we had always sent two extra horses to meet the coal on this hill. From here to Trewern the cart-rutted road zigzagged steeply all the way. So I waited for Justin, the old mare and Brown nosing in the grass by the gate, their chains clink-clanking with each movement they made. Justin had said he would be along about eight o'clock; and although I knew his ways so well, I had made sure that I would be there in time. If he would be late, well, that was just Justin's way.

I sat on the gate smoking and thinking. I hated this spot. I had dreaded the thought of it all through the day. And now, here I was, with the darkness like pitch around me, and the sound of the river like thunder in my ears. I tried to enjoy my pipe, but it was no good. Then I thought of Grett, trying to see her clearly in my mind. But I could only capture a sort of half-glimpse of her. I thought of her hair, then the curve of her lip when she smiled, or the swing of her body as she walked. But I could not see her completely, only feature by feature; and yet, behind each glimpse there remained a vision of her which I apprehended clearly but could not see. As it was, the only thing that I was perfectly conscious of was the river and the darkness, and the icy tremors that passed over me as I sat there straining every nerve to see or hear if Justin were coming. I thought of the old cart piled high with coal, the iron-banded wheels crunching their way towards me somewhere between here and Brynamman; and there, half-lying on a sack folded over the coal would be Justin, his bowler tilted low over his forehead as he sang or cursed his way along.

The minutes passed slowly, and I fell to thinking of all the stories I had heard of the pool below the bend of the road. I had heard them since my earliest days. Sitting at hime on the skew by the fire and hearing the raindrops spitting down through the wide chimney and hissing on the coals, it was easy to talk of Graig Ddu. There was the suicide back in the 'seventies when Catherine Jeffreys had walked to the edge of the pool on her wedding night, and had been found next morning in the whirlpool, her night-dress stained with the red mud, and with leaves and moss clinging to her hair. Graig Ddu! Graig Ddu! Like every place of wild and terrible beauty, it had its moods. There was its strident, hag-ridden mood such as it had on this night. Then, too, were nights when the moonlight threw the rocks and the twisted trees into gaunt shapes, and through a butt in the hedge you looked down and saw the river flowing hard and swift like a sheet of shining steel.

At last, and when I heard it my waiting for it seemed no more than a moment's pain, I heard the cart come creaking and crunching up the hill. I jumped down from the gate. I could hear Justin shouting and cursing as he urged Duke up to where I was waiting.

"Come, Duke! Dammo di!" As soon as he was level with the gate, he swung the horse over until the cart-wheels rested in the rain-rut that slanted across the road. I knew from the exultant note in his voice that he had had a glass or two on the way.

"Whoa!" The cart creaked to a standstill, and I scotched a flat stone behind each wheel.

"What a day!" Justin wiped his face with his white-spotted red handkerchief. The pale light from the lamps glinted on the polished brasses of the harness.

"Been waiting long?" He pushed his best bowler back over his head and grinned at me.

I grinned back at him. Now that he had come, he seemed to fill the place with his strength and vitality. That was how it had always been. Our Justin was like a rock. There was no one in the parish who could stand up to him. I shall never forget the first day I went to school. He was then in the top class, and I remember with what respect the other children regarded me, only because of the fact that he, Justin Peele, was my brother. No, there was no one like our Justin.

He came over and leaned against the gate.

"What sort of a day have you had?" I asked.

He gave me a quick, searching glance, but, as always, when there were only the two of us together, there was a twinkle of humour under his beetling eyebrows.

"All right! All right!" he laughed. "I know I'm late . . ." He laughed again and shrugged his shoulders. The light from the lamps shone on his teeth. "Couldn't help it," he continued. "I met some chaps over there. And then, I had a few at The Pandy. . . ." He looked at me again and laughed. "I must have been there an hour. . . . You know, old Duke needed a rest. Here, have one o' these"—he pushed a cigarette into my hand—"they're a change after that bloody twist."

He cupped a lighted match for me in his coal-grimed hands. I knew quite well what the attraction was at The Pandy. As like as not, he had been in one of the outhouses with one of the girls there. The Pandy was well known, and Justin was not particular.

"How was Sal?"

Justin said nothing for a moment or so. Then he turned to me slowly:

" 'Twould do you good to drop in there some day. . . . It's time you were a man now. Diawl! When I's your age I'd . . .''

I let him carry on. For a vivid instant or so I saw him and Sal together, the darkness of the outhouse hiding nothing from my imagination. I saw the white-washed walls, the heap of hay or fern in the corner; and there was Sal's face with her eyes laughing at Justin and her red lips parted. . . . And with that picture in my mind, my longing for Grett came over me again. I glanced at Justin's profile, and wondered what he would say if I told him about her. But he would never understand, never. Grett was too fine for Justin. What he wanted was some hoyden of a girl, someone like Sal at The Pandy, or like the girls he picked up in Brecon after the Mart or the Christmas market. So, while Justin rambled on about Sal, I let my thoughts turn again to Grett. To think of her was to feel myself carried along on some swift flood. A weakness would come over me as I imagined her in my arms and breathing against me. I half turned away from Justin and looked through the darkness up-river towards Rhos Dirion where she lived. I saw the white-washed farm-house with the ash and the high beeches behind it; the barn, the stables, and the narrow lane leading up to it from the riverside where we had lingered so quiet and secretly in the autumn darkness. I saw her leaving me as I stood under the alders until she was out of sight. She was like water in her lithe movements, she was so alive and sudden with impulse. Imagining and seeing her face as I leaned there against the gate, I could think of nothing but summer; summer with its warmth, its shadows, its mystery of dusk, and its slow, heavy, passionate hours.

It was Justin who made the first move to go. "Come on," he said suddenly, "we've got to call at the blacksmith's. I've got a sack of meal for him."

I helped him to hitch the two horses to the traces.

"Right ! let's go." Justin swung the horses round until they were in line. I stood behind the cart with a scotch in each hand ready for any emergency. A thrill of excitement went through me as I looked at the horses. They were in good condition, father saw to that, and the light from the two lamps shone on their smooth, glistening flanks. I fancied that they looked as though they knew what was expected of them. They would need another spell when they reached the top of the hill. Justin stood a little away from the leading horse.

"Come, Brown! Come, Duke! Gaseg!" His voice was loud, with a hard edge to it like father's, and the three horses strained forward, their hoofs pawing at the road, their bellies low, and their great necks arched downwards. Slowly at first, then gathering speed as the cart lumbered over the rut across the road, they began to take the hill. I felt the tears sting on my eyelids to see the way they responded to Justin's voice. And there was Justin half running beside them, his voice damning and encouraging them in turn. So, with the axle creaking, the hoofs at times striking sparks from the road, they reached the top of the hill. Twenty yards more and we were more or less on the flat. From now on it was only a gradual climb up through the village, and then home to Trewern.

We could hear the ring of the anvils long before we got to Howells the Blacksmith. What a warm, friendly sound it was coming through the darkness. Night after night, old Howells and his two sons worked on, long after the evening star—the "Workman's Star" as we called it—had risen. And there's strange it was on a Sunday night when we came from church to hear no sound coming from the smithy. The clink of the hammers and the ring of the shining anvils were part of the countryside. They were as essential a part of the parish as was the dull rumble of the millstones inside the Felin, or the sound of someone whetting a scythe on a summer's morning.

"They're still at it," said Justin. "I was afraid I'd be too late for them."

We were both sitting on the load. The grass on each side of the road was acid-green where the lamp lights shone on it. The horses were pulling the cart with ease, and we lay back against the soft sack of meal we had for Howells. When we turned the bend of the road, we saw the light streaming out from the open door of the smithy. Justin drew the horses to a standstill, and jumped to the ground.

"Hullo, there!" he shouted. "Howells!"

The clangour inside the smithy ceased at once, the last ring of the anvils dying away, and the purr of the bellows suspiring in a moan.

"Who's there?" Old Howells came to the half-door, his coarse, blue-flannel shirt unbuttoned round his neck and rolled up over his spark-pitted arms. He was over sixty, but still held his own with his two sons.

"Heisht there! Less noise!" He shouted over his shoulder as Twm and Rhys came up crowding and talking behind him. Like most blacksmiths on in age, he was a little deaf; probably the roar of the bellows and the continuous thud of steel on iron had something to do with it. He peered at us, his eyes, no doubt, too accustomed to the glare of the fire and white-hot iron to see in the half-dark outside the door.

"Oh! It's you, Justin. Been for the coal, is it? Come in for a spell, and have a warm."

He opened the door, and Justin walked past him, the sack of meal slung over his shoulder and weighing him forward. I followed him, eager for the gossip and clecs which I knew we would get there.

It was lovely and warm inside. The small flames from the two fires flickered up through the damp small coal in blue and yellow spurts. I went over to the half-cask of water that stood by the bellows and dipped my hand in it. There was nothing like the black, acid water of the smithy to keep away warts.

"Sit you there," said Howells to me. He indicated a low, smooth bench with a cobbler's last affixed to it. "I saw you going by about seven. I told you, Twm, didn't I?"

Twm, the elder of the two sons, nodded his bald head. He was a tall, stout chap of about thirty-five, blond of moustache, and something of a dandy even in his working clothes. I never saw him without he had on some fancy waistcoat or other, or a silk tie looped loosely around his neck—the cast-offs, of course, of the Squire. He was a good-natured wag and whenever he had a moment, would be out with his liver-and-white spaniels and his gun. He was as strong as a horse, yet there was no story, or even a whisper, that he had ever been in a fight or a quarrel with anyone. Twm always said with one and was always in the background, even as now, standing a little behind his father, and nodding and smiling his agreement with everything the old man said. His brother, Rhys, was a different type. Short, stocky in build, his black, curly hair growing close to his head, he was more secretive and dangerous. He was a good man at his trade, and had won prizes in shows for shoeing. He stood a little away from the lantern that swung from a beam over the centre of the floor, and leaned back against the horn-tipped handle of the bellows, looking at us without saying a word, only smiling behind his black moustache. Justin had no time for him; besides, he was too thick with Jeff Ellis and his crowd.

"How are things over the mountain?" asked Twm. His eyes twinkled as he looked at Justin. Justin winked back at him.

"Not bad, not bad." He smacked his lips expressively. Old Howells frowned at this: he was a chapel man and was very powerful on his knees.

"Now, now!" He coughed warningly. "No silly lol . . . But have you heard the latest?"

The old man was ponderously heavy in his speech. Behind him Rhys smiled, and Twm nodded his head gravely as though to prepare us for the news that was to come. I looked again at the old man. He, too, was smiling, and I could see the tremulous twitching of his lips in his eagerness to tell us the latest gossip.

"What is it?" asked Justin. "Anybody dead, or"—he grinned again—"is it the other way round?"

The old man nodded. "You are right, Justin Peele. You are right. Who do you think it is?" He wiped the broad anvil with the flat of his hand and sat down facing us. "It's Dili Morgan the Felin. Someone has filled her. . . . The talk is all over the place."

Justin laughed, and so did I. Dili had been asking for trouble ever since she left school. She was always laughing was Dili, and you could never go past the Mill without you saw her about somewhere, her yellow hair half-falling about her shoulders, and her skirts pinned up over her petticoats and showing her lovely legs. Of course, we knew who was responsible. She had been carrying on with the English servant at The Frô ever since the June Fair. Ah well, it was the same old story all the time. After all, what else was there for people to do? Nights were dark and long; lanes and woods were lonely, secret places; and supper and midnight courting in the best kitchens after parents had gone to bed did not help matters.

"Poor old Dili," said Justin. "I'm glad I'm not concerned. What about you, Twm?"

Twm lifted his hands in protest and backed away shaking his head. Old Howells pursed his lips.

"Don't joke," he said. "It's serious. The heaviest load is the load of sin. Remember that; and a maid's best dress is modesty. I tell you, Justin Peele, it's time the chapel took charge of things—the vicar just doesn't bother. There's too much of this sort of thing going on in the parish. She'll have to be turned out of the chapel. It's a sad, terrible think; but there you are, what can we do?"

I half-turned from the old man in disgust. That was the trouble with the chapel people: they had to interfere in everybody's private life. According to them, the chapel was only for the pure in heart, for those who had seen the light. I thought of the ceremony that would take place when the matter of Dili and Albert the Frô would be brought before the deacons. First, they would have to be excommunicated, "cutout" as we called it. Then, when propriety was satisfied, the two could be received back into Christian society. There would be the special meeting after the Sunday night service, and after putting the question to the congregation as to whether the two repentants should be re-admitted, there would be the usual showing of hands. I could see Dili sitting there in chapel with her lover, her golden head bowed in shame, not daring to meet the calculating eyes, the pursed lips and nodding heads turned in her direction. I saw it all very clearly; and as I imagined Grett and myself sitting there in such a position, I felt the blood pound in my veins and my jaw go stiff with defiance. But that was impossible, impossible. I put the thought away from me; besides, we were church, not chapel.

"Those buggarrs will work themselves to the grave," said Justin as we drove away from the smithy. "Old Howells is a driver and no mistake. He's as bad as the old man at home.

14

. . . Poor old Dili," he went on. "We're lucky we are not in that lot. . . . The last time I was with her was over a year ago. . . . Brecon Fair night, remember?"

I remembered all right. He had driven off with Dili in the trap, and I had had to walk the twenty-odd miles home. But I made no reply to Justin, and we drove along without saying a word further. I felt tired, hungry; and the movement of the cart, rocking and creaking from side to side, almost made me fall asleep. I leaned against Justin for warmth, and found myself measuring and timing the beat and rhythm of the horses' hoofs on the road. The wind had dropped and the clouds had pulled away to the mountains over towards Brecon way. Across to the east, the Van Rocks rose black and clean-edged against the stars. Ahead of us, I could see the loom of the Allt under the farm. But, first, we had to follow the road down to where the Lyswen cut across our way, and then follow the hairpin bends up to Trewern.

Now that the horses were on the last stretch of hill, they pulled in great style. Sitting there on the cart and feeling the warmth of Justin against my shoulder, I thought of journeys in my childhood: coming from Llandilo or Brecon and wedged in the front seat between my father and mother. There was always such a lovely warmth under the blanket-lined, waterproof rug. Now a trot along the flat, and then leaning forward a little up the hill, or backward downhill, so as to help the mare.

Year in, year out, there was no change. It was the same old road. I knew the shape of every hedge and tree on the way home. And now, at last, here we were at the little dip where the Lyswen flowed across the road. The horses splashed through the shallows, and I feared for a moment that the wheels would sink in the soft mud and sand. But nothing happened. There, rising in front of us, was the Allt, the dreaded dark wood of stunted oaks that clasped the hill under Trewern like a black hand. At my side, Justin sat with his legs dangling over the front of the cart, his bowler low over his forehead. An occasional strong reek of beer came from him. All around us the soft darkness lay heavily on the land. We creaked and strained along, the flickering lamps throwing spasmodic gleams on the ragged hedges. Then, so soon that I realized that I must

have dozed a while, we turned into the narrow lane that led
down to Trewern. Someone had left a candle burning in the
dairy window looking out on the lane; and as we came into
the yard the dogs came rushing and barking to meet us.

Chapter 2

TREWERN lay in a hollow on the side of the valley sloping
down to the Lyswen. Some tall firs and a large sycamore
screened us from the north-east. We were well sheltered
from the biting winds, though we caught all the rain-drift coming from over the Van Rocks. The lane passed by the end of
the house, some dozen or so flagged steps leading down from
it to our back entrance. The cowhouse adjoined the house, it
being only a matter of a few yards from the back-kitchen door
to the stairway that led up to the "dowlod" over the byres.
The outhouses were compact, built in the shape of a square
enclosing the cobbled yard. The farm had been in the family
for years, and if you looked in the church records, or read
the leaning headstones in the graveyard, you could see that
there had been Peeles in the parish for the last hundred and
fifty years. Little wonder, indeed, that the thin smell of our
well water, tainted as it was with the taste of moss and the
sweet earth, was like the breath of life to me.

We were not badly off as things went. The farm was ours,
and money had come down to us as one by one of our relations
had died. Yet, great as was our love as a family for the farm,
it remained our enemy. We fought with it in and out of season. We wrestled with the soil and its outcrop of stone; we
drained the old "wain" until it was criss-crossed with narrow
channels, and every April we carted and spread the manure until every field was black with it. And for all our sweat, for the
resilience of our bones and the fibre of our muscles, for all that
we gave it, the land only grudgingly returned us the fruit of
our labour.

Meanwhile, I unharnessed the horses and saw to their feed
and water. Justin had gone into the house with some goods
he had brought from Brynamman. A storm-lamp hung from

the eight-inch nail over the coffer where we kept the oats, and its soft light was like honey on the cobwebbed walls and the worn, polished mangers with the sloping hay-racks above them. I always enjoyed seeing to the horses. There was no place that was cosier on a winter's night, especially if the wind was howling through the old firs. The rain would make no more than a whisper on the thatched roof, and the dry hay smelt as rich as tobacco or brandy. Night after night, Justin and I would come out to do the chaffing in the loft overhead, and from below us would rise the biting smell of the stable floor, and the heavy, slow crunching of teeth on the hay or oats.

Justin came in just when I was giving Brown the last strokes of the curry-comb.

"Don't bother with that now," he said. "Mother's had supper waiting since nine. Leave them now; I'll come out with you after supper."

He sounded impatient, and I smiled happily to myself. Trust Justin to be full of consideration where mother was concerned! There was a great love between them. Once, when I was whilmenting through a drawer in the old dresser, I had come across a diary which he had kept when he was a boy. The writing was in heavy, laboured copperplate; our Justin was never much of a hand with the pen. Page after page contained some reference to mother: "Churning with Mam to-day." . . . "Helping Mam with the chickens." . . . "Mam bad in bed. Doctor stayed all night. I got out of bed to pray for her." And on one day, after accompanying her to the Christmas market, he had written in red ink: "Mam got top price for the geese to-day. We had a lovely tea at The Welcome. Mam bought me a new knife." There were references, also, to father: "Dad knocked the mare flat with his fist when she kicked him to-day. He hit her in the chops and she fell down like a tree. He is very strong. I wish he was nicer to Mam." So it went on in that little diary on the flyleaf of which he had inscribed: "Justin Peele, his book."

I followed him into the house and swilled my hands in the enamel bowl on the wash-house table. Because of the damp and the milk, together with the yellow soap we used, the towels in the wash-house always smelled sour. From the kitchen came the smell of boiled ham which mother always prepared by removing the rind and placing a layer of brown sugar on it, and then letting it crust in front of the fire so that the sweetness went down through it.

Mother was full of fuss, her eyes shining behind her glasses. She tried the crusted sugar on the ham with her finger. "It's just right," she said, licking her finger and then wiping it on her white apron. She was not tall was mother, and her brown hair had plenty of grey in it. Sometimes, when I went into her bedroom and saw her without glasses, I hardly could recognize her. And there's strange she looked without them. It was then you saw what a beauty she had been in her day. Her eyes were a weak, pale blue, and when she lay there in bed with her glasses on the small table beside her, she looked frail and defenceless. I always felt that I was seeing some other person, and the thought would come to me that this was some shadow of the girl who had once walked the dark lanes with her lovers, listening perhaps to the nightingales beyond Tavarn-y-gwynt, or watching the reflection of the harvest moon in the still stretches of the Sawdde by Allt-y-brain.

To-night she was in her element. It was always the same when father was out. There was nothing she liked better than to have a meal with one of us in secret, drawing the round, three-legged table up to the fire, and having a cup "on the sly" as she called it. On occasion, however, if you drove her too far, she could be tart, and her tongue would run away with her. But her temper never lasted long; she would soon laugh or cry; and when the little strem would be over, she would be herself again, just as if nothing had happened.

"Where is father?" asked Justin. "Parish Council?"

"Yes. He went off after milking. Come now, he'll be back soon. I thought you would be home by nine." She smoothed her apron, and sat down to pour the tea.

"Ha!" Justin half-sneered. "I 'spect he'll come back as pleased as a cockerel because he's floored someone again. God help us, though, if someone has crossed him!"

I looked at mother to see how she was taking this. She just nodded her head. No doubt, she was past caring. She carved

18

the ham with the worn-down carving knife, cutting it in thick slices and heaping them on our plates.

"You can talk," she said. "Why, you are the very spit of him!"

"Duw!" Justin swore good-humouredly. "If he heard you say that!"

"All right, all right!" She smiled across the table at us, and brushed a loose wisp of hair back over her forehead. "You know what I mean," she continued. "You and him are like two tupps, always backing away from each other ready to charge again." She turned to me, smiling. "How about you, Edwin? Did you have to wait long for Justin?"

Of course, she knew as well as I did that Justin had had a drop and that, as usual, he had been late. I nodded, and she gave an understanding toss of her head. We both looked at Justin and smiled. His dark head was bent over his plate. His close-trimmed beard hid most of his face, and his black hair had a slight wave to it. In looks and colouring he took after mother's brothers, the Vaughans of Llanifor, up Cwmwysc way. But there the resemblance ended. I looked from him to mother and then back at him, trying to make out wherein lay that vitality and strange, lovable attractiveness that was his. He was not tall, and his width of shoulder and depth of chest detracted from his five feet eight or so. And yet, for all his width and strength, there were plenty of his own age in the parish who were heavier and more powerfully built. I thought of Jeff Ellis—Grett's brother; Moc Mihartach, who was Justin's friend, and Lloyd Parry. These were strong fellows, and each had his own following and was held to be their champion. What they lacked, however, was that verve of purpose of Justin's which showed in every movement and action of his. Whatever he did, he did it with every ounce of his strength and energy. You could tell this from the expression in his eyes, a blue-black they were, and from the line of his lips and the set of his jaw. When looked at in profile, you saw how straight and almost vertical was the line from the black hair to the deep-set frown that lay between his eyes. The eyes looked at you, direct and fearless. They were eyes that would taunt or

dare sooner than avert themselves for the sake of peace. He
had a terrible temper, terrible because he indulged and con-
trolled it at the same time. There was, too, another side to him;
but he made but few friends, and boasted always that he had
never in his life been in love with any girl.

We had only just finished supper when we heard the dogs
barking, and father's voice silencing them. Mother got up at
once and got another cup and saucer from the dresser. A moment later we heard the bitch outside give a yelp of pain.

"What did I tell you?" said Justin. He filled his pipe slowly.
"Someone has crossed him again."

Mother looked anxiously across at him.

"Hush now, Justin. Let him have his say to-night. Don't
piggat him. . . . You don't understand him like I do."

Justin laughed. "He's always having his say, that's just
the trouble."

"All right, all right!" She ground the iron kettle down on
the coals. "You just be quiet to-night. It's me that will get the
worst of it between you. So keep quiet for once."

Father came in and placed his high-crowned bowler on the
chair nearest the door. He stood for a second or so blinking
at us, as though finding the lamplight too glaring for his eyes.
He shook his overcoat and then spread it over the back of the
skew.

"So you are back then!" He was very slow and quiet, and
he was smiling; a bad sign it was when he was like this. "How
long since you came now?"

Justin answered without looking at him:

"A good hour. . . . Must have been here about ten."

"Ha!" He turned to me: "Were you there in good time to
meet him?"

I nodded, and stretched my legs under the table to ease my
position in he chair. My father stood facing us with his back
to the fire. His well-polished leggings were splashed with mud.
I knew from his manner that he was in one of his slow, dangerous moods. Something had surely happened at the Parish
Council to upset him. What it was, I couldn't guess. Still, I
knew him of old. Sooner or later, in his own time, we would

hear all about it. So, without saying a word, we sat there in silence waiting for him to start.

He said nothing more for a while, but stood there with his feet slightly apart and his hands thrust deep into his breeches pockets. His baldness suited him, and unlike many others who kept their side-hair long and plastered it across the dome of their heads, he took a particular pride in having his hair cut very close above his ears and on his neck. His visit to the Mart was never complete without a visit to the barber's. His face glowed with health, he shaved every day, and his clipped moustache was still a pale-gold in colour. Not one of us took after him in feature. His chin and jowl were heavy, the nose a little fleshy and aquiline. He rarely shouted, and when he was annoyed it was then he was most quiet. He was dressed this evening in his best breeches and polished brown boots and leggings. The black coat buttoned high and cut very square in the shoulders with a double slit in the tail, enhanced his great width and bulk. He tipped the scale at over two hundred, and once when the shearers were at our place, he had walked across the yard with a fifty-six in each hand and with the same weights tied under each foot.

He must have known that we were waiting for him to start the conversation, for he stood there watching us and half-smiling to himself.

"What do you want for supper?" Mother's voice was a little anxious. She was fussing around the table, piling the empty plates on top of each other and making a show of laying the table for him in front of his high armchair.

He glanced carelessly at the table. He had an indifferent taste for food. He always ate what was put in front of him, and when we were boys he would never allow us to pass any comment on the food placed before us. "Eat it," he would say, "and no remarks!"

He crossed the floor and pulled the chair under him to the table.

"You boys had supper?"

"Of course they have." Mother's voice was sharp with her curbed impatience. "Haven't they been back an hour?"

"Hm! Back an hour, eh! Any trouble to-day?"

Justin shook his head.

"How much did you bring?"

"A ton and a half." Justin paused while lighting his pipe, and looked at father over the flame of the match. "It should see us through the winter," he added. "No good going short. . . . Besides, it'll save another journey. We still got about a ton left over from last time."

"Quite right, quite right!" Father nodded and chewed his food slowly. "But what about Duke? You must have half-killed him, as usual."

"Nonsense!" Justin half-twisted his chair from the table and thrust his legs out in front of him, one foot crossed over the other. "What's a ton and a half coming downhill all the way?" He turned to me. "Old Duke was quite fresh when you met me, wasn't he?"

The old man gave me a quick, suspicious glance as I nodded my agreement; and I wondered what it was he was leading up to. That he was nursing something against Justin was plain enough. This was just his way of preparing the ground. Any minute now, I thought to myself, one thing will lead to another, and then we'll soon know all about it.

"That's all right then," he said. "As long as you did not put on the old horse, it's all right. You know how you are with the horses." He munched quietly for a while, cutting the ham carefully with his knife and moistening his finger to pick up each stray crumb from the tablecloth. He picked up his white-and-gold teacup, but before drinking from it, he looked across at mother.

"Nice things I've been hearing to-night . . ." he began.

I sat up in my chair waiting for him to go on. Justin looked at him over his shoulder, the smoke wreathing slowly from his short pipe. Mother paused with the brown wheat loaf held against her blouse, her knife with the butter on it held in mid-air.

"What is it, Daniel?" Her voice trembled with anxiety. "Why don't you say at once what is on your mind, instead of throwing out these old hints?"

"Take your time, don't get so impatient. I've hinted nothing yet; besides, I've got no need to hint. I always speak out." He breathed hard as though he found the strain of keeping calm very difficult. "It's what others hint that make me mad. Have you heard the latest?"

I looked across at Justin, but he sat there smoking with his eyes half-closed as if he was uninterested in whatever father had to say.

"It's Dilys the Felin," continued father. "She is going to have a baby."

Mother opened her lips, but no words came from her. She turned quickly towards Justin, her eyes full of questioning.

Justin laughed.

"Don't worry, Mam," he said. "Ned and me are not in this. We heard all about it at the blacksmith's to-night. . . . Of course, everybody knows who is responsible. It's Albert the Frô. . . ." He looked across at father. "What's worrying you?" he asked quietly. "What have you been hearing about it? . . . Or about me?"

Father's face was a little pale, the colour always drained away from his forehead when he was upset.

"The Frô servant!" he mused. "The Frô servant! Well, well! Then it's lucky for you . . . very lucky . . . Let's hope he will marry the girl. But isn't it a nice thing that whenever a thing like this happens, people always manage to couple your name with it!"

"Who's been talking now?" Justin was still unmoved and contemptuous. "Any fool knows that I've had nothing to do with Dili."

"You were thick enough once. But I'll tell you who was talking." He paused for a moment or so and nodded his head slowly. "It was Ellis Rhos Dirion." (My heart sank at his words, and a heaviness like a bout of chill affected my limbs.) "We all came out of the meeting and we were talking about this, and I heard him behind me talking to Lewsin the Post: 'That girl has never been the same since Justin Trewern was with her,' he said."

"What did you say to that?" Mother's eyes flashed behind her glasses. "Why didn't you knock him flat?" she went on. "Ellis Rhos Dirion, indeed! A fine one to talk he is!"

23

Father cut mother short with a wave of his hand.

"I had to use tact," he said. "Tact! Do you understand? What was the use of taking him up about it? The whole parish would be talking about it to-morrow, and then, where would we be? Never mind, don't worry, I'll settle with Ellis in my way. . . . Plenty of time for that, plenty of time . . . !" He looked at Justin. "It's time you saw to it that you are not the talk of the place. It is only your luck that someone hasn't named you yet. . . ."

I got up and left them to it. The position was hopeless; the old quarrel between us and Rhos Dirion was as bitter as ever. A sadness came over me, and with it there was a feeling of dull, heavy anger as I thought of all that was against Grett and myself. I kept saying to myself that blood was thicker than water. Could it be possible, I kept asking myself, for any lasting happiness to come of our love when such a hatred existed between our families?

Justin did not come out to help me finish the horses. I listened once or twice at the stable door if I could hear the sounds of any quarrelling coming from the house. All was quiet. There was still a light in the kitchen; then, presently, I saw the candle-light up in mother's room, and father's shadow came between it and the window. By the time I went in, Justin, too, had gone upstairs, and the fire was half-dead, the sticks for the morning piled up on the tarred hob.

I lay awake for a long time thinking of Grett. But there was no secret ecstasy in the darkness as I imagined her breathing against me; the thought of the old quarrel was like a door between us. It had started when I was a boy. There had been some argument between John Ellis and father about the *arosfa* on the mountain. John Ellis had complained that father had coursed his sheep away from their pitch. Court proceedings were threatened, but nothing came of it except that, from that time forward, the Peeles and the Ellises were for ever at each other's throats. Justin and Jeff had always fought each other in school. Of course, now that they were grown up, they did not fight any more. Grett's brother had his following in the parish, and I dreaded each market day when Justin would have a glass or two, that he and Jeff would come to blows again. And here were Grett and I in love with each other. Once again, I tried to imagine myself telling Justin and father about Grett. It was terrible, and how would her father and Jeff take it? It was indeed a miracle that the story was not already round the parish. We had been meeting regularly since that night in September at Brecon; the twenty-third of September it was, the night of the fair. I went over it again, seeing the moon coming up over the Vans as I drove home that night with Grett's name singing in my brain. I saw her again as I had first happened on her that night. I had left the noise and glare of the fair thinking to while away a few hours until Justin would be ready to go home. And there, by the river, some little way above the bridge, was Grett Ellis. I wondered for a moment if I should walk past her or turn back. Somehow or other, I had not met her face to face since we had been at school together. And it was then, at that moment, that I saw her in all her loveliness. I stared at her. Her ankles were fine and shapely, her figure supple and high-breasted, and her face was framed by her dark hair. She was lovely, moulded in loveliness; and as I walked towards her, I thought how she would fit into some unwritten, four-line englyn. She looked up as I approached her, and I saw the colour rise and stain her cheeks, her eyes flashing a look of startled recognition as she saw me. Poetry came easily to me that night. The consonants of each word melted into each other, and the vowels of each phrase found its echo in the one that followed it. What was it we talked about? I could not remember; all I could remember was that after the first, shy, awkward words, we walked along the river path, the noise and music of the fair dim and faint in the distance. I was made with ecstasy that night, and all I could think of was Grett and her figure, the expression in her eyes, the sunburn on her cheeks; and with each minute the evening got softer and darker until, at last, the river was brighter than the sky, and the leaves of the alders and the willows were blue-black against it. And when Justin and I drove home over the Black Mountain, I insisted on getting out of the trap and bathing my face in the Usk. Soon, by dawn, the ripple I had kissed would be whispering under the alders at Brecon.

I thought of all this as I lay awake in the darkness, and before I fell asleep the oblong of the window was lighter than the walls of my room.

Chapter 3

OVERHEAD the seven stars of the Plough linked their ageless pattern against the sky. I looked up at my seven old friends; they were over the Black Mountain, just where Dynant flowed, and the long, quiet pool under the Ffalde was probably reflecting their dim gold. Except for the Evening Star and the North Star, they were the only stars I knew. I always looked out for them, and what a comfort it was on a lonely night to see them there; as like as not, they were exactly the same now as they had been when Amos wrote of them and of Orion and the Pleiades.

I paused for a while to look at them and to make the most of the trembling excitement that was on me. At last, it was Sunday evening; and in less than an hour I would be sitting in my corner seat under the stone arch watching the church door to see Grett as she came in. All through the day I had longed for this hour. A great love and high sense of beauty were on me. Dreaming of Grett, I saw beauty everywhere. Day after day was filled with wonder and wild romance. And although there were yet three weeks to go before Christmas, the trees and the mountains had already taken on themselves the mystery of the season. There was a stillness on the land, just as if everything were in a state of breathless waiting. It was the time of the year that I liked best. At about four in the afternoon, all colour would fade from the land; the rocks of Llyn-y-fan lost their purple and would stand clean-edged and symmetrical against the last light in the sky, and the outline of the Allt below the house became like a jagged mass of dark fire. These were great days on the farm. From now on, until the killing and the feathering for the Christmas market, there was very little to do. Justin was out every day doing some hedging and ditching, and I had already finished ploughing the gorse-land above the road. I spent hours every night in the cowhouse, sitting on the hollow seat of the milking-stool, smoking and trying to put all that I felt into some poem or other. And now, here I was on my way to church to see Grett. Father and mother had left soon after the milking, and I had left Justin half asleep in front of the fire.

I breathed deeply. There was a smell of pine in the air, and behind the tang of the frost I caught the bite of the hoar-frost rising from the river. Beyond the Allt I could see the lighted windows of the village. Along the road, going up past Tavarn-y-gwynt, went the bobbing, twinkling lights of a trap. It was probably the visiting preacher on his way to the chapel. That was one advantage the chapel people had over us: they had the opportunity of hearing different preachers once or twice a month. With us in church, it was always the vicar. Still, it was, perhaps, no disadvantage in the long run. His voice was part of the church, he fitted into the white-washed dignity of the old place; and though he only rarely worked himself up into any *hwyl*, you always knew just what you would get from him.

By the time I got to the steep hill leading up from the Sawdde to the church, the bell had changed its tempo. It had started ringing when I was crossing the river above Rhos Dirion, a slow, leisurely tolling, not as heavy as when there was a funeral, but having in it a warning note, as if bidding all who heard that it was getting time for church. It was now more insistent, and I half ran up the hill, fearing every moment that it would stop. Before coming to the churchyard, I wiped my boots in the grass on the roadside, and polished the toe-caps on the back of my trouser legs. The band of my hat was wet with sweat, and I felt myself blushing in anticipation of the moment when I would see Grett.

How strange it was that on a Sunday evening, never mind how dark it was, I never felt any fear at having to pass through the churchyard. I thought of this as I walked through the iron kissing-gates and along the gravel path to the porch. The crooked headstones and leaning crosses gleamed palely in the light coming from the narrow, pointed windows. The stained-glass window with its picture of Mary and the cattle was lit up from within and was framed by the darkness. And there's solid and looking for all the world as if it were a natural growth of the earth itself was the long, low mass of the church against the sky. It was as natural a growth as was a hillock or a clump of oaks; it had its roots in the red soil: the old earth sending up its Hallelujah of stone. It was as real and necessary to the background of my life as were the rocks of Llyn-y-fan or the forest of Blaen Ddol. It was part of Christmas, of Easter, and of the Harvest Thanksgiving; and the bell that pealed for every marriage tolled in turn for every burial we had. And what poetry abided in the graveyard. No, not in the texts that covered the gravestones, but in the names and ages recorded there. Here in a row were the Wynnes, the Lewyses, and there behind the church was the row of the Peeles; here, too, the names of women—the Margarettas, the Annes, and a Myfanwy, a Magdalen, Menna, Aels, or Megan: girls who in their heyday had flashed their dark eyes, perhaps from the same seat that Grett would occupy to-night. And for ever brooding over the scene were the rocks of the Van, some four miles away on the horizon.

The bell stopped as I made my way on tiptoe up the side aisle. Father and mother were already in their seats. And there, self-conscious as ever behind his flowered waistcoat and gold watch-chain, was Lewsin the Post in his conductor's seat by the harmonium. Father gave me a chiding look. He always insisted that we should get to church in good time. "The greater the haste, the greater the hindrance," was a favourite saying of his.

For a few seconds I did not dare to look around. I rested my head on the back of the seat in front of me. To have knelt on the floor would have savoured too much of popery for us: we used the hassocks only for foot-rests. When I sat back in my seat, I saw that the church was well filled. Each family seat had seven to ten in it. But the Rhos Dirion seat was still empty, and I feared that Grett would not be coming. I remembered how I had seen a light in Rhos Dirion as I made my way along the river. A feeling of intense loneliness possessed me, and I saw the endless days that would have to pass before next Sunday's evening service.

Soon, we were standing up for the chant; it was the Sixty-seventh, and we sang it to Poole in E flat. Father, Lewsin the Post, and Rhys Davis Dan'rallt were ringing the tenor part. Father had a high, clear voice, and his pitch was perfect. He always sat in the choir and opposite him, with the sopranos and altos, was mother. No voice ever affected me like mother's alto. There was something sad and rich in it. It wasn't a great powerful voice, but you could always hear her, for her sense of harmony was perfect. But to-night I hardly listened to the singing. Lewsin was driving it a bit, and once or twice I saw father look at him over the top of his Common Prayer. I half-leaned against the stone pillar behind me. To me, the church was empty; I could not make out what had happened to Grett. I half-turned and looked down the dark aisle towards the porch. There were a number of late-comers there, and as soon as the chant ended, there was a tiptoeing of feet along the stone floor. I held my breath in anxiety, convinced deep inside me that Grett was not coming; and then, in one glance, I saw John Ellis, Jeff, and there behind them, her face blushing as she hurried to her seat, was Grett. Her mother was not with them, and that explained the lighted window I had seen at Rhos Dirion. I stretched my legs half along the seat and rested my head back against the pillar while the vicar rasped his harsh-voiced way through the Lesson. I felt so wildly happy that I could not help smiling at the show he made of reading in English for the benefit of the English farm servants. He always read one of the Lessons in English, and also gave out the text in English. It was funny how he shied at the term "whoremongers" and referred to them as "ironmongers."

I was sitting there stealing an occasional covert glance at Grett, and thinking how in an hour's time we would be together again, when I heard a heavy footstep coming up the aisle. I knew at once it was Justin, there was no mistaking his tread. One of his boot-tips was loose, and as he walked past my seat I could hear its tinny clink on the worn stones. I could hardly believe it was him. He had not been to church for months. Yet there he was, crossing in front of the altar to take his place in the choir facing the altos and sopranos. Father's face reddened. I knew quite well what was passing through his mind. That Justin should clatter in so brazenly half-way through the service was in itself an affront to his dignity and, in his way of thinking, to us as a family. To-night, again, there would be a scene at home: father storming, Justin as stubborn and full of

29

mocking devilry as ever, and mother in tears. I shrugged my shoulders and tried to dismiss all thought of it from my mind. It was little wonder indeed that people said that if the Peeles had no one to quarrel with, then they quarrelled and fought with each other.

I saw that Justin was enjoying the stir he had created. The vicar looked hard at him, his clean-shaven lips pressed together in a thin, hard line. Justin sat back in his seat without even pretending to bow his head and pray. The vicar resumed his reading.

As I sat there I wondered what Grett thought of Justin, and once again the thought came to me of how terrible it would be if she were to fall in love with him. I looked across at him, admiring and envying him that he could sit there like that with everyone staring at him. In his serge suit and white shirt and stiff collar he looked, if anything, more square and solid than when in his stained breeches and unbuttoned shirt-neck. Now that he had damped and combed his hair so that it waved ever so little away from his side-parting, his eyes seemed more direct and challenging, his nose straighter and finer, and the black, close-bearded chin and jowl stronger than usual. I could well imagine how "those Peeles" were getting it at this moment. No wonder that the old man was mad with him. I couldn't see mother's face for she had her back to me; but her face was bent over her book, and all I could see was the bun of her hair and the red flush on the nape of her neck.

In the singing that followed I thrilled to hear Justin's bass rolling out in contrast to father's tenor. Their voices blended well, and I saw Grett look across at them. When I caught her glance she gave a lovely look, secret and full of promise. Seen in the soft light of the hanging oil lamps, her dark eyes and parted lips were a picture under the wide brim of her hat. Then Jeff looked across in my direction and I felt myself blush. Jeff Ellis had a heavy, domineering way with him. He was tall and well made, and time and again the drinkers up at the Tavern had spoken speculatively of a clash between him and Justin. What Jeff gained in height and weight was offset by Justin's width and stockiness.

The service over, I took my time in getting out. I saw Grett hurry out in front of her father and Jeff. She gave me one backward look before disappearing through the porch.

Outside the porch the young fellows of the parish were gathered in a half-circle facing the door. Everyone coming out of church ran the gauntlet of their glances and remarks. I tacked myself to the outside fringe of the group, but did not attach myself to anyone in particular for fear that it might be difficult later on to break away and meet Grett. One had to be careful. Tongues would soon start wagging. I was lucky it was winter; and I was already dreading the thought of the light evenings.

One by one the families followed one another out through the low-arched doorway. The lantern fixed above the porch threw its wan light on the faces turned towards it. Behind us the pallid gravestones leaned and sprawled out of the darkness.

Jeff Ellis was standing right in front of the group. As was usual, he had his clique around him. Rhys Blacksmith was there, Iori Allt-y-brain, Shinkin the Shingrig, Dai Alltwen and the others. A guffaw of forced laughter followed something Jeff was saying. I edged a little closer.

". . . I don't care a damme if he hears me or not," Jeff was saying. "Diawl, boys! Does he think he owns the place? Look at the way he came in to-night. I tell you, I would have been ashamed, really ashamed to clonk in like that. . . . No respect at all. . . . Typical of that set. . . . And old Peele thinking himself God Almighty?"

"Tut! tut!" Rhys Blacksmith laughed. "You arr a fine one to talk, Jeff. Diawl! You will be starting a revival soon. I can see him, boys"—Rhys softened his remarks by adopting a mock-hearty, devil-may-care frankness in which there was no real sting; it was nothing but rough flattery. "People bach," he continued, and he started to intone his words like a chapel preacher working up to a grand *hwyl*, "do you believe or not? Listen to me or—wallop!" Rhys illustrated his point by driving his fist into the palm of his hand. "The preacher with the mighty arm! The Reverend Jeffrey Ellis, myn diawl i!"

The crowd laughed again. A moment later Iori All-y-brain spotted me and whispered something to Jeff. Jeff turned and stared at me.

"Well?" He looked across at me, we were about the same

height, and his eyes dared and taunted me to say something. "Got anything to say?" he continued. "You are very quiet, gwas?"

I said nothing. I did not want a scene outside the church. My legs trembled and my stomach turned to water inside me.

"Speak up, Ned." Iori leaned towards me. I hated the false encouragement in his voice.

"Carry on," I said. I could hardly recognize the sound of my voice; then I cleared my throat of its phlegm. "Shout a bit more; Justin'll be out in a minute—perhaps he'll hear you. Carry on!"

Everyone was suddenly quiet. I looked up and saw Justin standing on the step under the porch. Someone behind me—I think it was Prosser Ty Unoos—called out protestingly: "Not here, boys, not here. Outside the gates if you want trouble."

I watched Justin as he came down the steps towards us. He had come to church without his overcoat, and his square-cut jacket was buttoned up to his collar.

"What's the fuss about?" He put his bowler on his head, his face in shadow against the light behind him.

I indicated Jeff. "Ask him," I said. "Strikes me he wants to start converting you."

"You!" Justin looked up at Jeff. "Always one for talking you are. What is it now?"

"I don't want no trouble," began Jeff. "Not here anyhow. I've got a character to keep, even if you haven't. See! But don't start thinking you have got it all your way. Diawl!" A note of reckless glory crept into his voice. "You think you can lord it here just like your old man, don't you? Well, think again, Peele. And don't forget, you haven't got Moc Mihartach or any of your set with you to-night."

"Shut up!" Justin wasn't shouting, but there was a hard edge to his voice. "I know you, Jeff Ellis, like your old man you are, all wind and bladder you are——"

"You keep my father out of it——"

"Aye, same as we've kept him off the mountain. See! Now just you listen here. I've had nothing to do with you for years, and I don't want anything to do with you. See? I don't see you

32

when I'm out, so keep out of my way and keep your mouth shut or——"

"Or what?" sneered Jeff.

Justin moved a step towards him and touched him on the chest with his forefinger, punctuating each word he said with a little tap: "Or anything you like," he said. "Or two of your sort, and anywhere you like. Here, outside, and whenever you like." He paused and looked at the others. "And if any of you fancy a go, don't worry that Moc Mihartach is not here." He laughed and turned to me. "Duw! If Moc was here to-night——"

"Boys! Boys!" It was old Prosser again. "Go home now. Have you no respect for the day? You, Justin Peele, it would be far better if you kept away altogether from church if this is what you come here for."

Justin looked round at the crowd. He nodded quietly.

"All right." He turned to Jeff. "Just remember what I said. Any time, any place, see?" He gave a side-jerk of his head for me to follow him. "Come on, Ned, we've got no partners here. And if you are like me"—he laughed—"you don't want any of them. Come on."

We went together down the path. After we had gone a little way we heard a laugh follow us from the group. Justin stopped.

"Come on!" I took his arm. "There's none of them got any stomach. You know that. They only sneer and laugh when there's no one around."

"You are right. Diawl! I'll mark that Jeff one of these days. I'll make him glad to keep the other side of the road when I'm about."

When we got on to the road, Justin paused and filled his pipe.

"Are you going home?" I asked him. I couldn't understand why he had come to church. He grinned at me, his eyes shining and full of mischief.

"No!" He puffed at his pipe until the tobacco glowed. "No, I think I'll go after Gaynor. Did you see her there near the back?" He gave an appreciative nod. "She looked all right, didn't she? Being away has smarted her up a bit, eh?"

I smiled and understood. Gaynor Fedwarian had come home after a year's stay in the mining valleys. What Justin said was true. She had brought something of the town style with her. If she was the same as when she went away, Justin would not be home until the early hours. Still, it was no concern of mine; trust him to look after himself.

"You be careful," I laughed. "Mind she doesn't catch you one of these nights."

"You look after yourself, boyo. And don't go you fancying yourself with Gaynor. It's you and young fools like you that get caught. Young blood and no timing. . . . You serve your 'prenticeship first. What are you doing? Are you going home now?"

"Of course! What do you think? Where else could I go?"

He gave me a slow, shrewd look.

"I don't know, I don't know." He half-closed an eye, and blew out a reflective jet of smoke. "You are a bit of a mystery, Ned. Anyway, be careful!"

He left me at that and hurried off up the road. I waited until his footsteps passed out of hearing. The vicar and the church-wardens were now coming down the path to the kissing-gates, father and mother with them. Jeff and his crowd were still by the porch door. I hurried away, my heart beating quickly, and as I ran along the grassy edge of the road, I felt my legs tremble with nervous excitement.

As I ran along I wondered if Grett would still be waiting for me at the top of the lane. It was now surely a quarter of an hour since we had come out of church. Overhead the stars were brilliant, and they showed up the shape of the hedges and trees quite clearly.

She must have heard me running towards her, for when I came to fir trees she was out in the middle of the road. I held her close in my arms, and her cheeks were on fire against my own. It was hard to realize that, at last, after the long waiting, she was here in my arms. I kept saying to myself over and over: this is not any slip of a girl that I have just met, but she, Grett, Grett Ellis. I strained her closer to me, loving every

34

touch of her, and loving the darkness, the stars, the trees, the dark comfort of the hedges, and loving too the secrecy and danger of our love.

"What happened?" she asked. "I thought you were never coming."

"I couldn't get away. . . . You know how it is. I daren't make it too obvious."

"I know," she said. "Tell me, did Jeff see you come up the road?"

I said nothing to her about the scene outside the church, there would be time enough for that before I'd leave her.

"Don't worry," I whispered. "Nobody guesses anything. How about you? You haven't heard anything?"

"Nothing," she said. "Not a thing."

We left the road and took the path across the fields down towards her home. As we walked along, I felt the pressure and warmth of her arm increase against my own. We did not speak, and I knew quite well where our steps would take us. Back in the soft autumn nights we had discovered the tree-sheltered dingle at the edge of the wood near the Sawdde. Whenever it was dry we made for this spot and lay there until it was time for her to go home.

We were soon there. Beyond us we could hear the soft splash and trickle of the river. Around us the ferns were dry and rusted, and as we made our way down into the sheltered hollow, the bare trees on the banks rose higher and higher against the stars. Grett stood looking at me while I took off my overcoat and spread it on the ground.

And now, at last, we lay locked in each other's arms. This was the end of all the days and nights of my longing for her. I tried to live each moment as if it were an eternity, but her kisses came between me and my dreams. Then, as soon as the last kiss was over and I rested my face against her cheek, the star caught between the stark fork of the oak above us filled me with its glory; and there, beyond the line of her cheek was the round breast of the hill across the river, soft and dark against the sky. Around us the wind rustled thin and sharp through the briars and tangled branches, but we felt no breath of cold upon

35

us. We were warm against each other, her breath was sweet in my nostrils, and her soft, fine hair smelled as fresh and sweet as rain-water.

I looked down at her, marvelling at her beauty. Because of Jeff, no one in the parish had ever tried to make fresh with her, none had ever dared to whistle after her or make to follow her from church; and, certainly, no one had ever hung about Rhos Dirion and thrown a pebble at her window. And here she was breathing against me; her feet, her knees, her whole body pressing close to me.

She wasn't tall was Grett; yet, because of her slimness and the way she had of walking, you thought she was much taller. She was high-breasted and long-hipped: she gave the impression that denuded of her clothes she would run with the long, easy grace of a hound. But to describe her beauty was beyond me. Because she was Grett Ellis, her hair was dark and soft; she was as dark and lovely as her name. How could she have been fair-haired and blue-eyed? It was unthinkable. And because she had spent her summers in the fields and lanes around Rhos Dirion, her beauty had caught something from the flower of the blackthorn, and her lips were as sweet and red as were the wild strawberries that grew in the shady hedge-banks. She was Grett Ellis, and when I whispered her name to myself she was all these things to me. She was the Sawdde herself, lovely and sudden; she was the blossom in a springing wood, the darkness that slid over the fields on a summer's night; and when I held her in my arms and kissed her, it seemed that some part of me stood still and quiet, and listened to all the rivers and brooks singing her praise.

So, lost in the ecstasy of our warmth together in that wintry darkness, we lay there while our stolen minutes slipped away from us. It was not many months since our first kisses, and I desired no more than to undo her coat and so draw her even closer to me. Thus, feeling her breathe against me, I felt we could lie together there for all time.

The minutes passed and I knew she must soon be going. I looked up through the dishevelled tangle of her hair at the stars —she had taken her hat off and it lay crown-downward on the grass behind her—and saw the Plough and the glimmer of the

36

Milky Way right over our heads. Where was Justin now? I imagined him with Gaynor. . . . I listened to the sounds of the night. There was no stillness anywhere. Faint rustlings disturbed the ferns around us, a seared branch rasped against another with a harsh, insistent sound. Far off, down towards Allt-y-brain, a dog barked, and then another from the direction of the mill. Grett stirred and half-raised herself on her elbow.

"This is terrible, isn't it?" Her voice trembled.

"Terrible?" I heard myself echo her word while I continued to look up at the stars. Somehow, it made me quite giddy to be looking at the inky void closing in on every star. I fancied myself standing on the very edge of the world and looking into a great depth.

"Yes. All this hiding from people, and both of us wanting each other. Aren't you tired of it?"

There was no shyness in her eyes. Instead, she met my glance with her eyes bright and shining. I nodded my agreement.

"Aye. I wish we could make a clean break. . . . We've been carrying on like this since that fair night. . . ." I saw the Usk again, and the way the last light in the sky had lingered on the waters.

"I'm game for anything," I went on. "We are both of age. I don't care a damme for our families, I'm tired of this row between them. . . . Just you say the word, Grett, an' I'll come up to see your father and mother right away; yes?"

But even as I spoke, I saw clearly the figure of my father voicing his hatred against Grett's family, and the memory of the scene outside the church this night was vivid in my mind. Justin and Jeff Ellis! There would never be any peace between them. Grett and I would have to break away completely from our families and start on our own. It was difficult because blood counted for so much. Even to me, Grett's people were still the Ellises of Rhos Dirion. Ever since I could remember, the thought of the Ellises had been a pall on my happiness. I remember how, on a sunny morning, I would stand on our yard looking over towards the rocks of Llyn-y-fan, seeing the mists rising from the Sawdde, the sun making the leaves of the poplars all a-dazzle; and then my eyes would fall on the hated fields of Rhos Dirion, and the thought of John Ellis and Jeff would come between me and the morning. And now, here I was with Grett Ellis in my arms, her breasts soft against me and her lips waiting for my next kiss.

After I had told her of the row outside the church, she was very quiet for a while.

"How was Jeff?" she asked at length. "No, don't tell me," she shook her head with exasperation. "I don't know what is wrong with them all. And your Justin is as bad as Jeff; they never miss a chance to fly at each other."

Her voice was filled with bitterness, and I did not contradict her.

We lay together again, very quietly, for all the passion had now gone out of our bodies. I heard the sound of the wind again in the branches of the oaks. It was thinner, sharper; and the air was colder so that I clung to Grett for warmth. The sound of the river, too, came clearer; crystal-cold it was, and I thought the night was like a black hand closing around us. We did not speak, and after a while Grett rose to her feet and smoothed her skirts and tidied her hair.

"I must hurry," she said. "It must be nearly ten."

I looked at my watch. It was only just turned nine, so we took our time as we walked along. And it was then as we walked along, Grett with her head resting against my shoulder, that the thought came to me how I might go away to the mining valleys. There was plenty of work in Merthyr, Aberdare, and the Rhondda. There was good money there, too. You had only to see the Shonies in the pubs on a fair day to see how well they were doing. Quite a number of the boys from the parish had already gone away to the valleys. I said nothing to Grett about it, but I could have a word with Justin about it.

When we got within sight of Rhos Dirion, we stopped. The kitchen window was not shuttered, and the glow of the lamp threw a soft light on the yard outside.

"Don't come any farther," whispered Grett. "I'll be all right now. Which way are you going home? Not along the road, are you?"

"Don't worry," I said. "I'll cut across the fields. I'll not meet anyone then. Will you be all right?"

I kissed her again, and once more my passion for her came over me like sultry wind. It was now, I thought, we should be together again.

Too soon, I was alone, listening to her as she hurried down the path towards the house. I waited there until I saw the door open. For a second or so I saw her outlined against the light that streamed out past her. Then the door closed. All I could see now was the greyish mass of the white-washed wall and the black roof against the sky. I crossed the river where it flowed noisily over the stones and made my way up through the fields to the village. All I wanted now was to get to bed, to lie in the darkness thinking of Grett and remembering how she had lain in my arms. I met no one on the way, and when I got home father and mother had gone up to bed. Justin was still out, and before going upstairs I quietly put some more coal on the fire in readiness for his return.

Chapter 4

THE next fortnight went by without incident and almost before I could realize it, the feathering was in full swing. Since early morning, the first of them arriving just after six, the women had been busy in the kitchen. Justin and I had been up all the night before killing the fowls, geese, and turkeys. I loathed the job. The reek of the poultry almost sickened me. Between us, we had killed over two hundred birds. The geese had been the worst. I could never overcome my dislike each time I held the long, sinuous neck in my hand, the warm, struggling body held between my thighs, and the slender, sharpened blade of my pocket-knife sinking into the downy neck behind the ear, the red stain of blood welling on the whiteness that was like snow.

It was now getting on for nine in the evening. As the women were in the kitchen, mother had prepared and laid the food in the best kitchen. Justin was already washed and changed. He had one of mother's best white aprons tied over his breeches.

"What a damme row! Listen to them!" He jerked his head sideways towards the kitchen. At that moment another wild,

raucous laugh rang out, followed by shrieks from the ot[h]
women.

"That's Mati Nanteos." He grinned. "Trust her," he c[on]
tinued; "she lives for shearings, funerals, and do's like t[h]
Good God! Listen to them! I bet Mam's shocked. . . . Y[ou]
know what old Mati's jokes are like!"

I helped myself to more cheese. The big round cheese [of]
sheep's milk that had been the rounding of a barrow wheel [had]
dwindled to half its size since the morning. But there you a[re]
the helpers had to be well fed. The table was still littered w[ith]
the remains from tea; we lived well, and whoever came [to]
Trewern for the feathering, shearing or harvest, had ne[ver]
cause to complain about the food they received.

"We will have to go and give them a hand again." I got [up]
and turned the large wheat-loaf top downwards on the bre[ad]
board. "It'll be a late night," continued Justin. "The old m[an]
has killed too many again. If they'd only shut up a bit a[nd]
get on with it, we could get the cart loaded up and get a f[ew]
hours' sleep. Mam will be dead-beat by to-morrow night. .[..]
There's no sense in the old man. Nothing but drive, drive [all]
the time!"

I agreed with him. It was nineteen miles to Brecon. Y[et,]
tired as I was, and with the prospect of only a few hours' sl[eep]
before starting, I found myself looking forward to the journ[ey.]
The excitement of Christmas was in the air. A grand rid[e]
would be over the mountain, leaving the twin forests of Bl[a]
Ddol on our left and seeing the Van Rocks coming up agai[nst]
the dawn. There was more than a chance, too, that I would [see]
Grett there. But this time we would not walk along the riv[er]
bank. Somewhere in my mind, I saw us wandering through [the]
darkened streets and turning into a church because it w[as]
the Christmas-tide. I wanted to be sitting with her in so[me]
gloomy interior, hearing music, and seeing the stained gl[ass]
and the candle-light gleaming on the brasses.

I followed Justin into the kitchen. A scene like a miniat[ure]
snowstorm met us as we went in: the place was filled w[ith]
flecks of down. The women, seated in a large circle with [a]
large brass pan in their midst which we used for mak[ing]
"brekki" for the cows were plucking for all they were wo[rth]

The stench of entrails and grease was strong in the room. On a long scrubbed table, as far as they could place it from the fire, mother weighed and priced each bird as it came trussed to her hands. Near her, the hampers were filled to the top, each fowl wrapped in butter-paper and decorated with sprigs of parsley. Father was busy cleaning the chickens. His hands were steaming from the warmth of the innards which he removed expertly and quickly. From time to time he dipped his hands in the pan of hot water that stood by him. He looked up as Justin and I came in.

"Come on!" he shouted. "You, Edwin, give a help with the feathering. Justin, you help your mother there."

"Why don't you go to bed, Mam?" Justin spoke to mother across the room. He turned in explanation to the women: "She should go, shouldn't she? She'll have to be off with father in the trap before six. She'll be done up if she don't rest!"

"That's right. You go, Mrs. Peele," said Mrs. Rees Nanteos. Mati Rees was a stout woman, low-bosomed, dark-eyed, her hair now white with down. She always came to help us with the shearing and the feathering, and never missed a sale or a funeral in the parish. She would stay with us now until we returned from market, seeing to the milking and the pigs, and doing all that was necessary. "You go," she added, "just like Justin Peele says. We'll manage all right."

Mother looked across at father. He nodded with good humour. In front of people he was always the same: jocose, easy-tempered, and ready to enjoy any joke.

"Go on!" He waved his hand at her, half in command. "We'll manage fine. You go and get some sleep."

"We won't keep him long," shouted Mag the Carpenter. "Keep the bed warm for him!"

Mother smiled and blushed, her eyes behind her glasses were moist and shy. But she was tired, there was no doubt about it. She wiped her hands on her soiled apron.

"I'll go then," she said quietly. "And thank you one and all for your help. Daniel will see you before you go. And make a good supper. There is plenty there for everybody, remember now."

She gave Justin a little smile as she passed him.

"Don't worry about saying your prayers," he whispered to her. "I'll say one for you!" The next moment, he started weighing and packing, fitting each fowl firmly into the hamper beside him.

From now on the jests became more suggestive and lewd. Some of the older women raised their hands in mock expostulation.

"Oh! Stop it now!" shrieked Mrs. Beynon from the village. "My stays is giving already."

"I'm soaking," laughed Mati Nanteos. "Oh dear, what a day we have had!" She looked round at us in turn. I smiled back at her. "There's quiet you are," she said to me. "Thinking of some girl, I'm sure."

I laughed. For a moment I saw Grett's face in front of me, her hair parted deep on the left side and sweeping over her forehead.

"He's blushing." Gwen Tŷ Gwyn, a young girl of twenty or so, pointed at me with a goose-quill. "You are giving the game away, Ned. Who is it? Come on, tell us, there's a sport."

"What game?" I tried to look surprised.

"Ah-ha! Your eyes are shining," shouted Mati. "You can't fool me, Edwin. I know that look in Rees' eyes!"

"Rees gets it once a year, don't he?" Gwen Tŷ Gwyn looked up from the goose she was plucking, her black eyes dancing with wickedness. She turned to me: "You don't feel like that, do you, Ned?"

Mati Rees tried to look dignified. She was the mother of eleven children. "You be quiet, Gwen," she said. "I'm married and you are not. You didn't ought to know about such things. . . . You young girls! Too impatient you are. Look at Dili the Mill now!"

"All right," replied Gwen. "But just you watch you don't run out of names. You ought to make a sack for Rees and tie it round his neck every night!"

"Now, now, Gwen!" Father shook his finger at her. "You let Mati Rees be. A good mother she is and"—he paused significantly—"she *is* married."

A silence fell on the group. They were thinking, no doubt, of Dili. The matter of her condition had been brought before the chapel on the previous Sunday, and she had been excommunicated until she should ask for re-admittance after her marriage.

"But aren't we getting away from the point? Who is this little girl they were hinting about, Edwin?"

Mrs. Beynon was a honey-voiced, diminutive, neat-haired woman dressed in black. Her fingers, nimble and quick from years of dressmaking plucked at the feathers as though they were harp-strings.

"Tell us," she insisted, "who is the young lady? Is she chapel or church?"

"He's been going very regular to church lately," said Mag the Carpenter. "A sure sign that is, isn't it?"

I looked up and caught father's eye fixed on me. He was looking at me as though I were still in my teens. Justin, too, was looking at me, his eyebrows raised and his eyes twinkling. For a moment I was tempted to shout Grett's name at them; I wanted to hear the sound of her name in our kitchen. But no, it wouldn't do; the time was not yet ready for that.

"P'raps it's Gaynor Fedwarian," I said. "If Justin would just step down, I might be able to get in there."

That started them on another tack, and they started to tease Justin, but he gave back as good as he received; and the time passed with their fun and laughter ringing through the house. I sat there with them, keeping the conversation going, in case they should come back to Grett and me. And the thought of her was with me all the time like a breath of honeysuckle from a June hedge.

Chapter 5

I AWOKE suddenly the next morning, my brain as clear as if I had had a whole night's rest. Father and Justin were already downstairs. I could hear them about in the kitchen, the purr of the little bellows coming up through the floorboards of my room. I got out of bed and lighted the candle. It was just on three. What a blessing it was that we had loaded the cart the night before! All we had to do now was to get breakfast over, and then we would be on the road.

The candle-light played on the shining chest of drawers that stood in the corner of my room. And there's warm and nice on a winter's morning was the sheepskin under my bare feet. The window was a patch of shining blackness reflecting my shadow and the candle flame. There was no sign of the dawn in the sky and the sharp tang of the air in the back of my nose told me it was frosty outside. Before I had finished buttoning my breeches, I could smell the bacon frizzling downstairs. I delighted in the sounds of the morning preparation, the purr of the bellows, the clatter of the cups and saucers, and the mutter of conversation that came up to me.

I opened the window and looked out. Lights were twinkling in many farms. In the far distance I could just make out the shape of the Van Rocks. The weather was perfect, the poultry would keep as cold and firm as iron. The roads, too, would be like marble. The mare's shoes had been roughed only two days ago; besides, in weather like this, we always took some frost-nails, a hammer and pincers with us. Justin could nail and clinch a shoe with the best of them.

"So you are up. Good! We'll be off in a wink!"

Justin was standing in the doorway of my room looking at me. He was already washed and dressed. His leggings were like glass, and he was wearing a blue tie with yellow horse-shoes printed all over it. He had trimmed his moustache and beard very close the night before, and the furrows made by the comb showed in his damped hair. He was in great spirits, and he leaned against the door-frame while I got my best shirt and stiff collar out of the drawer.

"Did you shave last night?"

"Aye."

"Right. Get a quick swill. The water's like ice, it'll take all the sleep out of you."

I followed him downstairs. Father was sitting on a milking-stool in front of the fire, his breeches unbuttoned at the knees, and the bellows in his hands. I could hear mother and Mati Rees in the dairy. The old man looked over his shoulder at me. He hadn't washed or shaved yet.

44

"Get washed," he said. "Breakfast is almost ready. Don't waste time now."

Out in the yard everything was frost-white and ringing. Justin had already broken the ice-crust on the rain-water barrel, and I had only to fill my bowl with the dipper that stood nearby. The cold water set my blood tingling though it was impossible to get a lather on the flannel. With cupped hands I splashed and sluiced the water over my face until my skin was smooth and taut.

For a half-minute or so I stood there taking in the unreal beauty of everything around me. It was unreal because it was not night, for I had had my sleep; and it was certainly not one of our mornings with the stars flashing overhead and Mati Rees here to do the milking for us. I felt I was in touch with the mystery and wonder of the Christmastide. With only two days to go you could feel it in everything: it was in the stillness, in the frost, and in the stars with the sky black around them. Breakfast this morning, too, would be different, the wood fire burning brighter, and the white cloth whiter than ever. As I stood there thinking these things, I paused in towelling myself to look at the friendly shape of the old house with the kitchen window alive with the flames and the lamplight; and down in the valley beyond the rise of the village I could just make out the pale mist rising where the Sawdde wound its way past Allt-y-brain and the Cwmsidan. Where was Grett now? I imagined her hurrying in and out of the kitchen at Rhos Dirion, getting breakfast ready and preparing for the journey to Brecon. And though I had never seen her in any other than her Sunday clothes, I imagined her in her white apron, the tapes tight round her waist, her arms bared to the elbows, and her white blouse rucked and taut over her breasts.

"Breakfast, boys!" Mother stood in the doorway, her apron showing up in the half-light. Justin answered her from the stable, and followed me into the house.

Half an hour later we were ready to start.

"Don't drive the old mare too hard now," said Father. "You've got a good four hours, plenty of time in front of you. Your mother and I will be there in good time. Take it easy till you come to the Usk, and walk up the hills, both of you."

"All right! All right!" Justin buttoned his overcoat and set his bowler jauntily on his head. He paused as he rested a foot on the wheel-spoke to get into the cart. "Get a stall out of the draught." He looked over his shoulder at father. "Remember now, Mam caught a cold there last year."

"Go on with you!" Mother laughed happily. She was just like a young girl. "I'll be all right," she continued. "Don't you worry about me. There is bread and cheese in the big hamper, in the top corner, and don't lose the cloth."

We were soon away, the mare pulling at the bit and trying to break into a half-trot. Justin and I sat on a plank resting across the cart with our backs against the hampers. Justin's overcoat collar was turned up so high that it tilted his bowler over his forehead.

We got down to the river in no time. The light from the lamps shone on the frost-webbed hedges. As we passed through the low water before coming to the bed of the river, the ice crunched like soft glass under the wheels. The river-smell was sharp and cold, and the tinkle of the water was like a spoon on a cup. Somewhere, so I thought, there was an englyn or some form of poem there behind the darkness, the water, and the cold breath of the morning. And following on such thoughts, there came a sweet longing on me again for Grett. What would I not have given to have her sitting beside me at this moment, holding the old mare for a minute or two just to listen to the sound of the water and to feel the warmth of her shoulder against my own.

Once through the river, we saw the candle-light shining through the window of Nanteurin. Outside the house, a low cart piled high with sacks and boxes, rested on its shafts.

"I bet old Parri has got some fine boots ready, eh? He's put plenty of work in this winter . . . should do well, too, fair do's. Come, Brown!" Justin slapped the mare with the reins. From here to the village it was a steady pull; we were, in fact, against water all the way until we reached the Usk.

As we left Nanteurin behind us, I thought of old Parri and his stock of hand-made boots. He was a fine craftsman was Parri. We swore by his boots, they were the only ones we ever had that were proof against the morning dew on the hay-

46

making; and no slush would ever go through them either. He could make a woman's boot, too, the leather as soft as a glove and with fancy work on the toe-caps. And what great nights we had there in his workshop. It was, I suppose, the most popular meeting-place in the village, next to the blacksmith's, whatever; the only difference being in the company. In old Parri's it was religion, poetry and music. Parri was a great one for remembering sermons. He could imitate the old preachers and would reproduce the "tonc" and the *hwyl* so well that you would forget the smell of the leather and think you were in a chapel or a sassiwn with the heavens opening above you. Then, again, Huws the Tailor would be there, reciting englynion with such sweetness and felicity that for days afterwards I would be haunted by the growing beauty of some line or phrase.

When we got to the village there were lights in almost every house. Soon, most of the cottagers would be on the road to Brecon, too proud and shy to turn round as a trap would overtake them, yet sure of getting a lift all the same.

"I suppose we are about the first," I said. There was no sign of a cart anywhere, no sound of hoofs on the road coming up from the mill or the road past the blacksmith's.

"Perhaps they are all in front," said Justin. "Anyway, they'll all be at the Tavarn. How about a drop when we get there? Just to warm us up, eh?"

There was something cosy in the thought of a drink. The Tavarn would be crowded with farmers. Except for the annual eisteddfod which was held in the schoolroom, and the sheep-dipping, no policeman ever came near us. And on a morning like this, well, it was "open-tap" at the Tavarn; and so it would be all day until we came home from the market.

We rumbled and swayed along the frost-bound road, the wheels occasionally getting out of the cart-ruts and then slipping back again with a jolt that made the hampers creak behind us. The trees on each side of the road were frozen-still, gaining height with each turn of the wheels until they towered over us and were gone.

I had got used to the jolt of the cart by now and, but for the prospect of a drink at the Tavarn, I would have let myself go to sleep. I was quite warm. The thickness of the sacks which we had wrapped round our feet retained the warmth, and I was wearing the thick woollen gloves which mother had knitted for me two or three winters back. How Justin kept warm with his bare hands holding the reins, I could not understand. But there it was, Justin never felt the cold. As he said, his beard kept him warm. I drew my hand over my face. I had shaved very close the night before. The hollow-ground had sung as it went over my cheeks. They were still smooth, not a bristle caught in the rough wool of my glove. Being fair, I would still be clean by the end of the day.

"Duwedd! What a crowd!"

As I looked up and saw the gleaming trap-lamps and the glistening flanks outside the Tavarn, I felt again that quickening stir of my blood in my veins. The yard outside the bar was crowded. And backward though I was in mixing with people, I felt I wanted to be one of the crowd, laughing and talking with a glass in my hand. This was where the Christmas really began. First, the dark of the winter morning, then the journey in the cart through the stirring, candle-lighted village; and now, like a landmark on this journey, here was the inn with its white-washed walls and unshuttered windows and open door.

Justin was first down from the cart. He stamped his feet on the hollow-sounding frozen ground. I was on his heels as he stepped into the stone-flagged passage leading into the bar. Jos Watkins was in his shirt-sleeves behind the counter. Jinnie and Nell were there, too, drawing beer for all they were worth.

"Here they are!" Jos waved a hand to us. He had a half-filled mug in front of him. He gave us a wink and a nod, and lifted his glass in greeting. "Jawch! We thought you had gone, didn't we, boys?"

He was all smiles; business was good. It was not often the bar was as full as this. Jinnie and Nell looked across at us with shining eyes.

"What are you having?" Jos half turned and threw out a fat hand to indicate the casks and bottles behind him. "Anything you fancy. Whisky-hot with a lemon and sugar? Rum and hot milk? Beer? Stingo?—there's plenty of body in that. What about you, Justin?"

"Aye. Stingo for me."

"You, Ned?"

I looked at the brown almost treacle-like beer set before Justin.

"No. Whisky-hot for me, a big one."

"Right you are!"

Jinnie, red-cheeked, and with her hair done in tight little curls, filled my glass for me. I watched her as she put the sugar, lemon, and hot water in. She blushed and dimpled as she handed me the glass.

"Iechŷd da!"

The whisky warmed me through and through. Another one like this and I might be able to fall asleep in the cart. Justin called for another pint.

"Same again for me," I said. Justin paid. "You keep your money!" He pushed my hand away as I tried to pay. "Have a good time after the market's over," he said.

He lifted his glass to me, giving me a sly wink at the same time.

"I suppose you've got quite a lot on the cart there, Justin?" said Owen Allt-y-grug.

"Aye! We've got a good load."

"Hm! It ought to be a good market. Those colliers will be there in crowds. Plenty of sovrans there—that's where the money is, eh?"

Justin agreed, but he was non-committal regarding how many fowls we had. Beyond an evasive "tidy few," he gave no one any information.

"Now then, boys!" Dai Pantglas banged his empty mug on the counter. "Which of us is going to lead? Come on, let us have the names now. You, All-y-grug, you have the hat. . . . A pencil, somebody, and paper. Right! First me . . . now you, Allt-y-grug . . . you, Justin . . . now Brynmair . . . you, Isaac Nichols . . . and you . . . and you . . ."

"Hope I don't get it," muttered Justin. "There'll be a hell of a crush behind us. I'd rather take our time, don't you think so?"

He was right. With the bulk of the carts in front of us, we could take our time without driving the mare. Father and

49

mother would be in the market long before us. There was no need at all to hurry.

"Isaac Nicholas!" Pantglas held the slip of paper in his hand. "Come on, Isaac, one last one, quick now. You've got to be away."

Isaac Nicholas Cefnwern, tall, ragged-moustached, and with a blue-striped celluloid collar round his long red neck, emptied his glass with one gulp. His Adam's-apple did not move as he drank. He must have just opened his gullet and poured the beer down his throat.

"Right!" He wiped his mouth with the back of his hand, and made his way to the door. "I'll lead"—he seemed proud of the honour to be first on the road—"I'll see you all in The Fiddlers to-night. Come on, on the road, boys!"

One by one the men left the bar. The rumble of the wheels told us that the carts were already taking the road. Justin looked round quickly. Everyone was outside now, old Jos had gone into the kitchen to have his breakfast. Justin winked at me, then he leaned over the counter and whispered into Nell's ear. "One little one," I heard him say. "Just one for the road, eh?" He made to put his arm round Nell's waist and draw her to him. Jinnie looked on smiling, her lips parted and her eyes dancing. Nell wriggled herself free.

"A slap you'll get, Justin Peele. Get on with you! Go and scratch!"

Justin smiled appraisingly at her.

"All right, Nell. I'll collect later," he said. "One of these dark nights, eh?"

Nell snorted and made a great ado of wiping the beer-streaked counter. But she was pleased. I could see how her pouting lips were half-breaking into a smile. She looked up suddenly, her dark eyes half-reproachful and shining.

"Go on with you," she laughed. "What about Gaynor? Besides, you are afraid of the dark!"

"We'll see, we'll see!" Justin turned to go. "I'll remember that, Nell fach, and don't you forget it. . . . Just you give me a chance one of these dark nights!"

He chuckled to himself as he made his way out through

50

the passage. "She's all right is Nell," he said. "Too respectable for me, though!"

I thought of his words as we took our place behind the long string of cart-lamps. In a way I envied him his easy way with women. As he said, he had never been in love with anyone. He whored promiscuously, taking his pleasure when and where he could. Women never troubled him. He rarely spoke of them except to repeat some bawdy story he had heard; desire in him seemed almost non-existent. A woman was nothing more to him than a being whom he could enjoy. Beer, a brawl; a half-hour or at the most a night with some hoyden—these were his natural relaxations from work.

We were soon on the mountain road. There was still no sign of the dawn. The stars were as bright as when we started. For nearly a quarter of a mile ahead of us the carts straggled on in a linked line of jogging lights. Shouts of laughter came back on the wind, and sometimes a song or a hymn sung in harmony. The whisky was now beginning to take its effect on me. My feet were on fire under the sacks and I knew from the pulse-beats in my temples that I had had quite enough. I answered Justin only in monosyllables.

"Why don't you have a sleep?" suggested Justin. He worked his back into a comfortable position against the hampers so that I could lean against him. I lay there against the wall of his back, and when I awoke we were rising up towards Trecastle. It was almost day. A greenish-blue light tinged the sky over the mountains. The Van Rocks were black and terrible against the paling stars.

Just before we got to Senny, father and mother overtook us in the trap.

"You'd better hurry," called father. "You can let the mare have her head now. I'll get the stall ready for you."

He was in his plaid cloak and high-crowned bowler. Mother was shawled up to her ears, her cheeks red from the cold and the drive over the mountain. She gave a little wave of her hand as father flicked the cob with the whip. They took the bend of the road just as if it were a circus ring.

"Trust him," said Justin. "He'll be there first. I bet the old buggarr won't let Mam have a cup of tea, let alone a drink before they get there." He spat over the side of the cart and breathed hard through his nostrils. "Drive, drive," he muttered, "that's all he can do. . . . It's time we had a servant girl. . . . Mam's beginning to break up. It's time he steadied up a bit! Just you wait, I'll settle this one of these days. What would five pounds a year be to him for a good girl?"

I did not say anything, but what he said was right. It was nothing but drive, drive, from morning till night. Up betimes in the morning, working until it was too dark to see more, we were uddered to the place. There was always the milking; and now, as soon as the new year came in, there would be the calving and the lambing; then the ploughing, the manuring, the shearing, the harvest, and the old man shouting and driving all the time. The soil exacted its labour all right, dragging us downwards until one grew bent with work; flesh and bone returning with each step to its own element in earth. We were moulded in earth, soil-bound to the farm. And sitting there beside Justin and feeling cold because the effects of the whisky had now worn off, I saw the years stretch out before me. Twenty, thirty, fifty years; father and mother lost in earth, removed from sight; Justin himself tempered by work and old age; myself and Grett. . . . Each day leaving its chisel-mark on us, and all the time, day in, day out, the land exacting its labour.

By the time we reached Brecon, it was turned eight. The market was a blaze of light. Father was waiting for us out in the street.

"At last! Where have you been? Come on! The dealers are already buying up everything. But I'll not sell. Oh no, they don't catch me. I'll wait and sell direct; just you wait until the Shonies arrive from the valleys!"

By the time we had carried the hampers to the white-scrubbed tables and unpacked the fowls, the people were already coming in to buy. Mother stood quietly behind the stacked poultry. In her white apron and black hat with the ostrich feather curled round it, she looked a little shy and out of place against the town people.

"Yes, they are all fresh and home-fed," she would say in

answer to a query. "All killed and cleaned yesterday, quite fresh indeed, ask him."

Father stood in front of the stall, smiling at everyone.

"Don't touch! Don't touch!" he chided. "You can see they are plump and tender. Just look at the fat there!"

He was everywhere, counting out change, wrapping each bird in grease-proof, and throwing parsley and sage away as though he were giving it for pleasure.

"A grand market," he kept whispering to us. "We'll be sold out before dinner. Now you and your mother go and have a bite, Justin and me will amanage. Don't be long though! We might have a rush. A quarter of an hour mind, no more!"

As mother and I hurried away to the refreshment-room we could hear him arguing with some buyer:

"Liver, mam? Damme it all, where do you expect it to be? Look inside, mam, look in there! Just where it belongs, eh?"

The morning went by quickly. As father had foreseen, the poultry was sold out by dinner-time. There was left now only the clearing up of the stall. Mother sat on an upturned box looking round her with a tired, contented smile. Father was in his oil, as we used to say. He had sold everything direct to the public. To a dealer who had approached him when the market was in full swing, he had cursed quietly, smiling all the time:

"Go to hell!" he had said. "I raised these; me, my wife, and the boys here. Think you are going to make on our backs, do you? Buggarr off and quick too, or you'll get some giblets down your throat!"

"All sold! What did I tell you?" He put his hand into his breeches pocket and pulled out a handful of gold and silver. "Here! It's Christmas!" And as though we were still boys, he thumbed a sovereign each to Justin and myself. "You, too," he turned to mother, "the same for you. Buy what you like!" He laughed and cocked an eye at Justin: "Don't you go and get drunk now. Gold is too good for that. Put it in the bank!"

Justin touched his hat. "Thank you, sir, thanks. Don't worry"—he spat on the coin and put it in his pocket—"it'll get to the bank all right."

"Aye, it will swell some tavern-keeper's account, I'm sure.

53

Still, better that than a hoyden's stocking. . . . You be careful now!"

After we had finished loading the empty hampers on the cart, I stood in the yard of The Goose and Cuckoo wondering what to do next. I wanted to slip away to have a word with Grett.

"I'm going to look round a bit."

Justin nodded. He was still in his shirt-sleeves, his hair falling sweat-heavy over his forehead.

"Right! Come round to The Fiddlers about seven. There'll be a randy-boo there. You are not in any hurry to get back, are you?"

I shook my head. I was seeing Grett and myself having tea together in some little tea-place, a small table between us, just as if we were in some little place of our own.

I went back into the market hall and started walking along the paper-littered aisles between the stalls. The reek of poultry was everywhere, and more than once I slipped on a piece of liver or fat. The place was still crowded; the vendors shouting and praising their produce; women and children trailing from one stall to another; men in black suits and dark caps, their hands and faces pock-marked with the blue scars from the mines—I had never seen such a market day; and the money flowed like water.

"Edwin Peele!"

I looked up, recognizing the voice at once. It was Parri Nanteurin. He sat there behind his boots with a bitter wepp on his face. By his side, very staid in her black shawl and grandmother's hat, his wife looked equally dispirited.

"I suppose you have sold out?" There was no mistaking the faint, underlying note of envy in the old man's voice. "A good market for some people," he went on. His wife smiled halfheartedly and gave a little toss of her head, as if she were too full of disappointment to speak. I looked at the rows of boots and understood.

"It's early yet." I wanted to encourage them both. "It will buck up by the evening. You know how it is—always a rush first thing for the poultry."

"Early! Nonsense! It is we are too late!" Old Parri spat on the floor in his disgust. "We are too late, Edwin Peele. Behind

54

the times, that's what we are. Those ready-made shops are killing the trade. Nobody wants good leather any more. Look at them!" He pointed at the feet of the passers-by. "Shiny boots, patent leather, machine-made. All for show! Not an honest stitch in one of them. 'Slaps' I call them. Slaps! Don't talk to me of boots! And to think of the work I have put in on them, hammering the wet soles till they were like iron. No, Edwin Peele, the day of the craftsman is going fast."

"It is true what he do say," added Mrs. Parri. "Not a pair sold, and it is nearly dinner-time."

I leaned over and felt the uppers of a pair of Sunday boots.

"Lovely!" I said. "Just you wait till the farmers finish selling. They'll be round here in no time. . . . Do you think any of us would buy a pair of machine-made? Be patient, man. It's we farmers know what is good. Let the town people buy their fancy stuff, country people want something better. Don't you worry, you'll be sold out all right!"

I moved on. It was the same at the woollen stalls. I saw Amos Morgan, Dili, and her mother standing quietly behind their piled-up shirts, rolls of flannel, stockings and skeins of wool. It was sad to see them standing there so shy and quiet while the women and town girls swept past them in their smart clothes. I didn't go up to them for fear that Dili might be embarrassed about her condition. She had a big loose coat on and there was a sickly paleness on her. And then, as I walked quickly down a side aisle, I saw Grett in front of me. The whole family was there with her: her father, mother, and Jeff. They had not quite sold out. I looked at their geese. Rhos Dirion was a good little place, and Mrs. Ellis and Grett had quite a name for their butter. Their geese to-day were plump and rich in colour. There was quite a crowd round their stall, and I could see that they would soon be sold out.

Grett saw me at once. She blushed and I could see how her hands were trembling as she held out a goose to a woman who seemed to be deliberating over her purchase. I felt a wave of strange pity sweep over me as I watched her. I felt as though I had surprised her unfairly. . . . I had never seen her before in her apron and with her sleeves rolled up. She was just as I had imagined her that morning. She soon regained her composure, and though she did not smile across at me, she gave me a soft, dark glance once or twice, looking up at me through her dark eye-lashes, then bending her head again over her work. I watched her quietly from where I stood behind a press of women. Her face was a little flushed with exertion, and her movements were quick and deft. I waited until I caught her eye again, then I motioned her to slip away. She nodded quietly and flashed her eyes towards the refreshment place. A few minutes later she spoke to her mother and put her coat over her shoulders. I walked away and waited for her near the tea-tables.

"I can't stay a minute." She was breathless with excitement. I followed her into the passage leading to the kitchens. "If they knew I was here, father and Jeff would kill me. We're terribly busy."

She was radiant; lovely, lovely. I looked at her as if seeing for the first time the oval of her face, her cheek bones, her fine jaw-line, and the way her eyes narrowed a little towards the corners. She was wearing a white blouse, and her belted skirt flared away from her hips.

"Let us meet somewhere this afternoon," I whispered. "You'll be doing a bit of shopping, won't you?"

She nodded and looked round over her shoulder nervously.

"Of course! Mother and I have got a lot to do. But I'll manage it. Where shall you be?"

"By the church. . . . The one on the square. Do you know it?"

"Yes . . . What time?"

"From two on . . . I'll wait there in the porch till you come."

"Right, I'll manage it somehow." She looked around again, peering past the women who bustled past us with huge tea-pots and plates of sandwiches in their hands. "I must go," she said.

"From two o'clock on then."

She pressed my hand and went. I lost her for a moment in the crowd; then I saw her again, her head high and her shoulders firm and buoyant as she hurried back to her stall. I waited a while in case someone might see me, then I sauntered back to the stalls. Amos Morgan the Mill was now alone in his stall,

Dili and her mother had no doubt gone to have some food. I went over to him for a chat, anything to kill time until two o'clock.

"How are you doing?" I asked. He looked up sharply through his steel spectacles. With his woolley grey hair, beard, and scarved neck, he looked like a very product of his own industry. He was ensconced in wool. His overcoat and suit were of his own weaving, and his almost bloodless hands were heavy with fat and stained with oil and dye. He was like every weaver I had ever known: pale, flabby, and reeking of oil and wool.

"Not so bad, not so bad," he answered. "I have seen it better, much better. There isn't the call for good flannel that there used to be. People are going more for fancy goods. . . . Take red flannel now." He picked up a roll of red flannel and ran his hand over the soft pile of it. "I remember the time when everybody lined their waistcoats with this, even the gentry. The best cure for rheumatic that ever was. But what is it now?" He threw the roll away from him. "Pills, patent medicines! People with no qualifications—quacks, I call them—coming to town with smart tongues. Look out there in the street. Cheap-jacks and quacks with little tables in front of them. And what's in the shops? Nothing but machine-made stuff! No, Edwin," he wagged his blue-nailed finger in my face, "times are changing. One of these days the old mill will have to stop. Why? I'll tell you; we can't compete much longer. To-day it is the battle of the cheap-jack and the machine against the likes of me. . . . But that is enough about me. Tell me, now, how have you done? Sold out you have, I am sure."

"Aye, everything."

He nodded quietly to himself, his eyes narrowing behind his spectacles and his lips pouting reflectively.

"That's how it is," he said slowly. "The belly knows what is good. You can't fool a man's stomach, good food he must have. Ha!" He snorted triumphantly. "That's something the machine can't make—good food! I——"

He paused and gave a quick glance in the direction of the refreshment-rooms.

"Come here, I've got something to tell you." He beckoned

me closer to him. As I bent my head to him I caught again the oily reek of the wool that clung to him like a damp mist.

"Listen!" He spoke in a whisper. "It is supposed to be a secret, but I want you to spread it about. Listen now, Dili and Albert the Frô are getting married to-day . . . Registry Office, after dinner. They told me not to tell. . . . But you tell everybody, Edwin. You tell everybody."

I looked at him with relief. For a moment I had feared he was going to tell me something about Grett and myself. The old man was smiling now though his eyes were a little moist.

"I want everybody to know that Dili is married," he went on. He shook his head and ran his fingers through his hair. "It is a pity it had to be like this, almost broken our hearts it has, cutting her out of the chapel and the disgrace. But there you are" —he gave me a guilty smile and shrugged his shoulders—"she isn't the only one by a long way. It was just the same with me and Lissa, and with plenty of others, too. . . ."

I left him there waiting for Dili and her mother to return; and as I made my way from stall to stall I found something very lovely in the fact that Dili was getting married this afternoon. A rush of tenderness came over me as I thought of her, her stomach beginning to get out of shape with the child she was carrying, and the bloom of her cheeks already gone because of the drain of sustaining that little life. I envied her and Albert. They were already in a little world of their own and had paid the price for the happiness that was now theirs. The thought came to me that Grett and I could easily bring matters to a head in the same way. The idea took such a hold on me that, for a moment, I imagined Grett and myself walking through the crowd; my lovely, dark-eyed Grett more tender-eyed than ever before, and with a secret smile of happiness on her lips because of the joy that was with her. In that moment I felt a new, terrible yearning for Grett. I wanted her in my arms with all the glowing smoothness of her body burning against me. It was a wonderful moment. I felt as if I had at once bridged some great distance that had separated us. Until now she had been Grett Rhos Dirion, the girl whose beauty was the talk of the parish, and I had been proud that I, Edwin Peele, was her lover. Hitherto, she had been a girl apart, removed from me because of her loveliness; and now, at last, I longed for her and wanted her with all the passion of my being.

I left the market as if I was in a dream. A throbbing ecstasy stirred in my very marrow, and I walked through the crowded streets hearing the cries of the street-vendors as though they were far away; and although I was not thirsty, I went into the sanded bar of The Crown so that I could sit down and dream.

Grett came quickly into the dark porch of the church, and for a moment the stone arch of the gateway held her against the light. To me, waiting for her in the shadows, the moment was eternal; there she was, arrested in time; her shape dark and alive against the afternoon light of that winter's day. The next moment she was in my arms. She was a little breathless from hurrying, but she returned my kiss before she put her hands against me to free herself.

"Come inside," I whispered.

She gave a quick, backward glance over her shoulder.

"I left mother in the draper's down the street," she said. "I mustn't be long."

The musty smell of the hymn-books and the tang of the pitch-pine came to meet us as we tiptoed through the baise-covered swing-doors. Although it was ringing hard with frost outside, the flagstones in the church were sweating with damp. The whole interior was mysterious and still with the colours from the stained-glass windows. The tramp of footsteps on the pavements outside were soft and muffled, and only a whisper of the street noises came in to us.

I took Grett to a shadowy pew right in the corner away from the door. From here we could watch whoever might come in and not be seen ourselves until they turned to leave. Sitting there, hand in hand, and not saying a word for a while, I felt a great peace come over us. We were away from the world, and I began to understand something of what our vicar had meant when he spoke of the sanctuary of the church. He was right: this was sanctuary; the world was outside these walls.

I looked at Grett, and seeing the line of her profile against the shadows beyond her, I imagined us coming here on Christmas Eve. I thought of the chanting, the candle-light falling on the gold and the brass; I saw us walking home arm-in-arm through the sleeping streets, the high buildings on each side rising up above us, and making a narrow roadway of the stars. I saw us lying together in bed in the waiting silence and stillness of the morning, lying quietly together because of the sweet holiness of the day. . . .

"Here!" I pushed a small packet wrapped in tissue-paper into her hand. "Go on, open it. It's for you."

It was a little brooch which I had bought at the jeweller's on the way to church: a leaf and spray of lily-of-the-valley in silver.

Grett's eyes dazzled, and my fingers trembled as I pinned it across the neck of her blouse.

"But I've nothing for you! I haven't had a chance!"

"Don't talk," I said. "Just let me have you, that's all I want, just you, Grett."

"Me?" She looked straight into my eyes. "You mean . . . ?"

"No, no!" I shook my head, but something leapt inside me at the expression on her face. "It's your love I want, just that."

She smiled and shrugged her shoulders.

"That's nothing," she said. "You know you've got that. I—I thought——"

"What?"

She gave me a long look and I could see that her cheeks were burning. I put my arm around her and drew her close to me.

"Say it," I whispered. "Come on, tell me."

"There's no need," she said. "You know, don't you?"

All I could do was to hold her closer to me and repeat her name over and over again. I felt we were already married, and an impulse came over me to take her up to the altar-rail and kneel there in front of the shining crucifix. The next moment, we shrank back into the corner of the seat. An old woman had come softly in through the swinging-doors. She walked almost the whole length of the church before she turned into a side pew where she knelt and put her hands together. I sat there feeling very uncomfortable. Back at home no one ever knelt in church except when they took communion from the vicar. Seeing the old woman there, in her shawl and black bonnet, made me feel as though I were trespassing and eavesdropping on a prayer.

Grett nodded, and together we went out quickly into the porch.

It had got colder since we had been inside; you could smell the frost in the air, and the voices of people talking were loud and clear. The afternoon was already darkening and some of the shop windows were lighted up.

"What about your brooch?"

She unpinned it and slid it under the palm of her glove.

"I'll have to say I bought it," she said, "then I can wear it."

I noticed that she was worried about something.

"What is worrying you?" I asked her.

She moistened her lip.

"When are you going back?"

"Late—I've got to wait for Justin."

"You won't get drunk, will you?"

I laughed. I could see plain enough how the thoughts were linking themselves together in her mind.

"Don't you worry," I assured her. "I'll not get drunk."

"You promise?"

"On the Bible. Drop dead!"

She smiled, her cheeks dimpling. "And keep that Justin of yours away from Jeff——"

I drew her into the corner of the porch and kissed her. This time she responded to me with her whole body. Then, suddenly, without even a word as to when we should next see each other, she broke away from me and hurried out of the porch. I hurried out after her, hoping to see her threading her way through the crowd. And there, standing on the pavement across the road, was Justin. His bowler was squarer than ever on his head and he was holding himself stiff and straight. He was drunk, but not too badly. I knew him well, this was only the first stage.

"Hey! You! Come over here!"

His voice rose above the noise and jostling of the pavements. People turned to look at him and smiled. But he paid no attention to them. He stood there glaring at me while I crossed the road over to him. But I didn't care. "At last, at last"—I kept repeating to myself—"I am coming out into the open." It was good. At last someone knew; soon, everybody would know. It was about time, too. Kissing in dingles and in church porches! It was time Grett and I had a bed to ourselves. I faced Justin smilingly. I only hoped he would not start shouting in front of the crowd.

Chapter 6

JUSTIN'S eyes blazed with temper. He looked at me for a few moments breathing hard through his tightened nostrils.

"Let's go round the corner," he said.

He turned, and did not wait to see if I was following him, but stalked off with his shoulders square, his hands clenched, and his feet stabbing at the pavement with their iron-tipped heels. He stopped some twenty yards down a side-street. I followed him leisurely. I was ready for whatever might happen. He stood watching me as I came up to him, his eyes looking me up and down.

"So that's your game," he started. He was quivering with rage, and I saw how his chest rose and fell with his temper. "Grett Ellis! Have you gone off your head, or what?"

He could hardly speak, and at that moment I hated him. He was the very spit of father, and I realized how the fellows in the parish must hate him. He moistened his lips, and his eyes dared me to answer him. He was just waiting for me to provoke him to let out at me.

"What about it? What if it was Grett Ellis? What's it got to do with you or anybody?"

I made no movement as his hand stretched out and grabbed the lapel of my coat.

"What about it?" His voice trembled and he lifted his fist as though to hit me. "You ask that? Diawl!" He was shouting now, his face so close to me that I caught the stench of spirits from him. "You'd make us the laughing-stock of the parish, would you? Can't you find some other bit? You've got a sovran in your pocket, haven't you? Look around you, man; there's plenty here in Brecon better than that——"

"Shut up!" I twisted myself loose from his grip on my coat. He looked at me sharply, and a worried frown puckered over his eyes.

"Ned . . . ? You're not . . . ? No, you are not in love with her, is it?"

"Of course I am! What do you think? Who wouldn't be? We've been going together since September."

It was out now, and I felt as though the whole world had slipped off my shoulders. Justin stepped back and leaned against the brick wall. He took off his bowler and fanned it in front of his face.

"Good God! In love with Grett Ellis! You poor, bloody fool, Ned! You know what it means? The old man . . . her people . . . Jeff! Damme, the whole parish'll . . ."

His anger was passing. He began to grin. I smiled, too. I could see that from now on I could count on him. I felt I could shout my defiance at everybody now. With Justin behind me, I could face the whole lot of them.

"Grett Ellis!" He shook his head as if he still couldn't believe it. "Grett Ellis," he repeated her name to himself. "Couldn't you find someone else? Brain! She's only a slip of a girl, a little shwli. . . . How old is she?"

"Twenty-two."

"Hm! Not bad, not bad. And you've been there since September you say. . . . Three months! That's a good spell."

His eyes twinkled as he looked questioningly at me. I knew quite well what was passing through his mind.

"You are off the mark," I told him. "I'm going to marry her. To hell with the family! What do you say to that?"

He did not answer immediately. He stood there leaning against the wall, his hands thrust deep into his pockets, and a bemused, pouting smile on his lips. It was getting dark now, and I thought of the hours that lay ahead of us before we set off on the cold, slow journey back over the mountains.

"Ah well!" Justin straightened himself up. "If you are set on this girl, I suppose there's nothing we can do about it." He looked at me, his eyes half-mocking yet friendly. "I don't know how you chaps get like this. I've never been bowled over, never! It must hit you hard. Duw!" He laughed and fetched me a nudge with his elbow. "There'll be hell from now on. Think of the old man! He'll get a stroke when he hears. . . . Can you see him? . . . And Jeff Ellis——" He stopped and I saw his eyes narrow, and his jaw hardened under his beard. "I reckon we'll have our hands full there. . . . He'll be awkward. You'll be getting into a fine family and no mistake! Diawl, Ned! They'll have to tie a few people up that day!"

He laughed again. His mood had changed entirely. I think he really enjoyed the prospect of trouble that lay ahead of us. He took my arm as we made our way back to the High Street.

"You've got more spunk than I thought. . . . The girl too." He winked, and gave an appreciative nod of his head. "She's a smart one; those Ellises are well made, eh? I bet you haven't had any late suppers there though. No good throwing gravel at her windows—you'd probably get a double charge of shot in your behind. Come on, let's go and get some food; we want a good foundation for to-night. And you are coming with me, too. We'll celebrate this, just you and me."

We had tea in a little place where the street ran steeply down to the river. The eating-room was filled with farmers and their wives. The tables were scrubbed white and the floors were sanded over.

"Look at them eating! You'd think they had never had a square meal in their lives."

What he said was true enough. The farmers ate as though they were famished. Their wives, too, though somewhat abashed at eating in a public place, were not behind. Still, I understood how they felt. I knew what it was to get away from bacon and broth. Day after day, it was nothing but bacon at home: fried for breakfast, boiled for dinner, and cold for supper. It was nice to have a change of food.

"Tell me," Justin leaned across the table. "What does Grett Ellis say about all this? Is she game all right?"

At last, I heard myself talking about Grett. I felt as though I was writing a poem about her. She was there in front of me while I spoke, and my words lent a new beauty and life to her: I had kept her in my heart too long.

"Game! She is game for anything. . . ." Now she was lying in my arms in the dingle. I felt the elastic touch of her skin under my hands; and I remembered, too, the expression in her eyes when she had looked me straight in the face inside the church. . . . "She doesn't care a bit about anybody. She'd marry me to-morrow if I'd ask her."

"Then you'd better start looking round for a little place. But don't count on anything from the old man. How much have you got saved?"

I had, all told, about seventy pounds. But I didn't worry about that. Even if I couldn't get a farm, there were still the pits. The valleys were rolling in sovereigns. You had only to look around to see how the colliers were doing. No, our livelihood was the least problem.

"I'm not worried about that," I said. "We'd go to the valleys before we would starve. There's plenty of money there. The land is finished anyway. What do you say? Aren't I right?"

A shadow passed over Justin's face. He smoothed his bearded chin with his hand. The thumb of his right hand was broad in the nail, thick and flattened with work. He shook his head.

"Don't talk," he said. "There'll be no need for that. We'll manage somehow. We must stay on. There'll be some good places going soon, and for dirt too. Look at the chaps who have gone off already."

He started counting them on his fingers: Twm Berthlwyd, Wat Ffynnonoer, Dic Glandwr, Dai Ynyswen. . . . There was no end to them, all fellows of our own age, and all doing well in the valleys.

"No," he went on, "there'll be plenty of places going soon. . . . You bide your time. Hang on. But watch your step!" He gave me a wicked grin. "Don't rush things, be careful; you know what young blood is. . . . You be careful!"

I told him about Dili the Mill.

"I'm glad," he said. "You watch nothing like that happens to you and Grett. Things are bad enough as they are, without anything like that happening."

Three hours later we were in The Fiddlers. I drank slowly

and made no attempt to keep up with Justin. He was drinking with everyone. He was having a quiet game with the barmaid, too. I could see us getting home for breakfast.

"You are drunk," she kept on saying to him. "You are drunk, it's too much silly lol you have!"

She was fair-haired, and her shiny black dress was creased around her. Justin had taken off his hat and overcoat, and stood swaying against the bar.

"Say 'Yes,' come on, say 'Yes,'" he pleaded with her. Those around him winked at each other, and laughed whenever he leaned over the bar to reach for the girl's waist.

"Look here!" Justin pulled a handful of gold and silver from his pocket. "Plenty of cash," he shouted. "And all to be spent or given away."

I watched him anxiously. He was properly in his drink now. He was a little dangerous; even when he laughed and looked at anyone, I could see the devilry that lurked under his glance, ready at a word or a gesture to turn nasty at anything he didn't like.

"Get on with you!" The barmaid laughed scornfully and lifted Justin's glass to wipe the counter. "That's nothing," she said when he pulled out his money. "There's plenty here could buy you up, farmer. I suppose you've sold a few chickens, eh?"

"Quite a few!" Justin was very grave. He regarded the girl through eyes half-closed and speculative. "Quite a few, my gel."

"Well"—she turned her back to him and spoke to him over her satin shoulder—"you'd better go and pick a little chicken for yourself on the street. Plenty about, just your sort. . . . And be careful you don't get feathered!"

A roar of laughter went up from the bar.

"Good gel fach!"

"There's quick for you now!"

"She is too smart for you, Peele. Too smart, my boy!"

"Watch you don't get feathered, beard and all you've got. Ha! Ha!"

Justin laughed.

"Aye, it's too good she is, too good!" He grinned across at her.

66

"All right, you win. And drinks on me, and a special one for you; one of the best!"

He threw a half-sovereign on the beer-streaked counter. The barmaid filled herself a glass of port. She smiled over the rim of her glass at Justin.

"Your health, sir. No offence, is there!"

"Not a bit. Come here!" He leaned across the counter and drew her to him and kissed her.

"You wait!" Her cheeks were burning, but her eyes were shining as she made a show of tidying her hair. I saw Justin wink at her, and although she pouted and flounced to and fro along the bar, I could see that she was not ill-pleased with him. With each breath she took, her breasts lifted a little; and whenever she caught Justin's eye she smiled with the corner of her mouth.

The conversation was mainly of the market. Now and again there would be a huddle of heads together. The barmaid went on with her work as though not hearing. Then would come the burst of laughter from the men, the teller of the story laughing more than anyone. I found myself laughing as well. The stories were dirty, but somehow or other they went with the drink. The thought of Grett came to me at times, but she didn't belong here; besides, I was not myself. I found myself looking at the barmaid and envying Justin his easy way with her. Then, in the midst of my desires, I would see Grett's face and hear the sound of her voice. "Keep outside, Grett," I kept saying. "You don't belong here. Keep away Grett, keep away!"

So it went on. Before "stop-tap" Justin was singing "Can y mochyn du," and I had to wait an hour for him after the pub had closed. The journey home was dark and cold. I drove all the way, while Justin slept and snored in the sacks on the floor of the cart.

Chapter 7

THE Christmas morning was such that it shall not pass. The years come and go, they will come and go, and the memory becomes dim; the darkness of many a winter's night, and the hoar-frost of many a morning comes between me and many a day; but the memory of that Christmas shall not pass. I was in love on that morning; the beat of my heart's blood was in tune with the twinkling of the stars, and the sigh of the wind and the sound of the river had their echo in my singing joy.

Mother did not get up that morning, she was still overtired from the exertions of the market. The rest of us got up in the dark and made breakfast quietly so as not to disturb her. Father set off for church before me; and I left Justin sitting in front of the fire, plying the bellows steadily and using the long iron tip of it to poke the smouldering sticks.

It was just after four when I left the house. The "Plygain" was at five, and as I went down the lane I saw the lights shining across the cwm from the church windows. I went down past the Allt without any fear; there is never any fear of the dark after the early hours. And there was something in the air that if I had been suddenly translated to the Allt from some great distance away I would have known at once that it was Christmas morning. The miracle of Christmas had already happened. The quietness of the dark spaces among the stars had come down on earth. I could feel it everywhere. The shadows in the depth of the wood were soft and dark as sleep. And when I came to the Lyswen, there's clear and lovely was the tinkle of the water against the stones.

Up I went through the village. The chapel people were still in bed, not a light showed in their houses. Ahead of me, I could hear the talking of those who were on their way to church. There was something wonderful to me about this Plygain, the "Mass of the Cock-crow" as the vicar had called it. I felt that my walk was a pilgrimage, and I was glad that I was alone; that the road was dark and lonely, and that at the end of my journey the windows would be shining because of the light behind them.

I did not follow the people who were ahead of me. Instead, I took the path over the fields and down past the Rhos Dirion. I could see the light in their window when I came to the Sawdde. I looked at my watch and in the starlight I could just make out that it was still before five. For a moment, I was tempted to wait there until I would see the lights go out in the house and then follow Grett and the family up through the woods to church. But I went on quietly. A great peace was on me. There was no desire on me at all. I wanted only to see Grett, to look at her; to go up with her and the others to the altar-rail and bend my head in her company in the same candle-light.

The smell of the frost was strong along the Sawdde. There was no sound anywhere, no dogs barking, no birds; nothing but the babble and splash of the river and the occasional snapping or moving of a dry twig in the hedge.

As I walked along I half-sang under my breath. I chanted; I made up a ragged verse about Grett and her beauty; and when, at last, I came to the church, I crossed myself because of the great mystery that was there.

There was a good congregation there, more than I had expected. To my surprise, Grett was already there with her father and mother. I peered at her through my fingers when I put my head down to pray. She had a new hat on, and her dark coat was open at the neck. She smiled openly at me when I sat back in my seat, and lifted her hand to show me the brooch at her throat.

Everyone who was late came in on tiptoe that morning, and I noticed how frail the old people looked. The stove was roaring hot, and the white-washed walls were darker than ever where the shadows thrown by the candles flickered to and fro across them.

No, that morning shall not pass. Grett with her dark beauty is there for ever, her face pale in the candle-light; the chanting goes on, too; and the old giants of the faith are there for ever, bearded, bald, stooping; bowing their heads at the altar-rail. . . .

I did not get a chance to speak to Grett, but in going out she turned her head and gave me her love with a noiseless motion of her lips. I brushed against her and felt the soft yielding of her against my elbow.

It was still dark when I got home; mother had got up, and Justin had finished the milking. Over the Van Rocks a greenish-blue light streaked the darkness, and with the dawn the mystery vanished as, one by one, the stars paled and faded from sight.

Chapter 8

THE New Year came in and the Eisteddfod went by. I did not get the prize for the Englyn because I was afraid to put Grett's beauty in it in case people would put two and two together; our choir, too—father was the tenor and Dico Lewis the bass—were beaten by the choir from Gwynfe. Oh, those tenors from Gwynfe! Like nightingales they were, and you knew from the way they grouped themselves on the stage that they were full of confidence because of the way they had been trained. I took Grett home that night. We left the Eisteddfod before it was over, and it was two o'clock before I left her. Even so, they were still competing in the schoolroom as I passed it on my way home.

The memory of that night was fresh on me when, a night or two afterwards, I sat on the low bench by the vice in Howells the blacksmith's. Old Howells was turning a coulter, tempering it into the hardness of steel by drawing it white-hot from the fire, holding it while it changed from its glowing red to red-green, blue-green, and then, at the right moment, plunging it into the cask of water that stood by the bellows. The acrid smell of steam and hot iron filled the whole smithy.

"There it is, right for any field; guaranteed to go through rock and stone like a knife through butter!" He wiped the anvil with his apron; then, idly, he polished the mirror-like head of his hammer with the flat of his hand and let it fall on the anvil.

"Like a bell," he remarked. "That sound has been in our family as far back as we can go."

The old gang was there in strength this night. Old Howells—Twm and Rhys were out; Twm, no doubt, in some singing practice, and Rhys up at the Tavarn with Jeff and Iori Allt-y-brain—Lewsin the Post, Eli Williams the Carpenter, with his rule in his pocket and his steel spectacles askew on his nose, Ebe the Factri, and Prosser Ty Unnos—they were all there, smoking and watching old Howells at his work.

"So poor old Meredith is gone," said Howells. "Sudden,

wasn't it? He was in here a few days before. . . . Didn't think anything then. How old was he?"

"Sixty-nine last Mihangel," said Eli the Carpenter. "He was the same age as Mag, only a day or so between them."

Howells took the coulter from the cask. It was still warm and a wisp of steam curled from the end of it. He regarded it with half-closed eyes.

"Was there any sign or anything?" he asked quietly. I looked at the old men. They shook their heads, and I felt again as I always did when they started to talk about the dead.

"I didn't feel anything," went on Howells. "Nothing at all. I've racked my head trying to remember if there was anything." He turned the pin of the vice and started to file the edge of the coulter with long, steady strokes. "He was here, as I told you, three days before he went. We had broth that day, but he wouldn't take a drop. Perhaps he was ailing then, eh? It was stoppage he had, wasn't it? The doctor said something about inflammation, too. . . . But for the life of me, I didn't notice a thing whatever."

Slowly the coulter grew like silver under his file. The edge caught the candle-light, and I imagined how it would shine after a day's ploughing. As old Howells had said, it would cut through the red earth like a knife. I felt I could smell the earth and feel the strain of the reins, and see the birds wheeling and swooping behind me.

"Now, when old Jeffre Hendrescythan went last November, I knew a day or two before."

"You did?"

"Yes!" Old Howells paused and blew on his file. "I was taking my bills out that night; I had one for him, poor chap."

I drew on my pipe. Whether the old man was playing up to me or not, I had no idea. But no, he was sincere. You could tell from his voice, from the note of awe that lay underneath it, that he meant every word he was saying. But before he could continue his story, a step sounded outside the door, and a hand could be heard fumbling with the latch.

"Press down, man, and give a kick," shouted Lewsin the Post. "Wonder who it is?" he said. "You ought to put that latch right, Howells."

The door opened and Dico Lewis stood there with a sack fastened over his shoulders and a lantern in his hand.

"Come in, Dico. Close the door!"

Dico came in peering at us in turn. He was a strong fellow was Dico, his heavy moustache making him look older than his years. He was, in fact, no older than Justin. Because he lived on the top end of the parish we did not see him often. He was a great singer, and if he had been trained there would have been no one to touch him; he could ground double C with a note or two to spare.

"Just passing," he said. "Had to drop in."

"We were talking about old Hendrescythan," said Howells, "how sudden he went, remember? And now here's old Meredith gone. What are you giving him, Eli?"

"Oak, solid oak; top, bottom, and sides," said Eli. "I'll be lettering the plate to-night. Mawredd! He'll be a load to carry mind!"

"He wasn't what you would call a big man though," said Ebe the Factri. "Not like Wat Ffawydden!"

"No! Wat was big; but, after all, it was nothing but water—dropsy, remember? Now Meredith is solid. What do you think he measures now?"

Prosser Ty Unnos stood up and raised his hand horizontally to about the level of his eyes.

"Five nine, I say; and about forty-two chest. Say seventy by thirty. Right?"

Eli spat on the fine dust of ash and filings that lay heaped between the stones round the anvil.

"Wrong! Hopeless you are. He was five eleven and over fifty round the chest. Solid, too. I tell you, some of us will be blowing a bit before we get to the church. They will have to call 'Change' every ten yards or so, or there won't be a bearer left before we are half-way. And that old bier is enough to kill one, let alone the oak box and the body. Jawch! He must be over ten score and more. . . . But you were saying about Hendrescythan, Howells?"

Old Howells was still filing the coulter. His arms worked with a long, steady rhythm. He was as steady as if he were setting a razor.

"Yes. Now that was a case where I *knew* something was going to happen."

Lewsin the Post nodded. "I heard you saying about it," he said, "I remember it well."

"Yes. I'd been up there with the bill. He was like a cricksin, trying to knock me down a shilling or so. Well, after supper, and a good supper it was, they had killed the pig that day——"

"Yes?"

"Well, I was coming down the lane from the house. You know, down to the river. Dark! I couldn't see my hand before me——"

"Yes?"

I heard myself, I could hardly wait for what was coming. My thighs were like ice, and I could feel my heart beating with suspense. Old Howells stopped filing, and sat on the anvil. He was staring past me, the candle-light shining on the sweat on his forehead. Outside, the wind whined through the oak trees and a lick of rain beat against the window and the closed door. The others were all listening; Dico was all eyes, his moustache bristling around his half-opened mouth.

"It was pitch black; you know how it is when you come out of the light. So I walked slowly, not thinking of anything particular till I felt myself sweating. Sweating, mind, and it was a cold night. I was in a wabbling of sweat . . . I felt I could hardly breathe. . . ."

"Y Cyheurath!" muttered old Prosser. "I've felt it, too!"

"Yes! 'Y Cyheurath,' the 'Toeli,' " said Howells. "I knew it . . . I was in a funeral!"

"Did you hear it, too?" asked Dico. His deep voice trembled as he spoke.

"Hear it? Yes. I got to the side of the road. I could hear the feet going by; dozens of them! I tell you, I could hardly breathe. I felt I was caught in a great crowd. . . . And, then, I heard the heavy tread of the bearers, and I could feel that the coffin was passing me."

Old Howells wiped his face with his hands; he was sweating, and his eyes were staring in front of him as if he were still seeing what he was describing.

"I pressed myself against the hedge, and in a few minutes

73

the air was light again; I felt I could breathe more easily. By now, they were getting near to the river, and I stood there waiting for the noise. Then it came, the Cyheurath. You know it, Prosser, like a thousand cats in torment." He turned to me: "You always hear that sound when they cross the water, even if it is only a little stream. Enough to make your blood run cold it is. Well, I knew then that old Jeffre would be going feet first that way in a few days. . . . Yes, it was him all right, and when the doctor pulled up outside here two days after, I looked at him and said: 'Well, I suppose you have come to say that Jeffre Tomos is gone!' You should have seen his face!"

"Tell me," I asked him. "You are sure you heard it you say? What if you only imagined it?"

Old Howells came over to me and put his hand on my shoulder.

"I heard it, Edwin. And others here have heard it. . . . Pray God that you will never hear it. If you do, you will never be the same after. Look at me now. I'm not afraid of any man or animal; but, I tell you, there are certain roads around here that I wouldn't walk after dark if you gave me a sovran for every step I would take. As they say: 'Better for a man the ill he knows, than the ill he knows not. . . .' Take the road from Allt-y-brain to The Pandy, just by the little wood there. . . . Then there's Graig Ddu, they say that Catherine Jeffreys do still cry there above the pool. . . . And there's twenty or thirty yards under the Allt, there; by your place——"

Even as he mentioned it, I felt a shiver pass over me. So, it was true, there was something along the road by the Allt.

"No, no! You are wrong, Howells." Lewsin the Post shook his head. "The road by the Allt under Trewern is harmless. I've walked it hundreds of times. Besides"—he gave me a sly look and laughed—"Ned's father here and Justin would put the fear of the devil in any ghost!"

"That sound you were talking about," said Dico. "Like cats you say?"

"Worse," said Howells. "Much worse! I said cats, because it's not human. Souls in torment, Dico; a sound of weeping and wailing. . . ."

There was silence in the smithy. Howells put on his coat, but made no start to pack up for the night. His thick legs clasped the anvil as though he were on a horse.

"Parry-Prys had the same experience a year ago." Ebe the Factri had a deep, slow voice. Starting quietly, heavily, he had been known on occasion to lift a prayer-meeting almost to a revival by his oratory. "I remember the night well," he went on. "We were in the Tavarn, a crowd of us. Your father was there, Edwin. You ask him about it." (I knew the story well, father was never tired of telling it.) "Well, you know what Parry-Prys was. No belief in anything, only in his money, his pint, and his strength. That man did not believe in God or the Devil, nothing but himself and women——"

But no one laughed.

"Go on," said Lewsin, "I haven't heard this story."

"Well, you should have seen him that night. We were all having a glass, and there he was at the door. I tell you, he gave us a start. You should have seen him. He was like a ghost. We got him to a chair. His hair was running with sweat, just as if he had come out of the river. 'What is it, Parry?' we asked him. 'What is it?' 'Ebe,' he said, 'I have been in something terrible. I could hardly breathe. Look at me! Something happened coming down the hill here. I was riding quietly, and then the cob shied right across the road. It was all I could do to hold her. And then I felt it: we were caught in a funeral. It was all around me. I could smell it and hear the feet going by, and the women crying. . . .'" Ebe paused and took his time to light his pipe, the spurting match showing up his great hooked nose and deep-set eyes. "I tell you, I never saw a man so frightened in my life. He was shaking like a leaf. 'Come out and see the cob,' he said. 'And we haven't even trotted.' We all went out, and there she was in a froth of sweat, and trembling like a jelly. Between us, we took Parry-Prys back into the Tavarn, and your father, Edwin, went home with him that night. Less than a week after that, his wife's coffin was being carried that way."

The talk continued. Now it was about Corpse Candles and the knocking that the gravedigger always heard in his tool-coffer before a death would occur. Some had heard the church bell at night, others had seen a bobbing light going over the fields, or heard music. And there was old Pali Dolguog, who laid out the dead; she always knew before a call came for her by the black coffin mark that appeared on her forearm. But it was the Toili that I dreaded most. I sat there longing to get home, yet terrified of the moment when I would have to start. And the thought came to me that I must marry soon and have children lest, in my old age, I should be lonely with no one to comfort me in my terror. For there was terror along the dark roads at night. We had lived too long under the shadow of the mountains and the Van Rocks. There was something in our very blood that was attuned to the spirit of the place. We were in touch with every emanation of the soil and the air. Loneliness had begotten a sensitivity in us so that every tree and turn of road or path had some deep significance for us.

"But it is not what it was in our fathers' time," said Eli the Carpenter. "The old people used to see things all the time. But there you are—a lot depends on the sort of man you are. . . . A coward will flee from his shadow; and the rustling of a leaf is enough to startle a guilty conscience."

"What were things like when you were a boy?" I put the question to Eli just to change the conversation. "Was there same life as we get now?"

"Much the same, much the same, wasn't it, Howells? But there's not the old characters about now as there was then. They were wilder. . . . Dear me, there was your grandfather; no, your great-grandfather, the old Justin Peele. I remember him when I was a boy. . . . Do you remember him, Howells?"

"Remember him?" said Howells. "Of course I do. There was a strong man now. I used to hear my father say that he could lift this anvil here by catching hold of the pointed end with one hand. A terror he was—your brother Justin is something of his stamp." He looked me up and down. "I don't know where you come in, Ned. You are more after your mother's family. . . ."

"Who do you say is strongest in the parish now?" I asked.

Howells played his tongue along his lips. "I . . . I'm not sure. Things have quieted down a lot. There's our Twm now. He's as strong as a horse, but he's got no stomach, too gwyrion by a long way. I'm not sure who is the strongest! Who do you say, Lewsin?"

Lewsin the Post did not hesitate. "Young Edwin's father

here," he said, "Daniel Peele. There's a man who never knew his strength. Of course, he's getting on now. . . . Then there's Moc Mihartach and Jeff Ellis. . . . But the strongest and most dangerous of the young fellows is Justin, your brother. There's blood there. . . . Yes, Justin's the strongest, I would say; and he's got 'go' in him, plenty of spirit . . . a bit of bad blood, too. . . . Ha! No offence, Edwin, no offence; but you know him, don't you?"

I was proud to hear their verdict. So Justin was cast in the mould of my great-grandfather, Justin Ddu—Black Justin they had called him because of his wildness, his strength, and his black hair. There was father, too. It was good to hear the old stalwarts of the parish referring to our family. We were a strong breed, the Peeles of Trewern. And where did I come in? On mother's side, they said; the mountain people. Ah well, even if I lacked the grit and sinew of father and Justin, there was something to be said for poetry and for the joy I had in moments of loneliness and ecstasy, rare though they were. But deep in me, lying below all my love of peace, there was a hard layer, like rock. I knew it was there, even as I knew when I walked by the Allt when it was dark that, if ever I should see something, I would damn it back to whatever shades it had come from. Deep inside me, I knew the madness and strength of my own terror.

Lewsin and the others rose to go. Howells gave the anvil another wipe with his hand, just like a musician giving a last caress to his instrument.

"Another busy day to-morrow," he said. "Banding wheels, over a dozen of them." He untied his apron and slung it over the bellows handle. One after the other we walked to the road.

It had stopped raining, and the wind had dropped a little. Then, as my eyes grew accustomed to the darkness, I made out the gleam of the road and the shape of the trees.

Dico and I left the others still talking there with Howells. We walked up to the village without saying a word. I knew quite well that as much as I would have given anything to have him walk with me up past the Allt, so he, too, would have given the same to have me go with him along the quiet stretch of Tavarn-y-gwynt.

77

I left him at the cross-roads, and I was quite easy in my mind until I heard the sound of his footsteps die away. There was left now only the tread of my own feet and the sound of my breathing. Before I had gone a hundred yards, my scalp was prickling with terror. From time to time an icy wave passed over my back, and I felt the sweat break out along my spine. I kept to the middle of the road. That was one bit of advice which Justin had given me: "I don't care a damme for all that nonsense about ghosts," he had said. "That's nothing but nonsense. What I'm afraid of is a madman. Always keep in the middle of the road so that he can't jump on you. You've got a fighting chance then." I thought of his words, and tried to bolster myself up with all I had heard about us, the Peeles of Trewern! So Justin took after old Justin Ddu. . . . I tensed my muscles and walked on. Soon, my jaw ached because of the rigid set of my teeth against each other. I was taut with fear. I tried to analyse myself. What was it I was so afraid of? I stopped and listened. There was nothing, nothing only the darkness between the high hedges and the sound of trickling water in the narrow ditches on each side of the road. Overhead, in a ragged tear of cloud, I saw a handful of wild stars, but they gave me no comfort, for the thought came to me: what if some dark shape should pass between me and them. Not once did I look behind as I made my way down to the Lyswen. I watched the bend of the road ahead of me. My terror was for something that I sensed rather than felt. What if? What it? This phrase kept recurring in my mind, and in my imagination I saw clearly what it was I feared.

Although the road ran steeply down to the river, I found myself breathing with difficulty. I used all my will-power to keep from my mind the word which I feared. No, I must not think of the Toili. I tried to whistle, but no sound came from my lips, nor could I sing. I tried hard and heard myself croaking breathlessly.

Now the Allt rose beyond me, and in the back of my mind I remembered the allusion which old Howells had made to it. "Y diawled," I said to myself, "the devils, what if they were only trying to frighten me?" All right, then, I would beat them. I would not go home by way of the Allt. I could cross the fields and then make my way home along the top road. For a moment or so I played with the idea. It would mean a roundabout route; I would not be home before midnight. But when I got opposite Nanteurin and saw the light in their window, my fears left me, and before I was aware of it I found myself crossing the foot-bridge over the Lyswen.

As I walked along I talked to myself. "The Toili," I said to myself. "The Cyheurath! Very well, come on! Come on, then; let me hear the pad-pad of the feet, let me get the reek of the varnish on the coffin, the pitch, and the sweet smell of the dead." I walked on gripping my stick until my knuckles ached and, there ahead of me was the Allt with its twisted oaks, huddled together; and although what wind there was made no noise in the leafless boughs, I could feel the silence that lay in the dark places under the spread of the branches.

From now on each step was like the step you make in a nightmare. I walked with every muscle tense, a band of ice across the nape of my neck. I tried to think of Justin, of his strength, how I would talk with him about the terror of the Allt and find out if he had ever experienced the same thing. And Grett; where was Grett? Grett! I invoked every vision of her that I could summon. I imagined her in front of me, gleaming in the darkness, her eyes smiling in acquiescence. . . . But all was useless. I was gripped by terror, and my blood pounded behind my ear-drums. I made the sign of the Cross, repeated the Gloria and behind it all I heard the echo of Parry Prys's words: "I have been in something terrible. . . ."

When I came out from under the overhanging shadows of the Allt, I heard my breath escape from me with a great sigh. At last, at last, it was all behind me. In front of me, I could see the uphill greyness of the road. I paused and looked back at the Allt. Everything was still and quiet, and I did not start with fright even when an owl hooted in the darkness below me. But I felt weak, and I was cold and icy with sweat.

Soon, I was within sight of home. There was a light shining in the back window. And now that all terror had left me, I felt the sweet calm and hush of the night. The very stillness in the air was like a soft hymn of comfort.

BOOK TWO

Chapter 9

BY MID-APRIL the blackthorn was a drift of white blossom, the chestnut trees behind the barn were spurting with green, sharp-pointed buds, and down in the wain a daffodil or two leaned away from the wind. The spring was early, at least a fortnight or three weeks before its time. Every morning, from about five to milking time, the trees around the house were alive and throbbing with birds. I could not remember such a spring. The sun was warm, and the rains came and went in slanting showers with clusters of shining drops on the vivid hedgerows.

It was a quiet day with us on the farm. The lambing was long over, and I had been carting manure right up to tea-time. It was a glorious day, too fine by far for April. Justin was up on the breast of the hill above the house, ploughing. I hadn't seen him since breakfast. Mother had taken his dinner up to him; he said he was going to finish the field before milking time. In a way I dreaded his return to the house. He and father had been bickering at each other for days, and I knew that sooner or later there would be another upheaval between them.

I felt tired. Spreading manure was hard work. Each soggy forkful took an effort to scatter, and I was glad to unharness the mare from the cart, and to know that there remained only the milking.

What a day it was! I sat against the hedge-bank chewing the stem of my pipe and looking down over the Allt. Every tree had a thin veil of green on it and the red earth was furrowed on every other field, catching the sun like a piece of corduroy. But although there was no cloud in the sky, I knew that rain was not far off. The sound of the river was too clear and the mountains had closed in upon us; every sheep-path and rock could be seen as if they were only a few hundred yards away. There was every sign of rain, too, in the wind that turned the sycamore leaves back on their stems, their whiteness ruffled every now and then; and the whisper of the wind was like the soft hiss of the rain itself.

Presently, I made my way to the house. As I went in through the passage, I smelt the tart on the bakestone. Mother was getting tea ready. I watched her moving to and fro across the kitchen. She was ageing. Father had done nothing about getting a girl to help her.

"Won't be long now!" She turned the tart. "It's nearly done: the first rhubarb this year. Where is Justin? I told him tea was at four."

It was Justin, Justin, with her all the time. He was the apple of her eye. It touched me always to see the care she took when ironing his best shirt, and the way she glazed his stiff collars and then strung them to air on the brass rod under the mantelpiece. I didn't mind. It had always been the same. The two understood each other well, and I knew that but for her Justin would have gone off on his own years ago.

A yard inside the door a stain of sunlight lay golden on the blue flagstones. All the promise of summer was in it. Summer! I thought of the lanes heavy with the smell of honeysuckle and dog-roses, the new-mown hay like mead, and the blue shadows of the night gathering around Grett and myself where we lay in some screened corner of field or wood. Lost in dream, I watched the oblique sunbeam quivering above the blue stones, the dust-motes whirling and hovering in haphazard movement and pattern. I thought of Grett and how she had changed in the weeks that had passed. The last time I had seen her, she was in her summer hat, the cream hat of fine straw with a rose or two on its brim which she had worn on the day I had found her at Brecon. All through the winter it was her face that had haunted me. But now, having seen her in a light frock, it was her figure that persisted in my mind. Wherever I went, I could see the line of her hips, the swell of her calf, the rich whiteness of her throat and the round high firmness of her breasts.

At that moment I heard father out in the yard, and then Justin.

"Then do it yourself," came Justin's voice. "I don't know what you expect. It's nothing but 'Don't drive the horses,' or 'Why isn't the work done?' all the bloody time."

"Be quiet! You'll do as I say. You know I don't want the horses in a lather. You could have put in an hour after tea instead of this rush to finish."

Father's voice was quiet, passionless. He had been in one of his black silences or "moods," as mother called them, for days. I remembered these days of his from my earliest childhood. For no apparent reason, a frost-like silence and self-consuming rage would possess him. Not one of us would dare speak to him when he was like this. And he had been like this all the week. Meal after meal, he sat in silence, masticating his food as though some rigor affected his jaws, swallowing each mouthful with a strained gulp. Justin did not help matters. He would sit there at the table with his eyes fixed on him. Time and again the old man would meet his glance, sneer with a contemptuous smile, and proceed to eat his food with studied care and niceness. They were each waiting for something to snap or break, Justin for ever daring him to make the first move. And now, at last, they had started.

I got up slowly and stretched myself. I was no longer hungry. Mother came in from the dairy with a print of butter on a plate.

"What is it?" she asked quickly. "Didn't I hear Justin and your father?"

I nodded. "They are out there," I said. "Father's on about the horses again."

She gave a worried toss of her head. She, too, was tired of it all. Time and again we had tried to start a conversation at the table, but it had been fruitless. Father sat there half smiling, a sort of pitying smile of contempt on his face as though such petty talk as ours was below his consideration.

From the back-kitchen, came the sounds of father washing his hands and face, snorting as he doused his face with handfuls of water, and making the wooden roller behind the door creak as he towelled himself. He came in and made a show of comparing his watch with the clock.

"Tea is late," he muttered. "I didn't know it was this time!"

"I had to wait for the tart," said Mother. "But why didn't you come earlier?"

But he was not to be drawn. He just smiled to himself and closed and unclosed his hands, regarding his open palms with studied interest. Justin came in straight from the yard and sat at the table facing him.

"Oh, Justin! Your hands now! Why can't you wash them? You are like a pig. I don't know how you can eat!"

Justin munched his bread and butter before answering mother. He was dirty, his hands were red with earth, and his hair was down over his forehead. He copied father's gesture and studied his hands intently, opening and closing them just like the old man.

"Someone's got to work!" He stared across at father as he spoke. "And if I start washing my hands before every meal they'd get soft. Dirt protects them!" He turned slowly to me. "What have you been doing, Ned? Have you finished carting that dung-heap yet?"

"Yes, before tea—what do you think?"

"Before tea! Good God! You must have half-killed the old mare!"

Before I could answer, father had put down his knife and rasped the floor with a sudden backward thrust of his chair. He had gone white, and a zigzag vein stood out above his bald temple.

"Enough of this! I've had enough! Baiting me like a young bull you are!" His voice had been evenly suppressed when he started, but as he went on his voice rose: "What do you take me for? Get out! Get out of this room! You'll not eat at the same table as me; you dirty, drunken, whoring blaggard that you are! Come on, get out!"

He was now on his feet looking down at Justin, his fists closed, and his chest lifting with each breath he took. Justin leaned back in his chair, his hands in his trouser pockets. He stared up at father with a shade of a smile on his lips.

"Do you hear! Get out!"

Father lifted his fist.

"Daniel! Don't be silly now. Have you gone mad, or what?

Stop it!" Mother tried to pull him away. He turned angrily towards her and shook her hand off his sleeve. Justin made a movement as though he was going to rise to his feet. All he did, however, was to settle himself firmer into his chair. For myself, I felt my bowels turn inside me. It had happened at last, just like a thunderstorm that had been gathering in heaviness and darkness.

"Don't you interfere!" Father's voice was softer now, and I fancied I could detect a lonely note in his voice, but I did not trust him. "Don't you interfere, Anne," he went on. "You know me. You know how I've felt all these days. . . . But you've left me alone. You've had enough sense for that, whatever. But this blaggard is not going to give any tongue, oh no!" He leaned towards Justin. "Now, will you leave the table, or must I put you out?"

Justin grinned up at him.

"What, you?" He laughed. "What are you so excited about? Keep cool! And don't go talking about putting me out. Don't you put a hand on me or——"

Father gripped him by the shoulders, and Justin's chair fell backwards with a crash. For a moment it looked as if the two would start fighting. I jumped up and put my arms around Justin. The next moment, I staggered back from a heavy blow in the stomach; and as I fought for my breath and tried to overcome the weakening feeling of sickness that arose in me, I saw Justin square up to father again.

"Justin!"

As I stood there bent double and holding my hands to my stomach, I saw mother go up to Justin and fetch him a resounding smack across his face. Justin at once stepped back and dropped his fists. He put his hand to his cheek and frowned, as though not understanding who had hit him. Father watched him in silence.

"There! You asked for it!" Mother was crying. The tears coursed helplessly down over her cheeks. "You made me do it and . . . and I haven't hit you since you were little. . . . Fighting your father, and hitting Edwin like that . . . ! Oh, Iestyn, I don't know what's come over you . . . I can't understand you!"

She took off her glasses and started to wipe them with her apron. And it was that, I think, that finished Justin. It was the most pathetic thing mother could have done. There she was, so helpless without her glasses, her pale, blue eyes streaming with tears. Justin walked over to the window and stood there with his back to us.

"He is mad! I don't know what is wrong with him!" Father sat down and poured his cold tea into the slop-basin. "He doesn't try to pull with us. Everything must be done just in his way, and in his time!"

"Be quiet!" Mother was roused now. It was not often she raised her voice. And as I saw her in profile turning on father, I caught again a glimpse of the girl she must have been before years with father had forced her within herself. "You and your moods," she shouted. She was still without her glasses, and her hands were clenched at her sides. "What do you think we are? It's we've got to put up with you, just waiting for your pleasure until you feel like talking again!"

Father smiled. "That's right," he said, "that's right! Blame it on to me as usual. Me again . . . ! You!" He shouted across at Justin. "You learn to keep a civil tongue in your head. I'm not too old to manage you yet, even if you do rule the roost up at the Tavern there. . . . You wouldn't have done it in my day, oh no!"

Justin turned round. He gave me an eager, solicitous look. I winked back at him. I knew quite well how he was feeling.

"All right, all right, have it your way." He sneered at father with his nostrils. "You are always right, aren't you?"

He gave mother a little pat on the shoulder as he walked out of the kitchen. Mother put on her glasses and went to the hob for the teapot.

"Come on, Edwin, finish your tea; and you, Daniel. . . . And the nice tart that I had made—the first rhubo this year!"

Soon, father got up and went out. We watched him through the window. He walked jauntily, his hands in his pockets, and his hat well on the back of his head.

"What an afternoon!" Mother sighed, as though overcome by all that had happened.

85

"Don't worry," I said. "It had to come to a head. Things will be better now."

"Poor Justin!" Mother allowed a fond, musing smile to linger on her lips. "I know him so well. . . . And I hit him!" She wiped her lips with her apron. "Ah, well; he'll understand . . . I had to do it! He would have been sorrier if he had hit his father . . . Don't you think so?"

"Yes, of course! Didn't you see how he looked at us when he went out?"

"Yes, and he patted me on the shoulder. Do you know what?"

I waited for her to continue. She leaned over and whispered:

"He should get married. There's not enough room for him and his father here. I would like to see him married to some tidy girl. It would sober him up. It's time he had a place of his own and a family. Your father was set up long before he was his age. . . ."

I got up and went to the window. The day was drawing in, the sun going down very pale, and the Van Rocks already covered with mist.

"There's no one he would marry," I said. "I can't see him settling down with anybody."

"He might get some girl in trouble," said mother. "That's what I'm afraid of always."

I turned round quickly at her words. She smiled to herself as she caught my glance.

"Mam!" The word broke like a gasp from my lips. She shrugged her shoulders and started to collect the cups and saucers into one pile.

"Don't pretend," she said. "I know him as well as you do. Do you think I'm blind? Many is the time I have thought we would have some girl's father coming up here. I don't miss much," she went on quietly. Then she looked at me with a mischievous smile. "And I'm not so sure of you either. You've got some of the Peele blood in you, too; not that my side of the family is any too tame either!"

I laughed with her, and tried to read from her expression whether she was hinting something about Grett and myself.

"Don't be silly!" I laughed again. "You are imagining a lot."

"Ah, well! We'll see . . . we'll see. You have been going out very regular for months now. . . . And I've a good guess, too. Go on now, don't start asking me questions."

She disappeared into the black-kitchen with the four cups closed in a cluster on the heap of saucers.

I went down to the well. It lay in a square, flagged pool some twenty yards down the garden, past the flower-beds and the privets. I could still feel the tremulous beating of my heart. So mother guessed! How many more in the parish were already talking about Grett and myself? Perhaps, at this moment, they were talking about us in the blacksmith's or at Parri's. Anyway, what did it matter? Come the June Fair, I would spend the whole day with her at Brecon.

I thrust the water-jack down into the black square of the well and let it gurgle and gurgle until it was full to the neck. Our water was always ice-cold. I could never drink more than a half-dozen cupped handfuls of it without feeling my teeth ache and freeze in their sockets. And on a summer's day what pleasure it was to fold a green hazel leaf until it was shaped like a pointed cup, and then to dip it into the water. It was like a draught from the heart of the earth. You could taste the sweetness in it of moss and earth; and always, especially in the morning when the sun was low and slanting across the garden, your reflection came up to meet you as you bent to drink from it. On quiet nights, sometimes, I could hear its cold trickle welling over the stones and running down the gutter past the beehives at the end of the garden.

I was sitting there, smoking and thinking, when Justin came up to me. He had been digging at the far end of the garden. It was he and mother who looked after the garden. It was nothing for them to spend a whole evening there, especially in May or early June, mother with her skirt safety-pinned up round her waist and her grey petticoat showing, and Justin in his shirt-sleeves.

"Well?" He grinned. "How is it going now?"

"All right," I said. "I'm all right. The point is, how are you? You went a bit mad, didn't you? I thought you and the old man would half kill each other!"

87

Justin drew at his pipe until it glowed. Plumes of soft, pure blue smoke wreathed up past his face.

"Aye! I lost my temper. I can't stand his moods. . . . Damme it all, if you got to smooth a man like you would a dog, never go against the grain, then it's time something happened." He stopped and gave me a quizzical look. "Did I catch you hard?" he asked. "I don't know what came over me. . . . You know how it is. . . ."

A glow of warmth filled my heart for him, and for a moment I wished he hadn't that close-cropped beard which hid most of his expression from us. I always felt that it was a barrier between him and us, like a mask. He kept so much behind it; all you could see was the set of his lips and the expression in his blue-black eyes. He was smiling now, the wrinkles crinkling up the corners of his eyes.

"Don't talk," I said. "You just lost your head. It was a good job you didn't hit the old man."

"You are right," he said. "A chap can't go hitting his father, can he? Poor old mother," he added quietly. He looked towards the house. It was beginning to get dark and we could see her in the candle-light moving about the dairy. "She gave me a beauty, didn't she? A real bonclust! I bet she was a spitfire in her day, eh? How was she when you came out?"

"All right. What do you think she said?"

"What? What did she say?"

"She said you ought to get married."

He pondered her words for a while, nodding his head and smiling to himself. "Get married, eh?" He ran the tip of his tongue over his lower lip. "Get married! Perhaps she is right. . . . But who is there around here? Look here, I've been thinking . . . I wouldn't mind going away. I've had a bellyful here. There's no room for us all here, don't you think so?"

His words fell on my ears like the funeral bell. That he should leave home was out of the question, impossible. The place would never be the same again; he was part of the farm, responsible for all the main work, the ploughing, the harvest. He was the main spring of the place. And mother would be lost without him! And the old man would have his will and say unopposed, there would be no one to gainsay him. There was something else, too. What of myself and Grett?

"You can't, Justin, you can't!"

He looked hard at me, his eyebrows lifting in surprise.

"You don't mean it," I continued. "I . . . I . . ."

But I couldn't go on. How could I tell him what he meant to me! It was impossible, and he might have laughed. I looked at him, realizing again how essential a part he was of my home, my life, and of my future, too. It was now getting dark, and I could see only the outline of his strong face. I looked at him. This was my brother. With him behind me I had felt that, together, Grett and I could dare the whole parish. And here he was talking of going away.

"You can't go," I said to him. "Besides, where would you go?"

"There's plenty of places going," he said. "I ought to get married, like mother said. . . . But, damme it, I'd never want to be stuck to one woman. . . . I couldn't stick it. What I'd like is a little farm and an old house-keeper, or, failing that —well, there's the valleys, isn't there?"

I laughed, trying to ridicule his words.

"You go to the coal-fields!" I scoffed.

"Why not?" He spoke with some heat. "I'm as strong as the next, stronger, by damme, and I'd soon learn the trade. Besides, the money's good. . . . Moc is already talking of going."

I did not say any more to him about his leaving home until we were chaffing that night. The cows were still in, and because our hay was getting low, we were mixing some straw with it and chaffing them together. Justin, as became the elder, was feeding, and I was turning the handle. We worked by the light of the lantern which hung by its wire handle from the beam running under the roof. The curved, scimitar-like blades of the chaff-cutter looked as if they were oiled from their contact with the hay and straw.

"Look here!" I crooked my leg over the handle and leaned over the machine. "I'm worried about what you said about going away."

Justin was on his knees gathering the pale chaff into the large brass pan which we used for carrying the feed to the cattle. It was as smooth as a gold watch inside, but its outside was as black as our broth-crock.

"What's it worrying you for?" He did not look up as he spoke, but went on heaping the chaff into the pan. "You can carry on here all right. You and the old man should manage all right . . . more peaceful than when I'm here, anyway. . . ."

"It'll be the finish of everything I've planned if you go," I said.

"What do you mean?" He got up and faced me. "What plans are you talking about?"

I made a movement with my hand; I felt I was begging some favour of him. "Me and Grett," I said.

"Grett Ellis! Good God. Are you still serious there?"

"Serious!" I heard myself give a short laugh. "Serious! Look here, if you go away, I'm finished. I couldn't leave the old people alone. The place would go to ruin—it's bad enough now. The old man would never manage. And how in hell could I ever get married? I could never bring Grett here! Think of it! Bringing an Ellis here to Trewern! There'd be a murder or a suicide here pretty quick!"

Justin didn't say a word for a minute or so. He just stared in front of him. The lamp threw the shadow of his profile on the white wall; the line of his forehead like a bastion, his nose straight, and his chin made sharper because of the cut of his beard. Below us, the cows chewed, splashed the dung on the floor, and rattled their chains as they moved their heads.

"Then why in the name of God aren't you doing something about it?" he said at length. He seemed to be weighing every word, uttering them as if he were working out some plan in his head. Then he gave me one of his sly, half-humorous grins. "So you are bent on getting married, eh?" He closed one eye slowly and lifted his other eyebrow. "Tell me . . . how far has it gone? You haven't got to get married or anything like that?"

"Don't be daft," I said. "There's nothing like that. I—I haven't touched her yet!"

"You haven't?" He seemed incredulous. He looked sardonically at me from under his mocking eyebrows. "Pretty slow, aren't you? Don't take it the wrong way," he added quickly. "I'm only teasing. But"—he grinned again—"you've been courting now since the autumn isn't it? Whew!" He pursed his lips in a noiseless whistle. "You're a funny chap, Ned; different to what I was at your age!"

"Shut up," I said, "I am serious. I want to get married, and to hell with everybody. I'm going to have her. . . . But if you go away, then I'm in the cart!"

"Aye! I can see that all right. . . . So you are thinking of taking a farm?"

"I'll have to," I said. "There's nothing else. This place will come to you after the old man. . . . Don't pretend, you know it's yours! Besides, think of mother. What do you think she'd do if you went away? You know how it would be, don't you?"

"Aye, I suppose you are right." He picked up the pan and started towards the steps that led from the "dowlod" down to the cowhouse. "But you'll have to get a bloody move on!" He spoke to me over his shoulder. "Don't think I'm going to stand by while you play 'kiss-in-the-ring' with her. Get on with it, get married! Stand up to it! Get a farm or clear off to the valleys. That'd be the best thing. I tell you, this place is finished. Farming is finished! In twenty years' time half the farms will be empty. You saw how it was in the Christmas market. . . . And this winter the clog-makers didn't come, did they? That shows how things are going. Take my advice: get a move on. . . . Put her in the way or something. . . . Perhaps that would force things a bit. It's time you woke up, Ned!"

I was still thinking of what he had said when I went down to the river for a walk after supper. It was a fine night, the moon was well up over the Vans. From time to time a puff of warm wind would come down the valley; warm it was and fragrant, like a breath on a June day. Everything was still, the moonlight touching the long fields and rippling on the river. It was because of nights like this that I read the old poets. Dafydd ap Gwilym was full of such nights, and even when he sang of the moonlight or the swan on Lake Syfaddon, you could be sure that, sooner or later, he would come back to the gold of Morfudd's hair or the redness of her lips. So it was with me; I saw Grett everywhere.

I was already looking forward to the fair. I had, at first, just after Easter, hated the light evenings. I wanted the lamplight at home, the starlight, the winds and rains to continue. I hated the interim between the seasons. I thought of the places where Grett and I had lain together and imagined that the summer would put its revealing brightness between us. But now, at last, the intoxication of the warm days made my blood beat faster and wilder. I began to think of the shadowed places in the secret woods. I thought of new-mown hay, of honeysuckle, wild roses, red campion, and foxgloves; and with the warmer days Grett would wear her thin frocks again and would be nearer to me when I clasped her to me.

Echoes of Justin's words kept ringing in my ears: Get married. . . . Put her in the family-way. . . . Farming's finished . . . even the clog-makers don't come now. . . .

The clog-makers! They used to come every year after the harvest. They always camped down by the Sawdde on Allt-y-brain or Cwmsidan fields. They were a rough crowd, and we found it difficult to understand their talk. During the day they worked on the alders, shaping the soles with their long, hinged knives, and smoking their clay pipes. At night, they kept together, going up to the Tavarn and singing on their way back. Years ago, Justin had fought with one of them. He had come home with his lips split and his thumb out of joint. He had been bested by their champion, but he was not in his full strength then. The clog-makers! How I remembered them! Annie the Mason had cause to remember them, too. Her little girl was still known as "Lizzie fach Clogs." And now, they had stopped coming; we hadn't seen them for three years or more. As Justin said, everything was on the down-grade.

The moon rose higher and higher. The fragrance of the trees and grasses was strong by the river. I walked slowly up over our fields, the loveliness of the night and the passion of my love making my heart ache with unexpressed beauty. I awoke in the night to the sound of the rain on the roof, and when I got up, a blue, lilac mist clung to hedges and the trees,

and you could almost feel the sap rising into every swelling
bud.

Chapter 10

THE days passed in high splendour. The corn sprang green
and close; and the clover and the hay grew so thick that the
winds darkened the fields with their down-sweep. For a week
or two, the may trees flowered in our hedges and my walk
through the soft dusk each night was a bridal. Twice as I
walked home, I heard the nightingale in the Allt, and where
there had been fear in the dark winter there was now only the
tranced spell of summer and the singing madness of my love
and passion for Grett. I was not quite myself these days because of the joy that was on me. Grett and I were meeting each
other two or three times a week, and each night found us
clasped closer and closer in each other's arms. This was the
high season on the farm. From now until the shearing and
the hay-harvest, life was leisurely; and, milking over, I would
walk indolently from one sunlit, pollened field to another.
There were days when the sky was a vivid blue above the green-
black fringe of the Allt, and across the dipping fields, dew-
dark and quivering with the sun on them, I could see the mauve
majesty of the Van Rocks. There were noons, too, when the
far horizons trembled because of the aerial flicker of the heat-
haze above the crests of our hedges. Then, towards the end of
May, came our outing to the fair at Brecon. This year, father
and mother did not come with us, and Justin and I set off together in the trap. I was full of excitement. I thought of the
September fair when I had first met Grett; and now, to-day,
she and I had the whole day in front of us.

Justin was in great fettle. I glanced at him with affectionate
amusement. He needed a hair cut badly. I don't think he had
had one since the Christmas market. His hair curled down over
the back of his collar and was one with his beard in front of
his ears.

"You'd better get a trim-up to-day," I said to him. He half-closed his left eye as he turned his face towards me. He was in that lazy, indolent mood that always characterized him when he was feeling his best.

"Don't worry!" He gave the cob a light flick with the whip. "I'm going to have a real slap-up 'do' when I get there. Uffern! They'll think I'm Robinson Crusoe or Twm Shon Catti!" He ran his fingers through the hair behind his ears. "I'll get some of that pomatum, too. You see if I don't!"

We were soon in sight of Brecon. The dusty, white road was splashed with the shadows of the trees and hedges, and on our left the Usk flowed smooth and velvet-brown through the long, flat fields. We passed trap after trap, people on foot, gambos and carts of every description. Everyone was bound for the fair. The villages on the way were deserted, not a shop open, and no ring of anvil breaking on the laburnamed silence. The inns, of course, were all open; still, even so, they were not doing much business. Not until late at night would they be busy; from ten on, the cobbled yards would be packed tight with traps and carts.

My heart gave a great jump as we rounded each corner, wondering if I would see the Rhos Dirion family in front of us. I imagined Justin and I overtaking them; Grett would be in the back seat facing us, and I knew that our cob had it in him to show them some fine action. But we saw nothing of them, not a sign all the way.

My plans for the day were quite simple. First, Justin and I would go round to the cattle market and the horse-fair. I was looking forward to seeing the horses; and I smiled to myself as I visualized the check-breeched grooms trotting their horses up and down the field, each man looking into his horse's face as he ran, and giving as excellent a display of "leg-action" as the horse or pony itself.

The town was gay with flags and bunting. The church clock on the square chimed the half-hour as we rattled in over the cobbles. It sounded like a prelude to the day in front of us, the soft notes rising on the air like bubbles until they were lost in the vast blue of the sky.

The Sun Inn stood off the High Street, its huge signboard depicting a sunflower-like orb rising above a sky-line of peaks

—perhaps they were a representation of the Brecknock Beacons. The brick-built arch leading into the yard enclosed a shadowed coolness, beyond which rose the acrid smell of old hay, urine, and stale beer.

It was getting on for one o'clock when I left Justin still watching the horse-sales.

"Are you meeting Grett to-day?" he asked quietly.

"Aye, after dinner."

"Where are you going with her?"

"Up along the river—out of town."

He nodded approval.

"Good!" And as he turned to go, he gave me a wink. "Be careful," he said. "Next February will soon be here you know!"

For a moment I did not follow his meaning. I started counting, then I laughed back at him.

"Right, you win," I said. "And don't forget that hair cut, and get your beard trimmed. You are enough to frighten the devil!"

I left him at that, and made my way into the streets. I wanted to spend a half-hour or so in the second-hand bookshop in the market. I wanted something so that I could treasure it and remember this day whereon I had bought it. The shop was dark and cool, and the smell of the old books was enough to quicken my pulse. I went from shelf to shelf, blowing the dust off the top of each book and slapping it against my thigh. There was a book, squat and bound in dark green cloth that took my eye at once. I went up on my toes and reached it down. It was a collection of Trebor Mai's poetry. I opened it eagerly; over three hundred pages, and two-thirds of it filled with englynion. Without looking at the price, I hurried over to the bookseller.

"Two shillings," he said, running his thumb over the top and wiping the dust on his trousers. "The greatest englynwr in the language. A real bargain. All right?"

Here, at last, was the book I had been looking for. Englyn after englyn describing the beauty and loveliness that I knew so well—the summer, the wind, a kiss, a young girl. . . . A line caught my eye:

"Yn oer ei lle, 'n'wr y llyn."

I read and re-read the line. . . . The moon itself quenched

and cold in the depth of the lake! It was wonderful, but it could not be translated; the mutations and consonants were like music. Every moon that had ever passed over Llyn Caerhafnant was caught in that line; the moon-spilt gold was there, the darkness, the lap of the waters and, even then, there was something more there. The ecstasy of the poet was there. I walked along the sunlit pavement from the market repeating the line to myself. I wanted no more from the book, not for the time being anyway. To-night, when I got home, I would write my name in it, copying the crabbed script of the vicar who wrote in such a fine scholarly hand. . . . To-night, I thought! How far away it seemed! The afternoon and evening with Grett stretched out before me in a blaze of sunshine and shadow of cool twilight. It would be morning before Justin and I would get home. By then, this day would be behind me. Gripping the green-bound book between my arm and my side, I turned into a little restaurant for some food. At two o'clock I would be waiting for Grett down by the river.

.   .   .   .   .

Flowing quietly beside us, the Usk drowsed under the willows, swirled round the green, moss-covered stones, and spread in widening circles whenever a trout leapt and snapped at a fly or hovering midge. Every ripple caught the sun, the river winked and dimpled with crystal brightness. Now that we had left the town behind us, Grett and I walked without fear of being seen. My arm was around her, and every now and again I felt her tremble against me. We walked up-river facing the sun, and time and again as I half-closed my eyes because of the sun-dazzle on the river, I saw the rainbow-flicker of green and blue-gold on my eye-lashes. The air was sweet and fresh with the smell of the river and the flowering trees. Of course, they were more forward here in Brecon than it was with us over the Black Mountains. It was always an overcoat colder up in our parts than in town, and our hay-harvest never started until early July, whereas up here they would start on or about the twentieth of June.

We were in no hurry. Grett was in a summer frock all flowered over with watery blue and white. She had bought another new hat and was wearing it for the first time. The white curved brim, with its cluster of purple and mauve flowers over the front of it, shaded her face and set off the texture of her skin. She had drawn her hair right back and her ears were quite uncovered. I had never seen her like this before, the long line of her jaw resolving to the lobe and curve of her ear. Her neck was of the creaminess of a rose-petal; and as she walked with her head resting against my shoulder, I saw how her eye-lashes curled dark when she closed her eyes.

"A whole afternoon and evening!" I said. I couldn't believe it; we had never before had so much time to ourselves. "What time have you got to meet Jeff?"

"He told me to be at the White Harp at ten," she said. "He thinks I'm with Mary Glandŵr!"

I held her closer to me, and trembled as I felt the supple lissomness of her body. Far behind us the church clock chimed. It was three o'clock. Only three o'clock. We had seven hours before us, seven hours during which the day would slowly darken; and when we returned the music of the fair would swell louder and louder to greet us.

"Where is your Justin to-day?"

I couldn't help smiling at the way she put the question. "Your Justin" indeed.

"He's on the spree. . . . What do you think?"

Grett looked up at me, her eyes twinkling.

"You two are not a bit alike," she said. She made a mock-serious expression and half frowned, though her cheeks were dimpling. "You don't go after women, do you?"

"What would you say if I did?"

She shrugged her shoulders.

"You men are all the same. Your Justin, Jeff, even you!" She pretended to toss her head in a huff of anger. "I wouldn't trust you with any girl!"

"And what if you were a man?" I countered. "Wouldn't you be the same?"

"Worse than any of you, I expect. Don't you think so?"

We stopped and kissed. I could feel the passion of her

whole body in that kiss. And when I drew my lips away from her mouth, her head still lay back against my arm, her lips parted and her eyes closed.

From now on, the wooded side of the valley rose steeply on each side of the river. Green in all its sun-touched gradations met our eyes on all sides. The river took on the willow and alder-green shade of the trees. Here and there among the hazels and gorse, a wild cherry flaunted its blossom.

It was so shadowy in the valley that we did not notice how overcast the sky had become until a faint roll of thunder made us look around.

"It'll soon pass," I said. "We haven't had enough heat for thunder."

But the afternoon light waned, and soon the sky was a mass of greenish-yellow clouds. Not a breath of wind stirred in the trees. Little sounds rose clearly in the still air. Occasionally, a bird called, and the sound it made only made the silence more hushed in contrast. The thunder came nearer, and a few drops of rain splashed softly on our faces. Ahead of us stood a white-washed building, right at the edge of the river.

"Let's run," I said, "before the rain starts."

The building was an old mill. We ran and reached it just as the storm broke over our heads. The river was pitted with rain-drops. A flash or two made us turn aside, and the crack that followed was like a whip-lash of iron. Then, in a few minutes the thunder rolled away and there was only the vertical down-pour of rain. The air was again fresh and light, and the mountains came into view, the sun streaming down on them through the breaking clouds.

The mill, or barn as it now was, was shadowy and cool. The hay was down almost to within a yard of the floor. I looked around, my heart beating wildly and my limbs trembling. I looked at Grett; and seeing the expression in her eyes, I took her in my arms. She, too, was trembling. Then, as gently as I could, I took her over to the far end of the building and spread my jacket to make a place for her.

Far away a faint roll of thunder sounded; and as I lay there with Grett in my arms, I heard the hiss of the rain on the river, and in the greenish light around us, I saw Grett with her frock half-opened at the neck, her breasts rising and falling as she breathed against me.

We lay close together while the storm seemed to circle back over us. Now and again, a sudden, greenish flash dazzled our eyes, and in a spasm of momentary fear we clung closer still to each other. We lay there for a long time until the gloom inside the old mill brightened. Through the doorway we saw the river rushing smooth in long green masses under the rain-heavy alders. Every leaf caught the sun, and one by one the birds started to sing again.

I looked down at Grett. Her cheeks were flushed and her eyes were dark and shining. She must have sensed what was in my mind, for she held out her arms to me and drew me to her again. Then, at last, at long last, there came a moment when everything faded from my sight, when the river ceased its noise and no birds sang; there was no sunlight, no shadow, there was nothing but Grett and her eyes shining, her lips parted, and her arms holding me.

. . . . .

When we rose to leave, the sun had gone down behind the crest of the valley, and the long shadows bathed the river. Grett stood up and smoothed her skirts. I was nervous of looking at her lest she should feel embarrassed, but she met my eyes openly and smiled happily. She undid her hair and it fell over her shoulders and her face so that she was a girl again.

"Edwin?" She paused with her comb in her hand and removed a hairpin from between her teeth. She looked at me with a little pucker of alarm on her forehead. I guessed at once what was in her mind. I shook my head.

"Don't worry," I said. "There's nothing to be afraid of."

"You are sure?"

"Yes, yes. . . . Nothing to be afraid of!"

She gave a sigh of relief and sat down again at my side. I parted the thick, dark hair from her face and kissed her.

"You are not sorry?" I whispered.

"Sorry!" She sat up and looked at me. "I am glad," she whispered. "I wanted you. . . . From now on, I am yours, yours. . . . Marriage or no marriage, I don't care!"

Mine! Grett was mine, and I was hers. A new, refreshing peace possessed me, and behind it, hardening like iron, was a new purpose. From now on, to-night even, everybody should know it. We were one. I could still feel in every nerve of my being the contact of her body. This was our consummation. At last, here was an end to the burning desires, to the hours of tortured longing. We were one, we were one! Yet, even so, we could not leave the mill. We lay together again, and all too soon the stars came out and we could see only the loom of the trees through the doorway. Grett put herself tidy in the darkness, and I used nearly all my matches trying to find her hairpins. Then, faintly at first, but increasing with each bend of the river-path, the music of the fair came to us. Soon, we could see the glow of the lights, and before we got to the town we were half-running in our eagerness and excitement to get to the fairground.

"Come on! Let's try them!"

Grett hung back for a moment as we stood alongside the slowing roundabout.

"All right! Let's go!" She gave a defiant, reckless toss of her head and stepped on to the vibrating platform ledge. We were both in a mad, devil-may-care mood. We had already seen a number from the parish. Whether they had seen us or not we didn't care. I was going up to Rhos Dirion the next day to see Grett's father and mother. I only hoped they would not hear the gossip before I could break the news to them.

Grett sat sideways on a champing horse of red and gold, and clung with one arm to the spiralled brass rod in front of her. I jumped up behind her, and held her close and safe with one arm around her waist.

The glare of the naphtha flares lit up the faces of the crowd below us until, as the circular platform gained speed and the music quickened its accompaniment, they became one indistinct merge of yellow. The lovely, galloping rhythm of the wooden horse under us gave a feeling of recklessness to our bodies. I felt we were riding away, Grett before me, on this flaming horse whose hoofs did not touch the earth. After a while, the first feeling of dizziness passed, and I looked down over my shoulder at the whirling crowd around us. Then they steadied a little, and as I bumped the saddle, riding as a farmer should in front of all these townfolk, I saw someone in the crowd pointing at us with his outstretched arm. I waited until we came round again and saw him as we approached. It was Parri Nanteurin, and his wife with him.

"Did you see that?"

"What?" Grett half-turned her head and looked up into my face. For two pins I would have kissed her there in the full light with the music thundering around us. But the roundabout was slowing down.

"Parri Nanteurin and his wife!"

Grett only shrugged her shoulders and nestled herself closer to me. I jumped down and lifted her off the horse. Someone whistled below us as the white gleam of her petticoat showed about her knees.

"What now? The coco-nut shies, is it?"

"Yes! Knock one down for me!"

We shouldered our way through the crowd towards the coco-nut shies. Grett carried her hat in her hand, and walked along with her arm crooked in mine, her frock showing up her figure and flaring around her calves.

"Well, well! If it isn't Edwin Peele and Miss Ellis!"

Right in front of us, barring our way to the stall where an auburn-haired gipsy girl with gold rings in her ears stood with a boxful of wooden balls before her, was Parri Nanteurin. I at once held Grett closer to me. Parri gave us a slow, steady look; then he closed one eye and smiled. He had a paper rosette in the lapel of his coat and his shoulders were covered with confetti. His wife, thin and quick-eyed, looked incredulously at us.

"You look surprised," I said. "Anything wrong?"

Parri gave a dry cackle. He came up to us and gave me a playful prod in the stomach.

"You young devil," he said, laughing. "So you don't care a bit who sees you!"

"Why should we?" said Grett. She hung on my arm and looked up into my face.

"Why, indeed! Good luck to you!" Parri nodded his head in vigorous agreement and turned to his wife. Though her thin, wrinkled lips were pressed hard and tight against one another, her eyes were twinkling with approval.

"The Peeles and the Ellises!" Parri's eyes opened and rolled upwards. "This is something new. But it's good stock. . . . Good stock, even if there is bad blood. . . . What do you say, Pali?"

His wife nodded.

"They have been very secret," she said, "very secret! And when will the engagement be, or is that a secret, too?"

I closed my left eye mysteriously and said nothing. Grett played up to them, too; for she spread open the fingers of her left hand and, with her head on one side, appeard as if she were already regarding a ring on her finger.

"Come on! Tell us now!" Parri's wife was insistent.

"All in good time," I said. "Good news travels fast, eh? Come on, Grett."

We made to go, but Parri put out his hand and gripped my arm firmly.

"Good luck," he said warmly, and I could feel the friendship vibrating from his hand. "And don't let them come between you." He turned and looked appreciatively at Grett. The naphtha flares showed up the lovely lines and shadows of her face, giving a sharp-edged delicacy to the line of her nose and chin; and her straight eyebrows were long and like jet above her eyes. "The finest girl in the parish," he went on. "Yes, you are; there's nobody to come near you! Good luck to you both, and"—he leaned across and whispered in my ear—"you stand up to your father; don't you let him have his way in this. And don't let parish talk put you off. Let the flies swell on their own dung-heaps!"

We left them there, and I fancied there was a speculative look in Mrs. Parri's eyes as she looked Grett up and down.

"She can hardly wait," I said to Grett.

"What do you mean?" she asked.

I laughed. "I bet she is counting on her fingers already. May,

June, July. . . . Yes, about February! Can't you see her counting?"

Grett gave my arm a convulsive squeeze. "Don't talk!" She laughed with me. "That would be the end of us. . . . Oh, don't talk about it. It makes me nervous to think about it!"

"Don't worry," I said. "I've told you it's all right. . . ."

Moving away from the coco-nut shies, we made for a group that stood watching a man who was swinging a heavy wooden mallet in front of the bell-ringing machine. He was in his shirt-sleeves, and with each blow he rang the bell fixed at the top of the high gauge. His blows were rhythmic, easy, and with each hit the weight coursed up the narrow groove and hit the bell with a clean smack.

"Mawredd!" I exclaimed. "He's used to that all right! Let's have a look at him!" We pushed through the crowd, and with a gasp I recognized the stature and build of the man with the mallet. I blinked my eyes for a moment or two, hardly believing that this clean-shaven, pale-faced being was my brother. Justin! It was Justin as I remembered him years ago: the same line of jaw and squareness of chin, the firm moulded lips; only now that the bones had set and all softness had gone from his cheeks, his face looked as if it had been chiselled from stone.

"It's Justin," I said to Grett. "Do you recognize him? He's had a shave, and look at his hair cut!"

Shorn now of its unkempt hair, Justin's neck looked stronger and more sinewy than ever. The back of his shirt was dark with sweat. He laid the mallet down and stooped to pick up his coat. The people crowded round him.

"Diawl! I thought you was going to crack the bloody bell, Justin."

Justin laughed and lurched slightly as he struggled into his jacket.

"Me!" His voice was tipsy. "I always ring the bell," he said. "Every time! Right on the bloody spot every time—you ask the girls!"

A roar of laughter followed his words.

"Justin!"

I called out to him from the edge of the crowd.

He turned round at the sound of my voice. Rhys Blacksmith, Iori Allt-y-brain, and Dai Alltwen stared at me as they saw me with Grett's arm in mine. Their mouths opened, and Iori pointed at me incredulously.

"Over there, look!" Jack Berthlwyd indicated us to Justin, and slewed him round until he saw us. He shook Jack's hand off his shoulder and came up to us. Self-consciously, he ran his hand over his smooth chin. He grinned admiringly at Grett.

"Good!" He gave a side nod of his head. "Good! That's the style! No more hole in the corner, eh?" He grinned again at Grett, and let his glance rest for a moment on the high, firm thrust of her breasts.

"We hardly knew you." Grett's voice was jocular, friendly. I loved her for that.

Justin again ran his hands over his face.

"I don't know myself yet," he said. "Perhaps I'll stand a chance to get a decent girl now. Diawch! With that beard I had, I'd have had some old girl in a shawl and a bonnet making eyes at me! What do you think of it, Ned?"

He struck a mock-heroic stance, thrusting out his chin and turning his profile to us. His hair, damp with sweat, fell over his temple.

"Where's your hat?" I asked him. I was doing my best to appear casual in front of all who were staring at us.

Justin gave a half-guilty smile. "I left it in The Coracle," he said. "The damme thing came down over my ears. I was like a cheap-jack. See here!" He thrust his hand into the large poacher's pocket inside his jacket, and pulled out a loud check cap. "How do you like that for a cap?"

I drew Grett a little back from him. She was getting the full blast of his breath. But she at once went up to him and gave the cap a little pat and tug of adjustment as Justin pulled the cloth peak down over his eye.

"So you are Grett!" He spoke quietly and moved a few yards away from the group. "Grett Ellis," he went on, "and I've never spoken to you! A bit silly, isn't it?"

Grett nodded. "It is," she said. "But you'll know me from now on. . . ." She indicated the crowd behind us by a side glance. "This will make them think a bit, won't it?"

Justin curled his lip derisively. "Them!" He snorted contemptuously. "Don't care a damme about them, nor anybody else either. The three of us together from now, isn't it? Damme! I'm glad you've come out into the open. Are you nervous?"

Grett wrinkled her nose and shook her head.

"Not a bit. . . . Are you?"

Before Justin could reply to her banter, Rhys Blacksmith came up, Iori and Alltwen behind him.

"Hallo, Ned." He spoke over his shoulder to me and kept his eyes on Grett. "Where's Jeff, Miss Ellis?"

Grett faced him coolly.

"Jeff!" She shrugged her shoulders. "It's no good asking me, I don't know; and what's more, I don't care. . . . Don't forget to tell him you've seen me, will you!"

The boys laughed at her reply.

"That's the style, Grett Ellis!" It was Dico Lewis. I hadn't noticed him there. He gave me a friendly nod. He pushed himself to the front. "You've got grit, young Grett. Diawl, Ned!" He turned to me, his moustache bristling. "If I was your age, I would try to cut you out. Drop dead, I would!"

"It's he'll need his grit," said Iori.

I bridled at that. "What's it got to do with you?" I shouted. "Just you keep your remarks to yourself!"

Dico leaned over towards me.

"Look out!" he warned. "Jeff is coming up behind you now."

I turned and saw Jeff Ellis striding towards us. He was in his check breeches, a dark brown coat, and had a new sleek bowler on his head. He carried an ash-plant, and looked for all the world like an auctioneer or gentleman farmer.

He came straight up to Grett and myself. I felt Grett's arm quiver a little. For a second or so no one spoke or moved, and it seemed to me that the fair and its harsh music and the hooting of roundabout engines passed into nothingness. The faces around us, too, became a blurred mass in the flickering naphtha light: there remained only Grett. I could see her clearly, her face taut and fine against the shadows behind her. And here at my side was Justin, cap on head, a half-smile on his lips, his shoulders square, and his jacket buttoned tight around him. Jeff's eyes were mad with temper.

"You!" He found his tongue at last, and caught hold of Grett to tear her away from my arm. "Are you mad, or what?" he shouted. Grett twisted herself free and shook his hand away.

"She's here with me!" I was surprised at the sound of my voice. Usually, I was soft-voiced, quiet; but this was the voice I used to the dogs and the horses. My nerves had suddenly become steady, there was no tremor at all in my stomach or in my limbs. "She's with me," I repeated. "And don't go making a scene here!"

Jeff looked me up and down. Then he looked round at the crowd. Rhys, Iori, and a few others were at his side.

"With you, eh?" Jeff's eyes returned to me. "Diawl! You are only a crot, and you say that to me!"

"Be quiet, Jeff. Listen to me!" Grett withdrew her arm from mine and faced him. "I'm here with Edwin from my own choice——"

Before she could say more, Jeff made a step towards me and raised his fist. I jumped back a step and put up my hands to defend myself.

"Enough of this!" Justin stepped up and pushed Jeff back. "Put your hands down, Ned, and take Grett out of this. Go on! Jeff and I'll have a little chat here."

Jeff made another movement towards me as I caught Grett's arm and drew her to me. Justin again stepped between us.

"Cut it out, Ellis!" He spoke quickly. "A scrap here and your sister's name will be mud." He looked over his shoulder towards the back of the caravans. "Come round here away from the crowd. It's time we straightened things out."

Jeff at once turned and walked towards the caravans, Justin following him quickly. Iori, Rhys, and the others were about to follow when Dico shouted:

"A private affair, boys. Fair play, now. We are not wanted there. Fair play now!"

I looked at Grett. She was white-faced and her eyes were flashing.

"I know those two," she said, and she tugged at my arm.

"They'll half kill each other. You know how they hate each other, and our Jeff will never give in."

The grassy clearing behind the caravans was quite deserted except for the two figures facing each other. Overhead, I could see the soft stars in the summer night. Justin had his face towards the fairground and the light shone on his face. Jeff had already taken off his coat.

"We'll settle this now," he was shouting. "If you think you and that crot of your brother can make a laughing-stock of me and my sister, then you are mistaken, Mr. God-Almighty-Peele. Come on, put your hands up before I lash you one!"

Grett ran on before me.

"Stop it!" she shouted. "You are off your head. Listen to me——"

"You keep out of this," shouted Jeff. "Out of the way, we'll settle with you at home. Just let me settle this blaggard first!"

Justin stood facing him with his hands in his breeches pockets. He was very still and quiet. How he kept like this, I don't know, for when he was like this a wrong word was like a whiplash to him. Justin, deadly quiet and seemingly calm, was far more dangerous than when he was roaring mad. He turned towards Grett, but kept his eyes on Jeff all the time.

"It's all right!" He gave a grim smile. "Don't worry, Grett, there'll be no fight . . . I'm not here to fight him." He turned to Jeff. "Do you understand?" he said. "I'm not going to fight you. But don't provoke me, or by God, you'll be sorry! Our little quarrel can wait. . . . Now, Ned," he motioned me to him. "Out with it, right now!"

"I'm coming up to your place to-morrow night to see your father," I began.

Jeff laughed. "To see my father! What, you? You?" He laughed again. "Good God, do you think you've got a chance with Grett here?"

"Yes! He's got me whenever he likes," said Grett. "And, what's more, we'll be married as soon as we can!"

"You are daft," sneered Jeff. "Just because you've been walking about with him to-day, you talk of marriage. . . ."

"Don't worry," I said to him, "we've been courting since last September."

He stared at me for a long time, and I watched his hands in case he suddenly hit out at me.

"You underhanded stoat," he said slowly. "Since last September!" He then looked at Grett, his eyes mocking and sneering at her breasts. She at once put her hands on her blouse as if to hide herself.

"And you think you can come up to our place to-morrow night! Just you try, my boy. Just try! D'you hear that? We don't want any of your breed up there."

"Who'll stop me?" I asked. "Not you or anybody else?"

The sight of Jeff was enough to provoke anyone to hit him. He looked across at me. We were of a height, but I hadn't his build or age. He was already in his strength.

"Now, take my advice," he sneered. "You've got no chance at all. Keep away from my sister, and don't you dare to come near our place to-morrow night, or any other night!"

The blood rose to my head. Who was he to talk to me like this?

"To hell with you!" I shouted. "I don't care a damme for you! Grett's mine, do you understand? Mine! And we'll be married whenever we like!"

In spite of the noise of the fair, the engine chuffing behind us, the blare of the roundabouts, the shouting and screaming laughter from the swing-boats, and the crack of the rifles from the shooting galleries, I felt a silence come over us. Justin pursed his lips and buttoned his coat. Grett took my arm again, and I saw that her face had gone drawn and tense. Jeff stared at her with something like horror on his face. And at that moment I felt sorry for him. What was it I had said? An echo of my words came back to me: "Grett's mine . . . mine!" But before I could say anything, Jeff turned to Grett:

"Grett!" He looked down at her, and I fancied his lip quivered as he spoke. "Grett, did you hear what he said? He said you are his. It isn't true, is it?"

She was silent for a moment. She gave me a quick glance, then she looked at her brother.

"Think what you like," she said quietly. "I'm tired of it all. Quarrelling over me like a pack of gipsies. Don't you think I've got my pride!"

"But is it true?" insisted Jeff.

"Think what you like," said Grett again. "It makes no difference what you think. . . . What Edwin says is right—we'll be married as soon as we can!"

"Uffern dân!" It was more of a cry of anguish than an oath from Jeff. The next moment he caught me flush on the mouth. "Take that, you Peele bastard!" he shouted. "An' that, an' that!"

I went down before I knew it from the blows he rained on me. I tried to get up and wrapped my arms in front of my face to protect myself. The next moment I felt my whole body turn weak and sick as Jeff's fist caught me low in the stomach. I fell forward with my head between the spokes of the caravan wheel. The lights of the fairground danced and flashed before me as if they had gone mad. Then things became clearer; there was the strident music again and Grett bending over me. I struggled to my feet. Justin was holding Jeff at arm's length.

"Sa' 'nôl, y diawl!" Justin drew his arm back threateningly. "You all right, Ned?" he shouted.

"All right!" I gasped. I was fighting to get my wind back. A feeling of nausea passed over me, and I would have given anything to vomit. I swallowed hard, and wiped the spittle from my lips with the back of my hand. A sour, acrid taste fouled my mouth.

Justin pushed Jeff away from him.

"I'll settle with you again," he said. "Now clear off, Jeff Ellis. I've told you, I won't fight you to-night. But don't start piggatting me, or I'll mark you for life, see?"

Jeff put his collar right.

"I'll take on each one of you," he said. "If you won't fight to-night, then I'll challenge you wherever I see you. Remember that! Wherever and whenever I see you. And keep that crot at home, and away from my sister!"

"He's coming up to your place to-morrow night, and I'll be with him," said Justin. "Keep your challenge till after he's seen your father. I'll be your man then, any bloody day!"

Jeff nodded. He measured Justin with his eye. And it was only then that I appreciated what was in Justin's mind: he would not fight Jeff knowing that, if he thrashed him, he would only worsen things between us, and so ruin my chances with Grett.

"Come on!" Jeff came over to Grett. "You are going home now."

"I'm going with Edwin," said Grett. She turned her back on Jeff, and took my arm. "Come on," she said to me. "You can take me to The White Harp."

I looked at Justin. He nodded and motioned me to go. When we looked back, Jeff was putting on his coat. Justin stood a yard or two away from him, his hands in his pockets, and the light from the fairground showing up the rugged lines of his face and the dark hollows under his cheek-bones.

. . . . .

At ten o'clock I stood leaning over the cool parapet of the bridge, looking at the sky-shot smoothness of my beloved Usk. The night air was still warm, and tier upon tier of stars rose into the night that itself was pale above the inky edge of the Beacons. The moon, three or four nights past her full, would not be up until well after midnight. I smoked there for some time, thinking of all that had happened on this day. Then, after a while, I crossed over to the other side of the bridge and looked up-river. Somewhere round the bend of the river, up there in the murmuring darkness and caressed by the cool flow of the river, was our mill. I stared up through the darkness finding it hard to reconcile the hours we had spent there with all that had happened afterwards. More than once, I had the feeling that I was dreaming, on inconsequential event following the other without rhyme or reason. I ran my hand over my bruised lip where Jeff had hit me. It was still sore and puffed, but it did not matter. Nothing mattered but my happiness, and that in itself was bound up in Grett. I tried to recature the ecstasy I had known with her in the green darkness inside the mill. But such rapture could not be recaptured even in imagination. A tremor of ecstasy would come when I imagined her lying with me. I caught the pallid gleam of her limbs and half-felt the thrill of her kisses and the warmth of her body; but as for recapturing the thrill of supreme and final ecstasy, that already belonged to the past and could not be known again until we would next be together.

I had no desire to return to the fairground. Now that Grett was in the kitchen of the White Harp waiting for Jeff to take her home, the town was empty for me. I already longed for the return journey over the mountain.

The church clock struck eleven before I made a move to go and look for Justin. It was a little cooler now, and I fancied I got a whiff of the mountain smell from the river. I thought of the narrow, winding stream on the Black Mountain, the quiet stretches of water reflecting the same stars that were mirrored here. Cold enchantment lay on the river where it whispered and clucked its way through the whinberry and heather-covered banks. Next to the Sawdde, there was no such river as the Usk. The only difference was that the Sawdde belonged to the parish, it had its source and mouth with us; but the Usk left us, and I knew nothing of its way down past Crickhowell and Abergavenny; though, indeed, the word Abergavenny rippled and lapped like a river itself.

The streets, almost empty now, seemed grotesque in the gaslight. I felt as if I were walking in a dream. This was so different from our lanes at home. There was a friendliness coming from the houses, they trembled with life, and the polished bar of brass against the bottom of each door caught the lamplight and spelled comfort and homeliness. And all the time, the music from the fairground and the distant roar of shouting gave an added intimacy to the hour. There was a secret joy, too, in the knowledge that Grett was still in town. I had wanted to stay with her until Jeff would return for her, but she begged me to go, fearing there might be further trouble.

I stood for a while in the main square opposite the church. People passed and re-passed. Traps came slowly out of inn yards, increasing in speed as each horse or pony set its head for home. From the public-houses came the sounds of singing and shouting. I looked around for The Coracle, not quite sure where it was. Then, suddenly, I saw Parri Nanteurin and his wife coming out of an arched gateway. I made my way across the road and into the tap-room.

The passage was crowded with farmers. They stood, glass in hand, their bowlers on the back of their heads, all talking and arguing together.

"Ned-w! Looking for Justin?"

It was Gwydd Evans from the top of the parish. He looked somehow out of place there with his square-fashioned double-tailed coat and high, starched collar.

"He's in the back room—all the boys are there. And, look here"—he thrust his face close to my ear—"you keep sober now, or you will never get home. He's on the proper booze to-night!"

"Right! Thanks, Gwydd!"

I pushed my way through. The reek of beer and vomit was heavy in the passage, and mixed with all this was the stench from the yard outside, the stables and crude urinal just outside the back door.

The "back room" of The Coracle was a long room with a bar at the far end. A few coloured pictures hung on the walls advertising whisky and gin. A thick haze of tobacco smoke clung to the ceiling. I had no difficulty in finding Justin. He was half-leaning against the bar-counter, his jacket and waistcoat open, and his arm circling the waist of a dark-haired girl who stood there with her head resting against his shoulder. Around him were a crowd from the parish. Dai Alltwen was slumped in a chair, his gaitered legs stretched out in front of him. And behind Justin, grinning all over his battered face, was Moc Morgans, Mihartach. I looked at Moc with curiosity. I had not seen him for months. He had only just come out of Carmarthen gaol where he had been sent following his last escapade before Christmas. Stripped to the waist, he had cleared the bar in a pub at Llandovery, finishing up with knocking the local policeman senseless. He was short, probably two or three inches shorter than Justin. With the dark muffler round his thick neck, and a broken-peaked cap drawn down over his forehead, he looked what he was—a typical mountain-fighter. Justin and he had always been close friends; and seeing them together this night, I knew the day was not yet over, not by a long way. When Moc was not in prison or away on a drinking bout which usually lasted a fortnight or until his ready cash ran out, he farmed a bit of land up near the Van Pools.

Justin turned a bloodshot eye at me as I came up to him. In his right hand he had a half-tumbler of neat whisky. Moc, too, was drinking whisky.

"Where's Grett?" asked Justin. "Gone home already?"

"Shut up!" I said. I didn't want Grett's name bandied about here.

"All right! All right, gwas! No offence!" He gave me a wink and a nod. "Sorry," he said. "Must keep the secret till to-morrow, eh?"

"When are you coming?" I asked him. "It's getting on."

"Getting on! Diawl, Ned, give us a chance! Going home! What do you say, Moc? We haven't started yet, have we?"

Moc emptied his glass and rapped it on the counter. But before calling for a drink, he caught hold of the water-jug and put it to his lips, rinsing his mouth round and round, and then throwing his head back to gargle before swallowing.

"That's the way," he gasped. "Wash out clean, and then the next drink tastes like the first."

He called whiskies for all of us. "What about Teg there? A little port, is it? Or a gin? Gin for the ladies, eh?"

The girl nodded, and made no remonstrance as Moc's hand closed round the shape of her breast.

Drink followed drink. I let myself go. After all, what use was it to be in a pub and not drink? At my side, Justin kept asking Teg to go outside with him.

"It's safe enough," he insisted. "You go first, then I'll follow."

But the girl would have none of it, though Justin kept plying her with drinks.

"Everybody's watching us," she repeated. "They'd soon put two and two together."

"One and one you mean!" laughed Justin.

Meanwhile, the landlord was trying to call "Time."

"Come on, boys. Past eleven, fair play now! Think of my licence! No, no, more! Llew Harris, you've had quite enough now, quite enough! You too . . ." But no one paid any attention to him. "TIME!" he shouted again. "Diawl! Is it a lot of pigs you are, or what? Swill, swill, all the bloody day and night. Come on, now: TIME, gentlemen!" He banged a pewter pot on the counter. A roar of laughter went up from Justin, Moc, and the girl, at some story they were being told.

"Look out, there's the Sergeant!" said Moc. His eyes narrowed and glittered as he pointed at the massive, pot-bellied, tight-buttoned figure of the police-sergeant.

"You go steady now, Moc!" Justin shook a playful finger at him. "Just you go steady, I want you with us over the shearing and not in gaol again." He leaned past the girl. "Just hang on," he said. "Old Seth is just calling 'Time' to get rid of the crowd. It won't be stop-tap though till we run out of sovrans. Remember last year?"

It was as Justin said. One by one the more timid left, and in a quarter of an hour or so the centre of the room was clear of people. I looked around to see who were left, and there seated on a bench near the door was Jeff with Iori, Rhys, and a few others. I stared at Jeff not believing my eyes. The thought that Grett was still waiting for him at The White Harp hit me like a blow. What was Jeff up to? He appeared to be quite sober, but Iori had a big dent in his hat, and Rhys was drinking steadily, saying nothing. He stared at me without any sign of recognition. Was Jeff mad enough, I wondered, to start again about Grett in front of us all? At that moment, he caught sight of me. He said something to Iori, and the whole bunch of them shouted with laughter.

"All right! All right! Keep cool, Ned. Keep cool now." Justin tapped me re-assuringly on the arm. "I saw them come in a few minutes ago. Don't worry, if it's trouble they want, Moc and me'll clear the bar in a wink. What do you say, Moc?"

Moc buttoned his coat. He drew his breath in and inflated his big, barrel chest. "Aye, and the bloody sergeant as well. Just my stamp he is, just my stamp!"

The girl, Teg, looked from Moc to Justin. A few of her hairpins had fallen out, and her hair was down about her shoulders.

"Shut up, you two!" She slurred her words. "Is it brawling you want, or what? . . . You want a fight, eh? Come on then!" She stood before Justin, her blouse open down the front, and before he could say a word, she hit him lightly on the nose. The blow, though light, brought the tears to his eyes. A roar of laughter filled the room. Some of the women started to pound the counter with their glasses.

"Go in, Teg!" shouted one. "Give him another. These bloody farmers think they own the place!"

Justin wiped the water from his eyes. "You bitch!" His lips hardened. "What d'you want to do that for? Damme. For two pins I'd turn you upside down."

He grinned and made a step towards her. In her drunkenness, the girl must have thought he was going to hit her, for she gave a scream and in stepping backward knocked over a small table cluttered with empty glasses. There was a crash and watery tinkle of breaking glass. The landlord came rushing out from behind the bar. His eyes, small and almost out of sight in the layers of fat that surrounded them, were glittering with temper.

"Out!" he shouted. "Out you go, the four of you!" He turned to the sergeant. "Put them out!" he roared. "They've had too much already. . . . And this piece, too. The street's the place for her!"

The sergeant put down his glass and wiped his moustache. He walked heavily across to Justin and Moc.

"No trouble now, be careful!" I whispered to Justin. He nodded. Moc Mihartach stepped back a yard until he was slightly behind Justin's shoulder. Everyone was silent in the bar. The sergeant stopped and looked down at Justin. He was a big man, well over six foot, and must have weighed upwards of eighteen stone.

"Well? You heard what Seth said, why don't you go now? Come on, we don't want any brawling here. I won't have it, even if it is fair night."

Justin looked lazily at him.

"What are you talking about?" he said. "Brawling? There's no brawling here. The girl just knocked against the table. Here!" He threw a half-sovereign on the counter. "That's for the glasses." He turned again to the sergeant: "But why should we get out? What about the rest here? My money's as good as theirs!"

"I don't want your money," interposed the landlord. "Out you go before you are thrown out. We know all about you and your butty there."

Moc spat and drew his thumb down over his nether lip.

"Aye! It's out you go," said the sergeant. He drew himself up and settled his helmet firmly on his head. "Out you go, or I put you on a charge."

Justin leaned forward and tapped the sergeant on his tunic with his forefinger.

"Right!" he said. "Get your little black book out then. Go on, put my name down, and don't forget the time and your own pint on the window over there. Don't think we are just yobs from the country! I know the law as good as you!"

The sergeant was quiet for a second or so. Then he replaced his note-book in his breast pocket.

"You are a rotten sport, you are. Rotten! Ah well!" He gave the impression that he was trying to recover his poise. "Then if you won't go out quietly, we'll have to throw you out. Understand now?"

"Just you try," said Justin. "Just you take your helmet off and try me, man to man, not like a bloody policeman!"

The sergeant shook his head.

"No! I'm too old. If I was ten years younger, I'd take you on like a shot. . . . But don't think we can't do it! Even if I can't, well, there are others you know."

"Bring him up! Bring him up!" Justin was beginning to shout. "Bring any man up here, and I'll back myself he won't put me out. Five pounds on it! Come on!"

He drew a handful of money from his pocket and counted out five sovereigns. An excited murmur ran through the room. Even the landlord began to show interest. I saw Jeff, followed by the others, come up to the bar. The landlord and the sergeant went into a whispered conference. They soon came to a decision, and beckoned to a young chap sitting on the other side of the room. I saw Moc look him over keenly and then whisper in Justin's ear.

"Makes no difference at all," said Justin. "He's just the man I've been looking for all day."

"Don't be daft," said Moc seriously. "It's Dai Probert. I

saw him in the ring at Merthyr last year. . . . A middle-
weight, and as tough as they make 'em. Used to work in Dow-
lais. He's handy he is, and no mistake!"

The boxer was about twenty-four or -five. He was a few
inches taller than Justin, and held himself jauntily. His ears
were small and misshapen, the cheek-bones sharp, and his nose
thickened and flattish.

"Call it off," I said to Justin. "He's professional, and in
training!"

"My money's good," said Justin. "If the landlord is agree-
able, I'll turn his bar into a boxing-ring. Where is this chap?"

The boxer, Dai Probert, stood a few yards away from him,
swaying lightly from his toes to his heels. Behind him stood the
landlord, the sergeant, and the rest of the drinkers. I looked
across at Jeff, Iori and the others. They were watching Justin
and casting occasional glances of appraisal at Probert. I caught
Iori's eye, and he shook his head at me as if to tell me to warn
Justin. Jeff, however, gave no sign of what was passing through
his mind. He stood there with his feet apart and his hands in
his pockets. I tried to hold his glance, hoping in my heart that
in such an extremity as this there would be something akin to
partizanship in his attitude. But his expression gave nothing
away.

The landlord rolled forward, his face flushed, and his podgy
hands pushing the people aside. He stood in front of Justin.

"Now, farmer, look here. Are you going out or not?"

Justin's answer was to take off his coat.

"Very well then!" The landlord turned to the crowd. "Don't
blame me, boys. We've given him every chance, right?"

Justin put the five sovereigns into a heap. He looked round.
He hadn't many friends there, only Moc Mihartach and myself. The girl, Teg, had already gone to sit with the other
women.

"Money talks," said Justin. "Cover that, Seth, and we'll let
the sergeant hold the money. I'll take your man on. Where is
he?"

Dai Probert came forward. He was very quiet, sober-faced,
and he smiled at Justin.

"Look here"—his voice was soft, gentle; to me it sounded

like a boy's—"you know who I am—Dai Probert. What about it, farmer? You are half-tight, and this is my trade, remember."

Justin smiled grimly at him.

"Thanks, Dai. But my money's down. I'd rather fight you than anyone here. This"—he indicated the sergeant—"and this, and this,"—he pointed derisively at Seth and others— "they are nothing but beer and wind!" He turned to Moc: "Slam anybody who interferes, Moc, and see fair for me. Yes?"

Moc took off his coat and placed his cap on top of it. He folded his arms and swelled his chest. His biceps were terrible, like the calf of a man's leg.

"Just let anybody interfere. Just let them try!" He doubled his fists and took up a fighting posture.

The sergeant took Justin's money. The landlord went from one man to the other until he had collected a like amount. Jeff gave nothing, nor did the others with him. I was glad of that.

The boxer peeled off his jacket and slipped his shirt over his head. His body was hairless and rippled with long, lithe muscles. Seen without his jacket and shirt, he looked as big again as when clothed. His shoulders were wide, smooth as satin, and his chest tapered down to his small, muscled waist. He tightened his belt a hole, and rubbed the soles of his boots along the floor.

"Some sawdust here," he said, pointing to a patch of spilled beer on the boards. The landlord scattered handfuls of sawdust all over the floor.

I marvelled at the boxer. I had never seen such a perfect body. With each movement he made, a muscle rippled; and yet, he was as white and smooth as a woman. There was a quiet confidence about him, even in the way he clenched and unclenched his fist. His face was expressionless, as though all feeling and emotion had been set aside. Only his eyes were alive. He looked round the room, his nostrils curving a little as in contempt of those who stood ranged in a circle around him.

"What is it to be?" he asked. "Rounds, or fight to a finish?"

"To a finish," said Justin. "The one who's finished, loses."

Justin had not removed his shirt. He took off his collar and tie, and gave them to me with his studs. He rolled his sleeves right up to the armpits, and his unbuttoned shirt-neck showed the black, matted hair that curled high over his chest.

Moc pointed at Justin's braces. "Take them off," he said. "They'll only hinder you."

I took his braces; they were greasy and dirty, and had stained his white shirt. Moc was now giving him advice:

"Go quiet-like for a bit. Wait till I tell you, then go for him with both hands. Don't worry about defence, he knows more about that than you do, anyway. And don't worry about his chin, you go for his guts all the time. . . . And fight, don't try to box. But wait till I give you the word!"

I stepped behind Justin and stood there with Moc.

The sergeant held up his hand.

"Now, boys, this is a game fight, just between us here. Don't let me hear any blab about it in the town. See? It's just a bit of clean sport. It's a fight to a finish. Moc Morgans here will see fair." He turned to Moc: "Everything ready?"

"All ready!" said Moc. "Keep back there, boys; and let me handle this. No interference now. Right? Very well then!" He turned to Justin and the boxer: "Right, boys. Start!"

Justin stepped out to meet Probert, his legginged legs slightly apart, and his left arm thrust out in front of him.

The boxer pranced lightly around Justin, his body swaying and bobbing as he changed his stance with each movement of his feet. Justin remained as solid and still as an oak. He still kept his left arm rigidly outstretched, his right arm drawn back and doubled ready to strike. A second later, the boxer's left whipped into Justin's face, and before Justin could recover from the sting of the blow a heavy right drove into the pit of his stomach. He doubled forward immediately, only to be jolted backwards by a vicious upper-cut.

"First blood to Probert!" shouted the sergeant.

Justin's nose was bleeding, and splashes of crimson spotted his shirt. I turned to Moc.

"It's all right," said Moc. "Justin can do with a little tapping. It'll cool him down."

The boxer was now circling round Justin and measuring him with his left. He feinted with a movement of his shoulder, and as Justin lifted his guard another right to the stomach doubled him up. The hubbub in the room was deafening.

"It's no fight," shouted someone. "Dai will kill him!"

"Farmer hasn't struck a blow yet!"

The next moment, Justin closed with the boxer, and I saw him sink his right into Dai's stomach. Justin's arms were going like flails, and I caught a glimpse of his face, bleeding from the nose, his left eye half-closed, and his teeth bared as he panted with each blow he gave. The boxer wrapped his arms round Justin, and leaned with all his weight against him.

"Careful, Justin!" shouted Moc. "Look out for him!"

His warning was lost on Justin, for as they broke away, the boxer upper-cut him with every ounce of his strength. Justin went down like a log. A cheer rose in the bar.

"One . . . two . . . three. . . ." Moc stood over Justin as he rolled over. With his left arm he motioned the crowd back. I watched Justin. To see him on the floor was terrible. Never in my life had I seen Justin put down before. I looked across at Jeff. He no longer rocked himself to and fro on his feet. His face was tense with excitement, and he was staring at Justin as though he, too, could not believe his eyes.

Justin rose to his feet before Moc finished the count, and this time it was he who rushed into a clinch. He shook his head once or twice, and before Moc could separate the two, Justin gave me a wink over the boxer's shoulder. And now the fight was on again. Once or twice Justin caught Dai with a right swing, but he rode it easily and countered beautifully every time that Justin led. I had never seen anything so cold and impersonal as the boxer's face. He was paler than when he started, and I had the feeling that his face was just a mask. His eyes, though, were like serpents. He peered and puckered at Justin, and never once did he blink as Justin's fist came near his face. He ducked, swayed, feinted, and used every trick he knew to evade Justin's blows.

Twice in the next few minutes he had Justin pinned against the corner of the bar. All Justin could do was to cover his face and crouched body with his arms, his chin buried deep in his left shoulder. The boxer was now raining blow after blow on him. He was like a dancer on his feet, his eyes searching for an opening, then measuring the distance and putting all the force and rhythm of his body into the blow. A wild rush of Justin's took them across the room, and this time it was the boxer who went down from a wild swing to the stomach.

"Now, Justin!" Moc's voice rose above the shouting. "Don't let go. Give it to him! Go in!"

A derisive chorus of laughter followed his words.

"He's beaten!" shouted the sergeant. "He'll be out through that door on his behind in a minute!"

I paid no heed to his words. Justin was in a terrible state. His face was bruised and bleeding, one shirt-sleeve red with blood hung over his fist. He tore it off and wiped his face with it while the boxer got on his feet.

Still keeping his guard, Justin shouted at him:

"It's my turn now. If that's all you had to give me, look out! It's my turn now!"

Moc gave a great curse as Justin leaped at the boxer. He seemed to have gone mad. This was the Justin I remembered. He was fighting now as I had seen him at home. His fists rained a torrent of blows on the dodging, ducking body retreating before him. Right up to the bar they went; Justin with his head down, his defence gone, and his arms going in and out like pistons. One swinging right caught the boxer on the side of the head and sent him crashing against the counter. Before he could recover, Justin gave him a right and a left in the stomach. The boxer bent at the knees and pitched forward.

"Go in, Justin!" It was Iori Allt-y-brain, and my heart warmed to him.

"Go in, Justin!" Rhys Blacksmith took up the shout. "Give the buggarr what for!"

The boxer struggled to his feet only to be felled again by a right to the mouth. This time he remained on one knee while Moc counted up to ten. Justin stood back waiting for him to rise, his right fist drawn back ready to strike.

"Come on," he shouted. "It's to a finish. The count don't mean nothing!"

The boxer made no attempt to get to his feet. His lips were bleeding badly, and a lump as big as an egg was forming over his left eye.

"He's finished," said Moc. "Outside with him!"

Justin lifted the boxer to his feet.

"Open that door!" he shouted.

Rhys Blacksmith opened the door and stood there grinning while Justin pushed the boxer in front of him and then pitched him down the steps into the yard.

"Now his shirt and coat," he shouted. He threw them after the boxer, and then closed the door and walked back to the bar. Only once did he look at Jeff; and his eyes, bruised and blackened as they were, mocked at Jeff and dared him to make a comment.

"Here you are, farmer. Ten pounds!" The sergeant handed Justin the money. "A good fight! Aye, a good fight!"

"Drinks all round!" shouted Justin. The landlord was busy behind the bar; and before he could serve the beers, I saw Jeff motion Iori and Rhys to leave with him.

"Diawl! Justin! You'll be champion of Wales next! Here's luck!" Moc blew the froth all over Justin. "Duw! I must have a go at you myself one of these days!"

Justin gave him a playful blow in the stomach. His eyes shone as he turned to me. "Just a little lesson for your future brother-in-law, that was. Now he knows!"

After a few drinks, Justin was taken through to the kitchen by Teg and the landlord to have a wash. Seth came back in a few minutes, and Moc and I had a couple more before Justin and the girl returned.

.   .   .   .   .

Half-leaning against me, his head bowed forward on his chest, Justin slept most of the way home. From time to time he shifted his position; and curses, foul and obscene, fell from his lips as he tried to make himself comfortable. I was glad to be out in the fresh air again. The time we had spent in the pub was like a dark valley between me and Grett.

Before we got to Senny, some men on horseback passed us. "How is Justin?" shouted one of them. It was Iori.

"All right!" I shouted. "Drunk as a lord, that's all!"

The night air had cleared my head. I was not sleepy at all. I wrapped the rug round Justin, its oilskin surface was quite moist with dew. Over the mountains the moon rose slowly into view. We clattered through Trecastle, and before we got to Pontyrhydfer, I could smell the mountain air. There was heather and gorse in it, and something, too, of peat and still bog-water. The little mist that rose from the river was keen and sharp in my nostrils.

The cob trotted where it was flat and dropped to a walk wherever the road rose. The wheels made a comforting sound on the road, and before me I could see the misshapen moon shedding its cold light on the mountain.

I gave no thought to the morrow. The pageantry of this day was sufficient. When would Grett and I lie together again? Tired as I was, I longed for her, wishing she were here at my side on this lonely, lovely journey through the night.

Too soon, we were crossing the Usk. Justin woke up at the rattle of the wheels over the pebbles and got out to bathe his face and drink some water. He looked ghastly in the half-light. His shirt was stained with blood, and his wet hair fell over his forehead. I helped him back into the trap, and by the time we turned into our lane above the Allt, the dawn was coming up behind us. I got Justin upstairs without any trouble, and took his leggings and boots off for him. He did not bother to undress, and before I could do anything more to help him, he was fast asleep, his face half buried in the white pillow.

Chapter 11

THE sun was well over Pen Arthur as Justin and I made our way across the fields to Rhos Dirion. I had thought the evening would never come. I had spent the day as if I was in a dream. My life seemed only a day old: everything dated from the day before. Justin's face had gone down a little, but his bruises showed up the more because of the paleness of his face. Father had asked no questions about our doings at Brecon. He looked quizzically at Justin when he came in to breakfast. "Who knocked your beard off?" he had asked. Mother, however, was full of concern, and when I described the fight to her, she took off her glasses to wipe her eyes. And though she tried to appear as if she were horrified at it all, she was, nevertheless, full of pride and asked continually: "And you say he was a boxer, a real champion?"

And now, here we were, at last, on our way to see Grett's parents. We were both in our Sunday clothes. Justin had shaved before dressing, borrowing my hollow-ground and cursing as he lathered his still swollen jaw. He was full of good spirits this evening. "There'll be no trouble from Jeff, mark my words," he said. "That little bout last night was more for his benefit than mine. Tell me"—he turned to me—"what did you think of that girl Teg?"

He was grinning in his old way. I smiled as I looked at him with his stiff collar, spotted tie, and a flower in his coat. He looked just like a bridegroom.

"What about her?" I asked. "You were a long time in the kitchen with her!"

"Not in the kitchen. Oh, no!" He laughed and swished his stick at a foxglove. "Damme, it was a good job I didn't go out with her before the fight! It would have been me that would have gone out through the door then!"

We walked on and missed the village by going through the fields. I walked carefully so as not to soil my brown boots. I had worked hard on them with mother's beeswax and a piece of old velvet. A bush of wild roses, white and tinged faintly with pink, stood out against the tangled mass of thorn and hazel looking like a bride itself. The hedge shadows were long across the fields, and over Myddfai the evening was blue against the rising mountains. I tried not to think of what was in front of me. It was no good going there with any prepared speech. I hadn't spoken to Grett's father since I was a boy in school. He would be very quiet, I knew that. John Ellis was always quiet, that was his strength; and if you saw him walk into church you appreciated at once the quiet power that possessed him.

"Feeling nervous?" asked Justin.

"No. . . . What do you think I'd better say?"

"It depends," said Justin. "Now, if it was me, I'd just tell him I was going to marry Grett, and that I'd be happier if he wasn't awkward."

I pondered his words as we came in sight of Rhos Dirion. It

was a compact, tidy little place. People said it was the best little farm in the parish. It was well watered and got the afternoon sun. They had a name for their cattle, and there was no better place for bringing the sheep down in winter. The house and the out-buildings had been white-washed only a few weeks ago, and the round ricks in the orchard behind the house were still intact. With the heavy crops down in the fields alongside the river, they were never short of food for the winter.

I felt a strange, proud emotion come over me as we took the lane leading up to the yard. It was here I had always left Grett on those dark nights when I had seen her from church. And here I was with Justin at my side, going at last to ask for her. Compared with what was in front of me, the telling of the news at home was as nothing.

The dogs set up a barking as we opened the yardgate. The collie bitch came yapping at Justin and he let fly a threatening kick at her. John Ellis came out of the stable and stood leaning on a besom looking at us. He didn't say a word, but stood there in his scrubbed corduroy trousers and flannel shirt waiting for us to speak.

Justin gave him a nod. "Go on"—he spoke to me under his breath—"it's up to you now."

"We'd like to have a talk . . ." I began. The nerves in my stomach were quivering, and I cleared my throat to get rid of my huskiness. John Ellis crossed the yard towards us. He was tall and lean, his hair an iron-grey, and I could see how Grett took after him; his eyes were dark and direct.

"Well, well!" He muttered and smiled to himself as he approached us. "So the Peeles have come to see me. Nothing wrong at home, is it?"

"No. The old man isn't dead yet!"

Grett's father laughed at Justin's remark.

"I wouldn't wish that," he said. "But come in, both of you!"

He led the way through the flagged passage into the kitchen. Grett was in a blouse and dark skirt, her sleeves rolled up above her elbows, and her hair dark and loose about her head. She blushed as we came in and gave me a quick smile. Her mother was sitting at the supper table. She looked first at Justin, perhaps not recognizing him at once without his beard;

then she looked at me and at once turned to Grett. I think she guessed at once what it was we had come for.

"Sit down!" John Ellis went to his chair at the fireside. Justin sat near the door, his hat on the ground beside him. Before we could say anything, Jeff came in from the back-kitchen. He looked at me and nodded to himself.

"So you've come then," he said.

"Yes. We said we would," I began.

"Just a minute!" John Ellis turned to Justin. "Now, Peele, what is the trouble? Let me hear it from you."

Justin indicated me.

"It's my brother here," he began.

"The young fool wants to marry Grett!" broke in Jeff. "I had it out with him yesterday, and warned him to keep away from here."

I coloured up angrily at Jeff's tone and words. Justin, too, went red in the face, and he looked hard at Jeff.

"Jeff's said it for me, Mr. Ellis." I coughed again, and shifted my position on the chair. "I want to marry Grett," I said.

"We've been courting on the quiet since last September, and now we want to get married. We are both over age, and we want to settle down and make a start."

Grett nodded her head in answer to the look her father gave her. He swallowed hard and shook his head.

"No, no!" he muttered. He looked again at Grett as though beseeching her to deny what I had told him. "It's not true, Grett? . . . Not you?"

"It's quite true. . . . I want to marry Edwin. Why can't we forget this old quarrel? What good does it do? Why should it spoil my life?"

She came over to where I was sitting and stood behind my chair. Her father shook his head.

"But you haven't been courting our Grett since last September!" Grett's mother stared at me, her eyes open with unbelief. "I can't believe it. I would have known. . . ." She looked reproachfully at Grett, her voice almost breaking as she continued: "Grett would have told me, wouldn't you, Grett?"

"It's a dirty, underhanded business!" interrupted Jeff. "How he's talked Grett round, I don't know! She's off her head, Mam! That's what it is. . . . Why, he's got nothing. Old Peele won't give him a penny to start with! We know him and his set all right!"

"Set!" Justin took up Jeff's word. "You ought to pick your words more carefully. You've got the advantage of us for once. We haven't come here for trouble!"

"Quiet, Jeff!" John Ellis waved an impatient hand at Jeff. "We've got to talk this out. . . . But it's out of the question, no sense in it whatever!"

"You are right, Dad!" Jeff gave a sneering laugh. "Just think of our Grett over there, or being mixed with them in any way! Why!" He looked across at Justin and me. "Why, they can't agree among themselves. Peele there and his old man are always at it. Let him deny that!"

"That has nothing to do with us," said his father. "And we don't want it to have anything to do with us either." He looked around. "Get the lamp, Grett. It's getting dark."

Not a word was said while Grett got the brass-bowled lamp and set it on the table. I watched her as she bent over the globe adjusting the wick. The light caught the saliency of her cheek-bones and made her hair shine like jet.

It was Justin who re-started the conversation:

"Whether the old man and I agree, or don't see eye to eye, has got nothing to do with anybody, and nobody'd better interfere," he said slowly. "But that's got nothing to do with my brother here. He'll get a place of his own, don't you worry. We've got our pride, you know!"

John Ellis nodded indifferently.

"What do you say to this?" he asked his wife. "Would you be willing to see Grett marrying into Trewern?"

Mrs. Ellis shook her head. "I don't like it," she said hotly. "No, indeed, I don't! It makes for trouble. We got to face facts. This is the time to talk, not after it's too late!" She paused and turned on Grett: "I might have guessed there was something up! All this dressing up and going to church every Sunday night. . . . But remember this"—she turned to me—"you know there's been bad blood between our families for years. And bad or good, blood is thicker than water. Do you think my girl is going to be happy while your people are so bitter against us? Love don't last for ever you know!"

"She's right," said John Ellis. "Things couldn't be worse. Mind you"—he gave me a sympathetic smile—"I've got nothing against you, not personally; nothing! But there you are, you are a Peele! And the Peeles and us have never made any go of it. No! I can't give my consent. Impossible! You must have known I wouldn't!"

There was every indication of finality in the way he brought his hand down on the arm of his chair.

"I don't care!" Grett's hands gripped my shoulders as she spoke from behind me. "I don't care what you say! If Edwin wants me, I'll marry him whenever he likes."

"Grett! Grett! Just a minute now!" Her father was thin-lipped, quiet. "I know you are both over age," he continued. "And if you make up your mind to get married then no power can stop you. No, no, Jeff"—Jeff had sworn—"it won't do, Jeff! Cursing and fists don't settle anything!" He looked significantly at Justin's black eye and puffed lips. "So you keep quiet a minute now." He turned to me: "Now, Edwin Peele, tell me this: what does your father say to this? Is he prepared to set you up on your own?"

I coloured up.

"My father doesn't know yet. . . . I—I——"

"You haven't told him yet!" I could feel everyone watching me in the silence that followed his surprised accents.

"No. I haven't told him yet. I came up to get your permission. That is all that matters to me. What my father says does not matter at all. I'll live all right without his permission. All I'm concerned with is Grett's happiness. I want to make things easy as far as she is concerned."

"Very smart," said Jeff. "Lover's talk! Nothing but hot air!"

"I back up what Ned says," interrupted Justin. "I'm with him all the way. Don't worry, we'll look after our side of the family. We are not paupers, you know!"

"What do you mean?" shouted Jeff. "Although you are visitors, there's no need to sneer!"

"Quiet, Jeff!" John Ellis got up. "I'm not going to say any

more. If Grett marries you, Edwin, without any care for our feelings, then let her do it. But don't forget, you are making a hard bed for yourselves. But what am I talking about!" He gave a harsh laugh. "I know Grett, just as I know her mood now. Marry you! Impossible!"

Grett walked across the room and opened the door. She looked across at her father, her cheeks red and her eyes dark with resentment.

"It's you are making things impossible," she said. "Instead of considering me, you are only thinking about yourself and what people would say." She turned to me: "Come on," she said, "let's go. I'll walk down the lane with you."

I got up.

"I'm sorry, Mr. Ellis," I said. "All I can say is that if Grett will have me, then I'll marry her as soon as I can!"

Jeff came forward to the door.

"Come back!" he shouted to Grett. "Will you disgrace us in front of these two?" He caught hold of her shoulder. She at once twisted herself free. In her anger, her eyes filled with tears. She looked across at her mother.

"Jeff! Leave her alone! Do you hear?" Mrs. Ellis was angry. "Let Grett alone! John!" She turned to John Ellis: "Tell him! I won't have this in front of visitors!"

Justin looked on, his forehead beetling with suppressed anger.

"Leave her be," said John Ellis. "She is not a child! She's old enough to know her own mind."

Jeff stepped aside.

"Come on!" Grett put her arm in mine. Behind us, I heard Justin saying "Good night" to Grett's father and mother. A moment later he was with Grett and me outside the house.

"I'll walk on," he said. "I'll be at the end of the lane. Don't be long: it'll be pouring soon!"

It was already spitting with rain. During the time we had been indoors, clouds had come over; and large drops, like thunder-rain, dropped slow and soft on our faces.

"Oh, Edwin!" Grett clung to me. I could feel her sobbing against me.

"Don't worry," I said. "It's up to you and me now!"

Soon, it was raining, and looking at her I could not tell which on her face were her tears or raindrops.

Chapter 12

I WATCHED the hands of the grandfather clock. It was now ten past the hour. At half-past eleven I would tell father and mother about my visit to Rhos Dirion. The supper things were still on the table. Mother was sitting there looking across at Justin as if she were still not reconciled to his clean-shaven face. The paleness of his face contrasted strangely with the deep brown tan of his neck. The old man was turning over the leaves of a catalogue on implements which he had received that morning.

Justin occasionally grinned across at me and wrinkled his forehead as if prompting me to get on with it and break the news to the old man. The minutes ticked by slowly, and all the time I could see Grett as she had stood at the door of their kitchen waiting to walk down the lane with me. Seeing her in her working skirt and blouse, had made me love her more than ever. I imagined her in a kitchen of our own, intimacy in everything she did, in the roundness of her bared arm when she would be clapping the butter, holding the loaf against her breast at the table. . . .

As the clock struck the half-hour, father put the catalogue aside and got up.

"Bed!" he said. "Time you two had some sleep."

He started to wind the clock, the chains making their familiar sounds as the weights were being lifted. Mother put the bread away, and started to collect the cups and saucers. I took a deep breath.

"There's something I want to tell you," I said.

Father turned his head at my words and looked steadily at me, still winding the clock. Mother stopped half-way to the back-kitchen, and then came back to the table with the pile of dishes still in her hands.

"What is it?" Father came back to his chair and sat down facing me. He looked at me, and then at Justin.

"Are you in trouble?" His blue eyes were hard and narrowed. "Come on, out with it!"

"I'm going to get married," I said.

I saw the colour rise to father's forehead.

"I thought there was something up," he spoke slowly, his voice almost dropping to a whisper. "Well? Who is it, then? Who have you put in the family way?"

"No one!" I felt myself going hard and cold inside me, and I met his eyes without fear. "I just want to get married!"

"But who is it, Edwin?" Mother's voice was almost tearful. "Not——"

"Yes! It's Grett Ellis," I said. And as I said her name aloud in our kitchen, I felt free and unafraid. It was as though Grett herself had come into the room, her loveliness breaking on the harsh drabness of our kitchen so that everything pulsated from the impact of her presence there.

"Grett Ellis? Grett Ellis?" Father repeated her name as if he could not believe his ears. He looked from me to Justin, and then at mother.

"I can't believe it!" he said. "You have gone off your head!"

He turned accusingly on mother:

"Did you know then?"

Mother gave me a shrewd look.

"I guessed something," she said quietly. "But I wasn't sure."

Father opened and closed his hand, looking at his palm as though he were reading it.

"I suppose you knew of this all along?" he said to Justin.

Justin nodded and puffed on his pipe.

In the silence that followed, I found myself counting the ticks of the clock. How was it, I wondered to myself, that we went through our days not hearing these sounds! And I saw the clock-face with its painted church and flowers like a mirror that reflected all our days.

"Grett Ellis!" Father repeated her name again. "And you want to marry her, eh? Why her?"

"Why do you think? Why do people want to get married?"

He smiled.

"Time will tell," he said. "We'll see."

"Daniel! Don't torment the boy." Mother was crying quietly to herself.

"Torment him! What are you saying? It's he is trying to torment me."

He was at his old game. He was smiling, and I knew he was playing with me.

"What do you think her people are going to say about it?" He put the question almost casually to me.

"We've been there this evening. . . ."

"Well?"

"They're against it. . . . But it makes no difference: we'll be married as soon as we can!"

He got up and came round the table to where I was sitting.

"You must be in a terrible hurry," he said. "And you say she is not in trouble! Ha!" He laughed. "Not in trouble, eh? I'd like to see John Ellis's face when his girl produces a little bastard!"

I made to get up, I had it in my arm to knock him flat, but he pushed me back in the chair.

"Steady, Ned!" Justin looked up at father from his chair. "Keep cool. He's only trying to provoke you. . . . Keep your head now!"

Father only laughed at him.

"I know," I answered. I looked up at the old man, hating his smile and the confidence he had in his physical strength. "You can think what you like," I said to him. "I don't care a damme about your quarrel with her family or what you say. . . . I'm going to marry her. Nor you nor anybody can stop me!"

"Be quiet!" He gripped my shoulders and ground me back in my chair. "First Justin, and now you. . . . I don't know" —he turned to mother—"I don't know what is happening to us! Think of it! We'll be the laugh of the parish. Look at the position he's put us in!"

"What do you mean?" asked mother.

"What do I mean? Damme! A Peele going over to Rhos Dirion to ask permission to get married!" He turned to me:

"Why in God's name didn't you tell us first and marry the girl?"

I stared at him in amazement. Justin, too, looked surprised. Father went on:

"I don't care who you marry," he said. "But how do you think I feel when John Ellis has told you to keep off the grass? I tell you, it's like fire on my skin!" He looked sharply at me: "Have you got any blood in you?"

"What do you mean?"

"Well, go and get her," he said. "To the devil with John Ellis! First, he gets the shame of seeing his own daughter taken from him by one of us. What a dab in the eye for him! A Peele in bed with his daughter! And me her father-in-law!"

He didn't say any more, but went upstairs in his stockinged feet, laughing and chuckling to himself. I looked at mother and Justin, not knowing what to make of it. Justin shrugged his shoulders and mother shook her head.

"Don't trust the old devil," said Justin. "He's full of spite against John Ellis to-night. . . . You wait till he's had time to think it over! There's no depending on him!"

"He only thinks of himself all the time," said mother. "All he's full of now is how he can score off Grett's father!"

We stayed up for a long time, talking about what would be best for me to do. Justin was all for my going away to the valleys, but mother wouldn't have it. It wasn't fair to Grett, she said, "and such a hand as she's got for butter-making. You look for a little place of your own. . . . Go down and see the squire one night, p'raps he could help you." So we talked, until, at length, father called down for mother to come up to bed. I sat on, even after Justin had gone up. A sense of unreality possessed me, my ears sang, and I felt lightheaded with happiness. "Grett! Grett!" I said her name aloud to myself, over and over. To-day in Rhos Dirion, and here at Trewern, and in every house in the parish, the news of our love was spreading like a bright flame.

BOOK THREE

Chapter 13

THE hay was heavy with dew, and with each sweep of the scythe a green wave broke over the curved, shining steel. Swish, then forward again with the left foot, a long rhythmic sweep of the arms, and another swathe lay darkly green at one's feet. The eight mowers moved in an oblique line across the steep field below our house; no one spoke, and the only sound to be heard was the swishing of the scythes through the short, thick hay, and the laboured breathing of the older men. High above us, revelling in the morning sun, a lark linked and looped its song in the wind-freshened air. The countryside, as yet, was not quite awake from its summer-night sleep. There was still a soft mist rising along the Sawdde. The woods, too, were half draped in mist and stood almost black against the sunrise. Six miles away, the rocks of the Van showed only a jagged shoulder through the cloud that had draped it since the evening before. Apart from this one cloud, the sky was clear. Down in the valley, from the direction of the squire's, the rachetting whirr of one of those new mowing machines could be heard. Up here with us at Trewern, it was impossible to use a machine on our steep fields: it was scythe work all through the harvest.

Step by step we followed one another. First was Twm Howells the blacksmith. He was steady was Twm, not too fast or too slow. He would keep the same pace all day. Behind him went Elias the Carpenter, his lean body and long arms moving effortlessly as though the scythe were a part of him. Then followed Justin, father, Moc Mihartach, Cefn Wern, Berthlwyd, and myself.

Father was in one of his great moods. With people around him he was at his best. His corduroys, held up by the belt which had slipped under the hang of his stomach, were as thick and massive as oak trunks. Mother had scrubbed his trousers until they were a yellow-white. He was scything well, saving his back as much as he could and leaving his arms to do all the work. His neck was burned red, and a roll of flesh formed ridge-like along the base of his skull as he glanced up from time to time to keep his distance with Justin in front of him. He was going steady, as I said, but by the afternoon, he would be on Justin's heels, his scythe flashing arc-like in the tail of Justin's eye.

The sight of the field was a joy to me. The mowers were moving like one, and the rhythm was the rhythm of the countryside. The sun was bright on the poplars at the end of the field, and the tiny, trembling leaves were twinkling like bits of glass. The heavy, fragrant smell of bruised grass and hayseed rose in the air. Seeing a molehill in front of me, I pressed instinctively on the heel of my scythe, and the dew-shining point of my blade missed it finely. Then on again, left foot forward, the backward swing to the right, then the sweep forward, and the purple and red clover flowers settling so gently on the flat of my blade. So we worked, aiming to account for a quarter of the field before breakfast, the dew wet and sparkling on my oiled boots, the hay flowing backwards over my scythe, and the sun flashing steely-blue fire from the whetted edge of my blade.

Now we were working back across the field. I could feel the sun on my back. How father could wear his waistcoat and thick flannel shirt I could not understand. He would have it that flannel kept the sun off his back. For myself, I preferred the old print shirts which mother had washed and washed until they were as thin as butter muslin.

In front of us, the sun caught the white-washed walls of the house. From the chimney an upright spiral of blue woodsmoke twisted up. Luck was with us this year; a fortnight of this weather and we would be finished with the hay. Of course, we would have to return the help of Cefn Wern and Berthlwyd. Moc, too, would need a hand. But Justin would be help enough for Moc. They always worked with a ten-gallon squatting on its end in the shadow of the hedge.

Soon, the mist disappeared from the river, and along the

hedgerows the heat-haze shimmered. And still the green-dark hay flowed backward in waves over our scythes. Step by step the mowers darkened the sunlit field with row after row of heavy swathes.

"Halt, then!"

Father laid his scythe flat on the ground and straightened his back. He eased himself backwards a few times to relax and loosen his loins. One by one, the mowers tested their edges. Eli pressed his flat, work-caloused thumb against his blade. A deft pinch, and the steel sang with a thin, pinging noise.

"Like a hollow-ground," he murmured. "Don't sharpen too much, Ned. It's no good putting a thread on the edge!" He turned to father. "A good crop, Daniel!"

"Yes. That rain in May saved it. Think we'll get done by to-night?"

"Easy!" said Moc. "As long as you've got enough to wet our whistles, we'll manage it all right."

"We'll manage that all right!" laughed father. "A good job we are not all like you and Justin. We'd need a brewery for that!"

I held my scythe by the point of the blade and gave it a few more strokes. Father looked his contempt at me. Since the night when I had told him a fortnight ago about Grett and myself, he had not spoken a word to me.

"Putting an edge on won't help you," he sneered. "You want to give a wider swing and keep her flat!"

I didn't reply to him. If the others heard, they gave no sign of it. They were all whetting their scythes, and the steely ringing noise was pure summer music.

Again the oblique line moved across the breast of the field. I could feel my shirt sticking to my back. Soon, tiredness would set in; aching, cramping tiredness, the thigh muscles pulling, and a line of pain across the small of the back as if a rope of iron were biting into one. Still, I kept in step. I kept the same distance between Jack Berthlwyd and myself. That was all that mattered, to keep my distance constant between him and myself.

Thoughts came and went through my mind in measured

succession, moving almost with the rhythm of my arms. A step forward again. . . . Grett in her white blouse and the lamplight shining on her hair. A sweep of the arms, the swish of the scythe like an indrawn breath. . . . Grett lying in the shadows of the mill. . . . The point of my scythe jarring on a stone made me swear, using one of Justin's filthiest oaths. I made a series of hurried strokes to recapture the rhythm I had lost. . . . Then, still keeping my distance from Berthlwyd, I again gave myself up to my longing for Grett. A step forward, a backward swing to the right, then the sweep forward to the left. "Grett! Grett!" I said. And with the blood pounding in my ears and the sun-dazzle on the poplars rippling like water, I scythed and dreamed of her loveliness and kept my place behind Berthlwyd without knowing half the time that I was doing so.

By eleven o'clock we had nearly finished the field. Twm was still leading. For once he had discarded his fancy waistcoat, and his shirt had almost worked itself out of his trousers. Justin was scything easily and keeping up a conversation with Moc. Once or twice father called on him to moderate his language. A blister broke between my fingers and I felt the bite of the sweat as it ran over the sore. I watched father's back. Was it possible, I wondered, that there was still enough vanity in him not to call for a rest? No one spoke now, even Justin and Moc were quiet, the sun was getting high and the butterflies in the clover were like flashes of sudden, spasmodic brightness. I looked at the sky from under my sweat-stinging eyebrows. It was pale and milky with heat, only in the distance, over the far-off mauve of the Van Rocks was it blue. When a little breeze came over the field, it came like a puff of heavy warmth, and all the time the hayseeds clung to the sweat that formed in heavy drops on my upper lip. The vast heat added distance to the hills, and the scythes cut monotonously into the standing hay. Some day the harvest would be over, but the thought of September with its crisp dew in the morning and its evening mists along the river was too far in the future. September! Where would Grett and I be then? The hopelessness of our love came down on me like a great hand, and when I heard my name called by Lewsin the Post, I turned round in my eagerness, and the point of my scythe jarred against a stone. Lewsin was crossing the field towards me.

"For you," he said. "You can bring me your answer to-night. It will be all right."

He thrust an unstamped letter into my hand.

"It's from Grett Ellis," he said. "She gave it me this morning."

I looked at the unfamiliar, upright handwriting. "Mr. Edwin Peele," it said. The others had not stopped, so I thrust the letter into my back pocket and tried to catch up with Berthlwyd. I scythed madly, my arms knowing no weariness, and I was soon up with Jack. One turn back across the field and we would be finished.

There are times when everything sings around you. You hear birds where there was silence before, the trees tell their whispered secrets, and the hedges sigh with one's heart. So it was with me on that last course across the field. I had no fears regarding the contents, whatever they might be. Grett's letter was in my pocket, I could feel the rumpled shape of it tight against my thigh, and in my eagerness to finish I gained on Berthlwyd, and the swing of my scythe only narrowly missed his heels. Father gave me a suspicious look as I left them all sitting in the shade of the hedge.

I went down to the end of the field where a trickle of water welled and spread from a clump of reeds. I slit the envelope carefully with my knife, for though I was in a feverish hurry to read what Grett had written, I was careful with this first letter.

Don't be frightened [she began]—I am only writing to you because I am so lonely without you. Oh, Edwin, they are watching me all the time, I could not even come to church last Sunday. I am giving this to Lewis the Post, and he has told me that if you give him a letter, he will give it to me privately. I saw you down by the river last Sunday from the window, and Jeff said that you were there on the Monday night, too. So they are not giving me a chance to slip out. I love you, Edwin. You know that, don't you? Do you still mean for us to get married? I am ready when you are. How I long to be with you on these long summer nights. It seems years since Brecon. But I will see you on the day of the Jubilee Sports. And I want you to come right up to me on the field and take my arm. I don't think Jeff will interfere in front of everybody. Tell your Justin to be careful, too. If those two start again, it will be terrible.

I love you, Edwin, and if I could only get mother's back, I would come right up to Trewern. (Is your father as terrible as they say he is?)

I must finish now. How lovely it would be if you were coming with the others to cut our hay next week! I would make you the best black-currant tart you ever tasted. Do write for me to have a word to-morrow. Nos da. Nos Da.

R'wyn dy garu,
GRETT.

P.S. Do you know, you have never given me one of your englyns. Aren't I pretty enough?

I lay back in the shadows of the hazels and lay there crowned with the wild roses overhead. Between the watery green leaves, I stared unblinkingly at the sun until the burning, blinding whiteness became a mass of pulsating blue. This was the first love-letter I had ever had, and my Grett had written it. The phrases and sentences of my letter to her were already forming in my mind. I would put all the summer into it, the scent of the honeysuckle and the wild rose would touch every sentence of it. I read her letter again, the words of it leaping at me through the black suns that danced on it. How long was it to the day of the Jubilee Sports? I felt I could not wait until then. I would haunt the river-bank under Rhos Dirion until I would see her. I had to see her. Even if she passed a field away, I must see her, my eyes were longing for the sight of her. . . . I re-read her letter again, marvelling at her script. Of course, her writing could not have been different, every bit of her was in the bold, round hand, even to the way she had written her name at the foot of it. My senses were heightened by the love of her letter. I could smell the cool, acrid tang of the sap under the mottled bark of the hazels; the trickle of water that laved the roots of the water-mints and foxgloves had all the sweetness of the earth in it, and the mown hay was the very breath of summer.

"Edwin!"

Father was getting ready to move off to the next field. I put my letter back in my pocket and rejoined the men.

"Hoi, Ned! You look as if you could tackle the wain yourself," said Elias. "What's come over you?"

I laughed happily.

"Was that Lewsin I heard calling you just now?" asked Twm Blacksmith.

"Don't be nosy, Twm!" Cefn Wern frowned in mock indignation at Twm. "Mind your own business."

The men were looking at me, kindly smiles on their faces.

"Don't you worry, Ned," said Elias. "We know all about it. Good luck to you, that's what I say."

"When is it to be?" asked Twm.

"Shut up, Twm!" said Elias. "Leave him be! Don't you take any notice, Ned. We have all been through it." He looked shrewdly at father. "He's got a grand girl there, Daniel. There's grit for you now!"

Father nodded grimly.

"Aye! She's got grit enough, if you can call it that. Face I call it! You know what the old people used to say: An angel on the highway, a devil on the hearth!"

"Nonsense! You are just full of spite, Dan. I'm for her if you like it or not!" Elias spat his defiance from the corner of his mouth. "There's not a better girl in the parish! Tell us, what is going to happen? There is a lot of talk going about you know."

"Don't ask me," said father. "Ask him there. I'll have nothing to do with it. If he is set on her, I can't stop him." He paused and looked at Elias. "So people are talking are they? What are they saying?"

"I can't help hearing gossip." Elias threw his hnds out impotently. "But people are saying that John Ellis will not let his girl marry into your family."

"Do they!" Father smiled. "Well"—he shook his shoulders and forced a laugh. "Ha! Ha! So John Ellis says that, eh? Won't let her marry into my family! Look here, Eli, you can tell everybody from me that we Peeles always get what we want. If that young fool there wants to marry the girl . . . Well, if I can't stop him, then I'm sure nobody else will!"

I caught Justin's wink. Berthlwyd smiled at me from behind father's back; Elias was nodding to himself as though he had scored a point. Father turned to me:

"Agree?"

"It was settled weeks ago," I said. Elias leaned over and clapped me on the shoulder.

.   .   .   .   .

The wain was sweet-smelling and muddy with seeping spring-water, and although the hay was thin it had a taste and fragrance that the cattle loved. We always kept this hay apart from the rest of the crop. By the middle of the afternoon none of us looked skywards when having a spell. The backs of our necks were blistered, and to protect my head I had knotted my handkerchief at each corner and made a cap of it. The sun came down on us like a hand of brass, and the hedge facing us marked the end of a long journey. I marvelled at father's strokes. His loins were reservoirs of crude strength. Twm Blacksmith had fallen back to third place, and Elias Carpenter now led the field. He still maintained the same easy swing of his arms as when he had started. Scything, he had told us at dinner, was nothing to planing oak. But his being short helped him considerably. Twm and Berthlwyd were each over six foot and had to bend with every stroke.

The Van Rocks had by now receded into the shimmering haze. They were our barometer. Whatever the season, they gauged the weather for us. On a morning in May you might see a spatter of snow shining on the peaks; and in the calm of an August evening the old rocks would come closer and closer, as if they would lean towards us and overshadow the land with purple, and by nightfall we would hear the sound of the river quite clearly and the morning would be rainy.

I looked frequently towards the gate leading into the field, and there's a sight it was to see mother and Mati Nanteos bringing the tea. The very sight of their white aprons and big straw hats was enough to make you feel cool at once, but Elias

Carpenter must finish his course before he laid down his scythe. The small of my back felt as though someone had given me a wad with a crow-bar. I wiped my blade with a handful of hay and nipped the blade just to hear its note.

Mother was excited and kept forcing everybody to eat. "Here!"—she cut a large piece of black-currant tart and slapped it on my plate. The tea from the sand-scoured jacks was scalding hot, and as I drank it the sweat broke out along the hollow of my back. The men lay back against the cool ferns in the hedge. What was Grett doing now? I imagined her bringing the tea to the field. Her hair would be dark and cool under her straw hat. I saw her round arms touched to gold by the sun, and the flash of her eyes and gleam of her teeth as she smiled. The men would be watching her next week when Rhos Dirion would be cutting, and I knew well what their thoughts would be.

"Have you had enough now?" asked mother. "Come on, I don't want to have to carry anything back. . . ." Her starched apron dazzled in the sun. Father looked at the men.

"What do you say?" he asked. "Shall we carry on?"

The mowers looked at each other dubiously. In spite of the shade from the hedge, the heat was almost unbearable.

"What are we here for?" replied Elias from under the red handkerchief he had spread over his face while he was lying down. "The sooner we finish here, the sooner everybody gets his own bit done. The weather won't last for ever. Easy it is to count the sheaves on the idler's field!"

Soon, the metallic rasp of sand on steel rose again on the air. In single file we went to finish what remained of the wain. Although we could feel no breeze, the hay waved and darkened like a sheet of water where the wind ruffles it lightly.

We mowed on until it was past eight. The sun was now touching the mountains, and our scythes no longer flashed with blue fire, but caught the fire of the sunset; and because of the dew, each cut was sharp and clean. Justin had thrown off his shirt, and I saw that his reddened skin still carried some of the bruises from his fight in Brecon. He scythed strongly, though his feet were a little too wide apart. The best mowers were Elias Carpenter and Berthlwyd; the heat had been too much for

Twm to-day. I envied them their easy style as I watched them in front of me. Did they think of nothing as they moved along? Did they know what it was to feel the urge of desire throbbing in their blood? I had spent the whole day with Grett, and while I kept my blade flat and swung with the sweep of it, I saw only her face and knew all the lovely mystery and beauty of her petal-smooth loveliness.

· · · · ·

I wrote my letter to Grett after Justin and I had come back from the pool under Nanteurin. My body was like marble, and as I sat at the black oak table in front of my bedroom window, the night air from the fields was sweet with the smell of hay. Moths came circling round my candle and at times their shadows would fall on my letter like the shadows that flit over a bright field when clouds will pass under the sun. All the while, I wrote with Grett's face in my mind. It was gone twelve when I finished it, and I read it through, liking the way I had set it down, imitating the parson's fine script. I imagined her face when she would read it, and saw her retreating to some quiet corner where she could be at peace and read it undisturbed.

MY LOVELY, DARK-EYED GRETT,

It is dark outside and the smell of the hay is coming in through my window; my candle throws the shadow of my nib on this paper, and down in the Allt an owl is calling. I got your letter this morning and read it in the hedge while we were resting. What are you doing at this moment? Are you sitting at your bedroom window looking towards me? I think you are, because I can feel your love around me. The darkness outside is your hair, and the sound of the river coming up through the Allt is your voice. Oh, Grett, you are everywhere: you are with me all day, and when I awaken from a sleep which has brought me no dream, even then, I feel you have been with me in that sleep, because my heart is so light and free. But I have longed for you, Grett. I love you with every beat of my heart. That is why I have written no englyn to you, why I will not write you one to-night because, somewhere deep inside me, there is a perfect poem to you. Perhaps, some night, when I will wake up and find you smooth and warm against me—perhaps that poem will burst to flower then. Yet, even if it does, Grett, it will have to remain unsaid for a while because I will be lost once more in the wonder and glory of having you in my arms. Now, in these long days, you walk on the waters, you drift with the winds, you are the darkness and the dawn; a thousand visions of you surround me wherever I go, but I would give it all just to have you in my arms now.

I know your lovely letter by heart now. Yes, Grett Rhos Dirion, we will go arm-in-arm on the Jubilee Sports Day. I can hardly wait for it to come along. Look here, from to-morrow night, and every night after, I will be down by your river. I will strike a match, and will you, Grett, light your candle in your room? You see, I want to be near you. I can't live without you.

Father is willing for me to marry you. I think he will give me a start, too. Justin says that if I get married, he will try and get Moc Morgans, Mihartach, to come and live here to help him. God help father with the two of them here with him!

I will write to you every day now. I am taking Lewsin some butter to-night; he deserves something for helping us, doesn't he?

Well, I must finish now. We cut two fields to-day. I thought of you when mother brought tea to the field. How I wish things were different between our families so that I could be one of the helpers at your place next week and see you coming through the gate with the baskets on your arms, and you, lovely Grett Ellis, in your print frock—the one with red flowers on it—and your skirts swirling around your ankles!

I am taking this down to Lewsin now. I will write you to-morrow again. Good night, Grett—Grett loyw-lan o liw lili—good night, I love you, and come what will, soon it won't be writing to you at midnight I'll be, but looking into your eyes and holding you close to me.

EDWIN.

I crept downstairs in my stockinged feet so as not to waken father and mother, and did not put my boots on until I was clear of the house. Justin had gone up to the Tavarn with Moc and was not back yet. The Allt was dark and friendly, and as I walked along I sang to myself, making up words as I went and thinking of Grett all the time. There was a light in the post office kitchen and Lewsin came to the door at once.

"I thought you would come," he said. "So I waited up."

"Don't give it to anybody but Grett," I said.

"Do you think I'm twp," he whispered. "Say, have you heard the latest?" And before waiting for an answer he told me that Shoni Maesifan had gone off to the valleys, leaving the old people to carry on with the harvest.

I walked home slowly. My back was aching and my thigh muscles pulled with every step I took. To-morrow we had to finish the big field above the road. I was half asleep when I heard Justin come up the stairs. He came quietly into my room, but I pretended to be asleep and he went out on his tiptoes. He had been drinking and my room reeked of beer for a long time after he had gone.

The next night I was down by the river watching the front of Rhos Dirion. Jeff and his father had already cut one field, and it smelled rich and sweet, their hay was much sweeter than ours because they had the river. I waited until it was quite dark under the trees before striking a match. I watched the front of the house intently. The white-washed walls were just a pale blur in the darkness, but the roof and chimney were as though they had been cut out of sheet-iron against the sky. By my side the river gurgled, splashed and went dip-dap-lapping on its way. A smell of fern and that evasive smell of trout hung on the air. The river was never still and by listening hard you could separate the different sounds one from the other. There was the steady splash where the main current swept into the pool below and the intermittent cluck of crystal which came from the stone that jutted up out of the water a little above me. Waiting there for Grett to signal back to me, I thought of the river coming over the quiet stretches of the mountain. What music was there like a river under the summer stars, the babbling and the liquid gurgling all through the dew-drenched silence of the night!

After a while, I struck another match and an instant later I saw an answering spurt of light behind the window over the front kitchen. Then, slowly, steadily, the candle-light filled the room and I saw Grett through the trees, standing behind her candle so that I should see her clearly. Before I knew what I was doing, I had cupped my hands to my lips and called like an owl. She gave a wave of her hand to show she had heard me. There was no other light in the house, her window was a picture framed by the night, and I stood there with my back to a tree watching Grett as she looked out into the darkness where I was hidden from her. How long I stood there, I don't know. I shifted my weight from one foot to the other. I tried to send my thoughts to her across the night-scented space that divided us, but she stood there without a movement and did not start to undress. I called again like an owl, and after a while she bent her head to the candle-flame, and where there had been a soft glow and the framed picture of my Grett, there was now only darkness. I waited, praying, imploring that she would let me see her again. I counted up to a hundred and the house was still a blur of grey with its roof sharp and dark. I imagined her lying there in her bed, her lovely limbs resting between the cool sheets. Overhead the stars were soft and far, far away. The river fretted and tinkled behind me and once a bat swooped within an arm-stretch from me. Then suddenly, I saw Grett coming across the yard. I could not believe my eyes. I waited, not daring to move, my heart beating and the blood pounding and roaring in my ears.

She came straight to where I stood. For a full minute she clung to me, her body trembling and her lips holding and returning my kisses.

"I had to come," she whispered. "I waited until I was sure they were asleep. . . ."

I could only repeat her name and hold her to me. Her hair was down over her shoulders and she still held her shoes in her hands. I waited while she put them on; then, with my arm around her waist, I led her into the wood where the shadows were thickest. The night seemed endless for I feared the dawn would come any minute. But each time I looked up, the stars were still there, and the river from time to time broke in on our ecstasy. We hardly spoke. In silence we came to each other, in silence I kissed her and held her to me. My eyes long accustomed to the half-light saw her clearly. I thought of the dreaming parish. We were, probably, the only ones awake. We did not feel the dew, and the touch of her skin was firm and cool. I saw the night pale through her hair that night; for ever more she would be Grett Rhos Dirion to me, for here at Rhos Dirion was our sweet bridal.

"Don't tempt me out again," she pleaded. "Promise! What if they found out!"

I promised, and waited there until she went back to the house. She lighted the candle when she got to her room, just to show me she was safe; then she douted the light and I went home. Father was up when I got in. He gave me a hard look, laughed to himself, but asked nothing as to where I had been. By the time I had washed, Berthlwyd had arrived. I felt clean and light and refreshed, as though I had come out of the river or been in some great wind.

Chapter 14

WE CUT another field before dinner; and all through the afternoon we turned the two fields we had cut the day before. It was light work after the scything, holding the diagonal rakes under our armpits and turning over the rows as we walked along them. It was warmer even than the day before. An oppressive silence lay on the land, it was too warm for the birds to sing; and after the morning freshness had gone, not a butterfly swooped or fluttered in front of us. Over beyond the Black Peak of the Vans there was a bruise in the sky, a nasty yellow and green tinge that made father shake his head when he looked at it. He increased the pace and the rest of us sweated to keep up with him. The day held good, however, and by the time we knocked off for the day the sunset promised well for the morrow.

That evening I went again to the bathing pool by Nanteurin, and as I lay half-floating on my back, the water warmer than the cool air on my face, I longed again for Grett. I got out and dressed quickly and took a roundabout way to Rhos Dirion so as to give her time to go to bed. Though I had not been in bed for two nights, I felt quick and fresh, and vaulted each stile and gate as I came to it.

I lay in the ferns watching Rhos Dirion as the dusk deepened around it. The sharp smell of the ferns took me back to my boyhood; you had only to lie face-flat in the sea of greenness that surrounded you and crush a handful of the long, fretted fronds in your fists, and you felt that you were part of the earth, that your own roots, too, were deep down in the red soil.

I woke up suddenly, wondering where I was. Above me the branches waved against the sky. I looked towards the house and noticed for the first time how light the sky is behind a black roof, even when it is night.

Rhos Dirion was in darkness. I was about to turn away when a sudden impulse brought a smile to my lips. I cupped my hands to my mouth and hooted softly, once, twice. I waited. The minutes passed, and times I held my breath as I fancied I heard the click of a bolt or a step. But the house remained in darkness and I did not dare call again. As I was going up by the mill an owl hooted down in the cwm. I half-smiled at the irony of that cry in the soft darkness. I called back to the owl and took the path through the kissing-gates up to the village, and on by the Allt. I was asleep as soon as my head touched the pillow, and when father called me I awoke fresh and ready for work, but it was raining strings outside. The Vans were lost in mist and the rain-pipe gurgled into the big cask under my window. It was already half-full, and the currant-trees in the garden were bowed low with the weight of rain on them. The sycamores outside swayed and tossed, and still the rain fell. I spent the day writing a letter in my mind to Grett and reading the letter which Lewsin slipped to me as he brushed by me in the passage.

By the end of the week we had carted in the three fields, and Justin and I had given a day each to Berthlwyd and Cefn Wern. I went to church on Sunday night. Only John Ellis was there from Rhos Dirion. At the end of the Credo I heard myself calling: "Grett! Grett!" though no sound came from my lips. I got some curious glances from the boys as I came out. They were all sunburned, their hair bleached from working in the sun. I hurried away, and that night I wrote again to Grett and sent her the consonant and vowel chiming englyn I had written for her.

.　　.　　.　　.　　.

The day of the sports dawned cloudy; but, as mother said, the wind was in the right place, and by dinner-time the clouds opened and sailed across the sky in great white masses, the sun catching their edges, and shining on every leaf and blade of grass. What a day it was! The air seemed as though the rain had washed away every wisp of mist and haze, and the old mountains rose green and paling into violet in the distance.

The sound of the brass band on the field came on the wind, and I quickened my step to it, and wished I had put on my trousers instead of my breeches so that I could compete in the races. When I got to the field, the people were coming out of the tea-tent. But for the milking I would have been in there with them. As it was, I had come without tea, but it didn't matter; I couldn't have eaten anything whatever. I was too excited at the prospect of seeing Grett; it was now nearly a fortnight since that night when she had come out to me from the house.

I saw mother just outside the tent. She was in her best grey and black silk, and beamed happily at me through her glasses. She was quite smart, holding herself a little self-consciously as though she felt that everybody was looking at her.

"Did you have your tea before you came?"

I shook my head, my eyes still roving over the field for a glimpse of Grett. There, leaning on his stick, his check cap stuffed into his coat pocket and his hair falling in a quiff over his forehead, was Justin talking to Cati Bronorwen. He gave me a wave of his hand, and said something to Cati that made her smile across at me as if she, too, were on our side. Near them, Twm Blacksmith was in a new fancy waistcoat, a dove-grey affair with green glass buttons on it. And there, beyond him was Jeff with Rhys and Iori. I could see no sign of Grett anywhere.

"Go and get some tea," urged mother. "Miss Nicholas will give you a cup in a minute!"

I still looked up and down the field. It seemed that every-body was there but Grett. I saw her father and mother talking to the vicar and Mr. Owen Roderick the preacher.

"Who are you looking for?" I fancied there was a little laugh in mother's voice; her eyes were twinkling and the dimples came and went in her cheeks.

"Don't worry," she went on. "I saw her a minute ago. She's with Gwenno Cwmsidan. You are not going to walk about with her here, are you?"

I felt her question was a dare: she was still smiling.

"Of course I will. Everybody's talking about us, so let's satisfy them!"

Mother nodded vigorously, her lips pressed close together and her eyes glinting behind her glasses.

"That's right!" she whispered. "If you want her, then you go and claim her!" She turned to peer round the field. The under tens were already forming up to run. Father was one of the judges. "He's having a great day," said mother. "Look at him! Always a leading horse or he wouldn't be happy. . . . You—you won't get into any row with Jeff Ellis, will you?"

"Don't you worry!" I gave her arm a little squeeze. "There'll be no trouble at all. . . . Just look at Justin over there!"

Justin was deep in conversation with Cati. He was, apparently, trying to make some arrangement with her for he took out his watch and then pointed with his stick towards the end of the field. Cati seemed reluctant; her lips were pouting with indecision, and she kept her eyes fixed on the ground.

"He's terrible—up to his old tricks again!" Mother gave a futile toss of her head. "The silly girl," she went on: "if she had sense she'd know that he's up to no good!" An indulgent smile softened her expression as she watched the two of them. "Don't you go and let Grett Ellis down!" She turned earnestly to me, her blue eyes troubled and concerned. "She is too good a girl for that. Who else would have the grit to do what she is doing, and with all her family against her and everybody talking? Go on!" She gave me a push. "Go and find her. . . . And give her my love!"

Grett was on her own when I found her. I had seen her white frock and leghorn hat across the field. She was standing by the gate behind the tea-tent and did not see me as I came up. She gave a little start as I put my hands around her waist.

Her work on the hayfields had given her a sunburn as rich as that on her arms. She was golden, sun-steeped, and the shade from her hat only deepened the rich texture of her skin. And as we stood there, not saying a word, only looking at each other, I saw how a new tenderness glowed in her eyes, and I had the feeling inside me that her nights had been spent in tears and that she was now come to the end of it all.

She held on to my arm as we made our way to where the crowd was gathered watching the races.

"I heard you that second night," she said.

"When I called from the river?"

"Yes. But I couldn't risk it. I felt sure I would be caught! Were you disappointed?"

I laughed happily. That was all in the past. Nothing mattered now but that we were together. Some day, children then grown up, would say how they had seen Grett Ellis with her lover on the Jubilee Sports Day. . . .

As we drew near the ropes that had been set up to keep the people on one side, I saw men and women nudge each other and turn to look at us. I met their glances proudly. It was no little thing to know that I was the talk of the place, and that Grett's name, of all people, was linked with mine. I think, though, that the majority of the parish felt kindly towards us. I know how I would have felt if I had seen someone like Grett daring the whole countryside and its gossip by walking arm-in-arm with her lover.

"Foot-race for over twenty-one!" Father was shouting the words through his funnelled hands. He could not see us because we were at the back of him. "Come on!" he shouted. "First one home wins a sovran!"

"Why don't you try?" urged Grett. "Win me a sovereign!"

"I daren't leave you," I said. I was sure I wouldn't win and could not bear the thought that she would have to suffer the shame of my defeat. In such a case as this, and on such a day, the lover of such a girl should carry everything before him; either that or nothing.

While we stood there a stranger wearing white shorts and a vest had lined up with the others.

"Who is that!" I asked the back of Elias Carpenter. His eyebrows lifted as he turned round and saw Grett and me.

"Well! Well!" He shook us both by the hand. "Well! Well! Just as it should be. Well done! Good girl, Grett Ellis, you deserve to be happy!" Then he remembered my question: "That's Dai Watkins, he's a professional from over the mountain. They say he is winning everywhere. But it isn't fair coming over here to run against our boys. They haven't got a chance."

Justin, Iori, Isaac Landwr and others, took up their position on the starting line. They had all removed their coats and made a show of rolling up their shirt-sleeves and tying their braces round their waists. Watkins stood a little apart from the others, bending and stretching his legs. The nearest to him was Ted Eyon Tŷ Gwyn, his tall, lean figure dwarfing everybody around him. Grett and I laughed to see his shirt front sticking out from his blue flannel shirt like a starched flap. He had tucked his trouser bottoms into his stockings. Squire Nicholas stood a little away from them with his whistle ready to give the signal.

"Are you ready?" The squire had a pair of brown boots on that were like butter. Do what I would, I could never get the same polish on mine. His toe-caps were just like the sides of father's saddle where his legs had worn the leather to a pale, golden-brown.

Dai Watkins was the only one who crouched as trained runners always do. He balanced himself on his toes and the tips of his fingers. His shoes had long spikes under them. The others stood with their feet touching the line, their fists clenched and right arm drawn back ready to swing forward.

Watkins was away like a shot, leaving the others almost standing. In the first few seconds he was easily ten or fifteen yards ahead. His action was perfect. We had never seen anything like it before: neck forward, arms working up and down, his legs stretching out knee-high with each step he took. Next to him was Justin.

"Come on, Justin!" Father's voice in his clear tenor rose above the shouting. There was resentment against the professional. That a grown man should appear in such trousers was an affront to almost everyone present.

Then Ted Eynon Tŷ Gwyn passed Justin, his legs flying and

his arms swinging, and drew up with Watkins. His stride was tremendous. He had no style, but he was in his stride now. Watkins half turned his head as Ted drew level with him.

"Ted! Ted! Come on, Ted!"

"Catch that winki, Ted!"

In the last thirty yards, Ted left the professional behind him. His stride must easily have taken him two yards at a time. Watkins came second, and Rhys Blacksmith third. Justin had seemed to slow down the moment Ted had passed him.

The excitement over, we walked over to Justin. He gave Grett a quick smile.

"What did you think of Ted?" he asked.

"Grand! I didn't think he had it in him, did you?"

Justin did not answer Grett, but gave us a warning look. Father was standing just behind us. His eyes swept up and down over Grett.

"It's all right," said Justin. "He'll not make any trouble."

Father came slowly towards us.

"You must introduce me, boys. It's Miss Grett Ellis, isn't it?"

His blue eyes went mockingly over Grett again. Whatever he did made me always feel as though I were a child.

"Ah, well! It's no tongues you have, is it?" He rested on his stick, waiting for us to say something. Grett's cheeks were burning, and I could feel her arm trembling against me.

"Come, come," said father. "The folk around here are enjoying this. . . . Don't let's have a scene. Introduce me!"

"It's you is making a scene," said Justin. "Duw mawr!" He gave a side-jerk of his head to indicate John Ellis and Jeff who were crossing over towards us. Father paled a little when he saw them.

"Stick your ground!" he muttered to me. "Stick to your guns now. And you, too, my gel. You've got nothing to be afraid of!"

People were staring at us.

"Next event: the wrestling match!" The squire was trying to draw the crowd away from us. I heard Justin swear again: he had set his heart on this competition. John Ellis came straight up to Grett.

"I don't want any scene, Grett." He ignored the rest of us. "Come with Jeff and me now. Everybody is watching you."

Grett shook her head stubbornly.

"I'm not a little girl," she said quietly. "And you are making me look like a fool!"

"Come on now! You know what I said——"

"I won't. . . . I don't care what people are saying. They'll have enough to say after this anyway!"

Jeff put his hand on her arm. "Come on!" he said.

"Jeff! Don't be silly! Let her be!" Her father's voice was low, almost without emotion. He still did not look at father or myself.

"Edwin!" Father's voice was hard, commanding. "Take your girl away out of this. If there is any argument, it can be settled later."

"Or now," added Justin.

"There'll be no argument," said Grett's father. "If you do this, Grett, you know what people will expect next, don't you?"

I answered for her:

"Yes! We both know: marriage. And nothing will stop it, John Ellis. Nothing nor nobody!"

John Ellis gave Grett a long, almost sad, regretful look; then he walked away. Justin stepped up to Jeff.

"What about the wrestling match?" he said. "You are full of the devil, aren't you? All right, then. Here's your chance to work it off! Are you game?"

Jeff looked at Justin as though he were taking his measure.

"Game!" he said. "As soon as you like!"

Grett turned to me. Her father was now some twenty yards away. The old man stood near us, smiling as he watched Jeff and Justin facing each other.

"Stop your Justin," said Grett. "Think of the disgrace. . . . People will say they are wrestling over us; besides, they won't stop till they've half killed each other!"

"Don't worry, don't worry!" Father smiled benevolently at her. "It will be a fair sporting trial. I'd have a go myself, but there!" He shrugged his heavy shoulders. "Perhaps I'm too strong for your brother! Justin's more his stamp!"

Justin and Jeff had already stalked across to the roped enclosure where Twm Blacksmith and Lloyd Parry (Iori's brother) were already locked in a grip.

The crowd seemed to have sensed at once that something was in the air by the way Justin and Jeff had made their way to the wrestling plot. Father followed them briskly, his shoulders squared and his step as jaunty as if he himself were out to challenge the winner.

Justin and Jeff stripped off their coats and waistcoats and rolled up their shirt-sleeves. I felt nervous, ill at ease, and a foreboding of ill darkened my mind like a heavy cloud. I felt that Grett and I were represented out there in front of us; and although I wanted Justin to win, I knew that if he did so, Jeff would be more embittered against us than ever before. I felt it, too, that Justin was out there fighting my battle. I would have given anything at that moment for his weight and strength, and for the glory of being out there fighting my own battle for Grett.

The boys of the parish knew nothing of the art of wrestling. With us the sport consisted of each man taking a grip round his opponent's back; then, straining and crushing, each one endeavoured to cave in the other's back. Two other pairs had now joined Twm and Lloyd and were scuffling up and down the scarred pitch.

"Come on! Here's another pair!" The squire did not show that he knew or guessed that anything was amiss; but he did glance at father as though he were questioning the prudence of letting Jeff and Justin oppose each other. I caught the whispering that was going on behind Grett and myself.

"It's all over Grett!"

"Jeff Ellis will kill him, remember how he threw Danrallt last year?"

"Kill Justin Peele! Not on your life! Did you hear of the fight he had in Brecon?"

"They started rowing as soon as these here in front came on the field!"

I took Grett closer to the wrestlers. Jeff and Justin were now facing each other. Jeff was red-faced and made no attempt to hide his feelings. Justin was bending and flexing his arms. His biceps were like Twm Blacksmith's, heavier, perhaps, and harder. On the other side of the wrestling pitch, facing Grett and myself, I saw mother. She was watching Justin and looked as if she was going to call out to him, but she put her hand to her mouth as if to stop herself. John Ellis stood a little away from the body of the crowd. Looking at him, no one would ever have guessed that his own son was there preparing to wrestle with the son of his bitterest enemy. His face gave nothing away, and in my heart I felt sorry for the humiliation which I knew he was suffering, and which he would suffer the more when Justin had beaten Jeff.

They did not start until Twm Blacksmith had beaten Lloyd Parry. The others were already out of it, and everybody was now waiting for Justin and Jeff to begin.

And now, at last, they took a grip on each other. Jeff, being taller, was at a slight disadvantage for he had to lower his arms a little in order to grip Justin across the small of his back. Yet, once he did get his grip, he would then be able to lift Justin off his feet and throw him. Locked together they swayed backwards and forwards, their boots ploughing and tearing the ground as they dug in and strove for a foothold. Once or twice it looked as if Jeff would lift Justin off his feet. The strange thing was that no one shouted. No one, it seemed, wanted to take sides openly. I looked at Grett, wondering what she was thinking. She was watching with her lips parted, and a flush of colour on her cheeks. Once, when Jeff half-lifted Justin off his feet, I felt her arm move convulsively, and I saw how her hands suddenly clenched themselves in her excitement. . . .

Justin, I noticed, was making no attempt to cave in Jeff's back; instead, he was exerting all the strength of his forearms on Jeff's ribs. His two legs, straddled apart, and his feet dug into the ground, made him look like an oak holding firm and strong against a great wind. Jeff tried time and again to lift him, bending him this way and that, but Justin still pressed inwards with all the strength of his short, brown, knotted arms. Jeff's face was visibly paling and his breath came in great gasps. In a frenzy of strength he lifted Justin off the ground, but Justin hooked his foot around Jeff's calf and the attempt failed. Again Justin straddled his legs and straightened the press of his arms on Jeff's ribs.

156

"Trip him and fall on him!" shouted father.

"Shame! Stop him! It's not fair!" shouted Howells the Blacksmith. "Justin Peele is not trying to wrestle! It's nothing but slow murder!"

"Stop!"

The squire tore the two apart. "You are not wrestling fair, Justin Peele. You are doing nothing but holding your opponent. You are not trying to throw him. Disqualified! I am sorry, but there you are. I don't want such goings-on on a sports day. You were crushing Jeff Ellis." He turned to the crowd: "Jeff Ellis stays in the final! Justin Peele disqualified for not trying to throw him."

It looked for a moment as if Justin would hit the squire. Then, as though realizing that he had virtually bested Jeff, else the squire would not have intervened, he went over to where his coat and waistcoat lay on the grass and started to dress.

"Thank goodness!" exclaimed Grett. "I'm glad the squire stopped them!" She half-turned towards me and looked defiantly at me. "But your Justin was not wrestling fair, was he?" I was glad that she tempered her statement with the smiling question at the end of it.

"Perhaps you are right," I said. "Anyway, those two can look after themselves all right. Jeff ought to win the final easily!"

I was suddenly tired of the sports and longed to get away where we could be alone. By this time the shadows of the trees stretched right across the field. Shrieks of laughter, the shouting and playing of children rose from all over the field. The band played all the time; the strains of "Comrades in Arms" stirring the blood and making one's feet itch to march.

"Let's go," I said to her.

"What if they see us?" Grett hesitated and looked round the field. "There's your mother over there talking to Justin——"

"She told me to give you her love."

"She did?" Her lovely face flushed red and her eyes became bright with tears. Mother must have seen us at that moment, for she waved her hand to us. Grett at once waved back, then we made our way through the crowd, thinking to slip out quietly through the gate behind the tea-tent. There were smiles and nods for us from everyone. The evening was now blue along the river, and the sunset gave a richness to Grett's complexion.

"Tug-o'-war!" We stopped at the squire's announcement.

"Oh, we must see it," said Grett.

I turned back with her to the middle of the field. This was the main event of the day. Year after year, the team of the "Top"—as we called the farmers from the mountain side of the parish—met the team from the village and its surroundings.

By the time Grett and I got through the press of people, the two teams were being picked. Father was anchor man for the Wern, Jos Watkins the Tavarn was at the end of the rope for the "Top."

Father already had Justin, Moc Mihartach, Twin Blacksmith, and Iori ranged beside him. Against them were Jos the Tavarn, Dico Lewis, Dai Alltwen, the two brothers Owen and Tudor Proth'ro, and Reesi Maesygwenyn. They were a heavy, powerful team. Jos the Tavarn alone scaled well over two hundred. Father turned round to the crowd; he still needed one man. The men all looked at him eagerly, each man fancying himself and ready to jump forward at the slightest beck.

"You, there!" Father pointed to Jeff. For a second it looked as if Jeff would refuse. He scowled at father and half laughed.

"Come on, Jeff. Pull your weight! You are big enough anyway, make yourself useful for once!" Elias Carpenter's remark brought a bashful smile to Jeff's face. Without saying a word, he crossed over and lined up with our team.

"That was a good stroke!" Grett smiled and winked wickedly at me. Father had, indeed, scored there. I don't know whether it was that I alone felt that a change had come over the day, but the air was at once lighter. People were smiling and the band played louder than ever.

The two teams were now complete. Three new ropes lay coiled on the ground beside them. With last year's experience in mind, when the teams had pulled so hard that the rope had snapped, the committee had seen to it that there would be two in reserve this year.

"Right now! Over here, please!" The squire spun a coin in the air.

"Heads!" called father. The choice of position fell to the Cefn team.

"We pull with the river," said Jos Tavarn.

Squire Nicholas scored a line with the heel of his boot and tied his white handkerchief to the rope. The onlookers moved up and down the narrow enclosure and ranged themselves alongside their six representatives. Grett and I found ourselves stationed opposite the handkerchief.

Each man now took up his position on the rope, rubbing his hands in the earth so as to get a better grip, and digging his heels into the trampled grass. Father at one end and Jos the Tavarn on the other, had looped the ends of the rope around their waists and then over their shoulders. The excitement was tremendous. The squire now took up his position, one hand poised on the rope where his white handkerchief hung like a furled flag; and the other, forefinger pointing, raised in the air.

"Ready?"

The twelve men dug their heels into the ground.

"Take the strain!" The squire's voice almost broke with emotion (you should have heard him presiding at a Gymanfa or an Eisteddfod, especially if the Gwynfe tenors had let themselves go), and the opposing teams became grim and set. The handkerchief fluttered like a leaf in a November gale.

"Pull!"

Father and Jos the Tavarn at once threw thenselves backwards. For a minute or so neither team gave an inch. The pull was steady, and the only thing that moved was the up and down quiver of the rope vibrating with the tension of the strain. I looked at Justin. His face was rigid and I saw how regularly his chest rose and fell with each deep, steady breath he took. His knuckles showed white through the black-brown sunburn on his skin. Behind him, Moc Mihartach pulled with all his strength and weight, his eyes closed and his tobacco-stained teeth resting on his lower lip. Then, slowly, first a half-inch, then an inch, the handkerchief moved towards the Cefn end.

"Together, boys! All together now!" roared Jos from the end of the rope.

"Dig in, the Wern! Hold them!" Father was now pulling

with all his might. His face was fiery and the veins running by his temples were like blue, knotted strings.

"Come on, Cefn! One inch—pull!"

"Hold fast, the Wern! Dig in, boys!"

I felt Grett's grip tighten on my arm as though she were hanging on to the rope itself. The two teams were now pulling like two men. Justin's arms were like wreathed iron. Behind him, Moc, Twm Blacksmith, Iori and Jeff were almost lying back on the rope.

Then our team dug in, and again the rope was as taut as a steel cable. The handkerchief twirled to and fro, an inch or so over the mark on the Cefn side. Then, using all his sixteen stone, father inclined himself backward until his great bulk was at an angle of forty-five or so with the ground. The Wern regained their lost inch.

Now it was the Cefn side who dug in. They stabbed and scored the ground with their iron-tipped heels. The band had stopped playing and had come over to watch the contest.

The minutes passed in still tension. All that could be heard was the panting of the twelve men. Father was again erect, and his five men held like grim death. Opposite them, the Cefn team held equally as strong. Jos the Tavarn was content to lean his great weight backward. He was grinning with confidence, not a tooth showing, and the clear sweat running in little rivulets over his cheeks.

"Watch now! Look!" I gave Grett a nudge as father took a deep breath and ran his tongue over his lip. Then he shouted:

"One inch—pull!"

Backward went each right foot and the rope quivered up and down as the handkerchief came an inch in their direction.

"One inch—pull!"

Father was shouting as he did when he was hauling wood on the timber-wagon. His voice had that hard edge to it which was always there when his temper was exultant and in its glory. I would have given anything to be there on the rope with him. One inch—pull! Then another inch—pull! How I would have pulled . . . ! But the team-work was magnificent. Justin was now grinning, and Moc was confident enough to turn his head aside and spit from the corner of his mouth. A convulsive sob of happiness and pride broke in my throat as I watched our team, and my eyes dazzled with tears. Justin, father, Moc; and there, next to father, was Jeff. Seeing his strained, set face, I saw for the first time how strongly he and Grett resembled each other. There was the same line of chin and jaw, even to the half-perplexed frown gathered between the eyebrows.

And now, at last, the Cefn team were stabbing at the ground trying to get footholds. Father was calling his commands in strict tempo.

"One inch—pull!"

"Come on, the Wern!"

"One inch—pull!"

"Dig in, hold them, the Cefn!"

"One inch—pull!"

Father was flat on his back as the handkerchief went over the foot-mark away from the line.

"The Wern wins!" shouted the squire. Everybody cheered and shouted. Jos the Tavarn unwound the rope from his shoulders. He had burst his shirt across the shoulders, and his white flesh was marked where the rope had chafed and cut into him.

"A good pull!" he exclaimed. "Jawch! Drinks on me tonight! Bring your team up, Peele!"

Justin and Moc sat on the grass smoking cigarettes. Jeff stood behind them struggling with his tie and his starched collar. His well-polished boots were all scratched and clogged with earth. He smiled as Grett came up to him, but frowned when he saw that her arm was still in mine.

"Great, Jeff!" said Grett. "You pulled like a giant!"

Jeff gave a wry smile. He seemed to be unwilling to show his pleasure in front of me.

"They nearly beat us," he said. "Look at my hands!" He opened his hands and showed us the ridges of the rope marks on his palms.

"Oh!" Grett's voice was full of feeling. "But you won all right. Excuse me a minute!" She turned and waved her hand to someone in the crowd. "There's Dili the Mill and her baby. I haven't seen her since she got married." She dashed away leaving Jeff and me together. I stood waiting for him to say something. The crowd was moving off now to another part of the field, and we were more or less on our own. The next event was the weight throwing. Jeff ran his hand through his hair.

"I suppose you think you are as good as engaged now, eh?"

I met his glance squarely.

"We are going to get married," I said.

Jeff shook his head.

"Never!" he said equally quiet. "Never! Don't make a mistake. Don't worry," he added quickly, "I'm not going to argue here. But understand this: we won't stand for Grett marrying you. . . . Remember that! And don't go parading about as if it was all cut and dried! It's not fair to Grett, if you think anything about her!"

He had turned on his heel before I could answer him. I watched him thread his way into the crowd.

"What did he say?"

Grett was back at my side. I gave her a knowing smile, realizing that she had crossed over to Dili only to give Jeff and myself a chance to get together.

"Nothing," I said. "He was quite decent."

"But what did he say?"

I took her arm and led her away towards the trees under which the band was playing. They were seated on two long benches set on the squire's four-wheeled hay wagon.

"He told me that we'd never get married. . . . I think he was afraid that I'd think he'd been won over because father had picked him for the tug-o'-war. It was just his pride, don't you think so?"

"Yes! He's so stiff." Grett half-turned and looked into the distance. "He and father are exactly the same!"

"So's Justin and the old man, too."

Without any further words, just as though we each knew what was in the other's mind, we started to make our way out of the field. The dew was heavy and shone on our toe-caps; and as we left the field a burst of clapping and cheering marked the end of the weight-throwing competition.

.   .   .   .   .

We took the steep path down to the river. The hedge was a pale mass of wild roses and honeysuckle. The foxgloves had already lost their red-purple and were like black bells in the dusk. Looking back we saw a line of firs standing black and sharp-pointed against the red and orange of the sky. Down below us, we could see the shining stretches of the river where it wound its way through Allt-y-brain's fields. The strains of the band passed over our heads and became fainter as we followed the twisting, rain-rutted path down to where the alders grew green and dark along the river. With each step we took, the light deepened imperceptibly. The trees were now blurs of soft darkness against the lighter shades of the fields and the skies. Where the river flowed over the shallows, the splashing waters were as bright as a scud of rain against a window. But under the trees the water was like dark velvet, and when a trout jumped the widening ripple was like a torque of silver.

There was no need to talk as we walked along. The stillness of the trees and the pale loveliness of the sky gave a feeling of peace and tranquillity to us. Back on the sports field the people would have missed us by now, and I knew what thoughts would have passed through my mind if I had seen someone like Grett Ellis stealing away with her lover. And now this day so sweet and so perfect in its midsummer loveliness was passing slowly by us, a day not to be suddenly remembered because of its joy, but known and appreciated at the very time because it was the heyday of our love. Then, as it will happen in the dusk of a summer's day, the stars were suddenly in the sky, and the spaces between the tree-tops became freckled with silver.

At last, we saw the wood before us. It was mysterious and still; and we trembled a little as we stood on the edge of it because of the passion and ecstasy that lay so secretly in its shadows. Once, when we groped our way through the tangle of hazels, and pushed waist-deep through ferns, I stopped and held Grett to me. We stood for a minute or so in silence, not even kissing, only clasped in each other's arms as though we were one body. Then we moved on and found the place we had been looking for.

It was Grett who saw the first shower of fireworks light up the sky. I turned and saw the violet, orange and green stars open slowly and then die away, and even after they had gone I still saw the colours against the darkness. Soon, the bonfires were burning on Llyn-y-fan and on the mountains up towards Brecon. The light around us was unreal, belonging neither to the day nor the night. I felt we were like two beings lost in some old legend with the mystery of fire and darkness ever around us. I looked at Grett and saw her like some phantasm of loveliness touched with flame; her dark hair was loose about her shoulders and her thin summer frock clung to her figure like the drapery of some goddess. I could only look at her, for now, because of the flickering glow around us, we no longer felt we were alone. At sudden moments even the trees themselves looked like watching, statuesque shapes between us and the bonfires.

"Grett!" I lifted her to a sitting position.

"What is it?"

"Will you come with me to see the vicar to-morrow night?"

"You mean . . . ?"

"Yes. I want to marry you. Now, at once. We've waited long enough. If we wait for your father's and mother's consent we'll always be like this. Are you willing?"

"Yes, of course. But how can we do it?"

"Let's ask him to marry us. We can do it in secret, or have the banns called. Whichever you like!"

We talked it over. Grett was all for going to the vicar and asking his advice, but as I told her, it was one of those matters on which the vicar could not advise us. He would do whatever it was we decided on; the responsibility would have to be ours, and ours alone.

We lay there until the fireworks were over and the bonfires were out. When we got within sight of Rhos Dirion, the place was in darkness. Her parents and Jeff could not possibly be home yet, so we leaned against the orchard gate until we should hear them coming up the lane.

"And we needn't be afraid we won't get a little place," said Grett. "Look at Dili and Albert——"

"Have they got a place then?"

"Yes, I thought I'd told you. They are going to the Birgwm on October the first. Davie John is giving up and going away."

So we talked and planned. Grett said she would meet me the following night in the field above the house. She would have to come as she was, without changing or anything lest her parents would suspect anything.

Presently, we heard voices coming up the lane, and Grett went—a pale, vanishing gleam in the darkness. I was well across the orchard before Grett's father and mother went by; and as I made my way up through the fields, the feeling came to me that the days were fast moving to their climax; and despite the tremulous happiness that possessed me as I thought of all that the morrow would bring, a shiver went over me, and I felt suddenly as though the trees had gone leafless and stark, and that the earth was desolate around me. I stopped and looked around me, and listened. There was nothing, nothing but the fragrant stillness of the summer night, the pale, soft stars overhead, and the sounds of the people going home from the sports. No, there was nothing, and I laughed to myself at the thought of the Toili and all that had terrified me on that winter's night in the smithy.

BOOK FOUR

Chapter 15

LOOKING back now, I see the days of that summer steeped in gold. But perhaps that was because the corn ripened with the unclouded nights of moonlight that we had; and with each day after the end of July, the sun lost its dazzling brightness, and when you woke in the morning you saw it golden in the window curtains, and the patches of light on the wall were tinged, though ever so lightly, with the richness of the harvest.

By day, it was high summer with the wind coming from the right quarter, and the weather-glass pointing to "Fine." Over and beyond Myddfai, and away to Ystrad Ffin, the mountains were touched with a soft blue haze so that you thought the sky itself had come down to rest on the purpling heather. And there's wonderful it was before breakfast going up to the fields above the road to get the cows in from the aftermath. It was worth losing a few minutes only to lean against the gate of the wain and to see the firs on the top of the gorse-land standing black and sharply scissored against the morning glory of the sky. There were colours in the sky that belonged only to a late August morning. The glow behind the hillcrest and the dark flames of the firs was a wash of gold that deepened and deepened in tone until you wondered how it became green and then paled and softened until it was lost in the blueness of the sky right above you. And rising out of their mists, the old Vans wore their purple like kings. There was a rich, trembling radiance on the land, and I felt that everything was in its last perfection for Grett and myself. Still, even so, I wished the days away. I lived only for the coming Sunday when the vicar would call our banns.

Justin was out almost every night now. He was drinking hard again, and I heard in the village how he and Moc were having a last wild fling before Mihangel when Moc was giving up Mihartach and going away to the valleys. Justin was beginning to look rough, too. Father and he gave each other a wide berth, and more than once mother looked across the table and shook her head as Justin came down to breakfast and pushed his plate aside without as much as looking at the fried bacon and egg on it. There were days when he would hardly say a word to any of us, and I wondered to myself if he was beginning to take after the old man. Then, by the evening, he would be almost his old self again; though, come what would, never mind how the work stood, he knocked off straight after tea each day and washed, shaved and changed. Then he would saddle the cob, and we would hear him tearing at full gallop down through the Allt. Mother was always afraid for him because he was not at all safe on a horse. He came home one night with his head bound round with his handkerchief, and blood all down the front of his coat. The cob had thrown him between The Pandy and the village, and he had to stay in bed for a few days until he was well again. But the old man said nothing. I think he was afraid that Justin would take it in his head to go away with Moc. Twm Blacksmith had already gone off suddenly to Porth to shoe underground.

I suppose it was lucky for Grett and myself that the vicar of the adjoining parish fell ill so that our vicar had to go over each Sunday and take the morning service there. I was indeed glad when Lewsin the Post brought me a note from the vicar telling me that he would have to call the banns in the evening service instead of the morning as is usual. I wrote a note to Grett at once and gave it, there and then, to Lewsin. It was, indeed, a stroke of luck for us. After all, it would have been a bit of an anticlimax to have had our banns called with the church only a quarter full for morning service. Justin laughed when I told him.

"I'll bring Moc along," he said. "Just in case Jeff turns nasty."

We started to count all who would range themselves on our side. I was surprised to find that we had so many friends, and couldn't help feeling sorry for the Ellises, knowing the reputation they had in the parish.

I watched father and mother set off across the yard after the milking. The old man went a yard or so in front of her, his back square and straight, and his cuffs gleaming as he swung his arms. Justin, as usual, was all behind. He had cut his chin shaving, and was cursing to himself as he dabbed salt on the cut to stop the bleeding. I was full of impatience to be off for fear that Grett should get to church before me and think I had jibbed it at the last moment.

At last, Justin was ready. His eyes were still a little blood-shot from the night before—it had been gone five when he came home, and I had got up to put him to bed.

"How are you feeling?" he asked me.

I was yawning and sweating in my anxiety and nervousness.

"What do you think will happen?" I asked. "Do you think there'll be trouble?"

He gave a slow grin and his eyes half-closed as he looked past me. "The old man will go up through the roof . . . but don't worry. We'll manage him all right, and the other side, too. . . . It's Grett will have to face the music when she gets home. The sooner you get married and bring her here or find some place for yourselves the better. . . . See her right first, then we'll manage Jeff and his old man. Just you wait, I'll see that they keep the other side of the road when any of us come by!"

To beat the church bell we ran down through the fields and up behind Rhos Dirion. Justin was blowing a little, and I eased up a bit so that he should not notice how fresh I was. It hurt me to see him out of condition. It would be a good thing when Moc would be gone for good.

The evening was glorious, wonderful; and, as I ran along, I had a feeling that I had dreamed it all before. I looked across at the Van Rocks and saw them bathed in purple and green; and seeing the evening light so soft and still and sad on the whole land, a dream that had faded in my mind came back to me in all its freshness. I saw myself going this same way, half-running or gliding over the gold of the corn, seeing the Van Rocks bathed in colours never seen before in summer or harvest-time; and then I was in our kitchen and Grett was with me. There was a sweet, lovely tenderness upon me and my face was wet with tears. . . . I remembered, too, that of late my dreams had been filled with colour and tenderness. And now, here I was, treading the golden-eared fields on my way to church. I had never seen the old rocks look so majestic in their blue, purple, and red. The sadness and small-aching melancholy of the late summer was on everything, and behind the pounding of my blood I could hear myself chanting or singing some unwritten poem to Grett.

The bell finished ringing before we were half-way up the hill leading from the river. We were a good five minutes late, and they were singing the Psalms when we got to the kissing-gates. I could hear father hitting the tenor, and the sopranos and the altos were there in strength. I pushed the porch door open and peeped in. The church was full, every family pew occupied. Anne Lewis was at the little organ, and no matter if Lewsin did rise half a tone, as he sometimes did, you could depend on it that she would rise with him, and only father and a few of the others would notice the change.

Grett, her father, mother, and Jeff were in their pew. I saw that Grett's shoulders were drooping a little and her head was low over her book. I turned abruptly to Justin.

"Come on," I said. "I'm going in. Grett must be thinking it's afraid I am."

I walked up to my seat behind the choir while Justin followed me noisily and crossed in front of the altar to take his place by father. Everybody stared at us, and I kept my head down for quite a minute before I sat up and looked around. Grett was in her dark blue costume, and her hat came down over one side of her head so that her face was set off against it. She was looking straight in front of her, and only those sitting in front of me could see the smile she gave me. I smiled back at her and noticed how Jeff turned red and scowled at me. Grett coloured a little, too; then she lifted her chin and I could see how her breasts rose as in defiance against all who were watching us.

While the vicar read the Lesson, father looked as if he were half asleep. He sat there with his great bulk filling the corner of his seat; mother, sitting with the altos, turned her head and looked quickly at me as if she were not sure of what was happening. Then I saw her peering across at Justin who was sitting like a rock in his seat, one arm outstretched along the back of the pew and a smile graven on his lips as he looked insolently round the church. Back in the seat nearest the door, I could see Moc with his quiff plastered across his forehead, and his deep starched collar, holding his head upright as though the muscles of his neck had been set in starch too.

All through the Magnificat I leaned standing against the stone pillar beside me, my legs trembling under me. The light was fading a little, but it was still light enough to see the words. Of course, the lamps were already lighted in readiness and they cast their splash of light on the white-washed spaces between the wooden rafters of the roof, and their reflections winked back at us from the brass rail in front of the altar; there was a ripple of flame, too, on the communion plates and on the slender gold crucifix. Mother's voice was more full and tender than I had ever heard it before, and Justin was grounding the bass with all his might. I saw the vicar turn to look at him; then he glanced over his glasses at me, as though to assure me that all was well and not to fear.

The Magnificat over, the vicar stepped out to the lectern by the organ, and before starting on the Second Lesson, he moved the candlestick and trimmed the wick between his thumb and forefinger so as to see better. I saw that he carried his black, shiny-covered announcement-book at his side, half hiding it against the folds of his surplice. I took one look at Grett as he read the Lesson and for one rapt moment it seemed that our eyes bridged the space between us. From far away came the sound of the vicar's voice, and then the silence that followed his reading. Grett's eyes were dark and shining, and her lips were parted as though for that moment she had stopped breathing and were holding her breath. I felt the sweat break out along my back as the vicar closed the Bible. He turned slowly towards the body of the church, glancing first at me, and then at Grett. Then, adjusting his spectacles, he opened his book; and as he gave his preparatory cough, I felt my nervousness leave me. A cold, nerveless rigidity took hold of me, and I leaned back in my seat waiting for his announcement.

"I publish the banns of marriage between Edwin Elidyr

Peele, of Trewern in this parish and Margaretta Anne Ellis of Rhos Dirion in this parish. If any of you know cause, or just impediment, why these two persons should not be joined together in holy matrimony, ye are to declare it. This is the first time of asking."

I looked at Grett. The shade of her hat-brim fell softly across her face.

"Vicar!"

Grett's father was on his feet. Everyone turned to look at him. I saw father make a movement as if he, too, would rise to his feet. Justin put a hand on his shoulder.

"Yes, John Ellis?" The vicar looked down at John Ellis. "What is it?"

"I can't permit these banns. I—I——"

"Wait!" If John Ellis's voice was hard and cold, there was a frost-like quality in the vicar's voice. "Wait!" he repeated. "Remember, this is the House of God. I will have no wrangling of family differences here. You can do that at home or on the road . . . I say again: If any of you know cause, or *just*"— he repeated the word "just," giving it added emphasis— "*just* impediment why these two persons should not be joined together in *holy* matrimony, ye are to declare it. . . ."

The vicar closed his book and waited. Grett's father sat down slowly and we stood up for the Nunc Dimittis. The singing was ragged enough. Lewsin had to step out from his seat by the organ, and swung his book in an attempt to keep the singing together. I leaned back against the pillar, feeling cold and calm. So it had happened. I had heard our banns called: Grett's name coupled with mine inside the old church. Somehow or other, the scene and the situation were as familiar to me as if I had gone through them a thousand times. I saw myself as a boy in my knee-breeches and Grett, big-eyed, with her black, gleaming pigtails down over her shoulders. I felt that I had known intuitively through the years that this hour was bound to come. . . . The singing was going better now. I could hear Justin, and father and Lewsin were leading the tenors. I looked at father in amazement and admiration. His poise and self-command were wonderful. To look at his smooth-shaven jowl, his great domed unwrinkled forehead, you would think he had nothing on his mind. He even moved his head from side to side in time to the beat; and with it, as always, came the tap-tap of his foot on the wooden boards. I tried to concentrate my ears on mother, but her alto was lost to me, if she was singing at all. Grett stood with her eyes fixed on her book. By her side, her father, mother, and Jeff did not sing a note.

I thought the vicar never would get through his sermon. He laboured his three headings or points, and when I thought he was about to finish, he began to gather up the loose ends of his discourse. I wondered once or twice whether he was purposely playing with us. I glanced at my watch; it was already nearly eight. The church was now flickering with shadows as the lamps swung gently on their black chains. But the vicar was not through yet. He was intoning his words vehemently, his voice rising and falling as his *hwyl* sustained him. It always made me embarrassed to hear him when he was in his jubilant stride. It was only rarely that he let himself go. We were not accustomed to it, and when he did so there was something too naked in the way he laid bare his heart and soul. And while I disliked the high, resounding glory of his oratory, the intonation and incantation of it tugged and tore at my heart, and a cry more poignant than ever would almost bring the tears to my eyes. I looked at Grett again, not caring any longer who saw me, but she sat there in her still quietness, her loveliness so still and rapt that I wondered to myself if this was not a dream that I was dreaming; thinking that it was impossible that I had heard my name called with hers in the banns. Margaretta Anne Ellis! I repeated her name over and over to myself, seeing it written on her school exercise books, seeing it inscribed in her round hand in the Marriage Register; seeing it, too, carved in stone and knowing that when that time should come I would have it so written: Margaretta Anne Ellis, wife of Edwin Peele. The Ellis part of her name should not die; it was a darker name than my own, and with it went her hair, her eyes, the nights we had lain together, and all the passion of our love.

At last, the service over, I walked over at once to Grett's side. Her father and mother sat as if they were incapable of rising. Jeff's eyes were wild with temper, but he could not push out past Grett. She stood at the end of the pew, pulling her gloves over her fingers; and when she saw me, she at once stepped out into the aisle and put her arm in mine. Before we could move away, the vicar came up to us, still in his soiled, rumpled surplice.

"I will walk out with you," he whispered. "Come on, one of you on each side of me. That's right!"

The congregation pushed out whispering and talking as though sensing that the climax of the evening would be reached outside the porch. As we made our way out, John Ellis and Jeff brushed past us. Behind us, I could hear father and mother talking in low whispers. Justin and Moc were already waiting for us in the porch. Moc rose his hand to his quiff as the vicar came up. No one said a word to us, though many of the women nodded smilingly at us and more than one elbow nudged me encouragingly as we passed out.

I was surprised to find it so light outside. The day was closing softly, beautifully. The trees were still, dark against what light there was in the west, and all over the churchyard was the brooding silence of a late summer evening. The Van Rocks had lost their purple and blue, and rose like the last ramparts of earth against the infinitude beyond them.

John Ellis and Jeff, and behind them, Iori, Rhys Blacksmith, Dai Alltwen, Lloyd Parry and the rest of them, stood facing the steps leading down from the porch. Then, before anyone could say a word, the squire came forward.

"My congratulations!" He shook Grett and me warmly by the hand. "My congratulations to you both. . . . Remember now, an invitation to the wedding. Don't forget!"

Father and mother came up and stood by us. Justin, Moc, Talsarn, Dico Lewis and a half-dozen others, among whom I saw Lewsin the Post, stood on the porch steps behind us.

"Grett! Come here!"

Her father came a step towards us. I felt Grett's hand tighten on my arm. John Ellis came up to us and took Grett's arm. She drew back, and Justin and Moc came and stood by my side. Jeff and his mother stood a yard or two behind John Ellis.

"Now, now!" The vicar looked gigantic in his surplice. The people crowded forward in a dark arc, pressing close together to hear his words. "All right!" His voice was full of authority. "This is none of my business I know, but here inside these gates I've got my say. Mark this, John Ellis, and you, Daniel Peele, and you, too, Justin Peele, and Jeff Ellis: I will have no angry words on this holy ground. . . . Come, now; you, Trewern, and you, Rhos Dirion, act like men. Everyone here knows about your quarrel. It is no secret from any of us. . . . Now, I beg you, let these young people go their way in peace. If you must quarrel, then do it on your own hearths. But no violence here, I will not have it!"

John Ellis turned to father:

"Daniel Peele, will you and your family come down to Rhos Dirion now? And you, vicar, will you come, too?"

Father and mother nodded without saying a word. The vicar made a movement with his hands as though to show that he would do all in his power to help.

"The first I knew of it," I heard father say. "The young——"

"Very well, then." The vicar took out his watch. "I must go to the vicarage first." But before going, he turned to the crowd. "Of course"—he smiled thinly—"you'll have plenty to talk about now, it's only natural. . . . Let me beg of you to be fair to these two young pople here. . . . Be fair in what you think and say!"

With that he motioned Grett and me to follow him. Justin grinned and shrugged his shoulders as we passed him. Moc stood there scowling, his under lip thrust wet and thick outwards as though he were disgusted with the turn of events.

Slowly, and arm-in-arm, Grett and I followed the vicar, taking the narrow grass-fringed path that wound in and out the gravestones, and stepping at times over many a grassy mound. I glanced back once and saw my father, mother, and Justin making their way slowly behind Grett's family as they passed down the gravel path towards the iron vee-gates.

Chapter 16

THE night was dark and sweet around us as we made our way down to Rhos Dirion. I walked with Grett's arm in mine, and the vicar did not talk much as we went along. We kept to the road all the way. I did not think of what awaited us at Rhos Dirion. All I knew was that, at last—like the end of a long journey—we were coming to the end of what had seemed interminable, and that beyond the darkness of this sweet hour a new life awaited us.

The little clumps of firs by Maesyfed corner were like spear-points against the sky, and as I saw them, I remembered how Grett had waited there for me in the dark winter nights. The air was sweet and heavy with the sadness of the last days of summer. There was a fragrance of damp reedy earth everywhere, and the blackberry-laden hedges gave a wine-like sharpness to the darkness around us. Then, at last, as we turned the last bend of the lane, we saw the lamplight in Rhos Dirion windows. And at that moment, I felt Grett tremble against me. The vicar stopped and groped in his pockets for his pipe and tobacco. Grett and I stood watching him in silence as he pressed the tobacco into the bowl and then held the spurting match to it.

"Well!" The vicar puffed hard at his pipe and the bouquet of his tobacco was such that I had never smelled from my own. "Well. . . . Here we are, then! How—how are you feeling, Grett Ellis?"

I put my arm behind her and she leaned her head back against my shoulder.

"I am glad everybody knows now," she said quietly. "And thank you, vicar, for coming with us."

"You leave everything to me," he said. "You leave it to your parents and me. . . . Remember, they cannot stop you getting married. So don't say anything to provoke them. . . . Of course"—he puffed at his pipe until it glowed—"they—they've had a terrible shock to-night. . . ."

Father, mother, and Justin were waiting for us at the gate leading into the yard.

"We wouldn't go in without you," said father. "Better for us all to be together."

Justin came over to me, and mother took Grett's arm.

"You are a good girl, Grett," she said. "I am very proud of you. Don't let them turn you, will you?"

Before Grett could answer, the vicar turned round and looked at father.

"One thing, now. No wild talk to-night. I've been asked to come along, so please leave things to me."

"Of course, vicar, of course!" Father was cool and smooth. So far he hadn't even given me a glance.

"And you, Justin Peele? What about you?"

"All right, vicar. Don't worry. If Jeff wants me, well, he knows where to find me. . . . No offence, Grett. But you know me. . . ."

The dogs set up a wild barking as we crossed the yard. John Ellis and Jeff came out of the house, the light streaming past them from the open door.

"Lie down there! Cwtch!"

The dogs skulked away at John Ellis's voice.

"Come in, vicar—all of you!" He held the door for us, and we went in past him; the vicar, father and mother, Grett and I, and Justin behind us.

Grett's mother was standing by the dresser. The table was not laid for supper. A large red cloth covered it, and the brass-bowled lamp was set in the centre. We stood standing and looking at one another until John Ellis came in and closed the door behind him.

"Sit down," he said. "You, Mrs. Peele, here by the fire. Vicar, you there. Daniel Peele"—he brought a heavy oak chair from the corner of the room and placed it near the vicar—"you sit here." He looked round at the rest of us. "Take a chair each; you, Jeff, get one from the parlour."

We all sat down. Grett went out into the passage and was back in a few seconds without her hat and coat. She refused my chair and went over and leaned against the dresser, half-sitting on the lower half of it. She was a little pale, and her hair and eyebrows were a shining black in the soft lamplight. Justin and I were near the door; Jeff and his mother sat round the table.

For a few moments we sat in silence. The wall-clock ticked loudly, each swing of the pendulum robbing Grett and me of a segment of time. A red coke fell from the grate, and a tarry mass of coal suddenly spurted a flame of pure white. Mother had half-turned away from us and sat there staring at the fire.

I could see the firelight playing on the gold rims of her glasses. She was nervous, and kept opening and closing the fasteners on her black kid gloves.

"Well," the vicar turned towards me and then to Grett, "I suppose it is up to me to break the ice. . . . Now, John Ellis, what is it that you have against Grett marrying Edwin here? The old quarrel, eh?"

John Ellis nodded.

"Yes. . . . What else? It is a sly trick young Edwin Peele has played on us." His eyes swept over me in cold dislike. "To do this without telling us a thing! We knew nothing about these banns. Why didn't he come to me and Mary like a man and tell us? Surely, we had a right to know, not taking advantage of us in church like that!" He paused and pursed his lips. "It is my belief that the Peeles knew all about it, judging by the way they are taking it. . . . But we knew nothing. Nothing! Just you put yourself in our place!"

Mother looked up quickly. She was a little red in the face.

"You are wrong, John Ellis. Daniel and I knew nothing . . . not a thing about it. You are not to go saying that we have been underhanded——"

"Anne! Just you let the vicar have his say with John Ellis. Our turn will come. . . . Plenty of time for us then . . . plenty of time!" Father's voice was deadly in its even, unhurried calmness. I could see that he had determined what part he was going to play this evening. He would goad Grett's father as far as he could with his smiling spengs and insults. He was for ever doing it to us at home, and lacked no practice.

The vicar turned to mother:

"Quite right, Mrs. Peele. You are right to point that out." He turned to Grett's father: "No, John Ellis, no one knew anything of this but myself. Your daughter and Edwin came to see me and it was their wish that the banns should be called to-night. . . . But, come now, surely, this can be settled quite easily."

John Ellis swallowed hard.

"You have shamed me," he said to Grett. "You knew all the time how we felt towards Trewern." He turned to the vicar: "I may as well tell you at once, vicar: my family will have no dealings with the Peeles. That is all I can say."

Grett stood up from the dresser.

"You are wrong, father. I am going to marry Edwin."

I marvelled at her. She came over and stood at my side, her hip against my shoulder. Justin looked across at her with shining eyes.

"Now, now!" The vicar put up a restraining hand as Jeff was about to shout something. "Please, now. You asked me to try to settle matters . . . Grett has said she is going to marry Edwin. Now, John Ellis, and you, Mrs. Ellis, are you going to go against this marriage? If you are, then tell us on what grounds?"

"Grounds!" John Ellis hit the table with his fist. "Grounds! Don't make me boil, vicar. Why, you know how we two families feel about each other. No good can come of this marriage; no good, I tell you! Blood is thicker than water. Grett will find that out, and then it will be too late. I am not going to let her spoil her life because she's lost her head!"

"Yes, yes!" The vicar tapped his pipe out on the fire-bars. "I understand your feelings. But you can't oppose a marriage on those grounds. . . . The young people are over age. They have got the law on their side. Indeed . . . you can't stop them from getting married. What do you say about it, Mrs. Ellis?"

Grett's mother looked at her husband, and then at Grett.

"I don't know," she said quietly. "All I am worrying about is Grett's happiness. That's all, but"—she gave Grett a reproachful glance, and then went on folding and refolding the hem of her handkerchief—"she should have told me. I am disappointed in you, Grett. I have never known you to be sly like this."

"There was nothing sly about it!" I turned angrily to John Ellis. "Grett and I knew you would never give us your consent, so we took things in our own hands. After all, we could have got married on the quiet. . . ."

John Ellis held my glance coldly.

"Right you are," he said. "Suppose we can't stop you then. What are your plans? Where are you going to take Grett? Tell us, what are your plans?"

Father coughed at this and cleared his throat. He looked at me with his fair eyebrows raised in cynical interrogation.

"She'll not live here or at my home," I said. "You can be sure of that!"

"Where, then?" shouted Jeff angrily. "You can't live on the parish——"

"I'm going away," I said slowly. "There's work enough in the valleys. We'll leave the parish——"

"Edwin! You couldn't!" Mother's voice almost broke. She turned quickly to father: "Speak up, Daniel. Say something!"

Father smiled across at John Ellis. Justin gave me a quiet wink and thrust his legs out in front of him.

"Well, things are moving very fast," said father. "First, I go to church and I hear he is getting married. And now he says he is going away. What can I do? As you say, vicar, he is over age."

"You can set him up in a farm," said Justin. His eyes dared father's. "We are not paupers."

Father thrust out his under lip and assumed an expression of calculating judgment.

"We are not paupers," he said quietly. "Far from it!" He turned to John Ellis, still smiling. "If I start my son, how much will the young woman bring with her? . . . Or is it the Ellises are the paupers?"

The room was suddenly quiet. The vicar closed his eyes and leaned back in his chair as though there was nothing further he could do. Father was still smiling, looking at us as if he were surprised at our silence.

John Ellis frowned, and the colour rose in patches on his forehead.

"My sovran is as good as yours, Daniel Peele. But let me make this clear: if Grett goes against my wishes, then she gets nothing from here. Do you understand that, Grett?"

"I didn't expect anything," answered Grett.

"But you won't get married," said Jeff. "Not as long as I can help it!"

John Ellis turned on Jeff:

"Quiet!" he said. "We'll have no shouting." He turned to father: "Daniel Peele, what are you doing about this? Tell me, are *you* for it, or against it?"

Father had to answer, and the smile faded from his face.

He went pale, and I knew that at last his temper was beginning to get the better of him. Mother looked anxiously at him, knowing the signs, and Justin sat forward, his eyes narrowed and every line of his face taut with suspense.

"I am against it. . . ." Father spoke slowly and weighed his words carefully. "You and me have had no dealings with each other for years. . . . You have kept out of my way and that has satisfied me——" Jeff scowled at this, but his father gave only a contemptuous flick of his eyelids. Father continued: "And now, here is this boy of mine wanting to marry your daughter. Well"—he paused and closed his fist as though gauging his strength, and I knew him well enough to know that here was the barbed speng he had been keeping up his sleeve all the evening—"well, if he has done wrong to the girl, then he should marry her, and I won't stop him——"

John Ellis jumped to his feet. His mouth worked and quivered as he tried to speak.

"Shame!" The vicar shouted the word at father. "Shame on you, Daniel Peele, hitting low like that!"

I looked at Grett. She had blushed and her lips were quivering. Mother and Mrs. Ellis stared open-mouthed at father who was again smiling in his chair. I said nothing. I hated him. I could feel nothing but a cold, passionless hatred for him. He was a terrible man. He was so confident of his strength and his power to inflict hurt that he had no thought for anyone else. The only person he feared was Justin, and that was because Justin was so like him.

Jeff got up and stood over father.

"Get out, you old blaggard! Get out!"

Justin looked for a moment as if he, too, would get up. But he changed his mind and lay further back in his chair.

Father looked up at Jeff.

"Keep cool," he said gently. "Keep cool. We'll be related soon, you know."

"Gentlemen!" The vicar rose from his chair. He looked coldly at father. "Daniel Peele, that was a cruel thing to say. You have insulted Grett Ellis's innocence in front of her family. . . . If you don't apologize at once, then I leave. This is no place for me!"

Father laughed. He looked at each of us in turn.

"Well, well!" He chuckled to himself. "The way you take on, there's touchy you all are! Times must have changed. Now, when I was young, we usually had to get married." (This again was a gibe at Grett's father and mother.) "Very well, perhaps I was wrong. . . . Time will show!" He turned to Grett: "Young woman," he said, "will you forgive me? I am very sorry."

Grett looked at him without saying a word.

"There has been enough talk," said John Ellis. "No good can come of this. . . . I can't stop the wedding. If Grett goes against our wishes, then she knows what to expect."

"And you, Daniel Peele?" The vicar was buttoning up his coat.

"I stand by my son," said father. "Don't think I am in favour of the marriage. But if Miss Ellis will take our name, then I'll see that she gets a good start with my son. That is my answer."

"One minute!" Jeff went up to Grett.

"I want you to give Daniel Peele the lie to his words," he said. "You owe that to us. You are still a maid, aren't you?"

My heart almost stopped at his words. I saw Grett's breasts rise and fall under her white blouse and the white sharp points of her knuckles showed through the taut skin. She made a swallowing movement with her throat.

"Of course!" Her voice was quiet. "What do you think!"

"Oh, Grett!" Her mother came up to her and put her arms around her. Then she turned to father:

"Now, Mr. Peele, you see! You shouldn't say things like that. It's a pity you haven't got a daughter yourself."

Father turned again to Grett.

"Miss Ellis," he said, "I did you a wrong. I am very sorry."

Jeff got up suddenly and went outside.

John Ellis gave his hand to the vicar, ignoring our family.

"There is nothing we can do, vicar. Thank you for coming." He paused, and looked at Grett and me. "Er—when—when is the wedding?"

"On the twenty-fifth," I said.

"The twenty-fifth . . . that's a month Thursday then!"
He turned again to the vicar, shaking his head.

"It is a bad business, vicar; a bad business!"

"You'll be at the wedding?"

"Yes, vicar, we'll be there. . . . No, no, don't be afraid.
There will be no trouble. We won't make it any harder for
her."

Grett came with me to the door.

"Come down to the river to-morrow night," she whispered.
Then she went up the stairs and I heard her close the door of
her room. Jeff was standing outside. He ignored Justin and
touched me on the shoulder.

"A word with you, gwas. Come here!"

I thought for a moment that he wanted to fight me, and I
felt ready for him. Justin stood by the gate watching us.

"What have you been doing to Grett?"

I looked straight at him and said nothing.

"If anything happens to her—you know what I mean, I'll
kill you. Just remember that. As your old man said: 'Time will
show.' "

He turned quickly and went back in the house.

Justin was waiting for me and together we followed the
others. It was quite dark, and the stars were watery and like
silver. The Rhos Dirion haystacks rose round and pointed
above the smudge of the hedge.

"What did he want?" asked Justin after the vicar had left us,
and we had fallen back about twenty yards behind father and
mother.

I told him.

"Hm! Are you worrying?"

"About what? About what he said?"

Justin stopped and looked at me.

"Look here, you haven't got to fool me. You know what I
mean. Are you worrying about Grett? Is she in trouble?"

"No . . . not as far as I know."

"I see. . . ." He grinned, his teeth shining in the darkness.
"Diawl! The old man was a devil to-night. But he shouldn't
have said what he did. Dampo! If I'd been Jeff I'd have
knocked the words down his throat!"

I saw the scene again, and felt the interval of time that had elapsed before Grett had replied to Jeff's question.

"What did you think?" I asked him.

"Think? What about?"

"Grett. Did she ring true when she answered Jeff?"

He shook his head.

"No. It was as plain as a pikestaff. . . . But don't worry. You know what parents are. They always think their children can do no wrong—all except our old man!"

I worried over his words as we went along. I thought of Grett left alone with her family. Get married we would, even if it meant going away to the valleys. And with that thought in my mind, my heart became lighter, and when we left the overshadowing gloom of the Allt behind us, I felt as if the road were gleaming bright in the darkness.

.   .   .   .   .

No word was said until after supper. The old man ate well and so did Justin, but mother only played with her food; and although we had cold chicken and the remains of the blackberry tart we had had for tea, I didn't want anything. I kept thinking of Grett, wondering how she was faring, what with Jeff and her father so bitter against us.

Mother made no move to start clearing the table, but sat looking at father, waiting for him to say something. He wiped his lips carefully with his best white handkerchief and looked across at me. He was not smiling any longer.

"You fool," he said at last. "Don't you think you have caused enough trouble already? I thought you had a bit more sense. And now you had to go and spring those banns on us. Damme! If I was John Ellis or Jeff, I'd half kill you."

"They're welcome to try," I said. "And don't talk to me as if I was a boy."

"No?" He sneered openly at me. "No, you are not a boy, far from it. And it seems to me as if you have been playing at being a man, a married man, too——"

"Daniel! Stop it! Don't say such things."

He took no notice of mother.

"Tell me the truth," he continued, "is she in trouble? Yes or no!"

"You heard what Grett said," I answered. "You are just trying to insult me, just to goad me into quarrelling with you so that you can get rid of your temper!"

"Yes, that's just his bloody game," put in Justin.

"Quiet, you. . . . Now, tell me the truth now. I want to know, I don't want to be the laughing-stock of the parish."

"Once again, then—no!" I answered.

"No?" He seemed incredulous. Then he gave a short, contemptuous laugh. "Then why in hell's name did she take such a time to answer? Ha! Ha! She didn't deceive me. . . . You are lying. I don't believe you."

"What if she is in trouble?" said Justin. "Isn't it the more reason why they should get married?"

"That's what I say," said mother. "You've got to help them. . . . You said you would. Don't try to get out of it."

"I will help them," said father. He looked at me again with his lips curled in a sneer, a sneer that he made no attempt to conceal, so that I should see his contempt for me. "Oh yes, I will help them, if only to put one across John Ellis." He laughed again. "A fine thing for John Ellis that the apple of his eye should take our name. . . . No, I'll not oppose it; and, what is more, you bring her here. A fine thing it will be for him to see his girl heavy with our brood!"

Justin got up from his chair and went over to him. The old man scowled up at him.

"Well? What have you got to say? You were quiet enough down there with Jeff about."

"Just this." Justin sneered down at him. "You be careful what you say or, father or no father, I'll give you the hiding of your life, and Mam shall come away with me. . . . We'll just leave you to yourself. . . ."

"Ha!" Father got up smiling. "You talk like that, eh? A fine place you'd have, myn diawl i! You to go away and take your mother with you! A fine place you'd have with one whore after the other sharing your bed. . . . And don't you talk of hidings. You'll never beat me. If I am too old to tackle you,

I'll still be your match with the first thing I'll get my hands on. You indeed!" He walked across the kitchen to wind the clock. "I'm going to bed," he announced. "You can all sit and cleck together as much as you like. Think of a good name for the little bastard that's coming!"

He went upstairs in his stockinged feet, and we talked together until the fire went grey and the owls started to call in the trees outside. When I got to bed I could not sleep for thinking of Grett alone in her bed at Rhos Dirion; my whole being cried out for her, not in passion, but in loneliness, in tenderness, and in despair.

Chapter 17

IT WAS a great day in the smithy. Howells had sent word up to us the night before, asking if Justin and I could come down to give Rhys and himself a hand with banding our cart-wheels. Now that Twm had gone away to the mines, they were a bit short-handed for a job like this. Following the night of the banns, the weather had broken and we could spare the time easily. It would not be time for the corn-harvest until the middle or end of the month, though news had come to us that it was in full swing down in the Vale of Towy.

Old Howells had the two fires going so that the heavy band was heated in two places at the same time. From time to time he moved it clockwise so as to heat and expand it all the way round. Howells and Rhys worked their bellows as though they were blowing some church organ. There was quite a crowd present. Eli the Carpenter, Lewsin, and Lloyd Parry were sitting on the bench under the vice. Outside, it was raining hard, the mountains a sour green and half hidden in cloud and mist. The dim interior of the smithy would occasionally be lighted up as the fire spurted, or when the band was moved round.

I stood leaning on the half-door looking out on the land. No one, so far, had said a word to me about the banns. That, perhaps, was because everyone knew how thick Rhys was with

Jeff. I watched the drifts of rain moving up the valley, riding the storm like witches with their grey hair streaming behind them.

The smithy door was one of the parish notice-boards; indeed, the only other was the one inside the church porch; the only difference between them being that the smithy door was plastered with tintacked stud cards and announcements of auctions and sales. It was marked in places also with charred impressions from various branding-irons. Our own "D.P." was prominent in the top left-hand corner.

Outside the smithy, one of Eli's heavy, hand-made cart-wheels was clamped down on the circular, iron tireing-plate. The moment that old Howells and Rhys deemed the iron sufficiently expanded to allow it to fit over the wheel, they would rush out with it, holding it between them with their tongs. Buckets of water stood in readiness nearby, so that immediately the band was hammered down on the wheel, we could at once cool the hot iron and cause it to contract tightly round the wheel.

It was difficult to hear well what was going on in the smithy. There was the steady, throaty roar of the two bellows; while all the time the rain slashed against the walls and drummed on the roof.

Lewsin was telling them something about the time when he had passed by Madame Patti's place in Craig-y-nos and had heard her singing through an open window—"all like gold it was, boys bach"—when the squire came by. He had a sack over his shoulders and another tied like a skirt around his middle and down to his ankles.

"Dear me!" He came in past me and swished the rain off his high-crowned hat. The raindrops hissed as they contacted the hot iron band. "What a day! Good job we haven't started the corn yet. This wind and rain is going to flatten some fields. . . . How many fields have you got, Justin?"

"The two under the road. If we get weather we'll finish them in a week easy."

"Very good, very good. Say, have you people heard the latest?"

"What? Whoa, there, Rhys!" The bellows stopped.

"James Nansharad is leaving."

"Leaving? Where is he going?"

"Where do you think! Why, off to the valleys! Where else?"

"Duw, Duw! James going! I thought he was doing nicely, too."

When is he going?" asked Lewsin.

"Selling up now, clearing out by Mihangel."

So James was going. I didn't wonder at it; he had been on his own ever since he lost his wife a year ago. The squire continued:

"He's going to the Rhondda, to his brother Llew. . . . Thinks he'll do better labouring in the mines."

"Ha! He will have to pay more heed to his pick and shovel there than to his poetry," said Eli.

James was a rare englynwr. He had won one competition after the other in the local eisteddfods. I remembered the evening I had spent with him at Nansharad when he had tried to explain to me the intricate rules governing the consonantal chimes that went to the making of the englyn. And now, here he was, leaving the old place for the valleys. . . . A sadness came over me as I thought of Grett and myself taking the same road out of the parish.

The band was now a dull red all round. Justin threw open the double doors.

"Right, then! Gangway there! Ready, Rhys?"

Howells and Rhys gripped the band with the long tongs, and lifted it clean out of the fires. They carried it horizontally over the anvils and out into the rain.

"Steady now. . . . There she is. . . . Now for the sledge!"

The smell of burning wood filled the air, bitter-sweet and stinging to the nose and eyes. Little flames curled up from the crude felloes while Howells and Rhys went round the wheel hitting at intervals with their sledges. At last, only a thin lip remained to be driven down over the wheel. A heavy blow from Rhys's sledge drove it into position.

"Now the water!"

We all took a bucket each and poured water on the wheel. Dense clouds of acrid steam enveloped us. All the while, Howells tapped the band with his sledge.

Soon afterwards, Howells and Rhys went in to tea, Justin went up to the post office with Lewsin to get some tobacco, Eli and Lloyd Parry walking behind them. The squire sat on the bench filling his pipe and not saying a word.

I leaned over the door looking out at the rain and the mist. I couldn't help thinking of James Nansharad going away to the valleys. I wondered how he was feeling at leaving the parish. In the last week, a deep strange love for the land had grown inside me. I felt I was looking on my last harvest as I walked the fields. Grett, too, had said as much when I had last seen her. The vicar had now called the banns for the second time, and in three weeks' time we would be married.

"What are your plans?" asked the squire suddenly. I turned round quickly; he was lighting his pipe, his eyes peering at me over his lighted match. He had used the second person to me, the subtle "Ti" instead of the more formal "Chi," and my heart warmed to the friendliness of it.

"I'm going away," I said.

He nodded his head, and looked at me from under his wrinkled lowered lids. Then, seeing that my pipe was empty, he offered me his oval, silver tobacco box.

"I think it is slackening," he said, getting up from the bench; "let us go out there under the tree."

The oak offered only little shelter. The leaves were heavy with rain and large drops fell on our shoulders.

"I wanted a word with you," he whispered. "You won't think me a busybody, eh?" His eyebrows shot up as he smiled at me.

"Ask what you like, squire." I remembered his warm handshake on the night of our banns.

"Well, look here," he gripped my arm with his hand. "Do you young people ever think of what is going to become of the parish? People going away from time to time. . . . The place is going down. Think how many have left here in the last year or so?"

I thought of them, one by one: Twm Berthlwyd, Wat Ffynnonoer, Dic Glandŵr, Dai Ynyswen, Twm Blacksmith, Moc about to go, a whole string of others, and now James Nansharad; and in a month or so, Grett and I would be gone. The old man's offer that I should bring her home to Trewern was out of the question.

"You ought to think," said the squire. "What is going to happen to the land do you think? One place after the other going empty. . . . I tell you, it is serious. And is work going to last in the valleys for ever? What about the time when machinery will come to take the place of men, and what if the coal gives out, or if the owners can't get markets for it? Think!"

"But that's impossible, squire!" I protested. "The age is advancing; besides, you can't use machinery without coal. One is a help to the other. . . . Anyway, what is there here for us? Take Grett and myself now. We've got to live, haven't we?"

The squire nodded his head ponderously. The rain, as he had predicted, was clearing off, and the sharp shoulder of the Van came into view, blue and purple with its streaks of red against the ragged lake of rain-washed sky behind it.

"What if you found a place here . . . ?" he suggested quietly. "You are enough of a farmer, aren't you?"

I immediately guessed what he had in mind. Of course Nansharad was his, James was one of his tenants. But the place was too small; Grett and I would half-starve there, and we could never hope to raise a family there.

"Nansharad?" I smiled as I said it.

"Yes, why not? Don't you think you could make a start there?" He was looking me straight in the eye, a little smile playing in the corner of his mouth.

"It's too small," I said. "What is it, those four fields and the wain? Twenty-five acres?"

He pursed his lips. "Twenty-eight, to be exact; but just think——"

"Yes?"

"Well, you know whose land it borders on——?"

"Yes, of course—yours!"

"Well?" He raised his eyebrows at me. "Can't you see?"

My eyes must have told him that I had read his thoughts.

"Right!" he went on quickly: "I am willing to rent you the four fields nearest the river. Four extra fields! Think of it? That will bring the acreage up to over sixty. All right?"

I nodded, too full to speak. The realization that here, within my reach, was a home for Grett and myself was almost too much to bear. Nansharad. . . . Nant Siarad, that was its right name, of course; Nant Siarad—the talking brook! It was well-sheltered, the river ran through it, and with the squire's four extra fields it was an ideal place, as good as any in the parish. I felt I wanted to rush to Rhos Dirion and tell Grett all about it. I shook the squire's hand in silence. Words choked in my throat. The coal-fields faded like an ugly dream from my thoughts.

"Now, not a word to anybody till James leaves. He is going in about a fortnight. There'll be a bit of a sale before he goes— private, if you take it over. You and I can settle the rent later, we won't quarrel over that. Tell your people and Rhos Dirion, of course. But, otherwise, not a word!"

He turned on his heel and went up the road, twirling his walking stick as he went, as if well satisfied with what he had done.

I stood there under the tree trying to gather my thoughts together. I wanted to run and sing. Nansharad . . . Nant Siarad! I repeated the name over and over to myself. Everywhere around me at this moment the clouds were lifting; and there, on the mountainside, the sunlight pushed the shadows before it.

"What's the matter with you?"

I turned at Justin's voice.

"You look as though you'd come into a fortune," he went on.

I winked at him, and fetched him a playful blow in the stomach. He bent double to ride with the blow, and caught me a clip on the ear as I lurched forward.

"Tell you later," I said. "I've had some good news."

It was two hours before we got away. Justin's face lit up when I told him.

"What about Grett?" he asked. "Do you think she'll like it?"

"I'm going down now," I said.

He shook his head.

"Wait!" he said. "See the old man first. No good raising her hopes if the old man won't help. . . . Get it over with him first. . . . You know I'm all right for about fifty, don't you? I'd give you more if I had it, you know that."

. . . . .

Father was in one of his grand moods that night. He was glad to have the cart-wheels before the corn harvest. Mother was as quiet as usual and had supper ready for us when we came in. She gave me many a tender smile these days, and was for ever asking me about Grett, and fretting as to what would become of us.

"Come on, Justin," she called. "You are not shaving to-night are you? Don't say you are going out again!"

The old man got up from the skew and sat at the top of the table. He looked critically at Justin as he came in wiping his face with the rough towel.

"Now don't tell me that you are going out courting to-night," he said. "Don't let's be having another wedding on top of this other!"

He chuckled at his joke and carved the meat for each plate. I looked across at him as he handed me my plate.

"Squire made me an offer to-day," I said.

He looked at me solid for a few seconds, then he proceeded to fill Justin's plate and then mother's.

"What was it?" he asked at length.

"He told me that Nansharad is going. James is going out at Mihangel. There'll be a private sale to the incoming tenant of the stock and the implements if he wants it."

"Well?" His voice gave nothing away.

"He said he'd give me four fields of his to go with it, if I take it."

Justin looked at father.

"It's a good offer," he said. "Plenty of water, sheltered, facing the sun, and the mountain close by for sheep. . . . What'll the acreage be, Ned?"

"Over sixty——"

"And the rent?" Father's mouth was set in a thin line. I could see he was already weighing the expense.

"He didn't say . . . said we wouldn't quarrel about that. . . . About twenty to twenty-five, I'd say."

"Damme! That's fair enough," said Justin.

"What about stock?" said father quietly.

Mother got up from her chair for the teapot and motioned me from behind father's chair to keep quiet. She put her finger to her lips, and then pointed down at father and winked. "Give him time," she lipped.

For a few minutes nothing more was said. I knew from the thin screech of father's knife on his plate that he was battling with himself. Justin, too, was quiet. He went on eating with his head bent over his plate. A coal fell from the fire and mother got up to brush it off the polished fender.

At last, father pushed his chair back. He crossed his legs and played with a lump of bread which he kneaded and crumbled between his fingers.

"I suppose you expect me to help you," he said.

I said nothing.

Justin threw me his tobacco tin.

"You promised you would help him," said mother. "You said as much that night at Rhos Dirion."

"Quiet!" He shut mother up without turning his head. "How much do you expect?" he asked me.

"It's up to you," I said. "I'll pay it back to you, every penny."

"From that bit of land? Never!" He laughed.

"You'll get it all back——"

"Be quiet! How much have you got saved?"

"About sixty to seventy . . . in the bank at Brecon."

He nodded approvingly.

"Seventy, eh? And you've worked about eight or nine years since you left school. . . ."

He took out his note-book and wrote some figures in it.

"I will give you a hundred," he said. "And you can have Doll and a cow or two, and fifty sheep. Will that do you?"

It was more than I had expected. I didn't know how to thank him.

"You'll get it all back," I said, "and interest, too."

"Be quiet," he said. "That is all you will ever get from me, so don't go waiting for me to die. That is your share and no more!"

"I'll give you the Leghorns and the Minorcas," said mother, "they lay beautiful. . . ."

"Don't forget, there's something coming from me, too," added Justin.

"I—I——" I couldn't continue. I saw the white table-cloth, the shining white and gold crockery and the fireplace through the mist of tears. The old man got up and went into the passage for his hat. He came back and looked down at me.

"Don't get sentimental," he warned. "I am doing this to save our face. If John Ellis does as much for that girl of his, you'll be all right. But don't expect anything more from me. Now, when is this wedding coming off?"

"On the twenty-fifth," I said.

"Then you will have to bring the girl here. You can't move into Nansharad until after Mihangel. . . . You can have our room. . . . Oh yes, the breakfast will be here. Food and drink for everybody." He laughed. "We'll show John Ellis how we do things!"

With that he went out and we heard him whistling to himself as he went round the buildings.

"Light up," said Justin. He gave me a wink and one of his open smiles, his eyes shining and his teeth gleaming. Mother wiped her glasses.

"You boys don't understand your father," she said. "He's got his pride, don't forget that!"

Justin changed and was soon away on his cob down to The Pandy. I changed, too, and set off to Rhos Dirion. The night was light and fresh after the rain, and the Allt echoed to my singing as I swung down the puddled road.

Chapter 18

Now that the early nights had come on us, it was like being half in winter and half in summer. By day it was golden, soft, and sad; a lingering tenderness lying on all the land, and the sunsets streaked with gold and bars of fire. Then the evening deepened, and with it the mists rose along the river and half hid the hedges. And when the darkness had come, you could smell the hoar-frost, and the rustle of the wind was a shade higher and sharper in the rusted leaves. There never had been such an autumn in my life. The cornfields were ready for our scythes, their gold already turning dark with ripeness. The skies were clean, and the stars took on a new brilliance, and when the wind rose at nightfall the hedges twanged like harps.

"What did Grett's father say to it?" asked Justin. He was riding the cob a few yards in front of me. I was on Doll, and we were on our way to The Pandy.

"He couldn't believe it. . . . Said we were lucky."

"Did you tell him what the old man is giving you?"

"Aye."

"Well? What's he going to do about it?"

"He hinted that Grett wouldn't come empty-handed."

"Good. . . . Was Jeff there?"

"No. Just as well, too. He might have spoiled everything."

We rode on in silence. As John Ellis had said, it was unbelievable. The only thing that worried me now was that I would no longer have Justin behind me. This was the break I dreaded, but when I thought of Grett's eyes and her body's loveliness, nothing else really mattered. . . . I thought of winter nights by my own fireside, hearing the wind in the trees around our new home like some wild animal not tamed or bridled. I thought of mornings when the frost would hold the earth in its grip of iron; I saw the seasons coming and going, and Grett and myself living in a world bounded by our hedges.

Justin hadn't changed this evening, he was still in his rib breeches and greased leggings. He had broken the stem of his pipe and was smoking the butt of it so that the bowl was under the tip of his nose. The cob was restive under him and shied across the road from time to time. It seemed he could do nothing with her. He had kept her in the stable for the last two days with the bit chained up as tight as it would go so that the flesh of her mouth was as raw and tender as a steak. Justin swore and brought his ashplant down on her head as she shied again. She reared, and then set off at a half-gallop and canter.

Down past Graig Ddu we went, along the road by the river, over the narrow bridge, and up the quiet stretch leading to The Pandy.

There was quite a crowd in The Pandy. Moc was in great fettle, and as soon as we came in, he and Justin started calling the rounds. The two girls joined in the fun, too. Sal was at the piano; and Justin, Moc, and the Gwynfe boys were letting their voices go in style. I went outside after a while. My head was like a wheel, and my temples had gone dead, a sure sign that I had had quite enough.

It was a grand, wonderful night. You could smell the first white-frost in the air. The big leaves of the sycamores behind the house were like blobs of pitch against the white-washed walls. The sky was alive with stars; the Plough standing out among all the others, and Orion glittering among the hundreds whose names I did not know. I stayed outside some time; and after I had been sick, I felt my head clear and I was quite ready to go back inside and join the others.

While I was in the wash-house rinsing my mouth and making sure that my coat and waistcoat were clean, I heard horses trotting up the road. They stopped outside the house. Even before I heard Iori's voice, I knew in my bones that it was Jeff and his crowd; and I knew, too, that there would be trouble before the night was out. I felt no misgiving at all; with Justin, Moc, and the Gwynfe boys, we were quite a match for them all.

The singing did not stop when they entered the bar. I imagined Jeff's face waiting for Sal or her sister to leave the singers and draw his beer for him. Moc was singing now. I smiled as I listened to him. Moc had the strangest voice I had ever heard. Looking at his great bull neck and barrel of a chest, you would have thought that he would be at home somewhere down in the region of double C. But there it was, he had a high, thin tenor; and when he sang falsetto, it was like a boy's voice that hadn't broken. He was sentimental, too. It was nothing unusual to see Moc with the tears running down his face in a Gymanfa, especially when the conductor would pull out the altos with a wave of his hand or give a nod to the heavy bassers when they had to rise an octave.

Justin had his back to Jeff and his crowd, and he gave me a wicked wink as I came in. I looked over at Jeff, ready to give him a nod, but he turned his back on me, and Lloyd Parry and Rhys Blacksmith rapped again with their coins on the counter.

Before Sal got up from the piano to go to the bar, Justin bent her right back and kissed her. She gave him an open-hander on his ear and he slapped her buttock as she flounced away laughing.

"How about riding over to Brynamman to make a night of it?" said Moc. "I've got to get over there to-night. Come along!"

Justin looked at me. I shook my head. I didn't mind making a night of it here in The Pandy, but to go over the mountain was a different matter. I didn't want Jeff to think I was on the spree either. Not that Grett would mind, even if he did tell her; but, somehow or other, it didn't seem fair to me that I should be having a wild, free time of it while she was kept just like a prisoner at home.

"No, I must get home," I said.

Justin looked at me and nodded his head understandingly.

"Not to-night, Moc," he said. Moc started to button up his coat. He jerked his head in Jeff's direction and looked inquiringly at Justin. Justin shook his head.

"Right, then," said Moc. "I'll see you at the wedding, then."

Jeff coloured up and put his glass to his lips.

"Wedding?" cried Sal. She came back to the piano and looked from one face to the other. "What wedding?"

Moc nodded in my direction.

"Edwin here."

"And who is the lucky girl?" asked Sal. She was full of the devil, and her sister nudged her to keep quiet.

Moc grinned over at Jeff.

"Ask him," he said to Sal. "He knows all about it."

Jeff put his glass down and came over to us. He looked down at Moc.

"There's no need for that, Moc Morgans. I don't want Grett's name talked here."

"Her name won't be talked here, Jeff," I said. "I'll see to that."

"You!" He looked me up and down. "To think it's you," he muttered.

Moc was still grinning at Jeff, his long arms hanging loosely at his side, and his eyes half-closed.

"Well, come on!" shouted Sal. "Why don't you all have a glass? Who is going to call drinks to the bridegroom?"

"All drinks on me," cried Justin.

He looked mockingly at Jeff.

"Will you drink?"

"Cer i ddiawl!" said Jeff. "I wouldn't drink with you or that crot if I was in a desert. To hell with you!"

"Ha! Must break your heart to refuse something for nothing," said Justin. "How about you, boys? You, Iori, Rhys, Parry, are you coming in?"

They reddened and looked at Jeff. Jeff shrugged his shoulders as if not caring what they did. But Justin suddenly roared out:

"No guts! Just a lot of sheep—wethers, too, myn diawl i! . . . Looking at Jeff indeed! Not a bloody drink at my expense for such a set!" He turned to Sal: "Fill up for everybody but this lot!" He flung a filthy word at them which Sal and her sister pretended not to hear.

They drank to me, not mentioning Grett's name, while Jeff stood with his back to us, the nape of his neck flushed red under his curling black hair.

A few minutes later, Moc left us. Then, as time went on, the Gwynfe boys left us, and soon there were left only Justin, myself, and Jeff and his crowd.

Sal was now behind the bar, her sister had gone into the kitchen, and we could hear her getting the supper ready. Sal flashed her smile from one of us to the other, her glance lingering a shade longer with Justin as he joked bawdily with her, regardless of who was listening.

We still drank steadily. I had reached the stage where each fresh glass made no difference to me. I felt I was watching myself; I was outside myself. It was well after ten when Jeff got up to leave. He drained his glass and motioned the others to finish. Then, without a glance at either Justin or myself, they left the bar.

Sal sniffed as the door closed behind them.

"I'm sorry you are marrying into that trash," she said. "That Jeff Ellis is a crunchy one! I hope his sister is different."

"Don't worry," laughed Justin. "She's a real girl; the pick of the bunch, isn't she, Ned?"

So we talked. I was a bit afraid that Justin would hang about so as to have some minutes alone with Sal. I saw them whispering together and Sal shook her head, glancing in my direction and averting her eyes. Justin did not press the question, and after another glass each, we left Sal and went out through the back door into the stable.

Soon, we were on the road, going along at a steady jogging pace. Being heavy in drink, I had the feeling that I was half-off the earth. My brain was like a whirlpool, and fragments of poetry came into my mind, only to be lost as soon as their beauty struck me.

We had gone about half a mile down the road when Justin's cob shied. I peered ahead as I heard Justin curse. There, blocking our road, was a low gambo, the shafts resting high on the hedge-bank.

We got off and started to move the gambo away. And then, suddenly, I saw Jeff and the three others. They were standing behind the cart. Before I could say or do anything, Justin was up to Rhys Blacksmith and was holding him by the throat.

"Want some fun, is it?" He swung his fist into Rhys's face and the next instant we were all in a free fight.

I found myself measuring up to Iori. Whether or no it was the beer in me, I don't know, but I felt full of confidence. And although Justin and I were opposed to Jeff and his crowd, I felt that I must win so as to acquit myself well in Jeff's eyes.

Iori had no science, and I knew before he struck a blow that he could not hurt me. He swung his wide haymakers at me and all I had to do was to jab my left in his face as I had seen Dai Probert do to Justin on that night in Brecon. True, he caught me a few times, but I felt nothing. I let him swing at me until he was blowing, and then I went for him; left, right; left, right; and when he crouched and tried to save his face with his hands, I hit him in the pit of the stomach with all the strength of my right. He fell forward and I looked round to see how Justin was getting on. Rhys Blacksmith was already out of it and Lloyd Parry was squaring up. Jeff, so far, had not taken part in the fight. I walked up to him.

"What about it?" I said. "Here's your chance, Jeff. You've been wanting to take it out of me ever since I started with Grett. Put your hands up!"

He brushed me aside with his arm and went up to Lloyd Parry and Justin. Justin had Lloyd pinned against the wheel of the gambo, his arm drawn back ready to strike.

"All right, Peele. Stop it!"

Jeff held Justin's arm, and Lloyd sank down on the floor.

"Diawl! So you want it, do you?" cried Justin.

"Steady on," said Jeff. He had made no attempt to put up his hands. Justin lowered his fists.

"Afraid, eh? I wouldn't have thought it of you, Ellis. Damme, you've been working up to this for months!"

Jeff took off his coat and rolled up his sleeves.

"Just to show you that I'm ready," he said. "But just listen to me first."

"What is it? Not feeling well?"

"Listen! We can have it out after. . . . You first or young Edwin——"

"Go on, then. What is it?"

"Just this. We were just having a joke, no hiding intended. Diawl! Do you think I would have stood by if we'd wanted to give you both a hiding? . . . Do you think we would have fought you one by one? No! You're wrong, Peele. You started on Rhys before we could say anything. . . . But if you still want to carry on—I'm ready for you."

Justin looked across at me.

"Leave it," I said. I was glad. The thought that a brother of Grett should try and set on us with three others had soured my inside. Justin turned to Iori who was now on his feet.

"Is it true what he says!"

"Drop dead it is. . . . Uffern! The four of us together would have killed you!"

"Right you are, I'm satisfied," said Justin. His nose was bleeding and he blew it violently in the hedge. "Of course," he turned round to Jeff: "if you still feel like a scrap, it's up to you."

Jeff shook his head.

"You hit first," he said. "Then I'll fight. . . ."

"Go in Jeff," shouted Iori. "Let's give them a hiding together."

"Shut up!" Jeff turned his back on him. "A fine show you put up, anyway!" He looked across at me: "You shaped well," he said. "Let's hope you'll stand up like that whenever you hear Grett's name mentioned in a pub again. . . ."

My heart suddenly warmed to him. He started rolling down his sleeves.

"Is it like that?" I said. I put out my hand.

"No shaking," he said. "Not with you!"

He turned to Iori and the others; Rhys Blacksmith was in a bad shape. There was a swelling over his eye like a duck's egg.

"Come on, boys; home!"

Jeff jumped on his pony and then wheeled her back to where we stood.

"Don't get thinking I won't fight," he said. "It will come sooner or later. . . ."

"Any time," said Justin. "Better hurry up, though. . . . We'll be related before the month is out."

"That won't matter . . . being related hasn't stopped you and your old man from scrapping!"

Jeff laughed, and the four of them rode down the road.

"Push the gambo back in the field," he shouted back to us, and they turned the bend of the road.

Justin was all for leaving the gambo in the road, and he cursed without stopping while I got in the shafts and he had to push behind.

"Don't worry," I said. "We gave them a shaking, didn't we?"

"Aye. You put Iori down in style. I'll have to watch out for you."

I was tingling with pride and satisfaction as we rode home. The side of my face was beginning to hurt where Iori had caught me, but I knew now that I would have no more trouble from him or from Rhys and the others. Jeff, I didn't mind; I felt deep inside me that he and I would never come to blows. What would happen between Justin and him was none of my business.

We got home just on midnight, and when I looked at my face

in the glass, I saw that the left side of my face was bruised and swollen. I hoped it would not be gone when I went to Rhos Dirion the following night. I was proud of my scars, and I had the feeling that Grett would not be displeased with them either. I fell asleep at once, and when I awoke next morning I wondered for a moment why it was that my stomach was upset and my face and arms stiff with pain. Then I remembered, and smiled to myself; and lay there until the old man started bellowing at us to get up.

Chapter 19

BEFORE the week was out I had settled with James for his hay, stock and implements. He gave me a sovereign back for luck, and the squire let me have the farm for a rent of twenty-six pounds a year. The squire also helped me by taking over the fowls and the two cows until Grett and I could move in.

I drove down to Rhos Dirion that same evening. John Ellis was in the yard as I came up. He gave me a quiet nod and waited for me to speak.

"I thought Grett and I could go up and see Nansharad."

"Is it right that James has moved out to-day?" he asked.

"He's gone," I said. "The place is ours as soon as we like. . . . The house will want doing out first, of course."

John Ellis nodded, then he noticed my swollen face and black eye. He came up to me.

"A nasty, dirty business," he said. "I didn't want anything like that. Who started it?"

"There was fault both sides," I began.

"Yes, yes, I know. But Jeff says they didn't mean anything. . . . I don't think they were out for trouble. You know how it is when your Justin and he get together."

"Don't worry," I said. "It had to come to a head. The air'll be clearer now!"

He smiled and smoothed Doll's neck.

"You are all right, Edwin," he said. "And I don't think you will get any trouble from Jeff after this. . . . If only your father and Justin were a bit wiser. . . . Ah, well, it is your life and Grett's now. . . . Grett!" He turned and called her name.

She came out of the cowhouse, her apron tight around her waist and a strand of hair falling over her eyes.

"Edwin wants you to go up to have a look at Nansharad with him. How far are you off finishing?"

"There is only Bron to do."

"Right. You go and change, I'll manage her all right."

While Grett was changing I went down to the river. The water was wild and lissom, blue-veined and green-shaded, and each stone changed its glassy course. I knelt down on the bank and played ducks and drakes with the flat stones. One that I threw, rose seven times off the surface of the water, and each fleck of spray that followed it was a shimmer of kingfisher blue against the sun. I looked up and saw Grett's mother standing by me. She was a little shy, and I had a feeling that she was worried.

"You are not worrying about Grett, are you?"

"As long as she is happy, I don't care much," she said.

"Then what is it?"

She looked past me, her eyes narrowing a little with age at the corners.

"It's your father I am afraid of," she said. "I want Grett to be able to go to your new home as soon as the wedding is over."

She came a step nearer to me and put her hand on my arm.

"Get it all ready now," she begged me. "Get what furniture you can. I'll give her all the linen she needs and some odd pieces. I want her to go straight to her new home . . . that is, unless you are thinking of going away for a honeymoon."

A honeymoon! I hadn't thought of it. I mentioned it to Grett as we drove up through the village. Lewsin waved to us from his gate and Dili's father gave us a greeting as we passed him on the road. Grett was bareheaded, dressed in her blouse and skirt. She had folded her coat over the back of the seat and I could see the lovely shape of her long thighs and legs as she stretched out and crossed her feet against the dashboard.

"Honeymoon?" Grett's eyes opened in surprise. "Do you want to go away?"

"What about you?"

She shook her head.

"I don't like the idea," she said. "Everybody knowing we are going away just to sleep together for the first time; you and me pretending to be old hands at being married, and spending our time throwing sand in people's eyes. What do you think?"

"As long as we are together, I don't care where."

"What about the old mill at Brecon then?" She was laughing, her eyes dark with mischief.

"Grand," I said, "but what about breakfast?"

We both laughed, and I saw her again half undressed in the green gloom of that afternoon in the mill.

"But serious now," she said, trying not to smile, "I hope we'll be able to go straight to our new home. . . . Think of it, driving up there in the trap that evening or walking up along the river; going home for the first time."

As we turned the bend of the steep lane leading down to the house, we saw the white-washed walls and the thatched roof. A small uncurtained window looked out on the road, and though the sun was slanting on it now and touched the white walls with a tinge of pink, I saw the window shining with candle-light as it would after a journey home on a winter's night.

We drove into the yard without a word, too full to speak. The ash in front of the house was still in leaf with only a splash of red or gold here and there. We sat for some minutes drinking it all in, Grett with her hand in mine. There was a brooding stillness everywhere, holy and quiet as a sabbath, for there were no chickens, dogs or any cattle about. And then I heard the tinkle and cluck of the river going by the barn. It endeared me to the place at once. I jumped down from the trap and caught Grett in my arms as she groped for the step with her foot.

The door of the house was on the latch, and hand in hand we entered the kitchen. The flagstones were blue and about six by three and I imagined their dock-leaf coolness on a July afternoon. The wallpaper was faded and showed where the pictures, the dresser and the clock had been. A low shelf suspended from the ceiling went right across the room and I saw my books there: Trebor Mai, Dafydd ap Gwilym, Myddygon Myddfai, Vicar Pritchard's *Canwyll y Cymru,* and Edward Richard and

Ieuan Brydydd Hir—there was room there for them all. Grett's eyes were shining with happiness as she started to plan her arrangements for the room.

"We'll have the table here—yes?"

I saw mother's long scrubbed table against the window; and there across the cwm outside I saw the mountain Fôl rising beyond it, and on it a solitary twisted thorn tree. The setting sun now shone on it and the fern and heather were a glory of rust and purple. The thorn tree enchanted me. I saw the moon coming up like a platter behind the sweep of the Fôl, and the fingers of the thorn wild and black against it.

There was only one big room downstairs and the dairy adjoining it. The upstairs was musty with the smell of the thatch, but as soon as I opened the window, the fresh mountain air poured into it like flowing well-water.

It was almost dark by the time we had been round the farm. The lie of the land sloped down to the river and had the advantage of facing the morning sun. The well was down by the river, just beyond the hand-railed foot-bridge that crossed over to the squire's fields. We took the winding, root-fibred path down to it, and the dusk was like velvet on the shadowed basin of each pool. In the half-light, the well was like an arc of silver where the water spouted out from the rock. I folded a hazel leaf for Grett. The water was icy, colder even than our well at home, and though it had not the mossy, earth taste of our water there was a sweetness in it that must have come from the heart of the rock itself.

We walked arm-in-arm back up the winding path and saw the roofs of the barn and the house standing black against the sky. The whole place was already familiar to me and I felt that it breathed the very spirit of home to us.

"You like it?" Grett was all smiles, as proud as a pullet. I saw how she looked around, no doubt seeing her washing flapping on the clothes-line, hearing the flip-flop of the butter in the churn. . . .

We stayed there in the yard until the first stars came out. Whether it was my fancy or no, the stars up here were more large and silvery than down with us, but that perhaps was because we were much higher up here; you could tell that from the thinness of the night air alone.

I lighted the trap lamps and let Doll pick her way as leisurely as she liked to Rhos Dirion.

Grett's father and mother asked me in to have supper, but as it was getting on, I said I would have to be going. Before I got back into the trap Mrs. Ellis came up to me and whispered:

"Do you have owls around Trewern?"

"Owls?" I echoed. Then, instantly, I remembered how I had called Grett out at night by shouting "Gw-di-hw" into my cupped hands.

"I—I think so. . . . Come to think of it, yes."

"Hm!" Her face dimpled in the light from the trap lamps. "We had them here terrible, night after night. . . . Did you hear them, Grett?"

"I don't take any notice of them," said Grett.

Her mother laughed. "Owls, indeed! Thank goodness, they won't disturb us any more!"

I smiled to myself as I drove up the lane. I was beginning to see where Grett got her sense of humour from. Little wonder, indeed, that John Ellis had had to hurry his wedding.

.   .   .   .   .

For the next few days we were busy carting furniture up to Nansharad. Mother gave me the old coffer from the parlour and all the furniture from my bedroom. Justin went to Llandovery and bought us a dresser, second-hand, with all the jugs and plates to go with it. The squire sent us a complete dinner-service, and Moc sent us a warming-pan, "for when you are old," he put in his letter. Father regarded all the proceedings with a half-smile. Mother went up to Nansharad with Grett and Mrs. Ellis, and together they did the white-washing and the papering. She said it was already beginning to look like home. Meanwhile, I got a cartful of odd things that were lying about the place and took them up one evening: a bake-stone, two milking-stools, some pictures including one of "The Last Supper" which I had grown up with; then a bellows, a copper kettle, some brass candle-sticks, a small grindstone, and a host of other things which Justin said the old man would never miss. So the days went by, and I thought with glee of those who were already counting the months on their fingers, thankful in my heart that for a while, at least, they would be doomed to disappointment. But one disappointment awaited Grett and me; try and hurry as we did, we realized that we could not possibly move into our home until a week or so after the wedding.

Chapter 20

I AWOKE at once and knew immediately what the day held for me. A flush of lovely green stained the sky over the Van Rocks. I watched it as it flushed to gold and then to rose, and with each minute the rocks took on colour and presently the mists drifted away from the mountain sweeping up below them; there was the hump of Mynydd Llan, and a skein of blueish-grey mist showed the course of the Sawdde. At last, a flood of gold threw the Vans into sharper relief and the walls of my room caught the first beams of the day. Although I had not fallen asleep until I had heard two, three, and half-past three strike, I felt quite fresh.

I looked at my watch and saw that it was only just after five, and as much as I would have liked to get up, I dared not do so for fear of disturbing the others. Mother had a hard day before her. The women would be along after milking to help with the breakfast.

I lay there thinking of Grett, wondering if she were already awake. I saw her dressing, going to church, coming in through the door to where I was waiting for her in front of the altar. . . . I must have fallen asleep again at this, for when I opened my eyes the sun was high and every leaf outside was dazzling with the dew. I jumped out of bed at once. The rest of the family was downstairs. I could hear the steady hum and drone of the separator and Justin singing to himself in time to it. I slipped into my everyday trousers and pulled on my working boots. Not until the last minute would I change into my Sunday best or risk splashing my brown boots with lather or washing water.

Mother was getting our breakfast ready. It was laid this morning on the small round table in the back-kitchen. The best kitchen was already set out for the wedding breakfast. Mother had taken down and washed the dresser the night before, and everything was shining and glistening.

"Hurry now," said mother. "You should have been up an hour ago. . . . Did you sleep all right?" She smiled shyly and came and kissed me. Usually so undemonstrative in her affections, she blushed and smoothed her apron self-consciously. It was years since she had kissed me. No doubt it was fear of father's contempt for sentimentality that made us all more or less reserved in our dealings with one another.

"I hardly slept at all," I said.

She looked critically at me.

"A bit pale you are," she said. "But you'll be all right after a good wash and shave. Hold your face in cold water for a while."

"I'm going in the river after breakfast."

"After breakfast! Not you! It's the worst thing you could do."

"What's that?" Father stood in the doorway, his cheeks a wabbling of lather. He held his hollow-ground in his hand.

"Edwin wants to go down to the river after breakfast."

"Nonsense! You go now. . . . Off with you or, damme me, you will have to spend your wedding-night in bed with your mother's shawl round your head and some hot plates against your stomach. Go on, now—a quick dip, and don't be long!"

I passed Justin in the dairy. His hair was tousled, and the stubble on his chin was blue and had bits of towel or blanket clinging to it.

"Coming for a twc?" I shouted.

"Right. Got a rough towel? I'm like a pig. . . . A good job I'm not sleeping with anyone!"

We ran down across the fields to the Lyswen. The dew was dark on the fields, and the sun was golden and warm as it streamed just over the brambly crests of the hedges. I saw the horizontal birches that I had ridden when I was a boy, gripping the smooth, silvered bark with my corduroyed knees and riding, riding to the swaying motion of the pliant, bending branch. . . .

The sun came through the trees and played like the hair of some woman on the floor of the pool. The water was brown, velvet-smooth, with one large foam-cake revolving slowly in the corner away from the cascade that poured into it.

Justin was soon undressed. He touched the water with his foot.

"Duw!" He swore and withdrew his toes as if he had touched liquid fire. "You go in first."

He looked me over with a grin.

"You don't shape so bad," was his comment. "By the time you fill out you'll be a tidy lump"—he grinned again—"that's if Grett won't kill you."

I gave him a push. He staggered, threw up his arms to recover his balance and, with a "Dammo di" went in head first. He came up red and blowing. I dived in after him, and with the first stinging shock of contact with the water, all the tiredness left my body. I rose to the surface a new being. The blood ran like fire through my veins. Justin was a yard or two ahead of me, floating on his back, his legs threshing the water like white flails. Ten minutes later, we were back in the house, our bodies glowing from the flannelling and scrubbing with red carbolic and the cold running water. I combed my hair before it dried so that the parting would stay. It was almost corn-coloured from the bleaching it had taken from the sun throughout the summer. I brushed it hard until it lay smooth and shiny on my head.

Father and mother had already started breakfast. Father's cheeks were as smooth and brown as saddle leather.

"Who is giving her away?" he asked.

"Her uncle from Trecastle, I think."

Father frowned.

"So John Ellis won't be there, eh?"

I told him that they would all be there.

"I hope they keep quiet. . . . What do you think, Justin?"

"They can do what they like," said Justin. "This is our day, and if anybody wants trouble, well"—he shrugged his shoulders—"Moc'll be there and our cousins from Cwmwysg——"

"Ho! So they are coming!"

"Don't worry," I said. "I don't think there'll be any randy-boo. We settled all that the other night."

Mother looked at us with some alarm.

"You are not looking for any trouble to-day, surely? It would be a terrible disgrace. But the vicar would never allow it!"

Father laughed.

"They can do what they like. But don't you worry. Roberts the Police is coming up; I saw him at the Mart last week." He looked up at the clock. "Now, come on. We must be away from here at ten. You, Edwin and Justin, in the flat cart. Your mother and me will go in the trap. Remember now, down through the village, then the top road by the Tavarn so as not to clash with the Ellises on the way."

Mati Rees, Gwen Tŷgwyn, and the other helpers had arrived by now, and what with the preparations for the reception, getting the horses groomed and dressing ourselves, we were all on top of one another. I felt empty inside and my legs were trembling under me; and in spite of it all, the old clock ticked unhurriedly and chimed the hour and half-hour with all the leisure in the world.

I turned to have a last look at the old place as Justin and I drove out of the yard. The morning sun struck full on the front of the house. The sycamore threw its large-leafed shadows over the flagstones and the cropped green in front of the parlour window; and as I sat there in the cart while Justin got down to close the yard gate, I felt a great love well up inside me. In a way I was saying good-bye to something, though in every splash of sunlight and behind every blue shadow there trembled the half-glimpsed impression of Grett's face. And it was back here for a week or a fortnight that I was bringing my bride. Grett Ellis was coming home to us, the Peeles of Trewern; and to-night, in each other's arms, we would hear together the sounds of the night in the sycamore; and the cries of the owls down in the Allt would arouse us to our love, and for once the dawn would be too sudden over the Van Rocks.

"Come on!" Justin jumped up beside me and gave Doll the end of the whip. "We've got over an hour, and if we take it quiet, we'll arrive spick-and-span with no sweat or dust on us."

I noticed every tree, every flower, every blade of grass that morning. The dew was webbed on the bramble bushes, and the blackberries were blue and shiny. Justin was starched and brushed up to his ears. He had done his best to curl the brim of his bowler back into shape. It had never been the same since the night he had fallen off the cob. Despite his efforts, it still gave him a rakish, shonny-like air, the brim coming down flatter than it should over his left temple. We both had a red clove in our buttonholes and our shirt cuffs were like snow around our red wrists.

We waited some minutes below the Allt so that father and mother could lead the way into the village. It was not long before we heard the crunch of the wheels coming down the red road. Father and mother sat stiffly side by side. Mother was in a black silk dress and wore a hat trimmed with a thin white band around it. Her lace gloves came up over her wrists, and she carried a large bunch of late roses, carnations and chrysanthemums in her lap. As was customary with father, he was carefully dressed and well-groomed. There wasn't a speck of dust or dandruff on the shoulders of his square-shouldered black coat. His collar was snow-white (mother had ironed all our collars and cuffs the night before and had strung them along the brass rod underneath the mantelpiece until the morning) and his large black stock with its gold horseshoe served only to accentuate its glazed whiteness and the smooth texture of his chin above it. The trap gleamed in the sun, the yellow spokes of the wheels and the shining brass on the harness caught the beams that slanted through the hedge. Suspended by its curved handle over the back of the seat was his silver-mounted walking-stick. Daniel Peele of Trewern was going to his son's wedding in style anyway!

Everyone was out in the village to meet us. Waiting at the cross-roads were Lewsin, Elias the Carpenter and old Howells. We adjusted the seat for them to ride behind father and mother.

Then, as we set off again, I nearly jumped out of my skin as a volley of fowling-pieces sounded from behind the hedge. So I was having a good send-off from the village. Everyone who had a gun was carrying it; and there, stretched across the road, was the rope to impede our progress to church. Father nodded his approval at this: it was part of the traditional ritual of the par-

ish. Justin and I had to unhitch the rope and it was some minutes before we were on our way again. But for all the fun, how
different this was from the weddings of twenty or thirty years
before. First, in those days, came the bridal party in twos,
forty or fifty couples wending their way to the church. The
bridegroom then had to call for the bride at her home, usually
to find that she had been hidden or abducted by his friends before his arrival. Then followed the search for her, and before
he could claim her release he would first have to recite the ap-
propriate verses set for the occasion. But that was all finished
with now, the times were changing; and apart from the oldest
in the parish, there was hardly anyone who could recite the
"Penillion Pen-drws" as they were called. Nevertheless, we
still had the ropes strung across the road and the volleys of
fowling-pieces to salute us.

Before we got to Tavarn-y-gwynt, the squire and his family
came up behind us and fell into line. The squire's wife had her
parasol over her head, and squire himself was in his light greys
and sable bowler.

From time to time I kept thinking of Grett's family. Would
they dare at the last minute to keep Grett from coming and
make us the laughing-stock of the parish?

"Don't worry," Justin assured me. "They wouldn't dare.
And, remember, for all they know—they've only got Grett's
word for it—she might be in the family way. They daren't risk
it, Ned."

There were a score or more traps outside the church when we
came up. Justin tapped out his pipe on his heel.

"A good crowd," he said. "There's Moc over there. Duw
Mawr! Look at that white chrysanthemum he's wearing! And
there's Llew and Dic from Brynamman. . . . Don't forget,
Ned, we are all with you!"

I followed Justin through the kissing-gates and into the
porch. There were smiles everywhere for me. I had one look
round before going in. Then, with the eternal blue of the Van
Rocks and the dazzle of the sun for ever imprinted on my eyes,
I followed Justin up the shadowy aisle.

The sun streamed through the stained glass, and the altar-
cloth seemed woven of divine blue, red, and gold, and other

half-tones. Vases of flowers had been placed in the windows. Anne Lewis was in her seat at the organ, and I could hear people walking into the church behind me.

Justin gave me a nudge as father, mother, the squire and his family, Lewsin and others came up to the front pews. I waited in a cold sweat for Grett to come in. I turned my head and saw that the church was packed. There was Allt-y-brain, the whole family of Berthlwyd, Dili with her baby and Albert; Talsarn, Ffynnonoer, Pantglas, Brynmair—they were all there; and back by the door were Moc, Iori, Rhys Blacksmith and the rest of them. Through the cool gloom of the porch I saw the Vans framed in the pointed stonework of the arch.

Justin took out his watch and showed me the time. It was not quite eleven. I could hear the whispering behind me, and a bird outside sang as if it hadn't a care in the world. My legs trembled, and every now and again I had to wipe the palms of my hands. Then, suddenly but quietly, here was the vicar with his white surplice freshly washed and ironed for the occasion, and with his book in his hand, coming up to the altar. He gave a nod to Anne Lewis, and as she started to play the congregation rose to its feet.

I stood up, Justin beside me, and saw Grett coming up the aisle on her father's arm. Behind them came her mother and Jeff. All I saw in that moment was that Grett was in a white frock and that she carried a mass of flowers in her hands. The whole family sat in the stalls facing father and mother. The vicar waited until the organ stopped, then he beckoned me out to the aisle. It was then that I saw Grett face to face. She was a little pale, her dark hair just showing under the large brim of her yellow hat. Where or when she had bought her white frock and hat, I had no idea; all I knew was that I had never seen her so lovely. Her eyes held me for a moment and I was suddenly aware that all the nervousness had left me.

Together we knelt on the red carpet in front of the altar. I tried hard to photograph everything around me on my mind. Yet, try as I would, it was only the small, insignificant things that I saw: the flannel sleeves of the vicar protruding under his coat-sleeves giving the lie to his white collar and surplice; the gold candle-sticks flashing where the sun caught their bevelled edges. . . . Then there was a shuffling of feet as some latecomer pushed into a pew, someone coughed, and a fly buzzed against the closed window.

The minutes passed. I heard myself repeating the words after the vicar, a note of exultation creeping into my voice. Then Grett's voice came to me, and I was proud that the whole parish was there to hear the words she said. The vicar gave us every help, whispering to each of us as our turn came to repeat after him. In answer to his question as to who was giving Grett away, a silence fell on us all as John Ellis stepped forward and gave her to me. Then followed my avowed troth to Grett Ellis, and as I heard her say that she, Margaretta Anne, did take me to be her husband, I fought hard with myself to restrain the happy sob that rose in my throat, and only its mist touched my eyes. I felt Grett tremble a little and put my arm round her to give her strength.

Justin was ready with the ring, and as I placed it on Grett's finger her eyes held me with all the passion and courage that was in her nature.

There remained only the prayers and the terrible injunction that none should ever attempt to sunder what God had joined together. And now followed the "Deus Miseratur" sung, as usual, to Poole's chant.

There had not been such chanting in the church since the Esgob came to consecrate the west window. The singing was heavy, like a great organ. Many of the chapel people were present and I doubt if there had ever been such bass in the old church before. By my side, Justin's voice caught with Dico Lewis's, and many a melting alto laid its burden of lovely sadness on my heart. Lewsin the Post had no call to-day to swing his book to keep the tempo.

The service over, the vicar led the way to the vestry. I did not kiss Grett, knowing that she did not expect me to do so in front of such a large crowd. Mother, however, put her arms around her and kissed her cheek; father shook hands with her. The Ellises did nothing. Mrs. Ellis stood behind Jeff and her husband, crying quietly into her handkerchief.

The vicar made the entry in the church register in his beautiful small hand, and then handed the pen to Grett and to myself.

He looked at father.

"You'll witness it, Daniel Peele, just there. Put your name there."

Father examined the broad relief critically and removed a minute hair from it. That done, he wrote his name carefully in his copperplate.

There was a half-challenge in the vicar's voice as he turned to John Ellis:

"Now, John Ellis, you sign here!"

Grett's father took the pen and wrote his name under father's, looping his signature underneath with a flowing line and two little circles which he dotted carefully.

As we walked down the aisle, Anne Lewis played something that was light and gay in six-eight time. Behind Grett and myself came father and mother, John Ellis and Mrs. Ellis, with Justin, Jeff, the vicar and others behind them. A stinging hail of rice met us as we came out of the porch into the sunshine. Moc had got hold of the bell rope, and was in his shirt-sleeves pulling and bending for all he was worth.

The people crowded around us. The squire shook my hand and then took off his hat and kissed Grett on her cheek.

"Good luck! Good luck!" he repeated over and over. Then he chuckled and whispered in my ear. "You have beaten them all, well done!"

Many jokes were levelled at us. Lloyd Parry shouted out that I was pale enough already; Berthlwyd told me to remember that the corn harvest was still to come and put his hand on the small of his back to illustrate his meaning. Grett took all this in good part. She was wise enough not to show any false prudery in front of them, and only when the jokes became a little too broad did she bend her head, raise a protesting hand, and turn aside.

We stood in a half-circle outside the porch waiting for father to give the word to start off. The old man beamed at everyone. He gave the impression that he was the proudest man there.

"Now, vicar," he said jocularly, "off with that surplice and into your coat and hat!" He turned to the crowd: "A welcome to you all at Trewern! Plenty of food and drink for everyone."

So far Grett's father and his family had not addressed a word to me or Grett. Mrs. Ellis was still crying. Jeff stood by her holding his bowler in his hand. Father crossed over to John Ellis. I saw John Ellis shake his head stubbornly.

"But you must," insisted father. The talking and laughter around us ceased abruptly. Father went on: "You, Mrs. Ellis, and Jeff must come. I won't take no!"

John Ellis looked across at Grett. Then a smile broke on his face and he came over to us and took her arm.

"Well, well! So you are Mrs. Peele now!" He turned to me. "Be good to her," he said quietly. "She's got courage. I wish you well!" He turned to Mrs. Ellis:

"Come on, Mary; and you, Jeff, get the trap ready. We'll go to the breakfast."

Before Jeff could say a word, the squire came forward. "Wait!" he said, bowing to Grett and me, "I want you, Edwin, and your wife"—a thrill went through me at his words, and I felt Grett's arm give mine a little squeeze—"I want you to ride in our carriage. Justin Peele shall drive, and Jeff Ellis is to sit next to him. Then Mr. and Mrs. Ellis in their trap; then Mr. and Mrs. Peele. . . . The vicar and the rest of us will follow how we can."

There was no gainsaying the squire, and Justin and Jeff got up on the front seat. I helped Grett into the carriage and for a second her lifted skirt showed the fine line of her leg and ankle. Justin settled his bowler a little on one side and held the whip in readiness to give the two chestnuts a starting flick.

"Right!" shouted father from behind. "Trewern next stop!"

Justin touched the horses, and with the touch of the whip and the shooting that went on around us, the two horses reared, and off we went.

"Dampo!" Justin swore as he put his feet against the dashboard and held the horses in. "The old squire's put a beauty across us, eh?"

Jeff turned round in his seat and gave Grett a smile. I smiled at him, but instead of returning my smile he gave me a slow, heavy wink and a side nod of his head. Grett half stifled a laugh and pressed close against me.

What a journey it was down the breast of the hill to the river and up to the village! Behind us came the traps and the singing of the hymns and old folk-songs. This was something I had never dreamed of—this participation of the parish in my wedding.

At last, the Allt rose into view.

"Home!" I said.

Grett pressed against me, and desire and warmth went coursing through me as she touched me with her knee. She held her gloves in her hand and every now and then I glanced at her ring. It was unbelievable, and there were moments when I thought it was all a dream: Justin and Jeff sitting side by side on the driving-seat in front of Grett and myself, the crunch of the carriage-wheels on the rutted road and the sun dazzling in blue sparkling blobs on the curved polished wings over the wheels. We splashed through the Lyswen and our hedges came into view, heavy with hazel nuts and almost touching in places where Justin and I hadn't had time to trash.

The last half-mile was taken in style. Justin gave the horses their heads and the dust rose behind us. We waited by the yard gate until the others came up.

Father came hurrying up to us and held his arms out to Grett and lifted her down to the ground.

"Welcome!" he said. "Welcome to Trewern!"

He then helped Grett's mother down and led her to the house.

By this time about a dozen traps were pulled up in the yard. Those on foot were still to come.

"Come upstairs!" Mother took Grett's arm; and, so, holding her frock above her ankles, Grett passed over the threshold of my home.

"Food in half an hour!" shouted father. "We must wait for the rest to come."

From inside the kitchen came the sound of women's voices, mother fretting and fussing about the food; and there, coming from the barn, was Justin with a four and a half in his arms. He was sweating, and bits of hay clung to his clothes.

"There's four more like this," he shouted as he passed us, "and port and rhubarb wine for the ladies."

He went staggering through the kitchen door, his feet feeling for the step leading down from it. A few seconds later, Gaynor Fedwarian came rushing through the door, her cheeks aflame and her hair half-undone. When she saw us she smoothed her starched apron and gave an embarrassed laugh.

"That Justin!" she said.

Father turned to the squire, John Ellis, and the rest of us, shrugging his shoulders.

"He gets worse every day," he said. "It will be a case of 'have to' with him one of these days, you mark my words!"

Some long tables placed end to end in the barn accommodated those who could not sit down to breakfast in the house. The crowd had now arrived and there must have been upwards of six score or more in our yard.

"It's just like a funeral," said Moc. "Never seen such food and drink since squire's brother died!"

Grett and I were seated at the end of the table with father and mother on one side, and Grett's father, mother, the vicar and the squire and his wife on the other. Lower down the table were Justin, Moc, Jeff, Iori, Rhys Blacksmith (I had not thought for a moment that they would have the face to come, and all our neighbours. John Ellis was trying hard to be affable. As was usual with him, he didn't say much, but he gave close ear to all that was being said around him. Grett's mother, however, seemed quite at home. She looked round our kitchen, noting, no doubt, the old dresser with its rows of gold-bellied jugs, the grandfather clock, the corner-cupboard with its quaint tea service and little ornaments and, more precious than anything else there, the age-black oak coffer which mother had polished with beeswax until its surface was like water. Jeff was very quiet. He made no attempt to join in the conversation. His black hair was heavily pomaded, and he looked well in his serge suit and white collar.

There was plenty of cold chicken, ham, mutton and beef on the table for everyone. Also, there were round cheeses and pats of butter with our own print of a cow on each of them within easy reach of every person. Father looked blandly up and down the table. The vicar cracked one or two gentle jokes and Moc had to cap it with a story that set all the young girls blushing and giggling into their handkerchiefs. I looked to see how the vicar was taking it, and saw him laughing and wiping the tears from his eyes.

"Very good, very good. I'll remember that, Mihartach! You must tell them that in the Rhondda!"

He caught father's eye, nodded, and rose to his feet, his glass in his hand.

"I want you to drink to the young couple. . . . Their love and courage has brought them thus far; may God speed them on their happy way through life!"

Father was the next to speak. He rose impressively from his chair and gripped the lapels of his coat. He looked round the table and I saw Justin regard him intently, the vertical frown between his eyebrows deepening; and he lifted his forefinger slightly as if to warn me to keep calm and steady. Mother, too, was apprehensive. She had laid down her knife and fork and was adjusting her glasses nervously and watching father with her lips parted. A silence fell on the whole table and whether it was my fancy or not, I don't know, but I sensed somehow that the atmosphere had suddenly changed.

Father looked at Grett and myself, his smile a little bit too thin.

"Well"—he coughed and reached out his hand to place his knife in position beside his plate—"well, I never thought I would live to see this day: my son married and this happy ceremony at Trewern here. As you all know, he surprised us all with this match—me, his mother, and you, John Ellis and Mrs. Ellis. But there you are"—he threw out his hands in impotent tolerance—"what can we do when the blood is young and hot? We must just stand aside and let youth take the bit in its mouth. . . . Now John Ellis and his family have done me the honour of coming here to the breakfast. I am very thankful to him for that. I am a father, and I know what it must mean to John Ellis to hand over his only daughter to my son. . . . Yes, I know well what his feelings are, and what his feelings will be when he leaves her here to-night. She is a lovely girl and this Peele blood of ours can do with a little of that strain——" I blushed at his words. He was rubbing it into John Ellis for all he was worth, and smiling all the time. Justin was red in the face and kept biting his lower lip. I dared not look at John Ellis; Grett sat quietly at my side, her face terribly pale and her eyes staring in front of her. Father continued:

"Now I want these young people to know that we here at Trewern are behind them. Although blood is thicker than water, and old sores take a long time to heal; in spite of all this, I hope they will not live to regret this step they have taken. That is all, just a word like that. I wish them all that is good. My son has certainly cornered the loveliest girl in these parts."

He sat down and John Ellis rose to his feet at once. He was pale and his eyes were hurt and bitter.

"Thank you, Daniel Peele." He turned unsmilingly to father. "Thank you for the good wishes you have given to Grett. Now, there is no need for me to go over old ground; but you, Grett, and you, Edwin, are bound to do well. You, Grett, have me, your mother, and Jeff behind you; and as Daniel Peele has said so generously, you both have him and his family behind you. And, now, one thing more; I don't want to throw any shadow on this day on your lives. You, Daniel Peele," he turned to father again, "you said that I must be feeling it very much that I have lost my daughter . . ." He paused and looked up and down the table. "Ladies and gentlemen, let me tell you this: I am a proud man, very proud. I am proud of the courage my girl has shown in marrying into this family . . . and I hope her courage will never desert her. I wish them both a happy life together."

Justin quickly scotched whatever back-biting might have followed by rising to his feet with a mug of beer in his hand.

"It is time I had my say," he began. "Father here has got the idea that we have done well as a family in having Grett come into it. Well, he's right; but, dampo"—he grinned his apology to the vicar—"he must remember that although she's changed her name, she is still an Ellis. . . . And that is what Edwin wants, isn't it, Ned?" The squire banged the table at this and most of the guests followed his lead. Justin went on: "It's because she was Grett Ellis that he wanted her. For myself, I don't know why she married him! Here am I, single, and I am sure Jeff there would have loved me for a brother-in-law!"

He glanced across at Jeff and everyone laughed.

"One last word before I sit down to start keeping up with Moc. . . . You all know how things were between us. . . . I suppose I was as bad as father, and Jeff there was as bad as his father. . . . What I say now is, let there be an end to this, if only for the sake of the new breed that will surely come one day. One drink, then, to the Peele-Ellis or the Ellis-Peele combination, whichever you like. Fill them up, Moc!"

Now the squire was on his feet. We all gave him a clap.

"It is a great pleasure to me," he said quietly in his lovely easy Welsh, "to propose the health and happiness of the young couple. I admire their courage"—and here he bowed towards us—"and I am sure that nothing but good can result from such a romance, for a romance it is—and such courage. And what I like more than anything else is that they are going to set up home here in the old parish. I am proud that they are taking over Nan Siarad. Do you know, there are far too many leaving us. Just look back over the last year. Do you realize the number of people who have left for the valleys? Of course, there is money there. But is it going to last? Ask yourselves that question. Of course, I know things are bad here in the country with us. Farms are going untenanted. Mr. Morgans the Mill was only telling me a day or two ago that the wool trade is going down. . . . Twm Howells is gone, and where there used to be a score of craftsmen in the parish here when we were almost self-supporting, what is the position to-day? The skilled craftsman is putting away his tools and is content to become a labourer in the mines and the steelworks. I tell you, friends, it is a bad sign. It is so bad that I daren't look ahead. The land is going to starve. The old country will have to depend almost entirely on imports from abroad. . . . This is a bad state, and I foresee a time coming when we will have to return to the land again. I . . . Forgive me! This is not the time or the place . . . Ladies and gentlemen, I give you the beauty of the bride and the prosperity of the young couple!"

So the speeches went on, Moc got so sentimental that he nearly cried; and when I got up to reply, my well-thought-out phrases got caught in my throat and I could only stammer my thanks. Father sat gnawing his lips, for once a little subdued; and John Ellis smiled from time to time under his moustache as though well-pleased with himself for the way he had turned the tables on father. By three o'clock the guests had all left, and I drove Grett down to Rhos Dirion to get the clothes she needed for her stay with us before moving to our new home.

Justin need not have taken his boots off to come upstairs that night, for Grett and I were awake. We heard him coming up over the Allt—it was well after two o'clock—but before coming in the yard, he unsaddled the cob and turned her loose in the field behind the barn; then he opened the front door quietly. He crept upstairs, missing the step near the top that always creaked, and went softly past our door. In a minute or so, we heard his bed creak, and then the house was still and quiet again.

Glory to the night and its stillness, to the loveliness it concealed and made more lovely; glory to the rivers of Wales that night so that our blood caught their wild singing and flashing tumult. Glory to the petalled smoothness of a woman's body, glory to her hair that is like silk, to the arms that reach out in the darkness to draw one to her mouth and her kisses; glory to each false dawn that gave us another hour of Eden, to the wakened bird that sang and was silent again because it was still night. Glory to the Van Rocks brooding over the parish; glory to every river and brook whispering their litanies under the soft stars; glory to the corn that awaited our scythes, and to the hay that filled our barns. Glory to all the singers and the choirs, to every hymn and chant caught in the rafters and stones of the old church. Glory for ever and ever to my mother for her quiet sadness and to the old man for his strength and the demon that possessed him at times; glory to Justin for his oaths and the earthy richness of his heart. Glory to the Plough and Orion and the Evening Star and to every pool in Sawdde that caught their gold and held it until the glassy alders came between them and their running mirror. Glory to Dafydd ap Gwilym and his dream of Morfudd's hair and Dyddgu's eyes; glory to Trebor Mai and his moon in the cold waters of Llyn-Caer-Hafnant. Glory to the mill at Brecon, to Dai Probert the boxer, and to Moc Mihartach. And glory, too, to the moment when desire can want no more, when the burning sword is lowered and the night is still and dark and filled with peace. Glory, glory to Grett, and glory to Justin my brother; a Gogoniant yn y goruchaf i'r Tad, ac i'r Mab, ac i'r Ysbyrd Glan.

BOOK FIVE

Chapter 21

ON THE last night but one before Grett and I were going to take over Nantssiarad, Justin and I set out for The Pandy for a last fling. He had spoken of it half-jokingly for days, and Grett had raised no objection to it; the old man warning her that she had better keep an eye on me.

The fortnight had passed pleasantly enough. It was something to see Grett about the place, to see the old man turn in his chair to watch her as she would come in through the door; the line of his mouth softening and his whole demeanour more courteous and charming than we could ever remember it. We had worked hard in the last week. The weather had held fine though the glass had gone down to "Change," and we were lucky to have had the corn in. We had carted even by moonlight; father and Justin on one gambo, and Grett and I on the other. In the distance the mountains rose blue against the moon and the Vans were as sharp and clean as if cut with a knife. From time to time, Grett would pause with a sheaf in her arms to listen to some englyn that I told her; and times I would pause midway in a line, content to let the music of it go while I looked and marvelled at her. It was almost unbelievable that Grett Rhos Dirion was here on the fields of Trewern, that she was the girl on the gambo: Grett Rhos Dirion in her white apron, her breasts round and pointed under her thin blouse, for the nights were soft and warm; her round arms bared to the elbows and her face all laughing and glowing in the moonlight.

So the days had passed. The down-sweep of autumn was as gentle and soft as a swallow's dip, and only the topmost branches in the trees and the untrimmed hedge-crests bore any trace of its presence.

And by now, too, Grett and I had taken the last load up to Nantssiarad. The house was now ready, the place aired and warm. Every room had been papered, and the dairy was set out with a dozen round shallow pans for creaming. A separator would come later; anyway, the skim from the pans was better than from a separator, and would help the pigs along fine.

Justin and I set off as soon as we could after milking. He was full of devilry, and I could hear him singing to himself as he changed in his room. It was good to see him in good spirits again. He had been in the dumps for the last few days, not saying much to anyone, and ready to cross the old man on the least provocation. But now that we were going out together, he seemed himself again.

"What time will you be back?" asked mother. She went up to Justin and brushed some dandruff off his shoulder. "You mustn't keep Edwin out late now," she added. "Remember!"

Justin grinned at her in his old way, then he gripped her in his arms and pretended to squeeze her. Mother struggled hard and threatened to give him a bonclust. When he released her, her eyes were shining and she smoothed her hair into place like a young girl. Grett stood smiling behind her.

"If you'll be reeking of beer," she said, "you sleep with Justin."

"Quite right," said mother. "It isn't fair that we women should have to put up with their old silliness."

We left them there, Grett already beginning to clear away the tea things and mother watching us, her eyes on Justin as if she were thinking to herself that even if I were married and going away, he, Justin, was still with her. He was the apple of her eye all right.

We rode quietly down through the Allt. The clouds had come up and I could feel an underlick of wet in the wind. What leaves there were whispered of rain, and the sound of the river was soft and muffled. Down over Gwynfe there was still an afterglow of light above Tychrug; but the rest of the sky was black and heavy, and something inside me gave a jump as a dog barked in Nanteos field. I felt it would be healthier if the rain would come; there was something too still and heavy in the air and I was glad that Justin was with me, though it was something to have Doll between my knees and to feel the sway and thrust of her shoulders.

"Have you heard from Moc?" I asked, just for the sake of talking.

Justin laughed.

"Moc write! Diawl! I don't think the old devil can write . . . Wish he was with us to-night, though!"

He didn't say more but rode on just in front of me. All I could see was the shape of him, and the reek from his pipe was like new hay. I wondered who would be at The Pandy to-night. I knew Justin had been down to the village in the morning, and he had hinted for days that there would be a real rally on our last night before I left home. Well, whoever would be there, I did not fear any repetition of our last visit. Things were quiet enough between Grett's people and mine now. True, none of the Ellises had been over since the wedding, though Grett and I had been there for supper two or three times. Jeff was still keeping out of my way. Grett said it was only his pride and that he would come round in time, especially when he would realize that we had not had to get married. Then, as if he had been keeping level with my thoughts, Justin pulled up a bit and reined alongside me.

"I wonder will Jeff be there to-night?" There was something in the way he said it that made me feel he was trying to make the question sound casual and carefree.

"What if he is?" I asked.

"Oh, nothing. . . . I just thought. . . ."

"What? Do you think he's still spiteful?"

"Spiteful!" Justin swore. "I don't trust him, not an inch. Anyway, now that you've got Grett, we haven't got to consider him——"

"Justin!"

"Aye? What is it?"

I swallowed my breath, and again I felt as if there was something too oppressive and fraught about the night. My heart was racing and I could hardly breathe.

"What's up?" he asked.

"No trouble," I said. "Don't provoke him. . . . It'll only make it hard for Grett. . . . You understand, don't you?"

"Don't worry," he said. "I won't make any trouble, but he'd better not start piggatin on me, that's all. . . . Come on, we're going like a bloody funeral."

He set the cob to a gallop, and I followed him. The exhilaration of the ride did me good. It was grand to feel the wind on my face and to see the black drift of the hedges coming towards me and slipping by. We tore down by Graig Ddu and up along the breast of the hill towards The Pandy. Doll was in a lather of sweat when I got off, and before following Justin into the bar I rubbed her down with some hay and slackened the saddle a hole or two.

The bar was full.

"Here he is," shouted Danrallt. "And about time; we've been waiting over an hour!"

So, it had all been arranged. I looked at Justin. He already had a pint in front of him, the skeins of froth still clinging to the sides where he had drunk from it.

"Aye, all arranged," he shouted. "Invites to everybody. Come on, Ned. You've got to get rid of a sovran or two before stop-tap."

I gave a half-sovereign to Sal and told her to fill up for everybody.

I looked around. Jeff, Iori, Lloyd Parry, and Rhys Blacksmith were on the far side of the bar. Jeff looked across at me, and I felt at once that he wanted me to ask him to drink so that he could refuse me. I didn't know what to do. His face was red from drinking, and Rhys kept smiling at me as though he knew what was going on in my mind. Sal and her sister drew from the cask behind them and set the pints in a cluster on the counter. Then, before I could ask the crowd to help themselves, Justin caught hold of three pints and put his hands around them and carried them over to Jeff.

"Drink up," he said. "It's a randy-boo to-night."

I watched him. His eyes taunted Jeff to refuse him and he was grinning. Rhys looked at Jeff, but Jeff said nothing. Iori helped Justin lower the glasses to the stained table. Jeff at last nodded quietly as though coming to a decision within himself and picked up a glass. The others followed his lead.

Justin came back towards me and gave a quiet wink.

"He's all right," he said quietly. "No trouble from him to-night. . . . Don't worry!"

The noise in the bar was deafening, everyone seemed to be talking and shouting at the same time. I saw Sal fetch someone a clout and push him into the passage. I drank my beer, thinking that if I splashed it down into my stomach I would get quickly drunk. I could see that the bar was in the mood for a wild, roaring night. But the beer was flat and sour to my taste. I knew that I could not hold it for three or four hours on end. I looked round the room again. Dico Lewis was there, and he and Justin were having a good laugh together. Over by the door a crowd of Brynamman boys had just turned in. They were more of Justin's stamp than the rest of them: thick-set, black-haired, and with that steady lurking devilry in their brown eyes. I motioned Sal to fill up for them, and whispered to her to give me a half-glass of whisky. The drink warmed me up, but I still couldn't join in the singing, and only made a pretence of laughing as one story followed the other. I looked at Justin again, wondering how he could come down here night after night. Oh no, I didn't blame him, perhaps I envied him that he could find happiness—or was it pleasure?—so easily. He was laughing with everybody, roaring his head off at every story: though, in the midst of his enjoyment, I saw how from time to time he would look over in Jeff's direction to see how things were.

Standing there, trying to enjoy my drink, I went back in my mind over the past year. It was strange that, apart from our visits to Rhos Dirion and once or twice to church, I had never accompanied Justin anywhere but to pubs. That was how it was, however, that was his life. As we used to say, he was in his oil in a pub: beer, fighting and women, these were his life, the only things that were naturally incidental to his existence. Well, it was the last time that I would be out with him and the boys. From now on my place would be with Grett. I saw the fire at Nantssiarad playing on the half-moon of sand-papered steel that was our fender and myself sitting by the fire, after Grett would have gone to bed, wrestling with a new poem and drawing strength from the darkness outside the window, though that indeed would not happen until the first early months of marriage would have lost their tingle and velvet softness. But it would come, it would come. . . .

I picked up my glass and went over to Jeff.

"Have another drink," I said.

He looked suspiciously at me. Then his nostrils distended a little and I knew that the movement of disdain, slight though it was, was conscious and intentional.

"Better if you saved your money," he said. "A good way to start a married life this is. . . . Where is Grett to-night?"

"At home. . . . Come on," I said, "don't be awkward. You know this is not my way of carrying on. This is just my 'good-bye' to it all. What about a drink now?"

Iori and Rhys were listening to us, all ears. Jeff motioned me away from them.

"Come here!" We stood in the corner by the door. I looked at him, trying to make out what he wanted. "Look," he began, "it's no good trying to be friends with me. You've got Grett now, and you'll get no trouble from us as long as you treat her all right. You can't hope for more than that. There's bad blood between us and——"

"But there needn't be," I said. "Justin's not out for trouble any more——"

"Don't talk," he said. "Neither Justin nor your old man will ever pull together with us, no more will we with you. . . . It's gone on too long for that. . . . We don't forget, nor do you, nor do we want to. . . . Look at Justin now! I ask you now."

Justin was wrestling playfully with one of the Brynamman colliers. He soon had him on the floor. The collier rose to his feet amid roars of laughter.

"It's too heavy for me you are," he said.

"Aye, you are right there, gwas," shouted Alltwen. "Peele is getting a real pot on him with all this swilling he's doing."

I felt myself go cold all over. Justin turned slowly on Alltwen.

"Pot-bellied, eh?" He inflated his chest and looked down at his waist. "Tell you what," he went on, "you fetch me a punch there, just to try. . . . Come on!"

Dai Alltwen shrugged his shoulders.

"Me? You are picking on a fine one, aren't you? Half your

weight I am. . . ." He looked round nervously. "What about your brother-in-law over there?" he shouted. "Jeff Ellis there. There's your man. Why don't you invite him to have a go?"

There came a hush over the bar. Everybody stared at Justin and Jeff. Jeff's eyes narrowed. Then he crossed the floor to where Alltwen was standing.

"No need to pick on me to fight your battle," he said to Dai. "Too fond of that you are!" Then he turned to Justin.

"It's up to you, Peele," he said. "You know how they are here. Everybody here would just love to see you and me fight it out. . . . It's up to you, whenever you feel like it . . . I don't mind."

Justin nodded.

"What you say is true," he began. "I know this trash." He clipped Alltwen suddenly on the side of the head. It wasn't a heavy blow, but Dai, drunk as he was, went down in a heap. "Anybody's welcome, even you, Jeff——"

"Justin!"

I crossed over to him and stood facing him with my back to Jeff. He looked at me frowningly. He had already had about as much as he could carry. His lips were dry and taut, and his face was a little pale. "Think of me and Grett." I spoke quietly so that no one else should hear her name. He nodded quiet understanding. He pushed me aside and grinned at Jeff.

"Come on," he said. "Drink up! I'll put you under with beer. Right?"

Jeff ran his tongue over his lips.

"As many as you can pay for," he said. "I'll pay my whack, too. But we'll make it a real drink." He turned and called to Sal:

"Two pints and a rum in each!"

They started, Sal placing the drinks before them as they stood facing each other against the counter.

Dai Alltwen came up to me. I was sorry that Justin had hit him; he was almost too drunk to stand. Rhys and Iori, too, edged over to us.

"Your Justin's had enough already," said Rhys. "Why don't you take him home? There'll be hell if those two break out to-night!"

But I knew better than to interfere with Justin now. He and Jeff were drinking steadily and not talking much. The Brynamman boys were round the piano and singing some English song that was new to me. Those colliers could sing well, and one of them had a voice that was the deepest I had ever heard. He would have been a match for Dico any day.

I still had the same glass that I had started with. I was out of sympathy and mood with the whole business. I looked at the clock on the brown-papered wall. There was still an hour and a half to go before stop-tap. They would have finished supper at home by now, and I thought of Grett lying alone to-night in the white bed.

"A happy wedding," said Sal in my ear. Then she nodded in Justin's direction. He had just emptied a rum into his beer and his eyes were bright and glittering. Jeff was like a turkey and his lips were swollen with drink. He emptied his glass in one gulp and looked challengingly at Justin. Justin did the same and called for another round.

"I think I'll get rid of the rum bottle," whispered Sal to me. "They'll both be helpless if they carry on like this. Don't you think so?"

I saw her slip the rum bottle under her white apron. She gave me a wink, and when she came back into the bar I saw that instead of hiding the bottle she had poured the rum away, leaving only a finger-breadth in it. I gave Sal another half-sovereign, and again announced to the crowd that the drinks were on me.

I felt that the tension was now passing. If Jeff and Justin would drink themselves into a stupor, then it was all for the best. I did not care what happened as long as they did not come to blows. The crowd, too, was leaving them well alone. Little groups had formed together; some were singing round the piano, and Sal was in and out among them, flashing her black eyes at everyone, and twisting herself like an eel to avoid the slaps aimed at her backside.

Dico Lewis came over and tacked himself to me. Like myself, Dico was no drinker. I think he came only for the singing and the company. He had an old coat of his father's on;

the square shoulders and double-slitted tail making him look almost twice his normal size.

"When are you moving in?" he asked.

I told him and he touched my glass with his and gave me luck. Behind us the Gwynfe and Brynamman boys were harmonizing "Y Ferch o Blwyf Penderyn" and Dico started singing the bass so easily that it sounded like a melody itself. That was his great gift. He could sing bass naturally and roundly; listening to him it wasn't so much a harmony as a contrapuntal melody, if that is the name for it. I was just about to go outside for a little trip when I heard Jeff roar with ironic laughter.

"That's the best I've ever heard! Where did you read that?" He laughed again. Dico and I turned round to look at him.

Jeff was still roaring his laughter from the edge of his lips. I could see that it was all put on, you can always tell when a man is laughing from his chest or just making a sound in his mouth. Justin was holding his glass midway to his lips. He wasn't laughing, and I could see the deep, vertical furrow between his black eyebrows.

The singing and the hubbub of noises stopped. Jeff looked round quickly and stopped laughing.

"Listen to him," he shouted, pointing to Justin. "The latest Peele boast! Go on," he shouted to Justin, "tell the whole room about it. See how they take it!"

I looked at Justin and felt my legs go weak under me. He was pale and quiet. He put his glass down on the counter and then pushed it so that its base was just inside a round beer-stain left there.

"Take him home," urged Dico in my ear. "He's getting nasty."

I didn't know what to do. Justin would not be humbled in front of such a crowd—I knew him too well for that; besides, he was too full of drink. Still, I went up and stood behind him. Iori, Lloyd, and Rhys came up and stood behind Jeff. Justin turned and looked at me. The expression on his face told me not to worry, that he was holding himself well in hand. Then he faced Jeff.

"Just a story, boys, something about my grandmother," he began.

"Grandmother's just about it," shouted Jeff. "Grandmother my——"

"Shut up!" Justin's eyes were glittering now.

"Drink up!" shouted Sal. "You haven't long to go."

No one paid any heed to her.

"Come on," taunted Jeff. "Let's have it again. Damme! You ought to have it on your coat-of-arms: a bull, a backchain, and your old grandmother!"

I couldn't make out what he was talking about. The allusions were completely lost on me.

"Right, listen, boys." Justin's voice was thin and hard and he was breathing heavily through his nose. The crowd pressed in around us.

"Listen, now," said Jeff. "Don't miss a word."

"Right!" Justin grinned at the crowd. "You know me, boys, I don't have to boast." He lifted his fist. "This can do all my boasting for me, but never mind that . . . I was telling Jeff Ellis a story about my father's mother when she was a young girl. . . ." (Of course, I remembered now; I had heard it from father many a time when he was in one of his expansive moods.) Justin went on: "It isn't much, just this. They had a devil of a bull at home there, nobody could do anything with him. . . . They used to keep him in the barn. . . . Well, one day, my grandmother (so the old man says) went in with a backchain, caught hold of his tail and lashed him round the barn till he dropped. . . . Now laugh at that!"

He turned to the counter and drained his glass. Nobody laughed. Iori and some of the others half-smiled, but when Justin faced us again they were all as sober as judges.

Jeff looked up and down the bar.

"Can you beat that?" he shouted. "All lies I say. . . . Lashing a bull with a backchain! I'd like to see anybody try that to-day."

A murmur rose from the crowd.

Dai Alltwen cleared his throat.

"It depends on the bull," he began, his words slurring into one another, "size, weight, and temper. Some bulls is wicked. Take our old Hereford now, we got to keep him in the *lloc* in the barn. Mari and the children can't go near him. . . .

There's a bull now that would kill a man . . . I always take the pitchfork with me when I go to him——"

"He's right there. . . . There are bulls and bulls!"

"Aye, no trusting them there is——"

"What age is he, Dai?"

"He's rising four. . . . Pure Hereford, you know what they are."

"Aye, but those black ones are the worst, though. Remember that black one at Carmarthen show last year, 'Deri Du y Fro'?"

Jeff turned suddenly to Justin.

"Tell you what, Peele. If your old grandmother could do it, why don't you show us how she did it? Dai wouldn't mind, I'm sure; besides, we'll all be there if there's any trouble. Diawl! Do that and I'll take my hat off to you!"

I went cold at his words. Of course, surely, he was joking. . . . Dai Alltwen would never allow it. I looked at Justin. He shrugged his shoulders and laughed.

"Why me?" he asked. "The Peeles, as you say, have done it once, even if it was my old grandmother. . . . Suppose you show us how you can do it? Come on, there's a chance for you. Quick enough you are to let somebody else do the dirty work, eh?"

The crowd laughed at the way Justin was turning the tables on Jeff, and I felt a great relief surge over me.

Jeff took another pull at his glass.

"Fair enough," he said. "I'm as good as a Peele any day. Fair enough. . . . What about it, Alltwen? Are you willing?"

I thought he was bluffing and so did we all, I think. Dai Alltwen did not answer; then Rhys put a word in, sly and quiet:

"Why don't you toss for it?" he suggested. "The loser to go in and show us how it's done."

"Don't be daft!" One of the colliers from Brynamman came forward, his blue-pocked face pale and hollow. "Don't be daft! Uffern!" He turned to Jeff and Justin. "Why don't you two strip to the waist and fight it out clean like we do over the mountain."

My heart leapt at his suggestion. A fight was better than this other thing. It had to come. I had known it all along. Justin and Jeff would have to fight it out; perhaps Justin would take a hiding just to help Grett and me. He had nothing to lose. His reputation was safe, especially after his fight at Brecon. The next moment I hated myself for the thought. Justin lie down for my sake! No, to the devil with it all! I would shout him on, proving to him that I wanted him to win. But Jeff paid no attention to the collier.

"What about it, Peele? Will you toss for it?"

Justin shook his head.

"I can lick you," he said, "and you are asking for it. Come on outside now. We'll do as the Shoni suggests."

He looked inquiringly at me, and I nodded my agreement with him.

"Outside for it!" shouted Iori.

Jeff turned round angrily on him:

"Keep quiet," he said. "I can't fight Peele. I've got to think of my sister. . . . Why doesn't he take up my challenge: either he or I go in and handle Alltwen's bull. . . . What about it, Peele?"

Justin still shook his head.

"There's no need for this fuss or this challenge," he said. "Jeff Ellis is drunk . . . he's not responsible——"

"Not responsible? Sal! More beer and rum!"

"There's no rum left," said Sal.

"Then whisky then, something with body to it. . . . So, I am drunk, is it, and you, Peele, are sober? Boys,"—he took us all in his glance, his eyes wild with drink—"listen to me. I dare Peele to toss the coin with me. . . . If he doesn't, then he's a bloody coward!"

I watched Justin anxiously. He moistened his lip with his tongue and shook his head as if he, too, were thick and fuddled with drink.

"It's madness," he said, "I——"

"Heads or tails?" shouted Jeff.

The half-sovereign twinkled in the lamplight. Jeff caught it and slapped it on the back of his hand.

"Call, Peele!"

My heart went heavy as Justin called: "Heads!"

Jeff uncovered the back of his hand.

"I lose," he said. He had gone a little pale; then he straightened himself up and laughed: "Well, I asked for it, didn't I?"

Justin crossed over to him.

"Forget all about it," he said. "If it had been 'heads,' *I* wouldn't have gone. So, listen, in front of the crowd here, I let you off the challenge. . . . Come on, have another drink. We are all drunk as it is!"

"Hear, hear!" shouted Twm Maesafon. "That's the spirit, Peele!"

Jeff shook his head.

"A challenge is a challenge," he said slowly. "And I don't want to be let off anything by any Peele. Where's Alltwen?"

He turned round to where Dai was standing behind him and gripped him by the lapels of his coat.

"Is it all right for us to go up to your place? Remember, it was you first mentioned your bull to us."

Dai was in a bad state. He could hardly stand.

"Come on, what about it? Are you willing or no?"

"It is up to you, Jeff Ellis," said Dai. "I'm willing enough . . . But I tell you this, it's dangerous. . . . It's as much as I can do to handle him, and he knows me."

"Right, then. If you can manage him," Jeff here looked down at Dai who came scarcely to his shoulder—"then I'm damme sure I'll manage him. Let's go!"

Justin was buttoning up his jacket. I turned to him again, Dico at my side.

"Stop him," I whispered. "I don't like it!"

"It is murder," said Dico. "You ought to know better, both of you."

Justin shrugged his shoulders.

"It's all right," he said. "A fright'll do him the world of good; besides, we'll all be there, and Dai, too. Don't you worry he'll be all right."

He put on his cap, the one he had bought that night in Brecon. The crowd was already moving out, Jeff in their midst. Behind us, Sal and her sister went round the two tables collecting the empty glasses. I walked out with Justin, and we went round to the stable and got the cob and Doll and walked with them down the road towards Alltwen.

Chapter 22

WALKING down the dark lane to Alltwen, I had the feeling that I had taken this same journey a long, long time ago. The sounds of voices in front of us and the noise of feet and hoofs struck some answering chord in my mind. I looked at Justin and realized that this was no dream. He was here at my side, the top of his head on a level with my eyes. He was very quiet, and once or twice he half lurched against me heavy from the drink that was in him. The air was not as oppressive as it had been earlier in the evening, but perhaps that was only my fancy, and because it was so fresh after the tobacco smoke and the warm reek of the bar.

"Are you coming?" shouted someone in front of us.

"Carry on," shouted Justin.

We were going down into the dip of the lane when I felt something heavy and stifling come upon me. I found myself struggling for breath, and through it all I heard the tramp-tramp of feet. I thought at once of the Toili and began to tremble. It was so dark now that I could only see the shape of Justin at my side. I put out my hand and touched him. Without a word he took my hand, his grip cool and firm.

"What's up?" he asked at length, because I was still trembling.

I took a deep breath. Of course, it was nothing. The tramp of feet was still there, the crowd in front of us pressing on in silence towards Alltwen.

"It's all right," I said. "It was coming out into the fresh air after drinking. You know how it is."

"Lucky you were not on rum and beer," he laughed.

Once out of the dip, I felt better. But the experience had frightened me. Was it some augury of what the night held in store for us, or was it just my anxiety affecting my nerves and imagination?

Ahead of us we could now see Alltwen with its stark high firs around it. The barn was a score or more yards away from the buildings, and while Dai went to the house for some lanterns, we caught up with the rest of them and tethered the horses to the railings.

Jeff was standing by the yard gate. He even grinned at me as I came up to him.

"Jeff," I said, "don't do it—think of Grett."

He gave me a long, quiet look.

"That's your job now," he said, "you've married her. . . . But don't worry, I'll lambaste that bloody bull till he drops. . . . Where is your brother?"

I indicated Justin where he was talking with Dico and the colliers.

Jeff's eyes narrowed.

"We'll have that fight yet," he said. "The parish is too small for us. . . . One of us will have to pack up after then."

We could hear voices from the house. Dai came out with the lanterns in his hands, four of them he had, the wire cages round them throwing dark patterns on the ground and on the white-washed walls. Behind him stood his wife and two children. Dai was arguing with her:

"Only going to see the bull we are. . . . We won't be long. . . . Go on now and get some supper ready."

Instinctively, the men hid behind the wall, myself and Justin with them.

"I don't trust you," we could hear Dai's wife shouting; "it is drunk you are. . . . Don't you and your friends go teasing the little bull. He has been quiet all day."

Dai waved her indoors, with a wide swing of the lamps. She banged the door to, and Dai lurched towards us.

He handed the lamps to the boys and then went to fetch some pitchforks and the pole with which to grip the ring on the bull's nose.

"Something new this is," said one of the colliers. "I can see us over there staging contests like this instead of boxing."

Dai was soon back with the pitchforks and the pole.

"Quiet now—we mustn't alarm him. Quiet as you can!"

We tiptoed up to the barn. It stood low and dark against the

236

night. To me, there was something strange and unreal about its silhouette against the clouds. It was more like some un-lighted church than a barn, so quiet and still it was, and all of us walking so softly up to it. I felt like crying out to the crowd to stop. But there it was, we moved forward as if impelled by some force stronger than ourselves. And Justin and Jeff were leading the way. The lamps cast a soft, honey glow around our feet, throwing the shape of each man into sharp relief as it passed in and out of the beams.

Dai unlatched the small door at the end. We would now, so he whispered over his shoulder, be able to go up the ladder into the hay-loft that looked down on the floor of the barn.

We went up the ladder one by one, and soon I was standing on the dowlod. The barn measured some sixty feet by twenty-five or thirty. I looked down trying to see the wooden pen. The lights from the storm-lamps shone on the tawny hay and on the grey cobwebbed walls. A sudden roar told me where the bull was. The lamplight gleamed on his eyeballs. I was near Rhys and Iori. No one spoke. A terrible silence followed the bellow of the bull, hanging over us like a dark, stifling hand. Dai was down by the pen, Jeff behind him with the backchain in his hand. Justin was on the edge of the hay looking down on them.

"Diawc! I don't like this," whispered one of the colliers be-hind me. "I feel same as I did before we had a 'fall' under-ground."

"Ssh! Quiet there!" It was Iori. Those in front near Justin had pitchforks in their hands, ready to jump in a second if danger threatened. I looked down again at Dai and Jeff where they stood near the pen. The pen, or *lloc*, was a stout affair of heavy, rough-hewn timber. The bull seemed quiet enough. He was in the far corner and Dai was trying to coax him towards the gate. Jeff had thrown his hat aside and was a dark figure in the shadows. The worn, close links of the backchain caught the lights and glittered like a thick, scaly snake.

I could only see Justin's broad back. He was standing there with his cap pulled well over his head. He was taut and still.

A wave of weakness passed over me as I heard Dai fumble with the chain that held the gate in place. He let it slip to the ground and kept up a wheedling, coaxing series of sounds to the bull. The bull at last moved quietly enough towards the gate. He was not as big as I had imagined he would be, but there was strength in the high, bunched shoulders and his horns were short and straight. His flank was caked with dried dung, and his tail swished quietly to and fro. I breathed a prayer as I saw Jeff stand back to let him out, and in that one moment I saw Grett waiting for me at home. I was about to call out to him when, with a yell, he caught hold of the swinging tail and struck the bull a thwack with the chain. The crowd around me roared as the bull plunged and tried to turn round on Jeff. But as fast as he turned, Jeff was behind him and flailing him unceasingly with the chain. The space was too confined for the bull to get up any speed and Jeff was in no real danger from the backthrust of the powerful hind legs. We were now all shouting, and Jeff's yells could be heard above everything. The bull curvetted and plunged, tossing his head and roaring as he turned and stabbed his forelegs in the soft floor, but Jeff was always well behind him.

"Enough! Back in the pen with him!" shouted Dai. The gate was open and Dai was there ready with the pole. But Jeff was in his glory. He was still keeping well behind the bull, gripping the tail with his left hand and belabouring him with the chain.

I saw the crowd around me, their faces lit up in flickering relief against the shadows behind them. All I could see were eyes, dark open mouths, here a high cheek-bone; those with moustaches were only noses and eyes.

I was seeing all this and watching Jeff and the bull circling below when it happened, just as I had known since before my birth that it would happen. Jeff fell sprawling, made giddy no doubt by the drink that was in him. The bull turned on him before I could even shout. Jeff gave one terrible cry as the bull gored him, and in that moment Justin sprang down from the dowlod on to the floor. The bull raised his great head as Justin landed near him

"Justin!" I heard myself shout his name as he advanced warily on the bull.

The bull lowered his head to gore Jeff again and I saw Justin throw himself forward, his hands outstretched to grip the horns. And even as I and the rest of them sprang down to his help, I saw Justin lifted into the air. He came down with a heavy thud, and even as he landed the bull was at him again.

I was now down by him, and there was the bull within a yard of me. The tip of his horn was dark and wet. A pickel flashed in front of my eyes and in the next instant I saw that Dai had got the clip of the pole fastened to the ring in his nose. The barn echoed to the deep-throated, tearing roaring of the bull. I looked at Justin. He was lying on his side, his knees drawn up to his stomach, and his cap fallen off beside him. He was very still and quiet. I felt for the beat of his heart underneath the warm, sticky blood that oozed from his side. I felt a faint beat. Behind me, I heard Iori say:

"Jeff's dead. . . ."

I remained there on my knees watching Justin's face. The eyelids fluttered once, twice, and I thought he would open his eyes. He gave a deep sigh, and I put my hand to his heart again. Yes, it was still beating.

"Don't move him," said Dico. "Run and get some blankets," he said to those behind us. "You, Parry, get to Llandovery for the doctor. Take Justin's cob, and gallop!"

What my thoughts were as I knelt there over Justin I do not know. I was watching his face, feeling his heart every now and again, and fearing every moment that I would find no movement there.

They came in with blankets, and when Dai's wife started to shout at us, she was silenced at once. She gave me a white towel which I pressed to the wound in Justin's side. The doctor could not possibly be along for an hour and a half, and the flow of blood had to be staunched. From the corner of my eye, I saw someone place a blanket over Jeff. . . . I remember once how the vicar said that pain and suffering brought with them their own anodyne; and it was quite true. I felt as if all feeling had left me. Father, mother, Grett herself; nothing mattered now but Justin.

The minutes passed and then, suddenly, Justin's eyes

opened. He tried to grin at me and his face grimaced with pain.

"That ——," he used a terrible obscene word. Then: "How's Jeff?" he asked.

I said nothing.

He nodded as if he understood.

"You . . ." He turned his head and looked straight at me. "Go home and . . . and tell Mam. . . ."

"But you?" I stammered. "I can't leave you——"

"Get home," he said. "Tell her . . . that . . . I'm . . . all right. . . ." He tried to grin again, but his eyes closed. I felt under the swab of the towel to see if he was still alive. His heart was still beating.

"You go!" Dico was kneeling by me. "We'll look after him. Lloyd's already gone for the doctor."

They made way for me; someone came with me, Iori I believe, and he took my arm.

As I stepped out of the barn and left the lamps, the silent crowd and the roaring of the penned bull, I felt as if I were coming out of a nightmare and would find myself in bed with Grett at my side. But no, the stars were alive in the sky and my hand was still clammy and sticky with Justin's blood.

Doll was there, tethered to the railing where I had left her. Though still dazed, I had the clearness of mind to tighten the saddle girth before getting on her back. I took a last look at the squat, evil shape of the barn behind me; then I jabbed Doll with my heels and gave her head for Trewern.

Chapter 23

I TREMBLE now when I think of that gallop home to Trewern. How Doll did it I don't know, though, perhaps, I did let her walk up Graig Ddu. When we got away from Alltwen, I fancied I could still hear the awful roar of the bull. And Jeff was dead. "Jeff Ellis is dead. Jeff Ellis is dead" : it was the rhythm of Doll's gallop, and I wondered to myself if the weal of the night would ever be erased from my soul. And Justin. . . . I could not bear to think that even now, at this very moment, he too might be dead. But no, it was impossible. Men of Justin's breed

240

did not die like that. I saw his face again, the wan lamplight playing on it; and with a prayer on my lips I kissed the dried blood on my hands.

As I went past Howells the Blacksmith's, someone shouted at me. I did not stop, nor did I pay any heed when a group of people standing on the cross-roads below the chapel scattered out of my way. There were times when I could not see the road or the hedges, and I was through the Allt before I knew it. Ahead of me, I saw the lights in our kitchen and instinctively I drew on the reins, realizing now that Grett must be told of Jeff's death. I started trembling, and a cold sweat broke out all over me. Jeff dead! Grett would never forgive me or Justin that we had allowed this to happen. A pall of foreboding came down on me and I wondered if the sun would ever shine on the parish again.

I got off before we came to the yard and left Doll by the wain gate while I went on foot to the house. It was no use thinking how I would break the news to Grett and father and mother. Something was weeping deep inside me, and although my home was here within a few yards of me and the light from the kitchen was bright on the cobbles outside, all I could see was the barn, the dark, savage mass of the bull, and those two lying on the floor. I went in through the front door and said a prayer and crossed myself in the passage. Then I went in the kitchen.

Mother and father were sitting each side of the fire, and Grett was sewing at the table, the lamp shining on her hair.

Father was the first to see me. His eyes opened wide and he stood up. Then Grett looked up and I saw her hand fly to her mouth. Mother turned round to see what was happening.

"Ned!" Father came quickly across the hearth to me. He pulled me to the table and held my hands to the lamp. Mother gave a cry and groped about her, feeling for the arm of her chair.

"What is it? Speak! Say something!"

Father was trembling as he spoke.

I could say nothing. Something rose to my throat and choked me. The tears began to roll down my cheeks, and I shook as if a fever were on me.

"Ned! Say something. What has happened?" Grett shook me by my shoulder. And still I could say nothing.

"Justin! Something has happened to Justin," cried mother. She got up and came to me. "Oh, say it's not true," she pleaded. "Nothing's happened to Justin?"

Between my sobs I started to tell them: "Justin's hurt . . . Alltwen's bull . . . he and Jeff——"

"Jeff!" Grett's eyes opened wide. I made to put my arms around her, but she shook herself free.

"Jeff? Is Jeff all right?"

I shook my head.

"Is he hurt . . . ?"

I looked at her despairingly, trying to tell her without uttering the words.

"What is it?" she whispered.

"A terrible accident," I said.

"He's——"

I nodded my head.

Grett gave one cry, and before I could stop her she was out through the door. We heard her feet flying across the yard. I turned to follow her and, as I did so, mother sank to the floor. Father stared at me, fear on his face and his eyes unbelieving.

"I'll see to Grett," he said. "Better me than you . . . I'll take her home. . . . You see to your mother. Where's Doll?"

I told him. He asked no further questions and went out of the kitchen. Mother was now coming round and I lifted her up and put her on the couch. She made little noises and moaned to herself.

Father came in.

"I've got Grett," he said. "I'm taking her home . . . then I'm going to Alltwen. You look after your mother. . . . Where's Grett's coat?" He looked long and hard at me. "What devil's work this is, I don't know. . . . It's the finish this is!"

With that he went out and left me with mother and the nameless terror and choking darkness that was on me.

.   .   .   .   .

Don't ask me how the next two hours passed. There are hours in one's life that one thrusts aside with a fearful hand.

They do not bear contemplation, not even when the years have softened their edge and dulled their pain. I told mother how everything had happened. From time to time she took off her glasses and wiped them on her apron, and all the time the tears streamed down her face. Then she would moan to herself and cry out: "Oh, Iestyn, Iestyn . . . and Jeff, oh my poor Grett!" And then start all over again, beating her fist on the table.

At last, I heard the slow, heavy rumble of a gambo coming down the lane. Mother ran out to meet it in the yard. I put the big kettle on in case the doctor would need hot water.

A terrible moaning met me as I went out into the yard. The gambo was drawn up by the door. Father was there with his bald head glistening in the lamplight. He stood very still, not saying a word. And I knew that Justin was dead. Mother was up on the flat-bottomed gambo turning back the covering which someone had placed over Justin. Behind the gambo I could see Lewsin, old Howells, Elias Carpenter, and a crowd of others. The doctor was there, too, holding his horse by the bridle.

I went up to father. He looked at me as I had never seen him look before.

"He's dead," he said. "He . . . he lasted only a few minutes after I got there."

I walked away to the back of the house. Justin dead! "Justin is dead," I said, "and Jeff is dead. . . ." Without knowing where I was going, I went to the well at the bottom of the garden. Don't tell me that people never realize immediately the awful, final significance of death. I knew it. I knew it and accepted it without question. Justin already belonged to the past. Quite automatically, I found myself referring to him in my mind as someone who had once existed. For evermore he would be in the past; Jeff, too.

I found myself uttering Justin's name over and over to myself. They would be carrying him in now, upstairs to his room. I saw him lying on his bed, the old dare-devil grin gone from his face. I started shaking violently again and a terrible bout of grief overcame me. Justin was dead. Now we were alone. He had always been behind us; behind me when I was a boy and right up to this hour. But things were different now: he was gone. It was then that my grief began to well up inside me. It hurt me physically. There was a pain in my throat, and as I began to think of his face, his voice and, strangely enough, how he had looked on the night he had foughtDai Probert—I began to cry. Then thoughts of Jeff came into my head. How was Grett, and should I not be with her at this hour? I knew, however, that I must keep out of her way for the time being. Even I had no place in her grief now. And this thought in itself was too much for me to bear.

I stayed by the well for some time. Pali Dolguog would not be along to lay Justin out until one of us went to fetch her. Before going back to the house, I bathed my face in the well so that the others should not see how red my eyes were.

.   .   .   .   .

When I got back to the house, the vicar was there. He must have arrived just at that minute. He was standing near father.

"I heard only half an hour ago," he was saying. He looked at father and caught his hand.

"It is hard, hard," he said. "Too hard even for you, Daniel Peele. . . . It is terrible, terrible for you and Rhos Dirion. . . ." He paused and shook his head as if searching for words to continue. "God help you," he said quietly. "We must leave it all to Him."

Father breathed deeply. Then he seemed to swell with sudden anger.

"God?" he said. "God?" Then he closed his fist and raised his arm. "God?" he repeated. "Don't talk of God to me, vicar. 'God!' you say! And a thing like this can happen! That boy of mine up there, dead; his life not half-lived. . . . And Jeffrey Ellis, too, at Rhos Dirion. . . . God? You talk to me of God?" His voice broke, and he turned his back on us so that we should not see his grief.

I looked at the vicar. He was standing there with his overcoat hanging unbuttoned from his shoulders. I went up to him. He gripped my hand silently, the very pressure of his fingers communicating his sympathy to me.

"Don't mind father," I said quietly. "You know how it is."

"He is a man," said the vicar. "I respect his grief; and, if I am not wrong, God respects him, too. He is no coward is Daniel Peele. He—he stands up to God like a man—Justin's father!"

Everyone nodded. Then the doctor called down for hot water. I poured it out into a white enamelled pan and father took it from my hands.

"You stay here," he said. "I'll bring your mother down with me, she is in her room."

He went slowly out of the room, and in a minute or so we heard him going into his room and mother's. We all listened. We could hear her crying. She was calling Justin's name; and then, low and firm, we heard father trying to console her.

Soon, she came downstairs. She was not crying now and looked at us calmly. The vicar went up to her and took her arm. "Sit you here," he said, taking her to the arm-chair by the fire. "Mair will be along any minute. She said she would follow me."

Father re-appeared at the door.

"I am going down to fetch Pali Dolguog," he said. He had his overcoat on and his ash-plant in his hand.

The doctor came downstairs at that moment. He was in his usual breeches, brown leggings, and Norfolk jacket. He was wiping his hands on one of the best towels that mother kept only for visitors. He came across to father and mother.

"A terrible business," he said in his broken Welsh, "terrible. But I don't think he suffered. . . ." He looked warningly at me. "He must have been unconscious all the time. . . . Nothing I could have done if I had been there when it happened."

He turned to me.

"Come down for the certificate to-morrow. . . . There'll be the inquest, too. . . ."

We heard him ride slowly up the lane, and all was silent again.

Squire had come by now and he rose to go with father down to Dolguog.

"Let me come with you," he suggested.

"No!" Father shook his head. "Thank you, squire, but I

would rather you stayed here." His eyes met mine. "Ned and I will go . . . I . . . I want to hear how it all happened. . . . You are all right, Anne?"

Mother nodded. There was no colour in her face and a little nerve kept twitching in the corner of her mouth.

I went out with father, and as we left the house we heard her starting to cry again.

.   .   .   .   .

It was over a mile down through the Allt to Dolguog. I followed father through the fields where we had ricked the corn only a week ago. There were no stars and a thin wind had sprung up. It carried with it the smell of fern and moss, and every now and then a tree would rasp its branches together and the dead leaves rustled over our heads and our feet made whispering noises in the grass.

For a while father said nothing. The lantern swung with each step he took and its light flickered in a jagged circle around us. Times my shadow reared like some dark spirit as we neared a hedge-bank or passed a tree. When the path got wider, I walked alongside him. It was unbelievable that here we were on our way to fetch Pali to lay out our Justin. No doubt Grett's father was on his way, too, to fetch someone to lay out poor Jeff, probably Sian the Coiti. When we were boys in school we had all of us been afraid of Pali and Sian, and even when I grew up I was always afraid that I would meet one of them as she went on her dread way. And now, soon, Pali would be coming back with father and me to Trewern. Though sleep and its sweet forgetfulness was a thing of the past, I felt that aeons had passed since Justin and I had riden off together after tea. I couldn't get over the awful chasm that separated the dead from the living. Justin dead and Jeff dead! I couldn't believe it, and yet I realized it. The knowledge of it was heavy on the darkness, it was over the parish like a black cloud; and I could feel it in the silence that lay upon me and on father.

"Now, tell me all about it. Everything. It will have to come out at the inquest anyway."

I told him and he did not interrupt me.

"And Justin was against it?"

"Yes."

"And he went to help Jeff Ellis?"

"Yes. . . . He was there before any of us could do anything."

We were now at Dolguog. The place was in darkness; old Emwnt and Pali were in bed long before. Father hammered the door with his stick.

The window above us opened.

"Who is it then?"

It was old Emwnt, his voice angry and ruffled from being awakened.

"It's me—Daniel Peele."

"Who?" Emwnt was as deaf as a post, and he bellowed down at us as though he was trying to hear his own voice.

"Daniel Peele!" shouted father.

"Oh, it's you. What is the matter then?"

Father turned to me.

"You tell him," he said. "Shout it out."

I made a funnel of my hands.

"Justin is dead," I shouted. "Justin is dead—killed!"

My voice broke as I heard father sob beside me. I saw his heavy shoulders shaking, and I turned away so that he should not know that I saw him.

"Pali! Pali! Wake up. Justin Peele is dead!"

Old Emwnt was talking to his wife in a voice of thunder. I heard the words: "Justin Peele is dead," and for all my grief and heart's heaviness, I imagined the echo of his voice rolling down over the parish. The rocks of the Van caught it, and it went from crag to crag and down through the dark places along the Sawdde, down past Allt-y-brain, Cwmsidan, past Graig Ddu, over our Allt and back to Rhos Dirion where Jeff lay still and cold; back to Trewern where Justin, too, was calm and quiet in his room.

It was the final pronouncement. At my side I heard father crying; terrible sounds they were coming from a man like him. And like some requiem, the leaves rustled thin and harsh around us, the dogs barked in the out-house, and from inside the house came the sounds of Pali getting ready to accompany us back to Trewern. I started to cry again, my heart finding ease in the tears that ran down my face. And all the time, still throbbing and jarring on the darkness, was the echo of Emwnt's voice: "Justin Peele is dead." That meant that I should never see him again.

.   .   .   .   .

When Pali had finished with Justin, Elias Carpenter measured him and hurried away. The house was now filled with callers. From time to time some heavy-footed neighbour would come to the door. We would hear the loud tone of interrogation; then, as he came in, his voice would drop to a whisper as he tiptoed to the chair set out for him.

People were still arriving at the house, and their subdued conversation followed me as I made my way upstairs to Justin's room. I had left father and mother sitting in the big chairs by the fire. The vicar and his wife were still there, and so was the squire—he had told me not to worry about Nantssiarad; he and the servants would see to everything until Grett and I felt we were ready to move in.

The candle-light from Justin's room showed out on to the landing. I hesitated a while before going in. Through the door I could see his chest of drawers, the mirror on it tilted upwards with a wad of paper stuck between it and the upright so that it should not swing. I breathed deeply and tensed myself. Although it was Justin who lay there so still and quiet, I was nervous of his presence. Then, holding my breath, I went in.

They had laid him out in his best blue suit, white collar and striped tie. And they had even brushed his hair so that it lay in a wave across his forehead. I looked at him tenderly. Now that Death was already moulding those strong features into a graven stillness, I saw the powerful beauty of his face. I saw how tender was the full-lipped mouth, all hardness and stubbornness now gone from it. So this was Justin. I looked at him, marvelling at myself that I felt no grief any more. I found myself breathing easily. There was a strange, lovely lightness in the room. But for the people downstairs I would have taken out my pipe and smoked. There was his gaff on the little oak table by the window, all shining and ready for the salmon when they would come up the river. I looked again at his stern profile and was suddenly aware that Grett was standing behind me. She stood there, pale as a ghost and leaning against the door. Without a word to me she came over to where Justin lay and bent down and kissed his forehead. I looked at her in amazement. Her eyes were red and swollen.

"Father is downstairs," she said quietly. "It was the least we could do after what Justin did. . . ."

I could only stare at her. She wiped her eyes.

"He gave his life for Jeff," she said, "poor old Jeff. . . . And now they are . . ." She came over to me and sobbed on my shoulder. When, at last, we turned to go, she looked again at Justin.

"He was grand," she whispered, "grand. Even father used to say so."

"He did!"

"Yes . . . 'That Justin Peele,' he used to say, 'he's as bad as his father, but he's got all the fineness of his mother, too.' "

We left the room. I turned at the door, and as I did so I saw again the relaxed lines of his mouth and chin. Grief welled in me again. I turned to Grett and we cried in each other's arms.

.   .   .   .   .

It was a sad thing to see John Ellis and father standing together, tears running down their faces as they shook hands. Pity, pity that their first-born should have had to die before the old sores could be healed.

.   .   .   .   .

It was close on four when I went to bed. Grett and her father and the neighbours had all left and we were now alone. How I fell asleep I don't know, but sleep I did. When I awoke there was a cold grey mist over the mountains. My pillow was quite wet where I had laid my face. The barrier of sleep, brief as it was, had put Justin more into the past than ever.

The dawn came slow and cold, and with no flush of colour. I could not remember such an empty, hopeless dawn. I listened hard. There was no sound anywhere. The silence from Justin's room had penetrated everywhere. After a while, however, I heard a step on the boards outside. I went to the door and saw father going in to Justin's room, his breeches unbuttoned at the knees and his shoulders quivering with grief. I went quietly back to bed and lay there thinking of the past. When, at about six o'clock, I hurried downstairs in my stockinged feet, I felt that I could almost feel the coldness and quietness in Justin's room, even through the closed door.

.   .   .   .   .

The squire had some hard words to say at the inquest, and the jury could do no more than bring in a verdict of "Accidental Death." His final words marked the end of the wild drinking in the parish, and the colliers from Brynamman swore they would sign the pledge that very day. Later in the afternoon, father and I drove to Llandovery in the trap. Mother was all right for mourning, because of late years she had worn almost nothing but dark grey or black. Grett was going with her mother on the following day, and I gave her ten sovereigns to cover the cost.

It was a wild, wet afternoon. It had started to rain after breakfast and was now a storm. The wind came up from the south-west, and at times the rain would seem to hover in the valley like grey, sculptured drifts, only to be lit up momentarily by a pale gleam from behind a torn cloud.

Father and I got fitted out at *The Gwalia* and we were ready to start back at about five. Then father remembered that we had to collect the certificate from the doctor. By the time we left Llandovery it was quite dark.

I found it strange to be going home without having to wait until after stop-tap. I sat with father, my coat collar up around my ears. It was a terrible journey. The river was in flood, and father was in two minds whether we should cross it under the village or take the top road by way of the Allt. He decided, however, to risk going the usual way.

We could hear the heavy roar and tumult of the river long before we came to it. But I didn't care. I could think only of Justin and of the frozen stillness in his room. Still, when we came to the crossing, I forgot everything for some moments while I clung to the sides of the trap. All I was conscious of was the black night around us, the wind howling in the trees and the awful roar of the waters. I can see father now, the trap lamps shining on the river, and the reflected dazzle lighting up his face as he stood up in the trap cursing and lashing poor Doll.

When we got to the top of the Allt we could see the light in the kitchen. One of the dogs barked as we came into the yard, and the sound of it made only more deep and significant the silence inside the house.

Elias Carpenter brought the coffin that night and, together, he and father afterwards brought it down from the bedroom into the parlour. I awoke in the night. The wind had dropped and the rain had stopped. I listened to hear if mother were still crying, but all I could hear was father snoring. I was glad that he could sleep. It was terrible to know that down at Rhos Dirion there was the same heartbreak and grief as here, yet must I sleep alone and not be able to comfort Grett until she could leave her parents.

We were all up early on the morning of the funeral. As the week-end was on us, father and John Ellis had decided that we would have to have the funerals on the Saturday. It did not give our relatives much time to travel from afar; but news travels quickly, and we had written to all we could remember. Father had killed three sheep on the day before, and we still had two hams which we had not yet started. There was plenty of food for everyone. And there's strange it was to see the long trestle tables laid out in the barn, just as they had been the month before for our wedding. Apart from occasional bouts of weeping, we went about our work quietly. Of course, there was no need for mother to do any work. There were plenty of women there all the time; Mati was with us from morning till night, and the squire's wife was seeing to all the arranging of the food.

It was a fine day. The fields were green and fresh after the rain, and the mountains were a blaze of brown and red fern. I went through Justin's things to see if there was anything there he would not have wanted mother to see. I took his diary—he hadn't written a thing in it for years—and I put away his old working clothes and the suit he wore on the night he had died.

I took his pipe, too, glad of the teeth-marks on the broken stem and the tarred edge of the bow. I stuck it in my mouth just to get the taste of it. It seemed some sort of a link with him.

By twelve o'clock there must have been over a hundred people on our yard. I moved among them trying to show a brave front and greeting all whom I knew. Everyone was very quiet. Little groups formed themselves, some going to look at the pigs, the ricks; others inspecting the buildings and looking over the hedges.

Mother broke down when Moc arrived. He had travelled from Merthyr that morning, getting a lift from Trecastle with my cousins from Senny. Moc was dressed in a black suit that was much too tight for him, and his new bowler was wider in the brim than the ones we wore. He could say nothing to father and mother when he came into the house, but stood there with his hat held up in front of his face so that we shouldn't see his tears.

Then came the families of Cefn Melgoed, Beili Glas, Y Wern, Ffynnonoer, Danrallt, Glasgwm, Brwynllys, Rhyd-yrhaf, Glyn Eithin and others; they were all there, even our cousins from Brynamman and Cwm Wysg, and they all had food either in the barn or in the house, just as there happened to be room. Then, at about half-past one because he would have to rush off ahead of the funeral to officiate at Rhos Dirion, the vicar came; and with him, too, came Mr. Roderick the preacher.

A strange, unreal hush fell on the yard.

The dogs had been locked in the stable, and I wondered if they knew what was happening, for they made no sound at all.

The stone-flagged kitchen was filled with chairs. Row after row of women sat still and upright, all dressed in black. The men stood against the walls except, of course, the very old who were seated. Father and mother sat in the big chairs by the fire.

I imagined the same scene at Rhos Dirion, and it was hard not to be able to be at Grett's side in such an hour.

The vicar took his place at the end of the table. The Bible, Common Prayer, and the hymn-book were open in front of him.

The service was brief. Father had asked the vicar to cut it

short. He did not believe in a lot of soft-soap at funerals, and because everybody knew what Justin had been, it would have been a mockery to try and whitewash him.

I don't remember anything of what the vicar read or spoke. The unreality of the scene had no actuality for me; I did not feel any emotion whatsoever. Justin was dead, that was all. That was why there was a great silent crowd out in the yard there; why our kitchen was filled with weeping women in black and vicar reading from the big Bible. All I wanted was to be away from the house. It would be nice to be out in the open, following the coffin to the church. I felt the house was killing me.

The prayer over, the vicar gave out the hymn, "Bydd myrdd o ryfeddodau," Lewsin took the note from his tuning-fork and led the singing. It started thin and ragged enough. Lewsin and the women had all they could do to keep it going. And then, like a surge of sound, came the singing of the crowd outside. I could hear the tenors from Gwynfe, and there was Dico Lewis leading the bassers, and the sopranos and altos were enough to melt you. It was then that I broke down. The beautiful singing of the old funeral hymn almost broke my heart. I saw Justin lying there in his coffin in the next room, and the thought that all his old friends were out there singing for him—this was the most terrible minute I had ever experienced. I felt like calling on them all to stop: Justin could not be dead, men like Justin did not die. . . . But Justin was dead, and Jeff was dead, too. My legs trembled under me, and if squire had not given me a chair, I would have collapsed on the stone floor.

The ordeal passed, and by the time the bier had been brought to the door, I was myself again.

Father called me out to the passage. Through the doorway I could see the blur of faces outside. There was Moc, his bowler square on his head and his eyes staring straight in front of him. I looked for Iori, Lloyd and the others wondering why they could not have come to my brother's funeral. Then I remembered: they would be at Rhos Dirion. . . .

Father and I took one end, and Moc and Dico took the other, and between us we carried Justin out of the house and placed him on the bier. The bearers then took their places: the squire, old Howells, Lewsin, and Parri; and as they went slowly up through the yard the funeral fell into place, two by two, until the lane seethed in a long black line with the sunlight glinting on the brasses and the varnished wood. So we went, father and mother, Moc and I, then our relations; down through the Allt, across the footbridge over the Lyswen, up through the village until at length we left Trewern far behind us.

As we came over the rise of the hill looking down on the Sawdde, we heard the singing of the funeral coming from Rhos Dirion. And as soon as we rounded the sharp bend of the road we could see in the valley below us the sunlight shining on Jeff's coffin and the long, straggling black column of people following it. This gave double sorrow to us, and we moved on until, at length, at about a mile from the church, the two roads converged, and Justin's funeral and Jeff's became one.

Many times did Elias call "Change" as we went up the steep hill towards the church, and each time he did so, so did the men fall out and shoulder the weight of the two coffins. Even Iori and Rhys Blacksmith put their shoulders under Justin, and I wept afresh at this last service of theirs to my brother. The bell tolled slowly as we neared the church, and the tramp of feet and the occasional sobs were all out of keeping with the bright afternoon and the swallows in the sky.

And now, at last, the service in the church was over. We had all sat in the same seat: father, mother; John Ellis and his wife; Grett and myself.

My grief had now wept itself away; and with Grett in my arm, I found myself looking over towards the Van Rocks and noting how soft and tender their symmetrical grimness had become with the sun so warm on their mauve and purple.

The two graves had been dug side by side, and as Elias put the webbing through the handles and under Justin's coffin, mother half-sank to her knees and but for father's arm would have fallen to the ground. All through the service he had not wept a tear or bowed his head. He glared at the people around us as if resolved to remind them that the Peeles still survived. I could not help thinking to myself that Justin would have looked at them in exactly the same way if one of us had gone, perhaps a little more insolently, his dark eyes provoking comment and wilfully antagonizing whomsoever met his glance.

One by one we all filed past the grave. Mother called: "Iestyn! Iestyn!" Then father brought her to where Grett was standing with me.

"Just a minute!" Everyone looked at him wonderingly.

"Here!" He handed me a long shovel; and then, taking one himself, he took a shovelful of earth from the mound nearby and let it fall as gently as he could on the two coffins. I did the same.

Soon, the inscriptions on the brass plates disappeared under the fine red soil, and in a minute or so we had put a barrier of earth between the dead and ourselves.

That done, father went over to mother and together they went down the path with Grett's father and mother. Through my tears I saw Grett come over to me. I looked once more down into the grave, but all I could see was the red earth that lay between me and Justin. The crowd made way for us and so, walking and weeping together, Grett and I left the churchyard and went slowly down the road.

That night after supper, I went out and leaned against the gate of the wain. Grett had left me after the funeral to go home with her father and mother. I had not dared to ask her when we would move into Nantssiarad. There was time enough for that, and the squire was behind us whatever we decided. Moc had offered to give up his job at Merthyr and come and work with father and mother, so that was settled; they would not be alone, and between the three of them they would manage the farm.

It was cold outside and the wind was blowing from the mountains. I looked over the Allt towards the church. Through the darkness, through the earth, I saw those two lying there; Justin so still and statuesque, that stern profile and tender mouth of his already touched by the coldness of the earth. And at his side was Jeff; peace between them at last.

And as I stood there seeing the dark lie of the land and the heavy drift of cloud overhead, I felt a new strength enter my being. Now that Justin was gone, the future of the family was with Grett and myself. Some day, it was bound to come, Trewern would be mine, Grett's, our children's. We would come back here where the memory of Justin's presence would still be with us.

I leaned there against the gate for a long time, not bothering to go in even when I heard a trap turn into our lane. What were condolences to us now! I continued to look across the parish towards the church and the dark shape of the Vans.

Presently, I heard footsteps coming towards me. I turned round and saw that it was Grett. She came to me and without a word took my arm.

Together we leaned against the gate and looked over the jagged crest of the Allt below us. We said nothing, not a word to each other. Then, like the beginning of a new life, the wind rose a little and became a live thing in the trees around us. Arm-in-arm we stood there, shoulder to shoulder, moulded in earth and rooted in the soil of our birthplace. Come what would—death, grief, sadness; come winter and its storms, come the seasons with what they would: we were together.

83
85